# PASSION

Intent only on Jewel now, on tasting, touching, feeling her, Brent plunged his hands into her hair and wrapped the long tresses around his fingers. As he crushed his mouth to hers, as she matched his urgency, Brent inhaled and was suddenly filled with her essence.

Their passion ignited, consuming them both. Entwined together, melting in the heat of their own desire, they spiraled down to the thick carpet. Jewel knew she was out of control, out of her mind, but it didn't matter. She was frantic to have him inside her, to have him fill the source of her heat and extinguish the exquisite flames.

Brent's kiss deepened as their heated bodies rolled across the carpet . . .

# GYPSY Jewel

## JUNE CAMERON

DIAMOND BOOKS, NEW YORK

This book is a Diamond original edition, and has never
been previously published

GYPSY JEWEL

A Diamond Book / published by arrangement with
the author

PRINTING HISTORY
Diamond edition / October 1992

ISBN: 1-55773-717-7

Diamond Books are published by The Berkley Publishing Group,
200 Madison Avenue, New York, New York 10016.
The name ''DIAMOND'' and its logo are trademarks
belonging to Charter Communications, Inc.

PRINTED IN THE UNITED STATES OF AMERICA

10  9  8  7  6  5  4  3  2  1

*For*
*Gloria MacIver Ruffing—*
*a rare gem of a mother,*
*jewel of my heart—*
*with all my love*

Special thanks to Joseph Barnett, for lending me his delightful hometown of Greenville, Mississippi, and for the lovely childhood memories I have of his home in California.

To Bobbie Wergen and her father, Maurice Scott, for the use of their minuscule, stunted, and totally unique little pinkies!

And to Joseph Thomas Reilly, for sharing his knowledge and memories of Mississippi.

# 1

*Chicago, Illinois*
*Spring 1876*

Her favorite college professor once said she was well-suited for her chosen profession because a woman could rationalize anything. Including murder.

Jewel Flannery had cause to consider that professor's words often. As an outstanding employee of the Pinkerton National Detective Agency, she had to rationalize her actions each time she took on a new case. This one was no different.

Jewel considered the possibility that this time she might have to shoot a man in the line of duty—a small-time counterfeiter at that—as she probed and twisted the stiletto in Matt Scottson's lock.

When it gave way, she took a quick glance up and down the hallway, then slipped into the hotel room and closed the door. After waiting and listening in the semidarkness for a moment, she was satisfied that she was alone. Jewel crossed the living room of the opulent suite and headed for the bedroom.

Carefully pushing the heavy oak door open, she followed a ribbon-thin path of light to the dresser. Her fingers trembling in anticipation of finding a link between Scottson and the bogus bills, Jewel reached for a nearby oil lamp and turned up the wick a notch.

A man's voice suddenly shattered the tension. "Don't scream."

Jewel stiffened against the walnut dresser. She heard the metallic click of a gun's hammer just before she felt the barrel being pressed into the soft hollow behind her ear.

"Now turn around," he ordered in a menacing whisper. "Nice and easy. No quick movements."

Jewel did a slow pirouette, burying the stiletto in the folds of her voluminous skirt as she turned. She raised her gaze to the owner of the voice.

Brent Sebastian Connors stared into her cool green eyes and sucked in his breath. Then he whispered another order. "You've got one minute to explain yourself. Unless you've got an engraved invitation to visit this bedroom, little lady, you're in a heap of trouble."

Jewel studied him, but no recognition registered. She didn't know who he was or why he was in Scotty's room, but she did know that the stranger didn't belong in this hotel suite any more than she did. Slipping into a slightly modified version of the role she was playing, Jewel smiled. "You mean this isn't my room? How could I have made a silly mistake like that?"

He slid the pistol down her jawline, caressing her with the barrel, and brought it to rest under her chin. "How silly of you indeed, little lady."

Gauging him, working on a plausible alibi for herself, Jewel pulled her shoulders back and forced a giggle.

Fascinated at the way her quivering bosom spilled over the top of her low-cut bodice, Brent grinned, then withdrew his gaze from the inviting cleavage. Suddenly more relaxed and confident, he went on. "I don't want to have to blow a hole in that beautiful face, and I'm pretty sure you don't want to be dead, so why don't you save us both some trouble? I want the truth. Talk—and I mean now."

Considering her options, searching for a sign of weakness, she centered on the man's voice and the hint of a drawl. If his roots were in the South, if he'd retained any part of his gentlemanly upbringing, he ought to melt under a "helpless female" facade. With painstaking precision, Jewel inched the knife toward his crotch.

Then, in spite of the frowzy blond wig piled high on her head, the oversized beauty mark painted at the corner of her upturned mouth, and the low-cut dance hall dress, Jewel transformed herself into a simpering, trembling excuse for a woman.

"Oh, suh," she pleaded in a barely audible voice. "Puh-leeze don't shoot me. I nevuh meant any harm. I only . . ." She batted her eyelashes and swooned against his broad chest. "Oh, I—I don't feel well. I think I may faint. Puh-leeze don't let me fall, suh."

In position now, Jewel took advantage of the gunman's moment of confusion and went on the offensive. She slid the blade along his pant leg until it rested—most threateningly. She gently pushed, and the knife pierced the expensive striped wool fabric of his trousers. Jewel increased the pressure and knew by his expression and the sudden tensing of his body that she'd made contact with the flesh of his inner thigh.

"Now then," she said, her voice suddenly bold. "Since I *don't* want to have to push this knife any deeper and get blood all over my new dress"—she paused, grinning at the shudder he was unable to contain—"and since I'm pretty sure you don't want to sing with the Chicago Ladies Choir, why don't you save us both some trouble and drop the gun? Then you can tell me why *you're* in this room."

"I can't do that. Drop the knife!" He didn't move a muscle.

"Sorry." She batted her auburn eyelashes again. "My mama raised me to take care of myself at any cost. You wouldn't want me to disappoint my mama, would you, now? Drop the gun."

"Drop the knife."

"You first."

Brent clenched his teeth and stared into her eyes. She

looked amused, as if she was enjoying his discomfort. Was she deranged enough to carry out her threat? The seconds were ticking by, and Scottson could burst in on them at any minute. How would Connors explain his presence in the man's room if his suspicions were unfounded?

"Tell you what. Why don't we both drop our weapons at the count of three? Then we can straighten out who does and doesn't belong in this room."

Jewel pursed her lips in concentration. He was a gambler; that much she could determine by his manner of dress. The fine three-piece suit of striped charcoal gray, the ruffled dress shirt, and the red cravat complete with diamond stickpin announced that he was a betting man, a dandy. If he were to shed his jacket, Jewel was certain she'd find a lady's garter constricting the muscles of his upper arm. Was he a thief as well? A liar? Probably both.

She looked up into his face and was caught by eyes the color of pure clover honey. He was a dashing figure with dark wavy hair and a sable mustache, cocky and handsome, sure of himself. *Too* sure of himself, she decided as the twin dimples in his cheeks began to deepen.

Gambler or thief, it didn't much matter. To Jewel they were one in the same. She matched his grin and said, "Sounds fair enough. Who counts?"

The dimples became caves. "Be my guest, little lady."

"All right." With a short nod, she cleared her throat and began. "One, two . . . three!"

Golden brown eyes stared into the cool green of hers. But no one moved. The Colt .45 remained pressed against her throat, the stiletto sandwiched between his thighs.

"Maybe it'll work better if I count," he suggested, sweat dotting his brow.

"I suppose that could work. Let's find out. Go ahead."

Again he stared into her eyes, wondering if what he saw was intelligence or dementia. Before he could decide or begin the count, the door to the suite crashed open.

Loud masculine voices argued from the living room.

"Take it easy," the first complained. "I said I'd give all yer money back to ya."

"You'll be doin' more than that, Scotty. You'll be payin' more than that. You've fleeced your last honest gambling man. You're lower than a gopher-fed snake's belly drug through the bowels of hell! It's time you got your comeuppance."

In jeopardy of discovery, Jewel and Brent froze as the men quarreled. Then the crack of gunfire exploded from the other side of the bedroom door. Like an oak tree split by a sudden bolt of lightning, the pair sprang apart.

Her fist still curled around the pearl handle of the knife, his thumb perched atop the hammer of the Colt, Brent and Jewel crept to the door and peeked into the other room. A man in a black suit, his back to them, knelt by a body on the floor. He issued a hoarse laugh as he stuffed some bills and coins into his pockets, then rose and made a fast exit.

"Damn," Jewel muttered as she impulsively reached for the doorknob.

"Son of a bitch," Brent spat as he prepared to ram his way through the opening.

In the last second before she touched the knob, as he lowered his right shoulder, they were drawn together by a singular thought: What's *your* interest in Scotty? They stared at each other for a long moment, Jewel's eyebrows arched high with surprise, Brent's knotted together in puzzlement. Then he shook his head and kicked the door opened.

The centerpiece of the living room was a chandelier that could only have been called gaudy. Now that great glass sculpture burned brightly. Huge pear-shaped drops of crystal hung from every available brass curlicue and sent glittering light bouncing off the ceilings and walls.

A few of those beams skipped across the face of Matt Scottson. He stared lifelessly at Jewel and Brent as they approached him, his expression one of shock, of disbelief. His eyes, flat and cold like stones discarded from a miner's pan, were wide open, gawking but not seeing. His mouth formed a perfect circle, as if he were preparing to whistle for his horse. Prisms of light danced across his shirt, flickering and drawing attention to the small crimson hole in his chest. Scotty was deader than a snakebit rat and twice as surprised.

"Son of a bitch," Brent complained again as he stepped across the body and jerked open the heavy outer door. Sticking his head through the crack, he surveyed the hallway. Deserted. Ducking back inside the room, he slammed the door and turned back to the girl.

Jewel dropped to her knees, ignoring the gambler's raised eyebrows. She grabbed Scotty's collar. "Wake up, you yellow-bellied son of Satan! Get up and take your medicine like a man!"

Brent stared down at the dance hall girl as she tried to force some life back into the corpse. Again he wondered about her interest in the dead man, her obvious distress. Had Scotty been a customer? Had he run out on her without settling up, perhaps? Or was it something else? With lazy deliberation, Brent reached into his vest pocket and withdrew a toothpick. Twirling it through the thick hair at the corner of his mouth, he inquired, "Begging your pardon, but if you don't mind my asking, I was just wondering—did ole Scotty try to stiff you, little lady?"

Jewel ignored his inquiry. She released her grip on the body and let Scottson's head drop to the floor. Finally resigned to the fact that the suspect was dead and that she'd failed in her mission, she struggled to her feet, disregarding Brent's outstretched hand as well as his inquiry. Grumbling in exasperation, she turned and stomped toward the door.

"Not so fast, little lady." Brent caught her by the elbow. "I asked you a question. I expect an answer."

A sassy reply was perched on the tip of her tongue, but Jewel kept it to herself when she saw the flecks of determination mingled among the bits of gold twinkling in his honey-brown eyes. She jerked her arm away, then slipped back into her helpless-female mode.

"I—I really can't talk about it, suh." Jewel reached between her breasts and pulled out a lace hanky. Dabbing at her nose, she struggled to produce the necessary moisture, then added, "You see—that is . . ."

"Now, take it easy, little lady. Just tell me why you broke into this room and what Scotty meant to you."

A manufactured tear finally rolled down her painted cheek. Jewel nearly swooned as she said, "Well, suh, it's just that . . . you see, Scotty was my long lost father."

# 2

Jewel stared out the third-floor office window belonging to the founder of the Pinkerton Detective Agency. Below, the dusty streets of Chicago swirled with early morning activity and industrial soot. Tradesmen jockeyed for position along the plank sidewalks, hawking their wares and fighting for the right-of-way against fancy carriages and hansom cabs. A young boy dressed in navy blue knickers and white knee socks cried out in pain as his mother swatted him alongside the head. Jewel watched, full of empathy, but nonetheless amused, as the woman boxed her young son's ears all the way up the street and around the corner.

A plump matron dressed in black silk caught Jewel's attention as the woman stepped from a cab across the street and entered the offices of the Pennsylvania & Reading Railroad. Reminded of her mission, her failure, Jewel heaved a heavy sigh and turned to face her employer. "I'm sorry, Allan. I was so sure I'd catch Scotty with the goods. Maybe if I'd—"

"You ought to know by now that maybe's and what if's don't do us one bit of good in this business, girl. You're one of the best operatives I've got, male *or* female, so sit down and stop fretting. You're making me nervous."

Her smile humble, Jewel glided across the room. Careful not to crush the chocolate silk fabric draping her bustle, she perched on the edge of a Queen Anne chair. "I appreciate your confidence in me, Allan, but I feel as if I missed

8

something on this case. Some little thing I failed to notice that might have made all the difference in the world.''

''Nothing I noticed.'' Pinkerton glanced at her written report, running a crinkled finger down the margin as he searched for pertinent facts.

Giving him time, Jewel picked at the black jet beading on her basque and regarded the Scotsman she'd come to cherish. Not for the first time, she lamented a cruel fate that had robbed her of a man like this to call her father. His hair, lightly waved and growing sparser every day, was rapidly changing color. The few accents of pepper he had left would soon turn to salt, join the white strands, and become as solid as Lot's wife. He was aging. Becoming more . . . fatherly.

Jewel impulsively reached for her little finger and began pulling at it through the fabric of her glove. A paternal genetic defect, the baby finger on each of her hands was half the normal size, more embryo than newborn, definitely stunted by anyone's standards. Jewel flipped the bit of rust lace at her throat back and forth, disgusted with herself for even thinking of the bastard who'd spawned her in the same moment she'd thought of Allan.

Looking across the desk to her employer again, she said, ''Well?''

''I see nothing here to warrant your attitude,'' Allan commented, stroking his beard. Thicker than his hair, more salt than pepper, it was cut in the fashion of the late President, Abraham Lincoln, a man Allan had revered—a dear friend whom he'd been able to save from an assassin's bullet once, but not twice. Still scanning the papers in his hand, he shrugged, ''It looks as if you searched Scotty's room and belongings thoroughly and were unable to turn up any sign of the forged stock certificates. I don't know what more you could have done.''

''I don't know, either. I just hate to come up empty-handed.''

''Umm, my sentiments exactly.'' Allan started to stuff the papers back into the folder but stopped at the last moment. His brows drew together above kind, intelligent blue eyes. Then he glanced up. "Is this all you found out about the fellow who confronted you in Scotty's room? Just his name?"

Jewel rolled her eyes, and her mouth twisted into a frown. The gambler. She suddenly remembered the mirth in his golden brown eyes and the perpetual grin he seemed to be shielding beneath his thick mustache. She thought of his warm breath and deep melodic voice, his firm muscular thighs—and the little reminder she must have left behind with the tip of her knife. She recalled his expression when he realized a stiletto was within an inch of his precious manhood, and nearly laughed at the sudden image of his sweaty brow and silly smile as he tried to regain the upper hand. He'd looked as if he had a chicken feather stuck inside his drawers.

The frown vanished, and Jewel swallowed her laughter. "Up and disappeared without a trace," she said crisply. "All he left me was that lousy excuse for a name—B. S. Connors. Rather says it all, doesn't it?"

The two detectives shared a hearty chuckle, and then Allan tossed the folder on a pile at the edge of his desk. He folded his hands, his expression growing serious. "Let's close the book on this one, then. Ready for your next assignment, my shining Jewel of many colors?"

There was a warning in his words and manner, but she couldn't be sure what he signaled. She proceeded with caution. "Maybe . . . maybe not. I've been thinking I could use a little time off. What's up?"

"You're a hard one to corner, Miss Flannery." He laughed. "I've got a special little job for you in Kansas. Topeka, to be exact."

Jewel draped her elbows across the arms of the chair and collapsed against the cushion, bustle be damned. "Oh, Allan," she groaned, "I don't want to go west to the land of dust storms and failed crops. I want to go east. Can't you find an assignment for me in New York? I hear the town is jumping with parties and celebrations for the centennial.''

"I can certainly understand that, but I've received word that Jesse James may be back in business. He's been spotted all through Missouri and Tennessee. In fact"—Allan straightened in his chair, and his color rose—"in Nashville the scoundrel had the guts to enter his horse in the state fair. He rode the beast himself and won first prize!"

"Then why wasn't he arrested?"

"Because," Allan grumbled, his rosy cheeks darkening, "the sheriff was the idiot who awarded him the prize! It wasn't until later, as he sat staring at a wanted poster, that he realized what he'd done. I tell you, Jesse's flaunting his lawlessness, and I'm going to get him if it's the last thing I do."

Jewel flinched as her boss's fist slammed down on the desk. Then she shook her head. "If you don't calm down, it very well may be the last thing you do."

Allan's smile returned, and his eyes sparkled. "I like to get my man, that's all."

"Me too." She laughed. "But why can't I look for him in New York?"

Relaxed again, his color back to normal, he said, "Tell you what, girl. You take this job in Kansas just long enough to find out if James has really been spotted in the area and I'll make sure you're in Philadelphia in time for the opening of the Centennial Exhibition on May tenth. What do you say?"

"But that's only a few weeks away!"

Allan shrugged. "Shouldn't take a sharp operator like you more than a few days to sniff out a skunk like Jesse James."

Frowning, Jewel avoided looking across the desk. As usual, Allan Pinkerton knew her answer would be yes, but she kept her silence, too stubborn to admit it just yet.

Allan decided to help her verbalize her decision. "While you're thinking about taking the assignment, add this to the pile of kindling—I have it on good word that Handsome Harry Benton may show up in the same general region.''

''*What?*'' Jewel sprang out of her chair. ''Why didn't you say so in the first place? You could have saved us both some time!'' She pressed her palms against the glass-topped desk and leaned over. ''Spill it—all of it. Where's he been seen? What game is he up to? Is he working alone or is—''

''Hold it!'' Allan laughed, his hands stretched out in front of him. ''Now who needs to calm down?''

''I'm calm,'' she murmured, self-conscious. Jewel straightened her spine and centered the brown velvet hat in her thick auburn curls before she trusted herself to speak further. ''Fairly calm, anyway. I don't know what came over me, sir.''

''Oh, I think I do.'' Allan squinted one blue eye at her. ''Same thing that comes over you any time Handsome Harry is part of the conversation. He's getting to be an obsession with you, Jewel,'' he said, more seriously. ''Better watch it before it gets you in the kind of trouble you can't get out of.''

''Thanks for your concern, Allan, but it's really not necessary. I can take care of myself, and the day I can't, I won't be taken down by a lop-eared mongrel named Harry Benton.''

''Make that *Handsome* Harry.''

''Says he.'' She sniffed. Says he and any widow or spinster over her own twenty-five years, she grudgingly acknowledged to herself.

Allan shrugged. ''Whatever. I just thought his name would sweeten the pot. If that's still not enough to send you packing, I've also got reason to believe you couldn't find those certificates because Benton was Scotty's partner on this little venture. Apparently Harry double-crossed him and made off with the goods before Scottson even knew what had happened.''

Jewel frowned. ''What would Harry be doing with a counterfeiter? His specialty is helpless women and their money.''

Propping his fingers tent-style, Allan offered a theory. "Maybe he's just trying to throw us off the track."

"I don't know. It seems to me that I would have noticed someone of Harry's caliber no matter what he was up to. I would have *felt* his presence."

"Could be his disguises are getting to be as good as yours."

"That does it. Harry is not going to slip through my fingers again." Her mind filling with questions, she circled the chair. "What's the attraction in Kansas? Why is Harry back in the States, and why in God's name would he go to Topeka?"

"First off, the centennial. Folks from all over the world will be converging—"

"Never mind," she said, holding up her hand. "Everyone who is anyone will be in Philadelphia next month. Stupid of me not to have thought of that myself. But *Topeka*? People there don't exactly shake diamonds off their fingers the way a duck sheds water."

Allan laughed. "No, but he may want a little warm-up before he heads to the big city. An important poker tournament will get under way next week at the Golden Dove Hotel. If he's operating as usual, Harry's going to become best friends with the most likely winners."

"Then I expect he and I are going to become very close." Jewel spread her arms and twirled in a lazy circle, the pleated flounces of her polonaise following the movement like the last skater in a whip. "Do you think I'll pass for a winner?"

"As always, your dress is as lovely as you are, Jewel, but I'm afraid that's not what I have in mind."

"It's not?" She dropped her arms to her sides. "What's wrong with it? This is my best dress, save for the ball gowns. Am I supposed to be a Vanderbilt? If so, you'd better raise my salary."

"That's not it at all." He laughed. "You look much too

rich and successful. For this assignment, you'll have to become a bit . . . plainer.''

''Oh?'' Jewel cocked a suspicious eyebrow. She returned to her chair and perched on its edge again. ''Just how plain, Mr. Pinkerton?''

Allan began to examine his immaculate fingernails. ''I have to admit it's not going to be as glamorous a job as some. Not like dressing up in fancy dance hall costumes or high-society ball gowns. Not like that at all.''

''Like what, then?''

He tossed a newspaper across the desk and pointed to an advertisement he'd circled in bright blue ink. ''You'll be dressing according to the whims of an Englishman named Fred Harvey.''

Puzzled, she glanced at Allan, then read the help wanted ad: ''Young woman 18 to 30 years of age, of good character, attractive and intelligent, as waitresses in Harvey Eating Houses in the West. Good wages with room and meals furnished.''

Jewel wrinkled her nose. ''I've never heard of this Harvey or his restaurants. Why can't I be a lady gambler or keep my dance hall girl disguise? It will put me in touch with more of Harry's cohorts than serving meals in some pie and coffee hole-in-the-wall.''

''It would also put you in a position of attracting too much attention. For this—these,'' he corrected,''criminals, I think we should try a fresh approach.'' Allan leaned back in his chair and linked his hands across his remarkably youthful waistline. ''I have a good friend named McIntyre over at the Kansas First National Bank. He says the restaurant in Topeka is the first of several Harvey plans to open along the railroad lines. It was finished just a month or so ago. Best of all, McIntyre tells me Harvey's credentials are impeccable.''

''So?''

''So, missy, you'll blend in with the woodwork, so to speak. This ad only tells the half of it, from what McIntyre says. Harvey's restaurant is a remodeled train depot, and it's serving gourmet meals prepared by French chefs. He also said"—Allan leaned forward shaking his head as if he didn't believe it himself—"that one of those French chefs makes more money than he does, and McIntyre is the president of the bank!"

Jewel issued a long low whistle. "I'm starting to get impressed, but why would I have to be plain if the food is fancy? Wouldn't I be more apt to get the job dressed like this?" She spread her arms, and then another thought occurred to her. "Or have you already arranged with this Harvey fellow to hire me?"

"I'll answer your last question first. While I trust McIntyre's judgment, I haven't had the opportunity to meet or assess this Fred Harvey for myself. I think it would be wiser in this case if you get the job yourself. You'll also have the responsibility," he added with a wink, "of finding a way to *keep* it."

Flashing her employer an injured expression, Jewel lifted her chin and said, "Are you suggesting I'm not capable of serving a few plates of fried ham and eggs?"

"Not at all, dear girl. What I am suggesting is that you may have a bit of difficulty abiding by Harvey's strict rules."

Her chin snapped down and her eyes flew open. "Rules? What kind of rules?"

Allan pushed out of his chair and lumbered over to the door, half dragging his game leg, and called to his secretary, "Maggie? Would you please ask Mac to step in here for a minute?" With a short nod into the other room, he turned and made his way back to his desk.

"Harvey has rules the likes of which you've never seen," he finally answered with a chuckle. "That's why I want you as plain as you can get. Harvey's been losing his pretty waitresses in record numbers to the lonesome cattlemen who hang around the depot. He's beginning to hire plain girls instead of pretty ones. We can't have that beautiful face of yours messing up your chances of landing this job.''

''You'd flatter your own mother if you thought you could get her to go under cover for one of your escapades.''

Laughing, Allan rested his hip against the edge of his desk. ''Once Harvey's hired you,'' he continued, ''you're only halfway there. He'll tell you how to dress, when to talk, and most difficult to accept, where to live.''

''But how can I—''

''That's one reason I've decided to send MacMillan along with you on this job. We'll try to get around that little rule with his help. Besides, it can't hurt to have two of my finest people chasing after two of the best criminal minds we've ever run across.''

But she knew him too well for that, understood that he was somehow concerned for her safety as well. Jewel stood up. ''This is going to be tougher than I first thought, isn't it?''

Allan averted his gaze and stared down at the floor before he finally said, ''It could get real tough—real nasty, too. Harry Benton is a swindler, pure and simple. He doesn't concern me, but Jesse James does. To my knowledge, Jesse's never shot a woman, but then, he's never been the object of such an intense manhunt before, either. I'll understand if you don't want to accept this assignment.''

With a barely perceptible nod she informed him she did understand, then strolled over to the window. The sun had fought its way through the fog and split the horizon. Gripping the windowsill, Jewel leaned forward and closed her eyes. She'd been in danger before. Even the report she'd just turned in related the incident with the Connors fellow and his gun at her throat. Danger was part of the job.

Was it really Jesse James and his ruthless disregard for the lives of others that concerned Allan so? Or was he closing in on the truth about her insatiable thirst for information on Harry Benton—her obsession, as he'd said—to track the man down?

Jewel took several mind-clearing breaths. The soft, comforting aroma of fresh-baked bread called to her, mingled with the sharp, fresh scent of cedar permeating Allan's office. The combination was as reassuring as it was intriguing, made her feel anxious and comforted at the same time. Then Archie MacMillan burst into the room.

"Looking for me, boss?" he said through a sparkling grin.

"The one and only!" Allan gripped his hand and called to his thoughtful operative. "Jewel? Have you made a decision?"

She turned until she was facing the desk. Mac, a scant inch taller than her own five feet four inches, stood level with his employer. Although at fifty-two he was four years younger than Allan, nature had rescinded its loan and snatched back most of his pure white hair, leaving Mac with a ring of short, sparse stubble. This connected with an elongated mustache and oversized sideburns, circling his bald head like a silver moat. His eyes, a pale dove gray, held none of Pinkerton's intensity but more than made up for that with a glimmer of his sheer joy for living. There was no question in her mind as to what her decision would be.

Jewel marched across the room with her hand extended. "I'm looking forward to working with you again, partner."

"Ah, Jewel, I just knew you couldn't resist, even if you do have to dress like a homely old spinster."

"Humph," she muttered, shaking his hand. "There are those who already call me a spinster. I don't think I'll be changing that much."

"Don't worry about what others have to say about you." Mac grinned, sure his next comments would cheer her up. "Why, one look at you ought to tell those folks you're a spinster by choice, not by circumstance."

Jewel gave him a sideways look. "Thanks . . . I think."

"All right, you two." Allan pushed himself away from the desk and walked back to his chair. "Both of you, have a seat and let's get down to business. We have a lot of plans to make and not too much time in which to make them."

* * *

Ten days later Jewel and Mac sat in the austere but very efficient office of Fred Harvey and waited for his decision.

"Highly irregular. Tsk, tsk. Very irregular." The Englishman thumbed through Jewel's documents, then glanced up at the couple. With a wave of one thoroughly scrubbed hand, he said in a thick British accent, "Would you stand, please?"

Wearing the most demure expression she could muster, Jewel delicately stood up and clasped her hands together.

"Whirl around, if you please." Fred Harvey made a circle with his index finger.

Slowly, fighting a scowl, Jewel spun around like a ballerina on a music box. She was dressed in a drab traveling suit of taupe trimmed with deep blue braid. Her glorious auburn hair was parted in the middle and tucked into a severe bun at the back of her neck, but most of its lush texture was covered by a large dark blue bonnet. She wore no makeup, not even a dab of powder to cover the dusting of freckles on her cheeks. She had most definitely achieved the status of a mousy spinster—even before she'd added the octagonal spectacles that made her eyes look like a pair of spoiled eggs.

"Hmm. You may sit." Harvey turned his attention to Mac. "Everything seems to be in order except your request to house your daughter in the Golden Dove Hotel with you. That's a highly irregular request, sir, one that I'm not sure I should even consider. I have a reputation to uphold. I'll not have it tampered with."

"Meaning no disrespect," Mac explained, spinning his bowler hat in his lap, "but I have these terrible spells. If my girl's not close by, I fear one day I may not make it through a rough one. Surely you can understand that. If you'll let her stay in my suite with me, I guarantee on her dear departed mother's grave she'll be confined each evening to her room by . . . ah, by what time?"

"Ten-thirty sharp, sir. Eleven-thirty on weekends, though I'm not sure even that is really within proper bounds."

"Ten-thirty it is, Mr. Harvey, even on the weekends." Out of the corner of his eye, Mac could see Jewel stiffen, but he went on. "If you'll just give her a chance, I know you'll be pleased with her work and her attitude."

"Well . . ." Fred Harvey raked his gaze over Jewel one more time, then shrugged. "All right, Mr. MacMillan. I'll give her a try, but just once. Let her slip up one time, and—"

"It's done. I know the rules, and so does she." He rose and slipped his hand under Jewel's elbow. "Come, daughter. Let's not waste any more of Mr. Harvey's valuable time."

"I'll be delighted to see you to the door." Harvey slid out from behind his dark walnut desk and strolled over to the door. After ushering them into the reception area of the Santa Fe depot, he said by way of farewell, "It's been a pleasure to meet you both. Miss MacMillan, I'll see you at seven in the morning. Sharp."

"Oh, thank you, Mr. Harvey," Jewel managed in her best innocent-little-girl voice. "My father and I will be eternally grateful for this opportunity."

Fred Harvey had closed the door to his office before the last syllable was out. As she turned to Mac to comment about the man's hasty dismissal, Jewel noticed an abrupt movement from one of the people reclining in the waiting room.

Turning her head toward the source, she was suddenly gripped by a sense of doom. Then her gaze connected with a pair of golden brown eyes. The owner of those eyes studied her over the top of a crumpled newspaper, his expression inquisitive.

The gambler!

Jewel's eyes darted back and forth as she looked for an avenue of escape.

The gambler's paper slid even lower as he continued to study her, cocking her head this way and that.

Jewel was unaccustomed to the glasses, which blurred her vision, and she had to hold out her arms to regain her balance. When she was able to see clearly again, she noticed a gleam of recognition in the gambler's eyes, a lazy smile spreading across his face.

A moment later the cocky man's grin had grown so huge it suggested his drawers were lined with ostrich plumes.

# 3

Brent Connors grumbled to himself as he studied the editorial page of the *Topeka Herald*. The news in Kansas was as dull and dusty as the farming communities that dotted the flat countryside. Welcoming the distraction, he peeked over the top of the paper when he heard a woman's voice. Something—not the tone certainly, but the breathless quality mingled with the hint of a deeper intelligence—stirred his memory. Something also didn't fit. The profile she offered didn't match his expectations, and her manner was all wrong, almost subservient. Had he heard right? Had she really referred to the balding gnome at her side as her father? *Another* long lost father?

Brent mentally replaced the blue bonnet with a nest of blond curls, then tore open the bodice of her modest dress to expose her lush, full breasts, and that gave him the clear picture he needed. He straightened his spine and let the newspaper fall onto the marble table beside him. Grinning as those cool green eyes found his from across the room, he stood up and smoothed his waistcoat. The town of Topeka, Kansas, had brightened considerably. His stride deliberate, as confident as the man, he crossed the reception area.

Jewel watched in horror as the gambler approached. "Here comes trouble, Mac," she whispered out of the corner of her mouth. But it was too late for further explanation. He was already upon them.

"Begging your pardon, ma'am," Brent said as he slid his

fingers into the valley at the crown of his Stetson and tipped the hat. "But haven't we met before?"

Jewel didn't have to work to produce the twin blotches of color on her cheeks. Anger and frustration at being caught by this arrogant bastard again supplied more than enough blush to her skin. Looking suitably embarrassed and coy, she covered her mouth with her fingertips and turned to Mac. "The gentleman must be mistaken."

Mac's gravelly voice took on an indignant tone as he faced the stranger. "I am afraid you must have my daughter confused with someone else, sir. Now, if you'll excuse us . . ." He linked his hand through her elbow and turned as if to leave, but the gambler persisted.

"I apologize if I have made a mistake, but I am quite certain the lady and I have crossed paths. It's not often a man has the good fortune to gaze into a pair of emerald eyes as beautiful as hers." Again he tipped his hat. "They are truly unforgettable—as sharp and penetrating as a well-honed stiletto."

Jewel stifled a gasp and avoided his gaze. Trying to look offended, as if she had no idea what he was talking about, she pointed her nose to the ceiling and took a step toward the door.

Wavering, wondering if maybe he *had* somehow mistaken her for the girl in Chicago, Brent blocked her path. "Please don't rush off, little lady. I mean no disrespect." She brushed against him as she tried to circle around him, and he caught her scent. Violets. Expensive violets. The very same tantalizing fragrance worn by the dance hall girl.

Convinced he'd seen through her masquerade, he pushed onward. "I'm almost certain we have something in common—perhaps a mutual acquaintance?"

"Sir," Mac cut in, "I believe my daughter has set you straight. She does not know you."

"Again begging your pardon, I believe it's possible her memory has failed her. I request your permission to jog it."

"I hardly think that will be worth your time or ours. If you'll excuse us—"

"It's all right, Father." Jewel regarded the gambler, wondering if it wouldn't be best to acknowledge him and get it over with. The last thing she and Mac needed was to have him following them around Topeka asking questions and making a general nuisance of himself. Besides, she didn't know enough about him, or about his occupation, to ignore him completely. She shrugged and patted Mac's arm. "He's starting to look a little familiar. Maybe we have met."

"I'd like to think I'm more memorable than that," Brent said with a chuckle. "I certainly had no trouble remembering you. In fact, those cool green eyes are almost as unforgettable as the cold dead eyes of a man you said was your father back in Chicago."

He paused dramatically, then went on, lapsing into his native southern twang. "Why, it truly boggles the mind just thinking about how many men it must have taken to sire a fine specimen like you, ma'am. How many fortunate gentlemen do you call Father—that is, if you don't mind my askin', ma'am?"

"Now see here!" Mac said as he tried to step between them, but Jewel pressed a gloved hand against his chest.

"I'm sure he's only making a joke . . . Father. I believe it's possible that I have made his acquaintance." She glared at Brent, then turned back to Mac. "Would you give me a moment alone with the gentleman, please? I'd like a few words with him."

Glancing first at the stranger, Mac issued a silent warning, then addressed Jewel. "As you wish, daughter, but I won't be out of your view. I'll wait for you by the door. And do be quick about it."

She gave him a short nod, then waited until he was out of earshot before she turned on the gambler. "I am not really convinced that I know you, sir. I simply didn't want my dear father put through any more of your silliness. Just what is it you expect to gain by besmirching my good name in his presence?''

''First off, I don't even know your name.'' He pulled a toothpick from his vest pocket. ''Second, from what I've seen of you so far, there isn't a hell of a lot left for me to besmirch.''

Jewel caught her breath and clenched her teeth. She couldn't afford to let this lousy excuse of a two-bit gambler ruin her first appearance at the Harvey House and perhaps jeopardize the entire mission. She swallowed and produced a wan smile. ''You don't know what you're talking about or with whom you're dealing.''

''I don't?'' His eyes lit up as if this amused him. ''You're right. Maybe this would be a good time for you to inform me just whom I am dealing with, and while you're at it''—he reached out and lifted the brim of her bonnet—''let me know what you did with your yellow hair and the big brown mole you had just about there.'' He flicked his fingertip across her upper lip and grinned.

Jewel slapped his hand away and stepped back. ''If my father knew what you were saying to me, if he knew what you were doing, why he . . . he'd—''

''What?'' Brent held his arm out, taking a long-distance measurement of the stubby-legged man, then drew his hand to mid-chest. ''Will he run over here and kick me in the shins until I crumple into a heap and cry for help?''

Jewel bit her lip and glowered up at him, but he became a blur as she strained to glare through the thick glasses she'd donned for the assignment. Her eyes began twitching and blinking with involuntary spasms.

Brent jerked his chin back and stared at her. ''What's the matter with your eyes? You're not going to pull that fainting act on me again, are you? I'm warning you, if you try it, I'll just let you fall.''

''My eyes are fine. They're a little tired, that's all.'' But they kept on blinking, in spite of her efforts to calm them.

"If you're quite through harassing me, I believe I'll join my father."

"Indulge me a moment longer, if you will. I don't believe I remember hearing your name—the real one. And I would also like to know the name of the man with you."

He had no right to know the answer to either question. She had no obligation to give them. But as she studied him, remembering the first time they'd met, she knew he wouldn't give up easily. He was as determined as he was handsome, as perceptive as he was cocky. If answering the questions—with the fabrications she'd settled on for the assignment—would appease him, it might be worth giving in to him. If her instincts were right, he wouldn't rest until he thought he knew all about her. Silently cussing him, she settled on a plausible story for their earlier meeting.

"All right, sir. I can't hide the truth any longer, but please . . . don't tell my father about— you know . . ." With a dramatic sigh, Jewel whispered, "That horrid little affair in Chicago."

Brent rolled his eyes to the heavens. "I wouldn't dream of such a dreadful thing, ma'am. Do go on."

"Of course." She choked back an imaginary sob. "My name is Jewel MacMillan. And that man is my true father, Archie. Everyone calls him Mac."

"And dear departed Scotty?"

"He, ah . . . Well, it's a truly painful story, sir."

"I'll try not to cry."

Her nostrils flared and her green eyes widened, nearly filling the lenses of the spectacles perched on her nose.

Brent squinted and leaned back. "I don't mean to be indelicate, ma'am, but do you suppose you could remove your spectacles until we've finished talking? I believe if I have to look into them much longer, I'll be gooch-eyed for life."

If the man hadn't been so damned insufferable and nosy, Jewel would have thanked him for the suggestion. As it was, she merely pursed her lips and plucked the offensive glasses from their perch.

"Thanks, ma'am. Now then, as you were saying? Scotty was your . . . ?"

"He was my nothing!" she snapped. "He forced me to accompany him on a wild gambling binge—kidnapped me, if you will. I was happy when he was killed and I could return to my father and the genteel life I was used to."

Brent arched an eyebrow and pushed the toothpick to the far corner of his mouth. "Genteel? I somehow doubt that. But back to your father—ah, this newest one, that is—does he know of the indignities you've so recently suffered?"

"Ah, no, sir, he is blissfully unaware of my adventures in Chicago. I'd be eternally grateful if you'd just forget all about my sordid past and never mention it again."

"That, little lady, is the first thing you've told me that I believe may actually be the truth."

Even though she had to do it with clenched teeth, Jewel gave him her best smile. "Then I hope I can trust your word as a"—she nearly choked on the word—"gentleman to keep my little secret."

"I give you my word, my dear," he said with a grin that surpassed hers. "And please do rest assured that my word is every bit as good as yours."

It was a struggle, but she managed to keep a pleasant, if somewhat frozen, expression. "Thank you again, Mr.—ah, I seem to have forgotten your name, sir."

"Connors," he said, his dimples receding. "Brent Sebastian Connors of the Mississippi Connorses—at your service ma'am. Most folks call me, Brent."

"Yes, I'm sure they do . . . among other things." She gave him a sassy curtsy, adding, "Thank you for your discretion, Mr. Connors, and good day."

"No need to say good-bye just yet. I'll be surprised if I don't find we're staying at the same hotel. Yes, sir, mighty surprised indeed."

Jewel tilted her chin and drew her brows together. "You're not staying at the Golden Dove."

"Of course I am, little lady. Where else?"

"Where else indeed."

Brent bowed and offered his elbow "Allow me to escort you and your father to your lodgings. It seems Topeka has had one of those torrential spring downpours, and the streets are extremely muddy. Perhaps I can be of some assistance in getting your luggage to your rooms."

And because she couldn't think of a good reason to say no, Jewel lamely accepted, "I'm sure Father will be beholden to you."

Later, in their hotel suite, Jewel sank into the cushions of the settee and removed her dreary little bonnet. "What else could I do?" she called out to Mac. "Besides," she added thoughtfully, "I think it would be better for us to stay close to this Connors fellow. If he's as crooked as I think he is, it would be in our best interest to keep track of his every move."

"I don't know, Jewel." Mac shook his head as he lugged the heavy bags across the large living room and into her bedroom. When he emerged, she was loosening the knot of hair at the back of her neck. "He seems dangerous to me."

"Dangerous?" Mulling over everything she knew about the gambler, Jewel sighed and rubbed her scalp with her fingertips as the last of her locks fell free. Just who was this Brent Connors? He was insufferable and opinionated, impertinent and much too handsome for his own good, and yet he kept her on her toes and made her think fast and hard to stay one step ahead of him. He tickled her funny bone and made her feel something she couldn't, or wouldn't, identify. No one, especially no man, had done that for as long as she could remember. Maybe never.

Jewel rested her neck against the back of the sofa, relishing the comfort, and thought back to earlier conversations, to the man himself. He was, if nothing else, a worthy adversary. Was he also a hazard, a threat to her assignment, perhaps her life? Probably not.

Jewel smiled, then yawned. "I think Connors is nosy rather than dangerous. He strikes me as just another gambler— although one to be reckoned with. I'm sure he's here for the championship game like everyone else. Fifty thousand dollars is a powerful reason to make a trip to Topeka."

"I don't know. I still don't feel right about him. We should at least keep him under surveillance."

"Oh, I intend to do better than that." Jewel sat up, refreshed by the thought of the hunt—of the quarry. "I'm sure you'll find him milling around downstairs tonight, sizing up the competition. When you do, I want you to challenge him to a friendly little warm-up game of poker. The minute he takes the bait, I'll head for his room. Before you can drop your aces and say 'read 'em and weep,' I'll know more about that man than his own mother does."

"I don't know if that's such a good idea." Mac shook his head and pressed his lips into a thin line. He weighed his objections carefully, knowing if they sounded the least bit protective, she'd come at him with her speech that began with 'I've managed to live for almost twenty-six years without a father. What makes you think I need one now?'"

Mac opted for reason. "If Connors is what you say he is, I don't see why we should jeopardize our strategy over him. Why don't we just watch him from afar?"

"I believe this is where Allan would say, 'Better safe than sorry.'" Her mind already made up, Jewel pulled herself off the comfortable sofa and started for her room. "I don't see how we can take the chance of jeopardizing our plans by *not* checking him out. I'll be ready to go in fifteen minutes."

Mac shrugged, sighing as he said, "All right, but if anything goes wrong, I'll leave you to answer to Allan."

Thirty minutes later Mac and Jewel strolled into the grand foyer of the Golden Dove Hotel. The walls, awash with scarlet and gold wallpaper and brightly burning glass lamps, made a silent statement of affluence, daring to overwhelm even the most prosperous of visitors. Unimpressed, the Pinkerton agents moved past newly arriving guests lining up at the registration desk, and headed toward the doorway with the large gold letters—Saloon—perched above the lintel.

The steady plink-plink-plink of piano keys pounding out "Buffalo Gals" beckoned reveler and teetotaler alike, but Mac held out his arm just before they passed through the doorway.

"You'd better stay in the lobby, daughter dear. If Fred Harvey should frequent this establishment, I don't think he'd take too kindly to finding one of his pristine waitresses in the saloon."

"Oh, pooh," she grumbled, but knowing he was right, she turned away. "Just be sure to let me know when you've got the gambler set up. I'll be over in the corner trying to blend in with the wallpaper."

Mac took in her Quakerish appearance and chuckled. "In that getup, you won't have to try." Then, with a tip of his low bowler hat, he disappeared into the gay atmosphere of the saloon, leaving Jewel to her own devices.

She stood tapping her toe against the polished wooden floor for several minutes, longing to join the merriment, wishing she were dressed like the fashionable ladies in the lobby. In keeping with her assignment, she wore a calico dress of dragon green with a plain little prune-colored bonnet hiding her crowning glory. She still wore the spectacles, but had learned to push them as far down her nose as possible, eliminating the need to look through them often. She was drab, dull, and decidedly bored.

With a sigh, Jewel strolled over by the stairway and sat on a wooden settee. She picked up a copy of *Godey's Lady's Book* and absently thumbed through it as she studied the visitors sprinkled throughout the lobby. Most of the guests were men, and most, she concluded from their manner of dress, were here for the championship. She scanned their faces, searching for one in particular, finding no one she recognized. She'd seen Harry Benton only once, three years ago in New York City. He'd sported a full beard and coal-black hair back then, and he'd cut a fine figure. Had he changed? Was his hair gray? Would she recognize him if she came face to face with him?

Yes, she thought with a scowl. She would know him by his small beady eyes, his calculating manner, and his aloof—

"Is everything all right, daughter?"

Jewel's head snapped up, knocking her bonnet askew. She straightened the hat and managed a feeble smile when she noticed the gambler standing beside Mac. "Yes, Father. I—I was just thinking."

"I sincerely hope you were thinking of someone other than me," Brent said with a tip of his hat. "If looks could kill, I fear I should have to order my gravestone."

"Given your penchant for sticking your nose in other people's business," she blurted out as she rose, "I would think that to be an excellent idea regardless."

"Jewel!" Mac complained. "Where are your manners? Mr. Connors had just consented to a game of cards. I would like him to think he'll be playing with a gentleman who has raised a fine daughter."

"I am sorry, Father. I don't know what came over me." Digging deep into the bag of tricks she'd acquired during her college drama course, she turned to Brent and managed to apologize as if she meant it. "Please forgive me, sir. I must be more tired from our long trip than I thought. I believe I shall retire." She gave the gambler a quick nod, then turned to Mac. "Good night, Father. And good luck."

"Good night, daughter." Mac leaned forward and kissed her cheek. "Don't wait up for me. Mr. Connors and I may attract a few other players."

Again she smiled and gave them a short nod. Then Jewel began to climb the long stairway.

After forcing herself to wait until she'd reached the first landing, she finally spun around and glanced throughout the lobby. Mac and Brent were gone. Moving quickly, Jewel hurried back down the stairs and pushed her way through the crowd to the reception desk.

"Excuse me?" she called to the clerk as she removed a blank piece of paper from her reticule and folded it in half. "I have a message for Mr. Brent Connors. Would you please see that he gets it?"

The harried man snatched the paper from her hand, barely glancing at it or her. "Sure, lady," he said as he turned and pushed it into the slot of room ten.

"Thank you," she said airily. "You'll just never know how grateful I am." Then she waded back through the crowd and dashed up the stairs.

When she reached room ten, Jewel stopped and looked up and down the hall. Satisfied she was alone, she lifted her skirt and removed the pearl-handled stiletto from the leather holster strapped to her right thigh. Moving quickly, carefully, she maneuvered the tip of the blade inside the lock until she heard a click. She turned the knob and slipped inside the darkened room.

Waiting for her eyes to adjust to the dim light, listening for any kind of movement, she stood stock still for a full minute. Then Jewel reached for the wall bracket and turned up the wick on the lamp. She made a visual sweep of the room, noting its impressive size, sparse furnishings, and burgundy flowered wallpaper. A large brass bed with one side table seemed almost lonely against the long back wall. Across the room, an oversized chiffonier stood near a small closet door. The only other piece of furniture was a full-length looking glass in an ornate freestanding frame of dark walnut.

Jewel headed to the closet and opened the door. It was pin neat, with not so much as a handkerchief out of place. She lifted her skirts and replaced the knife, then made a quick search of the suits hanging in front of her. She found nothing in the pockets. She closed the door and concentrated on the high chiffonier. Beginning with the bottom drawer, Jewel started to pick through the assortment of socks and handkerchiefs when she heard the distinct clink of metal against metal. Someone was using a key to open the already unlocked door!

With no time to consider her options, Jewel slid across the floor and under the bed. The intruder stepped into the room just as she pulled her feet beneath the mattress.

Brent sauntered across the threshold, his expression expectant, and began singing. "Oh, Buffalo gals won't you come out tonight, come out tonight, come out tonight, Buff—" He interrupted the song when he noticed the lamp. "Strange," he muttered, his voice unnaturally loud, "I could have sworn I turned that wick down before I left."

He swiveled, taking in all corners of the room, then grinned and approached the closet. With a jerk, he opened the door and peered inside. His clothes stared back at him. After taking off his Stetson, he sailed it up to the shelf and ran his fingers through his thick, coarse hair. Had he been wrong?

Puzzled, he crossed the room and sat down on the edge of his bed. He was positive he'd been set up by the girl and her father, or whoever he was. And if his instincts weren't enough to convince him, the old man had nearly choked when he'd claimed a sudden headache and excused himself from the game before it began. So where was the girl? She couldn't have gone through his things and robbed him that fast. Again he wondered if he had misjudged them.

Drawing a deep breath, Brent collapsed against the pillows with a low groan. Maybe he was getting overly suspicious, becoming incapable of judging anyone since he'd taken up this idiotic search for the scoundrel Harry Benton. Yet, he consoled himself, the girl had presented herself as two different women in two completely different circumstances. What else could she be but a confidence artist or a thief?

Brent took another long breath and froze. Violets. He sniffed the air again. Devon Violet te Eau de Toilette, to be more precise, his trained nose told him. Grinning, he sat up and began whistling the tune he'd been singing earlier. Little Miss Jewel, whoever she was, couldn't resist bathing in her favorite perfume no matter what manner of dress she donned. She'd been here all right, he thought to himself. And if he didn't miss his guess or the strength of the aroma, she hadn't yet left.

Bouncing off the edge of the bed, Brent continued whistling as he crossed the room. Just before he reached the door, he dropped his pocket watch and bent down to retrieve it. A quick glance under his bed confirmed his suspicions. If he strained, he could just make out the heel of a lady's shoe near the edge of the burgundy coverlet.

Coughing to hide a sudden burst of laughter, Brent stood up and removed his jacket. Now what? He ought to just march across the room and drag her out from beneath his bed. He could have her arrested for trespassing. He had every right to threaten to expose her and the old man for what they were and demand they leave town. There were lots of things he *could* do, but as he rubbed the spot on his inner thigh where her knife had left its mark, he decided none of those things came close to what she deserved.

Grinning broadly, Brent settled on a plan. Before the night was over, this little Jewel with the emerald eyes would think twice before she tried to rob him or stick a knife in him again. Brent opened the door to his room and rang the bell hanging on the jamb.

A few minutes later a young lad appeared at the opening. "Yes, sir, Mr. Connors. What kin I git for you?"

Brent dropped several coins into the boy's hand. "I'd like a bottle of chilled champagne and two glasses. And make sure," he tossed in as he added more coins to the pile, "that the prettiest little gal you can find working in the saloon brings it up to me. Tell her she'll be staying awhile."

"Yes, sir, and thanks!" The boy shoved the coins in his

pocket and ran down the hall before Brent could get the door closed.

Beneath the bed Jewel stifled a groan, thinking, Dear God, what have I gotten myself into? She listened to the sounds of fabric rustling as the gambler removed some of his clothing and made himself comfortable for his female visitor. She heard him open a drawer of the chiffonier, followed by several sharp slaps. Shortly the essence of bayberry drifted under the bed and assaulted her nostrils. It promised to be a very long night.

When a light tapping sounded in the room, Brent smoothed the sides of his hair and opened the door wide. "Do come in," he said pleasantly to the dance hall girl.

Balancing the tray on one hand, she brought the other to her mouth and giggled. "Evening, sir. Is this what you ordered?" She was clearly referring to her body, not the spirits.

Brent smiled at the girl and said, "You'll do just fine." He closed the door and relieved her of her burden. After crossing the room, he deposited the tray on the side table, sank down on the mattress, and patted the spot beside him. "Come on. Join me, won't you, sugar?"

"'Course honey!" The girl skipped across the room, all bouncing breasts and flame-red curls. As she neared the bed, she sprang onto the coverlet beside Brent.

The mattress sagged, coming within an inch of Jewel's nose. She began praying: Just let me out of this one, God. Let me out of this room before they do . . . it, and I swear I'll never ask for another thing as long as I live.

A loud pop, followed by hysterical girlish giggles cut into her desperate thoughts.

"Oh, honey!" the girl cried through her squeals of delight. "If you're near as lively as this here bubbly, you and me are gonna have us some good time!"

"I've never had any complaints, with or without the champagne," he said as he filled the glasses.

Then you've never been with a woman you didn't have to pay, came an unbidden thought from beneath the bed.

Brent held up two glasses of champagne and offered one to the dance hall girl. "To you . . . what's your name, sugar?"

Accepting the drink, she giggled again. "Lilly—but not because I'm lily pure! I'm more the 'gilded' type."

"I'll drink to that!" Brent clinked his glass against hers and downed the sparkling wine in one gulp.

Placing his index finger under Lilly's chin, he regarded her. "Say, you know what? You remind me of someone. A little dance hall gal from Chicago named . . . named—" Brent snapped his fingers and shook his head. "Funny, her name escapes me, but it was something like Opal. No, that's not it—Ruby? No. Maybe it was Esmeralda. No. Oh, Well. It was some kind of jewel—say, that's it! Her name was Jewel."

"So?" Lilly shrugged. "Why do you mention her when you got me?"

"Why indeed?" Brent said, slapping his knee. "Why, that gal couldn't hold a candle to a beauty like you. She had blond fuzzy hair, but I happen to know," he added, his laugh low and bawdy, "her real hair color is kind of reddish brown, if you know what I mean."

"Oh, I got you all right." Lilly giggled. "You're a bad one, you are!"

Beneath the bed, Jewel fumed. And she resumed praying: Please, God. If you'll just let me at him for ten minutes, I swear I'll never ask for another thing.

"And Jewel's eyes—they're really strange," Brent continued, enjoying himself immensely. "They're sort of pea green, but when she wears her glasses, they look a lot like some sowbelly I once had go bad on me."

Five minutes, God, Jewel prayed. Just five minutes and a bullwhip. That's all I ask.

"Say, if this gal is such a mess, why do you keep talkin' about her?"

"Oh, I don't know, Lilly. It sure isn't because I found her attractive. It must be because the wretched little thief stuck a knife in me."

"Oh, you poor man," Lilly gasped. "Where?"

"Would you really like to see? It's in kind of a private spot, but I suppose it wouldn't hurt to show you. Maybe you can kiss it and make it all better for me." Brent moved around on the mattress, more for effect than anything.

Beneath the bed, the prayers ceased: All right, that's it! I don't care what happens to this assignment, I am not going to lie here and listen to that dandy assault that cheap saloon girl any more than I'm going to listen to her moan and groan and tell him how wonderful he is. Allan, forgive me, but—

A loud pounding at the door cut off Jewel's thoughts and the movement above her.

"Hold your horses," Brent called as he climbed off the bed. "I'm coming." When he opened the door, Mac stood in the entry, his hat in his hand.

"Excuse me, Mr. Connors. I don't mean to disturb you, but you seemed so sickly when you left the table, I thought I'd look in on you."

"Well, that's right neighborly of you, old boy." He slapped Mac on the back, pulling him into the room in the same movement. "Isn't that the most neighborly thing you've ever heard of, Lilly girl?"

Mac looked around the gambler's broad shoulders to the woman perched on the bed. It wasn't Jewel. Somehow he and his partner had managed to miss each other going to and from their suite—or she was still trapped here in this room. He took a quick inventory. If she had been trapped, she would have to be in the closet or under the bed. Whatever had happened to her, he knew there was nothing he could do but leave.

Mac replaced his hat and covered his concern with a friendly smile. "I'm sorry to disturb you, Mr. Connors. I didn't realize you had company. I'll just be going."

Lose someone? Brent thought before he trusted himself to

speak to the other half of this obvious team of thieves. "Thanks for worrying about me, but as you can see, I'm well taken care of. Lilly here is known for her . . . massages. If she can't get rid of my headache, nothing will. Have a pleasant evening. See you tomorrow."

"Ah, yes. Good night," Mac sputtered as he backed out of the room.

Suddenly angry, Brent had to restrain himself to keep from slamming the door. After closing it quietly, he wheeled around and stared at Lilly. Now what was he going to do with her?

With a heavy sigh, he started toward the bed. "Tell you what, darlin'. The more I look at you, the more you remind me of that wretched little gal back in Chicago. So much so that I'm afraid I couldn't possibly share anything more than a glass of champagne with you."

Beneath the bed, Jewel gritted her teeth, out of prayers and resolutions, devoid of patience.

"Are you sure, honey?" Lilly asked as she got up off the mattress. "I can work magic on even the most stubborn little ole—"

"That's comforting to know, darlin', but I do still have that headache. Besides, you're starting to sound like that Jewel gal, too, and her voice screeches worse than a rusty gate hinge. Be a dear and run along."

"Well," she pouted, "all right, but—"

"I'm way ahead of you. Time is money, right?" The girl's eyes lit up as Brent pulled several coins out of his pocket and dropped them into her palm. "Maybe some other time."

"All right, honey." Lilly sashayed over to the door and let herself out.

Suddenly exhausted, tired of the game as well, Brent made a decision about the unwelcome guest beneath his bed. She hadn't suffered nearly enough or long enough. His mind made up, he stalked over to the door and began pushing coins into the crack between the edge and the jamb.

The little green-eyed bundle of dynamite might try to escape once he nodded off, but she wouldn't get away without waking him up. She could just lie on the hard floor until that happened. Then he would quite happily have her arrested.

Beneath the bed, Jewel listened as he rigged the door, knew he'd done something to make it impossible for anyone to sneak into his room—or out. She heard Brent return to the bed, recognized the sounds of buttons popping on his shirt and trousers, and realized by the further rustling of material that he'd stripped down to nature's own. Then he pulled back the covers and launched himself into the center of the bed. The mattress sagged and lurched, brushing the tip of her nose on one downswing, before he finally settled for the night.

She heard his exaggerated yawns, weary groans, and heavy sighs. Then, silence.

Jewel lay there for what seemed like hours before the sounds of light snoring finally reached her ears. Bridling the impulse to scoot out then, she waited until the snores became deeper, more rhythmic, before she acted on her revised plan.

Before the first light of dawn trickled in through the open window, Brent woke up, startled and confused. Something was wrong. He breathed deeply, already sensing there was no longer a hint of violets in the air.

He leapt from the bed and checked the door. All the coins were in place. Perplexed, he turned back to stare at the bed. Was she . . . or wasn't she?

Impatiently he crossed the room and dropped to his knees. Lifting the coverlet from the floor, Brent peered underneath.

The only thing hiding beneath the bed was a lot of lint.

# 4

A light sleeper by necessity, Harry Benton woke at the grating sound of wood scraping against wood. The rustling of fabric near his window alerted him to the fact that the noises were probably caused by an intruder. Quietly reaching beneath his pillow, he withdrew the derringer nestled there. Then Harry sat up, his catlike eyes searching the darkness.

When a form glided by the foot of the bed, he demanded, "Who goes there?"

"Oh, ah . . ." Jewel mumbled as she crept across the room. "Hotel security. No need to be alarmed. Everything's all right now."

"Hotel *what*?"

But by the time Harry got the words out, his door had opened and closed. The intruder had vanished.

Beside him a sleepy female voice said, "Was someone just in here with us, H.C.?"

"Hush!" he whispered as he climbed out of bed. "Whoever it was just went out the door. I'm going to have a look around."

Harry tiptoed over near the doorjamb and pressed his ear against the wood. He heard the patter of fading footsteps skipping across the carpeted hallway, then silence. A burglar? Or had the law somehow gotten wind of his return to the States? His eyes more used to the dark by now, he made his way to the window, then slammed it shut and locked it. Feeling uneasy, a little less confident than usual, he crossed back over to the bed and slid beneath the covers.

More awake now, the countess DeMorney sat up and said, "Will you please tell me what that was all about?"

"I'm not sure," he said as he pushed the small pistol back under his pillow. "The woman said she was hotel security, but I wouldn't bet your jewels on it."

"What on earth would a woman guard be doing in here?" she asked through a yawn.

Ninety percent sure the intruder had been nothing more than an inept member of his own profession, Harry relaxed and sighed. His features well hidden by the moonless night, he broke into a knowing grin and said, "Probably something to do with the poker tournament."

"So they guard us from *inside* our rooms?"

"My dear, you really can't be too careful these days," he warned as he gently pushed her back down on the mattress. "Why a big pot like that is bound to draw its share of crooks and swindlers."

"Well!" the countess said in a huff. "At least she could have knocked."

"I don't think you understand. It is generally unwise for thieves to announce their presence." At her gasp, Harry explained further. "If that young lady was a security guard, I'm the duke of Kent," he laughed, nearly strangling as he remembered he'd once passed himself off as that very member of the nobility.

"Maybe you'd better get up and check your money clip," she suggested.

"I doubt she was after anything of mine, dear lady." Barely able to suppress the urge to laugh, he said, "You are the one wearing the jewels. I imagine a person with less than honorable intentions might think you're just ripe for the plucking, Countess."

"Oh, don't be silly," she scoffed. "I don't have anything to worry about as long as you're with me, H.C. And by the way," she added playfully, "you don't have to call me Countess. My name is Penelope."

"I'd be delighted to call you Penelope, my dear. And you may call me . . . Harry." He leaned over and kissed her bare shoulder. "Now then—where were we before we were so rudely interrupted?"

"Sleeping." She laughed.

"Were we?" he said, feigning astonishment. "I must have been having a very vivid dream. Would you like me to show you what happened in it, my dear Penelope?"

"Oh, Harry, I don't know."

"Allow me this small indulgence, my sweet." Without waiting for her reply, he reached beneath the sheets and slid his hand along her nude body. After gently coaxing her fleshy thighs apart, he whispered, "If I recall, one of us was reciting a little rhyme. . . . *This* little piggy went to market—"

"Oh, Harry!" The countess giggled.

"And this little piggy stayed home. But *this* little piggy went whee, whee, whee . . . all the way *home*!"

The countess gasped, then groaned, "Ohhhhh, Harry."


Standing above them in the hallway on the third floor, Jewel trembled at the door to her suite. She rapped against the wood again, calling as loud as she dared, "Mac? For God's sake, wake up and let me in!"

The second a space appeared near the jamb, Jewel pushed her way inside the room and slammed the door shut behind her. "Holy hell if I haven't had myself a night!"

Trying to rub the sleep as well as the guilt from his tired eyes, Mac said, "Where have you been all this time? I looked for you, but—"

"I know you did. I recognized your shoes," she joked, finally able to relax a little. Pulling off her glasses, Jewel crossed the entryway and headed for the sideboard. "Have we got anything to drink in here? Some brandy or cognac? I could definitely use a belt."

"Sure," he said, joining her. "You sit down. I'll get it for you.'' As he worked, he continued his interrogation. ''So you were under Connors's bed?''

''Uh-huh.'' She groaned as she eased her aching body down onto the soft couch. ''For hours and hours. Now I know what it feels like to be stretched out in the morgue.''

''We'll get you warmed up in a minute here,'' he said, studying the row of bottles. ''How did you get out of his room? Peach brandy all right?''

''Sounds wonderful, and through the window.''

''The window?'' Mac wrinkled his nose, then poured two large snifters of liqueur. Balancing the drinks, he walked back to the couch, his head cocked. ''Pretty steep drop from the second floor, wasn't it?''

''Not if you crawl along the ledge and duck into the first open window you come to, it isn't.'' Jewel accepted the drink. Without waiting for Mac to join her, she took a long, slow pull on it. Then she leaned her head against the back of the couch, closed her eyes, and waited for the brandy to loosen the tight knots her muscles had become.

From beside her, Mac's kind voice inquired, ''Did he ever see you or realize you were in his room?''

''Who?'' she said lazily as the liqueur spread its fire through her system. ''Brent Connors or the unfortunate fellow I woke up?''

Mac laughed. ''Both.''

''We'll start with the stranger,'' she said, laughing along with him. ''He most assuredly knew I was in his room. I passed myself off as hotel security, but God knows what he thought when I waltzed across his bedroom and swept out his door! He'll probably wake up in the morning and think he had a really strange dream.''

Through a chuckle, Mac said, ''And Connors? Surely the experience was a little more . . . disturbing than a gay stroll through the room.''

Jewel inched her eyelids open, her green eyes darkening along with her thoughts. She lifted her glass, drained the contents in one large swallow, then held the empty snifter out to Mac. "Again, please."

"Jewel, I don't—"

"Please, Mac?" she pleaded. "I'm beat, and I figure I've got maybe two hours before I have to report to my new exciting job. I intend to sleep the sleep of the dead for those two little hours, and Mr. Peach Juice here is going to see that I do. If you won't get it, I will."

"No, no. You stay put." Mac grabbed the snifter, then hurried back to the sideboard. As he refilled the glass, he said, "I—I saw the girl Connors had in his room. I hope you weren't subjected to, you know, too much—"

Jewel laughed out loud, cutting off his words, unraveling the last of her tension. Mac approached her, his brow drawn, and gave her the drink. "Sorry," she said, still laughing, "but our handsome, cocky Mr. Connors was—how shall I say it?—unable to perform."

Instantly sorry he'd even broached the subject, Mac looked away from his partner. He cleared his throat and said, "Maybe he realized you were in his room. Is that possible?"

Jewel hesitated, closing her eyes again as another swallow of brandy trickled through her veins. The thought had occurred to her, especially when Brent had been telling the girl about his experiences with the "dance hall gal from Chicago." She knew that if she studied his behavior from every angle, she would most likely conclude that he'd known she was there all along.

The trouble was, she would also have to accept the fact that he'd bested her. If he *had* left her to rot under his bed while he slept the night away, his actions would warrant an elaborate act of revenge from her at the very least. Jewel thought back to the things he'd said, remembered his condescending attitude at the Harvey House, and decided it didn't much matter if he'd known or not. In either case, she owed him one.

Jewel tossed the rest of the brandy down, then struggled

to her feet. "That's it. I'm off to bed. Good night, Mac—or should I say, good morning?"

"Try to fool yourself and say good night." Mac collected the empty glass, then caught her attention one more time before she disappeared. "What time would you like to get up?"

Hesitating at her bedroom door, she looked back over her shoulder. "Mr. Harvey likes his girls plain and unattractive. I don't need to spend much time getting ready for this job—six-thirty ought to do it."

At one minute before seven Jewel passed through the depot waiting room and into the Harvey House restaurant. Fred Harvey stood by the door, holding his watch fob in his hand.

"Good morning, Miss MacMillan," he said as she approached. "Just go on into the kitchen and report to Mrs. Jahner. She will show you what to do."

"Thank you and good morning to you, Mr. Harvey." Jewel made half curtsy as she passed by the man, then bit her lip and forced herself not to yawn as she reached the kitchen.

She stood in the doorway, trying to look interested in her new surroundings, and studied the assortment of chefs and helpers as she glanced around for her supervisor. When a large, thick woman elbowed her way through the workers, then stomped in her direction, it was all Jewel could do to keep from spinning around and running out through the front door.

"I'm Maggie Jahner. You looking for me?"

Jewel nodded and produced a shy smile. "I'm Jewel MacMillan. Nice to meet you." She stuck out her hand, but the big woman ignored it and went on with her speech.

"In the future be in this kitchen at ten minutes before the hour." She stood back, gripping her own pointed chin between two meaty fingers, and examined her newest charge. "Hmm," she grumbled. "I s'pose you'll do, but don't forget that Mr. Harvey expects perfection from everyone who works for him. If you get so much as a speck of egg on that white apron, have someone watch your station while you come in here and change it immediately.'' Maggie lifted a slablike arm and twirled her finger. ''Let's have a look at your skirt and blouse.''

Still fighting the urge to yawn, Jewel did as she was told and turned around in a slow circle.

''Guess that'll do, but don't be sitting around getting all wrinkled up. Just 'cause you got on a black skirt don't mean the creases won't show. Come, I'll show you to your station.'' As they walked, Maggie glanced at her watch. ''The first train arrives in about a half hour. You got till then to acquaint yourself with the other waitresses and find out the best way to do things, but once we get some customers in the place, not another word between you—understood?''

''Between who? Me and the other waitresses or—''

'''Course, you and the other girls. Nary a word—hear?''

''Yes, ma'am.'' Jewel managed to resist the urge to salute, but she opened her mouth, sucked in a huge gulp of air, and yawned instead.

Maggie leaned her bulk forward and stared at the dark rings under Jewel's eyes. ''You make it to bed before curfew last night?''

''Oh, yes, ma'am,'' she lied, blinking in an effort to moisten her tired eyes. ''I didn't sleep too well in my new surroundings, though. I'll be perkier tomorrow.''

''See that you are.'' Maggie looked away from her and pointed to a section of the dining room. ''Those tables are yours, and it looks like you got your first customer. Here—take him this menu and keep his coffee cup filled. You got to learn sometime, might as well be now.''

Jewel straightened her shoulders, nodding to her supervisor, and marched stiff-backed to the table where a man sat reading the newspaper. ''Good morning,'' she said sweetly. ''Welcome to Harvey House. May I get you some coffee?'' The paper fell to the table, revealing the man's features.

"Morning, little lady," Brent Connors said through a broad grin. "I appreciate the offer. Make it two cups. Looks like you could use one yourself."

Jewel bit her lip and closed her eyes. Not this morning, she prayed silently. Please, God, not this morning! Grumbling to herself, she took a deep breath and stared down at him. "What do you want?"

"Breakfast—like most folks who stop by here. You have some kind of problem with that, little lady?"

"I've got a problem with you," she spit out.

"Tsk-tsk," he said, his dimples carved into his cheeks. "You're a bit on the testy side this morning. Lose some sleep last night?"

Refusing to be baited, even though she now knew he had realized she was under his bed, Jewel gave him a smile that was little more than a grimace and said, "I slept just fine, if it's any of your business. Here. If you can read this, decide what you want." She tossed the menu on the table, adding as she walked away, "I'll be right back with your coffee."

Laughing to himself, he watched her retreat, taking particular delight in the stiff back and angry gait. But then something about the way she moved, the way her round little bottom effortlessly guided the bustles beneath her plain skirt, caught his attention and cut off his breath. Damn, he thought to himself, acknowledging a spurt of desire, too bad the little lady's a thief.

Brent shifted in his chair and reached for a toothpick. Knowing she'd broken into his room was one thing, he thought, admiring her ingenuity, but getting her to admit it was going to be quite another. Suddenly looking forward to the diversion, the challenge, Brent spread his linen napkin across his lap and picked up the menu just as his quarry returned.

"Sugar and cream are on the table," Jewel announced as she poured steaming coffee into the fine china cup. "Have you decided what you'll have for breakfast yet?"

Brent looked up from the menu, through her octagonal

glasses, and into her tired green eyes. With a lopsided smile, he said, "I believe I'll have some, ah . . ." He squinted, pulling the toothpick from his mouth. "A pair of fried eggs. Please make sure they're fresh."

"The only thing fresh around here is *you*!" The knowledge that she was very close to losing her temper, her control, and even worse, her job wasn't enough to help Jewel muster up the necessary calm. In a voice much louder than was proper, a tone lacking any respect, she demanded. "Make up your mind you two-bit gambler. Just what is it you want?"

Brent raised his eyebrows and cocked his head as he began a slow perusal of her body. "It was easier to decide that when we met in Chicago. I liked that dress a whole lot better than this frigid spinster getup."

Jewel banged the pot down on the table, splattering the fine linen with coffee, and shook a finger in his face. "Listen, you overblown puffed-up dandy. I've had just about all I'm going to take from you."

From behind her, Jewel heard a distinct ahem! She lifted her chin, turned around, and was not surprised in the least to find Maggie Jahner jabbing her with a pointed gaze.

The stern-faced woman approached. "Is there some problem here, Miss MacMillan?"

"Oh, ah, the c-coffee. I, ah . . ." Jewel sputtered, chagrined to realize that she'd put her job in jeopardy. "I seem to have—"

"It's my fault," Brent offered. "I'm afraid I stuck my boot out at an inopportune moment for the young lady. Please forgive me"—he looked straight into Jewel's green eyes—"sugar pie."

Sucking in an angry breath, she glared back at him, but somehow managed a sweet sigh and a breathless "Don't give it another thought, suh. I'll just bring you a clean tablecloth. Would you like anything with those eggs besides fried potatoes? Bacon perhaps? Or ham?"

"Oh, no question about it—I'll have the . . . *ham*."

Her smile forced, Jewel said, "Right away, sir. Excuse me, Mrs. Jahner?" She curtsied and bounced off toward the kitchen as if she didn't have a care in the world.

As Jewel gathered the fresh linens, she cursed the fact she'd ever laid eyes on Brent Connors, then made herself a promise. She simply could not allow that insufferable man to draw her into any further conversation, nor could she let him jeopardize her job again. From now on, she would draw on her considerable acting talents whenever he was near, and behave as if she were a mute.

Her mind made up, Jewel glided back into the dining room and began moving the china and fine silver to one edge of his table. Although she kept his outline in the corner of her vision, she did not make eye contact with the gambler.

Amused by the sudden change, challenged by this new stoical exterior, Brent pushed his chair back from the table and crossed his legs. "How's your debonair father this morning, sweet lips?"

Jewel pulled the soiled cloth off the table and rolled it into a ball. Her mouth was set and determined.

Brent persisted. "What do you suppose your father's up to while you're slaving away in here? Robbing hotel rooms?"

Jewel spread the new tablecloth. She raised the corner of her upper lip just the slightest bit, but she remained calm.

"Perhaps he's robbing little old ladies of their egg money," Brent went on, "or marking a fresh deck of cards for tonight's big game."

Jewel replaced the silver and fine china. The freckles on the tip of her nose wriggled as she frowned, but she remained silent.

Brent leaned forward and sniffed the air. "Hmm, violets, isn't it? A lovely scent. I seem to recall it from . . . Where was it I recently . . . Why, I believe it was in my own room, just last night!"

Jewel gasped as she reached for the coffee pot, and in

spite of her vows, chanced a look into his warm brown eyes.
So that was it, she thought, almost laughing out loud. She
smiled, offering a silent That's one point for you, Mr.
Bayberry Cologne, then quietly refilled his coffee cup.

Touched by what he saw in her eyes, more confused and
more interested in her than ever, Brent played out his hand.
"By the way, sugar pie, you snore like a grizzly in
hibernation."

"I do not!" she snapped, all vows forgotten. "If anyone
snores, it's you! You sound as if—" Again banging the
coffee pot down on the table, she blanched and spun around,
partly to ensure the safety of her job, but mainly to avoid
admitting she'd fallen into yet another of his traps. Maggie
was nowhere in sight. The few customers sprinkled throughout the restaurant seemed unaware of, or uninterested in, her
tantrum.

Jewel turned back to Brent and went on with her tirade.
"Good Lord, Mr. B. S. Connors, you really ought to go by
your initials. They certainly say a lot about your character.
You are the most—" The shrill whistle of the approaching
train cut off her words and reminded her of the job she had
to do. Furious with herself for the lapse in her professional
demeanor, Jewel pressed her lips together and turned to
walk away.

Brent reached out and caught her wrist. "Not so fast,
little lady." He cocked his head, listening as the train
chugged into the depot. "You may have been saved by the
whistle this time, but you and I are going to have the rest of
this conversation soon!"

"Let go of me!" she insisted, tugging at her arm.

Brent tightened his grip. "I'm not through with you yet.
I've got a warning, and you'd better hope your dear sweet
daddy has enough brains to rob someone besides me today.
I don't cotton to uninvited guests in my room. Next time it
happens, I intend to prosecute."

Her green eyes flashing, Jewel ground her teeth. "I don't

know what you're talking about. Now for the last time, let me go.''

''And for the last time—if you want to visit my room, just ask. I promise you'll be a lot more comfortable.'' He winked, raking his gaze across her bosom, then lower. ''I might even let you lie down on *top* of my bed.''

''Oh, that's it!'' She tore her wrist out of his grasp and stomped off to tend the passengers filing into the restaurant.

''Welcome to the Harvey House,'' she forced herself to say over and over, even as the sound of Brent's laughter rang in her ears. ''And how many coffees here?''

Jewel fell into the routine then, grateful for the rush of customers, and traded Brent's table to one of the other waitresses. She kept pace with the more experienced girls, serving countless plates of biscuits and gravy, mopping up spills of honey and grits, and running from table to table with a full pot of coffee. When at last a lull seemed to settle over the crowd, when all were at some stage of filling their bellies, Jewel wiped her brow with the back of her hand and looked around the room. Brent, she noticed, still lingered over his breakfast, his face buried in the newspaper. All of her customers seemed content.

Her glance skipped to the other stations. Jewel dropped her waitress mien and began to study the patrons like a detective. As her gaze roamed the room, eager to settle on someone, anyone who might resemble Harry Benton, the familiar features of Jesse James suddenly filled her vision, stopping the search quicker than he could fleece his victims.

Slicked back, greasy-looking brown hair, close-set muddy brown eyes, stubbly days-old beard. She could have written the wanted poster. The man was most definitely the leader of the James gang. Slowly inching her way across the room, Jewel glanced at the other men at the table. The outlaw sat with his brother Frank; Jewel didn't know the three other gang members. All of them appeared to be close to finishing their meal, she noticed with alarm.

Mary Elizabeth, the waitress for the James table, emerged

from the kitchen carrying two platters of sausages and biscuits, and Jewel settled on a plan. Feeling a twinge of regret, but lacking the time to seek another solution, she grabbed a pot of coffee and headed into the unsuspecting girl's path.

"Oh, my Lord," Jewel gasped as she collided with Mary Elizabeth, spilling the contents of the plates all over the poor girl's crisp white shirtwaist and apron. "How terribly awkward of me!"

"Oh!" the young waitress squealed. "Oh, my stars!"

"Don't worry, dear," Jewel promised as she bent down and began cleaning the mess off the floor. "I'll take care of your station. You go change into fresh clothes."

"Oh—oh, my! Yes, I'd better run and do that. Thank you." Mary Elizabeth put her fingers to her mouth and backed self-consciously out of the dining room.

After she'd done her best to clear the floor, Jewel grabbed a fresh pot of coffee and advanced on the James brothers.

"Morning, gentlemen. More coffee, anyone?"

Jesse looked up at her and smiled, his dark reptilian eyes shining with excitement. "Hobbs? Bill? Everybody all set?" He turned back to Jewel. "Thanks, but we're all full up—with coffee, anyways."

"Maybe I can get you something else," she said, the model of efficiency. "Some pie or—"

"No, gal. The only thing you can get now is out of our way."

The James boys chuckled in unison, but Jewel didn't budge. Jesse glanced over at Frank, then slid his hands along the sides of his hair. "Go on now, gal. Skedaddle on outta here," he repeated as he straightened his tie and stood up.

Jewel took one step back, then stood her ground.

Jesse straightened his broad tie and addressed the roomful of diners.

"Welcome to Topeka, ladies and gents," he began, his scruffy beard the only thing out of place in his otherwise gentlemanly appearance. "Me and the boys here are a kind a welcoming committee. Ain't that right, boys?"

The rest of the men stood and bowed as they slowly turned, surveying the crowd.

Rapidly searching for a way to bring the situation under control, to arrest the outlaws without endangering the lives of the customers, Jewel remained not two feet behind Jesse.

Unaware she was still there, Jesse continued his speech, his grin easygoing and friendly. "How many of you are here for the big poker tournament?" At the overwhelming applause, he glanced at his companions and gave them a short nod. The four men split apart, each heading for a corner of the room.

"The boys and I are mighty glad to hear that. So glad, in fact, we've decided to save you the trouble of going into town. You can lose your stakes without ever leaving the depot!" Jesse drew a battered Colt .45, his grin suddenly a deadly leer, and barked an order. "Now everybody pay real close attention and no one'll get hurt! Put your money and baubles on the table. Soon as you've made your donation, put your hands on top of your head."

Stepping away from the table, he glanced around the restaurant. "The boys ar͝ ͟ing to come around and collect now. Don't no one try ͟ be a hero. Anyone makes a move for his gun gets a ͟ ͟lyfull of lead."

Behind him, Jewel's mind raced at top speed. She recalled each fact from his file, no matter how insignificant, and searched for the best way to approach him. She centered on his marriage of less than a year, hoping he still carried that newlywed glow and adoration of the fairer sex deep inside his black heart, then settled on a plan.

"Oh, my," she said in a breathless sigh.

Startled, Jesse spun around.

Jewel fell into his arms. Sighing again, she batted her thick auburn eyelashes. "I—I believe I'm going to faint."

Jesse's first instinct was to release her and let her fall to the floor. Then he made the mistake of gazing down at her

alabaster skin, following the trail of freckles across her cute
nose, and looking into her big green eyes as they stared up
at him like those of a sleepy kitten.

"Aw, hell," he grumbled, catching her waist and pulling
her snug against his hip. "Try to hang on long enough for
me to—" Jesse cut off his own words as he noticed a man
at the back of the restaurant duck out the side door.
Guessing he'd be facing a self-appointed posse of one when
he stepped outside, Jesse decided to use the waitress's
misfortune to gain an advantage.

"Boys, I think it'd be best if we use this little gal as a
hostage. Make a run for it. I'll be right behind you."

Resting her head against his shoulder, Jewel tried to
ignore the stench of a man on the run, the foul odor of old
sweat mingled with sage and stale tobacco. She concentrated on his words and her next move. Being a hostage
could work to her advantage, she decided, and would
certainly favor the safety of the customers in the restaurant.
Once outside, away from the others, she could simply
pretend to faint, then remove her gun from her left thigh
and, if necessary, the stiletto from her right. The shock of
her turning on him, armed and ready to kill, would surely be
enough to guarantee the arrest of Jesse James, if not the
others.

"Now remember," Jesse warned the diners as he seized
Jewel's waist and began dragging her backwards, "we don't
want to see no heroes. Put your heads down on the
tables—now!"

After the initial rustling and clatter as the customers
followed his orders, the restaurant became as still as a
graveyard. One by one the outlaws backed out the front door
until only Jewel and Jesse James were left standing in the
adobe building.

"I strongly suggest," Jesse said by way of a final order,
"that you all count to one thousand and don't get up off
them tables before then. If I see so much as a whisker
peeking outta this place, me and the boys'll be obliged to

give you the shave of your life—and it'll be your last one, too!'' Then, viciously jerking his hostage behind him, he jumped through the doorway and headed for the waiting horses.

Using her body as a shield, he half dragged and half carried Jewel as he made for his mount. Swiveling around, looking for the man he'd noticed sneaking out of the depot, Jesse climbed astride the horse with Jewel still hanging from his hip.

She began to struggle, frantically working on a way to alter her original plan, but her thoughts and wind were knocked from her as Jesse kicked the horse in the flanks and took off after his men.

From the side door of the depot Brent crept around the corner. Hunkering down behind a load of firewood, he removed his hat and looked around for a better vantage point. Then the outlaws took off, heading right for him.

Brent drew his pearl-handled pistol, then labored to steady the barrel as he peered down the sights. The gun continued to shake in his hand as the riders swept by him, unaware of his presence, and before he knew it, the final rider and Jewel were in his sights. He stood up, waving the gun in the air, and shouted, ''Stop or I'll shoot!''

Lowering his head so it was level with Jewel's, Jesse propped the barrel of his gun on her shoulder and fired twice as he rode past the man in the black suit.

Brent dropped back down behind the firewood, unscathed, but out of options. Struggling with an aim that he'd never been able to master, he followed the silhouette of the outlaw with the gun sight, closed his eyes, and squeezed the trigger.

A woman cried out. Jewel dropped to the ground amid flying hooves. Jesse James turned in his saddle, screaming in pain, and fired three rounds in Brent's direction. Then all was quiet save for the fading thunder of the stampeding gunmen.

The weapon in his hand shaking like a buckboard over a

rock-bed creek, Brent swallowed hard and jammed the weapon back into its holster.

"Jewel?" He choked the name out of a throat so tight he could hardly breathe. Looking through the dusty veil around her, he saw that she lay sprawled in the dirt. One sleeve of her crisp white blouse was streaked with blood. "Jewel!"

After jumping to his feet, Brent catapulted over the stack of wood and rushed to the spot where she lay. Squatting down beside her, he reached out, thinking to turn her over, but suddenly he couldn't seem to touch her. What if his lousy shooting had hurt her badly? Killed her, even?

"J-Jewel?" he said tentatively, still unable to assess the damage. "Hey, little lady, are you all right?"

Her face buried in the loose dirt, Jewel struggled to regain her wind. Her left arm felt as if it were on fire, and her lungs begged for oxygen. Her right ear was ringing, echoing the retort of James's Colt, the sound ricocheting off every corner of her skull. Finally the painful ache in her ribs began to diminish. Then she became aware of the gambler and the fact he was sputtering above her.

Able to breathe at last, she slipped her right arm beneath her body and began to push herself to a sitting position. Strong hands gripped her shoulders and helped pull her upright.

"Jewel?" Brent said, brushing the dirt from her face. "Are you all right?"

Again using her good arm, she pushed away from him and looked down at her bloodied sleeve. "Do I look as if I'm all right, you fool?"

"I'm sorry if I hurt you," he said, relieved to see she wasn't mortally wounded. "I never was much of a shot. If it makes you feel any better, I think I got the thief with the same bullet that hit you."

"That makes me feel a *lot* better," she spit out as she struggled to her feet.

Standing up and reaching out for her, again he apologized. "It's not as if I planned on hurting you, you know. I had to do something. I couldn't just let those guys ride off with you, could I?''

"So you decided to blow a hole in me? Good thinking, you two-bit sharpshooter. I think you broke my arm!'' Jewel whirled around and began to stomp off toward town, complaining loudly as she progressed down the street. "That miserable no-good gambler! He actually shot me!''

Brent stayed one step behind her, still trying to apologize. "I said I'm sorry. I don't know what else you expect me to do. After all, I did save you from those hoodlums. The least you could do is thank me.''

"Thank you?'' Jewel planted her feet and turned on him. "Thank you?'' she repeated. "I had things under control. I didn't ask you to save me from anyone, and I sure as hell didn't ask you to shoot me. No thanks to you, Jesse James got away—again!''

"Jesse James? Are you saying *I* shot Jesse James?''

"Yes, you great big hero,'' she said with a smirk, "but don't forget—you shot me, too, you sharpshooting dandy!'' Jewel spun around and resumed her march toward town.

"There's no need for name-calling,'' Brent said, still following along. "You're just a little upset, probably shaken from the fall. Let me take you into town to see the doctor.''

Over her shoulder she said, "You're not taking me anywhere, you hear? Just stand right there. If you try to touch me, I'll scream.''

"But—'' Brent's vision picked up a glittering object near his foot. He bent over, retrieved the item, and called to Jewel, "Hey! Wait up. I found your glasses.''

Determined this would be the last time, Jewel wheeled on him. "Keep them. Take them home to your kids as a souvenir of the day you shot Jesse James, or—poke them up your nose. I really don't care what you do with them. Just leave me the hell alone!'' She began to back away, glaring at him, daring him to follow her. When she was sure he understood how serious she was, Jewel turned around and stalked off toward town.

"That idiot actually shot me. *Me!*" she muttered to herself. "I can't believe it, I can't believe any of this. Wait till Allan finds out I had Jesse James in my grasp, and I let him get away."

She kicked at pebbles as she walked, biting her lip with each new wave of pain in her injured arm, but managed to keep up her tirade. "It's most definitely Brent Connors' fault. *All* his fault, and if it's the last thing I do, I'll get even with the dirty bastard. *More* than even!"

# 5

---

*Philadelphia, Pennsylvania*
*June 7, 1876*

Harry Benton stepped out of the hydraulic elevator and onto the thick wool carpeting of the fourth floor of the Fairmount Hotel. As he reached the door to his suite, he noticed a young couple bickering in the hallway next to his room. Taking his time fitting his key to the lock, Harry eavesdropped as the auburn-haired beauty gave her companion the boot.

". . . So let's leave things the way they are, Richard. Thanks for a wonderful time—the exhibition and all the parties were lots of fun."

"But, Jewel," Richard protested, "last night was just one of those things. I had a little too much to drink, I guess. I'll do better tonight if you'll just give me a chance."

Jewel stared at him, considering his proposal, wondering what her real objections to the handsome young Pinkerton agent were. Was it the wispy blond hair? The fact Richard did not have dark wavy locks? Or was his skin too smooth and babylike, lacking so much as a stubble where a thick, lush mustache should have been?

Richard smiled just then, drawing her attention to his mouth. His lips could have been painted lines; they were incapable of curving into the crooked smile that made Brent Connors look as if he had a feather in his drawers.

Somehow, she realized with a sudden flash of insight, that feather had moved over to her own undergarments. Because of it, of *him*, she'd spent the last few weeks of her forced vacation trying to relieve that itch and wipe the memory of Brent Connors from her mind. Nothing had worked. Not Richard, and not the marvelous excitement of the exhibition, with all its newfangled machines. Damn that miserable son of a bitch, she thought. How had Brent managed to worm his way into her mind and her dreams so easily?

"May I come in, Jewel?" Richard asked. "I promised Mr. Pinkerton I'd keep an eye on you while you were here, and besides, I uh . . . I—I think I'm falling in love with you."

She snapped her head up and took another long look into the pale blue of his eyes, noted the puppy dog droop to his expression. Love? How had he gotten love out of a few shared meals and laughs? That notion surely couldn't stem from his awkward and drunken attempts at lovemaking last night, could it?

Love. The word alone turned her stomach and darkened her thoughts. Love, if there really was such a thing, was for idiots and the feebleminded, people who were unable or unwilling to manage on their own. Love was something that could never happen to a strong person like Jewel Flannery.

Trying to hide her irritation, she raised her voice an octave and said, "I'm sorry to hear you feel that way, Richard. I hope I didn't give you the impression that I . . . that we could be more than . . ."

Jewel hesitated, disturbed as much by the tinny sound of her voice as by his undisguised adoration. Then she suddenly realized eyes other than Richard's were gazing at her. She turned and spotted a distinguished-looking gentleman standing one door away. He looked totally intrigued by the situation between her and Richard—and completely amused.

She abruptly turned back to the Pinkerton agent and

brusquely said, "As I tried to tell you, Richard, I'm sorry you feel that way, but I must say good night. Thanks again for all the fun, but I'm afraid you and I have come to the end of the road. I'm simply not interested in having anyone love me right now. Good night and good luck."

Harry laughed to himself as the young woman, hampered by a cast surrounding her broken arm, struggled with the lock, then disappeared behind her door. Sympathetic as well as tickled, he called to the frustrated man left standing in the hallway, *"C'est la vie!"*

Then Harry waltzed into his suite, calling out as he entered, "Oh, Duchess? Where are you hiding, my dear sweet girl?"

From behind a lacquered Oriental screen came a giggle followed by a husky feminine voice. "Jack? Is that you?"

Harry stopped to think a minute, then grinned and said, "I think so."

"I'm bathing so I'll smell like springtime and roses for you—and by the way, please stop calling me 'Duchess.' Someone might hear you and we'll both be in trouble."

"Whatever you say, Carlotta my love. I'll be waiting for you—in bed."

Harry quickly checked the leftover dinner tray he'd insisted on keeping in the room, and breathed a sigh when he saw his mashed potatoes still occupied a corner of the plate. Making certain his guest was still in the tub, he cocked his head and listened. Tiny waterfalls spilled intermittently, signaling all was clear. Working fast, Harry helped himself to the house key Carlotta kept in her evening bag, then pressed it into the center of the potatoes. After checking to make sure the impression was clear, he wiped the key clean and replaced it in its nest of black velvet.

Whistling to himself, he shoved the plate under his bed, stripped, and climbed beneath the sheets. Casually skimming the handbill he'd picked up at the saloon downstairs, he reread the information as he waited for his companion: "Sebastian Steamship Line proudly presents the debut of the *Delta Dawn,* the biggest, most luxurious floating palace ever to grace the waters of the mighty Mississippi River. Accommodations range from the finest of luxury suites to perfectly comfortable staterooms for one. Maiden voyage to begin from St. Louis on June 18, 1876.'' Below was a list of gambling devices, entertainments, and specialty menus.

Harry let the paper fall from his hand and took a deep relaxing breath. Maybe a few weeks aboard a ship was just what he needed, he told himself. A tonic of sorts for his unusually low spirits. Had he finally tired of the game—lost the special thrill of the hunt? What had happened to that delicious burst of adrenaline he always felt as he plotted a way to separate the haughty bitches of the world from part of their unearned fortunes?

Harry shrugged. Maybe he'd finally managed to repay Elizabeth, queen bitch of them all. Betty, as she insisted he call her, the only woman he'd ever loved. Betty, the hard-hearted beauty who'd used him, then tossed him aside like tattered underwear. Perhaps he was finally ready to forget the hurt, the pain. Then again, he thought as he listened to Carlotta's off-key rendition of ''When Irish Eyes Are Smiling''—maybe not.

Harry picked up the handbill again. Perhaps he should book passage—for one. He could use a break. A little vacation might just put the light back in his eyes and the spring in his heels. Even if he felt ready to work before the trip was over, what better place to find a new love than aboard a floating luxury palace?

''Oh, Jack?'' Carlotta called out in a seductive voice. ''What do you think of this?''

After glancing her way, Harry smiled and folded the handbill. ''My, my,'' he said, whistling appreciatively. ''What a naughty little girl you are.''

Carlotta floated across the room wrapped only in a thin scarf of red gossamer and a cloud of rose-scented lotion. Her body still damp from the hot bath, she stood before him and pouted. ''If you'd accept my offer and follow along on our trip to Southhampton, you'd see a lot more of this naughty little girl over the summer. We could be naughty together. Say yes, Jack—I'm begging you.''

Harry raised slender ebony eyebrows above his startling smoky green eyes. ''Now, you know that I cannot leave Harrison Enterprises unattended for that long. You'll just have to make do without me.''

''But, Jack,'' she cried as she climbed in bed beside him, ''surely you can find someone on your staff to care for the business. I need you.''

''Darling, Jack Harrison *is* the business. Enough of this talk. You're going to make me feel that I'm unworthy of you, that I'm not as successful as your husband.''

''Oh, Jack, never say anything like that. Edward may make more money, but you're much more of a man than he could ever be.'' Carlotta rubbed an appreciative fingertip over Harry's perfectly groomed mustache and sighed. ''I just love your skinny little mustache, Jack. It's *so* European.''

''Really?'' Harry slowly ran his tongue along his upper lip. ''Is there anything else you love about me?''

Carlotta laughed from deep in her throat and ran her fingers through the graying hairs at his temples. ''I absolutely adore the little rhymes you're always making up. Tell me another, Jack darling.''

''I don't know if I can think of one tonight. Why don't you give it a try? You might have some . . . hidden talents you're unaware of.''

Then, using his diminutive pinkies which would have been considered stunted by anyone's standards, Harry lifted the sheet and beckoned Carlotta to slide under it.

''Oh, Jack,'' she crooned, lifting an eyebrow. ''You're such a naughty one.''

''My dear,'' he said with an indecent grin. ''I'm much more than naughty. I'm downright dangerous.''

With a lusty chuckle, Carlotta snuggled up beside him

and began to recite the rhyme she'd settled on. "Jack be nimble, but not too quick. Jack has a great big—"

The rest of her poem was lost as Harry pulled her across his chest and crushed her mouth to his.

Back in Chicago one week later Jewel stuck her head inside Allan's office. "Hi, boss! Do I need to throw a white flag out, or am I welcome back here yet?"

"Good Lord, girl," he grumbled good-naturedly. "Get on in here. Of course you're welcome."

"I wasn't sure after that fiasco in Kansas," she said as she glided into the office and took her usual chair across from Allan's desk. "I apologize again for letting the James gang get away."

"Forget it. You didn't do any worse than the rest of us have from time to time—including me. How's the arm?"

Jewel shrugged. "All right, I guess. The doctor took the cast off this morning. The arm feels kind of strange, as if it doesn't really belong to me, but I'm fit for duty, if that's what you mean."

"No, you're not," he countered, spearing her with an ice blue stare. "I've had my share of broken bones, and I happen to know removing the cast is just one step toward complete recovery. You've got a long way to go before you'll be able to defend yourself properly."

"But, Allan, I can't just—"

"No arguments, Jewel. I know what I'm talking about, and I cannot allow you to jeopardize your life or the life of any operative who may be working with you."

"I know." She sighed, absently rubbing her wounded arm through the peach organdy sleeve of her blouse. "But I feel so ready, so impatient to get back to work. Isn't there something I can do besides sit around the office and read reports?"

"I think so," Allan said with a smug grin. "I may have stumbled across a little something you should be able to handle without too much trouble." He tossed a handbill across his desk and invited her to pick it up. "You can read up on the steamship later. For now just let me tell you what's come to my attention while you were having fun in Philadelphia."

Jewel glanced at the paper announcing the maiden voyage of the *Delta Dawn*, then stuck it in her reticule. She had something to settle with her employer, something that couldn't wait. "I want you to know that I appreciate the paid vacation and that I did have a lot of fun at the exhibition. But before you tell me about the new assignment, I'd like to clear the air about another little problem."

"Of course, Jewel. What is it?"

She glanced down at her hands, curled them in her lap, then looked him straight in the eye. "I'd like you to do me a favor, please. I'd appreciate it if in the future you won't try to set me up with any more of your operatives."

Allan looked away from her and began picking at an imaginary hangnail. "You don't spend enough time taking care of your personal life. A woman your age should at least have a semipermanent beau."

"Even if she doesn't want one, Allan?"

His gaze still riveted on his fingers, he shrugged. "I thought Richard might be a good match for you."

Jewel rapped her knuckles on the desk. "Did you really Allan? Come on now—the truth."

He let out his breath and finally looked back up at her. "No, I don't suppose I really thought he was right for you, but he's as close as you'll probably find. I'm not sure there is a proper match for a strong-minded woman like you."

"Now, that's where you're wrong." She laughed, surprised she'd verbalized the thought. "There most definitely is a match for me. He and I have already butted heads a couple of times."

Raising his bushy eyebrows in astonishment, Allan leaned forward and pushed the papers aside. "Why is this the first I've heard of him? Who is he? Where did you meet him?"

Again she laughed. "You've heard of him, but who he is doesn't matter. Brent Connors and I are a match made in hell, not heaven. If I ever lay eyes on him again—and that's not too likely—I'm just as liable to blow a hole through him as look at him."

"So that's it," Allan said with an amused grin. "The fellow from Topeka. The one who shot you and—"

"Forget about him, please. I have," she said, aware even her considerable acting talents couldn't hide the lie. She straightened her spine and put on her most professional expression. "Enough of that. Tell me what you found out while I was gone. What's it got to do with the debut of this steamship?"

Allan continued to stare at her, alternately grinning and puckering his mouth in speculation. When a long moment of this drew no response from her, he leaned back in his chair and continued to regard her. Four years of working with Jewel had taught him one constant about her personality: When she closed up, that was it. No amount of prodding from him or anyone else could get her to open up and talk about herself.

Uncertain whether he felt more admiration or sorrow for her tough hide, Allan pointed to the papers on his desk and explained the assignment. "It seems our good friend Harry Benton was probably among the patrons, if not the players, at the poker tournament in Topeka."

*"What?"* Jewel popped out of her chair. "But . . . but how could I have missed him?"

Smiling, Allan opened the file lying on his desk. He ran a finger down the page, then stopped at the name he sought. "It seems that Countess Penelope DeMorney finally came forward and announced that she'd been relieved of several priceless heirlooms while in the company of a man called, H. C. von Maximus."

"Let me guess," Jewel said with a frustrated groan. "It took the lady this long to report the theft because she was seeing Harry on an in flagrante delicto basis."

Allan laughed. "Aptly put, my dear."

Her attention was centered on only one thing—Harry—so Jewel didn't even smile. She ignored Allan's laughter and pushed on. "What makes you so sure the man was Harry? How was he dressed? What kind of description did the countess give the authorities?"

"Sit down, Jewel," Allan said, his tone dead serious. His gaze fixed and somber, he waited for her to comply before he went on. "When I've finished, I'll give you the full report I received and you can decide for yourself whether the description fits Harry or not. For now I will tell you I'm satisfied that he is probably is our man."

"I'm sorry, Allan. I didn't mean to contradict you or—"

"No apology necessary. Just see if you can be less emotional over the capture of Harry Benton." He cocked a thick bushy eyebrow to make his point, then went on. "You can read the report at your leisure. I'll send it along with you."

Smiling again, Allan leaned back in his chair and linked his fingers across his chest. "How would you like to take another vacation—this time aboard the newest steamship the Mississippi River has to offer?"

"The *Delta Dawn?*" she said, remembering the handbill.

"Precisely. The advertisement I gave you was one of hundreds distributed throughout the Golden Dove Hotel and Topeka in general. This same handbill has been seen throughout New York and parts of Washington as well. If everything advertised is true, the maiden voyage of this boat will attract the elite from near and far."

"And Harry? You got word he was planning to make the voyage?"

"No, it simply struck me as a place he might want to be."

"Oh," she said trying not to sound disappointed. "What makes you think that he or this von Maximus person will be aboard?"

"I can't know for sure," he hedged, "but it's as good a guess as any. I've procured a passenger list, and there are some very, *very* influential people aboard. Vanderbilts and Astors, to name a few. I would imagine those names might draw Harry like a polecat to a henhouse.''

Allan handed the passenger list to Jewel. She scanned the names, impressed with the caliber, but feeling more and more discouraged as she neared the end without recognizing any of Harry's known aliases. She sighed and began pulling at the little finger on her left hand, twisting and turning it until she bit her lip in frustration. More and more she felt that she was chasing a ghost, a figment of her imagination who evaporated every time she got close. Would she ever find Harry Benton? Corner and confront him as she'd dreamed of doing?

Vexed, as she always seemed to be when Harry was the topic of conversation, Jewel sailed the passenger list back to Allan's desk. ''Isn't there something else for me to do? Some assignment a one-armed detective can handle?''

''I'm afraid it's this or office work,'' Allan said softly. ''If you should get lucky and stumble onto Harry during this little trip, the worst danger you'll face is a possible broken heart. Harry may be a lot of things, but he's never  orted to violence of any kind. If you guard your feminine n  ure and remember that he can charm the fangs off a rattler, you shouldn't be in any danger.''

Jewel's laugh was bitter as she listened to the unnecessary warning. Harry Benton had done much worse than break her heart. He'd sealed it off, strangled the emotions, and destroyed the delicate capacity to love, then left it to dry up and vanish like a puff of dust. The heart she carried in her chest now was nothing more than a machine, an organ that beat only to sustain her life. How could Harry Benton possibly do it any further damage?

''What do you say, Jewel? Ready for a trip down the Mississippi?''

With less than her usual enthusiasm, she resigned herself to the new assignment and gave Allan a tiny smile. ''I suppose it's better than sitting around here watching the dead skin flake off my arm.''

"Oh, Jewel!" Allan said with a grimace.

"Sorry, but that's what seems to be happening."

"Just keep lotion on it. It'll be back to normal in a couple of days." Allan reached into his desk drawer and pulled out a sheaf of papers. "Now that you've decided to accept the job, I have to tell you that you'll have one small problem on this assignment. Given your talents, I'm sure you'll find a way to solve it."

"Oh?" Her interest finally piqued, she pulled her chair closer to the desk and cocked her head for a better look at the paperwork.

"This is your steamship ticket, but unfortunately it's only good for a round-trip on the *Illinois Eagle*, leaving here in the morning. It arrives in St. Louis the night before the *Delta Dawn* shoves off. That's where your problem comes in."

Jewel regarded his sheepish expression, the bad-boy glint in his eye, and said, "Let's have it."

"I'm afraid I was unable to secure passage for you on the *Delta Dawn*. The maiden voyage is sold out."

"For heaven's sake, Allan," she said with a huge sigh, "I thought I had a real problem." Jewel grinned, alive with a sense of adventure. "I'll find a way to get on that ship if I have to sign up as a cook."

"I sincerely hope you're able to find another means," Allan said, shuddering as he recalled the only time he'd had the misfortune of eating one of her home-cooked meals.

Knowing exactly what he was referring to, Jewel lifted her chin defensively and said, "You think I couldn't pull it off? Besides, my cooking isn't so terrible if you consider I never set foot in a kitchen until I graduated from college."

"Tell it to someone else," Allan said, laughing. "I've eaten your biscuits, remember? They plugged up my entire system for a month. There's a reason you were never allowed in the kitchen back home."

"Yes, there is," she snapped back in jest. "But just because a girl is raised in a houseful of servants, it doesn't mean she can't learn to cook."

"In your case it does."

Jewel began laughing and conceded, "Maybe I'd better look for some other kind of employment aboard that ship." She reached for the papers and pulled the handbill out of her reticule. "Interesting . . . It looks as if this boat has a little bit of everything going by way of entertainment. There's even mention of a couple of circus acts."

Allan shook his head. "Too dangerous until your arm is completely healed. Maybe you can get a job as a singer."

"The steamship company would have to be pretty desperate to hire me. I cook better than I sing." As she spoke, Jewel studied Benton's file. Even though she'd read it often enough to repeat it verbatim, she picked through it, looking for something, anything, to use as bait. Maybe if she stopped chasing Harry, encouraged him to seek *her* out, he would be an easier weasel to snare. "What do you see mentioned on this handbill that would satisfy Harry's hedonistic nature? If he actually signed on for this maiden voyage, there must be something that will bring him out of hiding, force his hand—and snap him into my handcuffs."

"Just about everything and anything, as long as it has to do with money and women. But don't forget," he warned. "Whatever you decide on will have to help gain your passage at the same time."

"I realize that," she concurred, looking for the perfect combination.

And then, although she'd known about this peculiar personality trait for years, it leapt into her mind as if for the first time. Jewel grabbed the Benton file and hastily read through it again. When she found the words she sought, the simplicity of the solution practically slapped her in the face.

"That's it!" she cried out, knowing she'd found Harry Benton's Achilles' heel. "God, why didn't I think of this before?"

Allan cocked his head and followed her finger as she trailed it across the paper. With a thoughtful frown, he glanced up at her. "You're not thinking of—"

"Oh, yes, I am!" Her green eyes alive and sparkling with enthusiasm, she ran her tongue along her upper lip. "That man doesn't have a prayer, Allan."

"But are you sure you can pull it off."

Her expression predatory, confident, Jewel assured him. "Harry Benton hasn't got any more chance with me than a snaggle-toothed spinster with a big bank account has with him."

# 6

From his lofty perch in the pilothouse, Brent Connors kept a nervous watch as Captain Randazzo maneuvered the *Delta Dawn* away from the crowded dock. Even though he was aided by two pilots, 340 feet of steamship was a tremendous bulk to guide into the traffic lanes.

Paulo, a veteran pilot who'd promised Brent he knew every old snag and low-limbed cottonwood tree along the banks of the river, gripped the immense wheel along with the captain. Watkins, a cub whose knowledge was limited to textbook descriptions, kept a lookout for other ships and small craft.

Brent held his breath until the steamship backed into the main canal, then started down river, before he released an uneasy sigh of relief. He had sunk every dollar he had in the world into this boat, he thought as his fingers searched the nearly empty pockets of his gray-striped trousers. Had he chosen the crew wisely? Or would this newly formed team run the paddle wheeler up on the first sandbar they came across—or, worse, sink her in the deepest parts of the river?

Captain Randazzo—Dazzle, as he was called—turned and smiled at his boss. "We managed that without a collision. 'Spect we can get her downriver in one piece— that is, unless her boilers blow."

"Good God, Dazzle," Brent said, flinching. "Don't even think a thing like that, much less say it. You trying to bring us bad luck?"

The captain opened his mouth, and his laughter, deep and rumbling, seemed to roll up and spew out from his round belly. "I've had both your share and mine of bad luck over the last few years. I'm due for some good. Why, when I think of last year and the time that tornado tore them stacks right off the texas deck of the—"

"Some other time, please," Brent said, his voice wavering. "No disaster stories today."

With a sharp salute and short nod, the captain walked over to his specially built high chair and climbed up the step. Settling onto the wooden seat, he glanced over his shoulder. "You're looking too much the southern gentleman to be hanging around in the wheelhouse. Why don't you go on down and mix with your passengers? We can handle her."

Brent shrugged, then straightened his long-tailed coat of the finest broadcloth. Glancing at his reflection in the wheelhouse window, he tilted his shiny black top hat just a bit to the left and smiled. He was, he decided, as fresh and crisp as the new coats of blue paint on the decks of the *Delta Dawn*—and as much a maiden as the ship when it came to navigating the waters of the Mississippi.

Still concerned about the perils ahead, Brent approached the captain. "You sure you don't need me up here? I don't know a lot, but I can keep watch on the—"

"Begging your pardon, boss, but what I don't need up here is another pair of virgin eyeballs, if you get my meaning."

"I admit I don't know much about snags and things, but I can watch out for other boats."

"That's why we got a cub aboard. Believe me, Mr. Connors, if I'd a needed another mate, I'd have asked you to hire one." Dazzle narrowed one ebony eye at his boss, then lit a fat cigar.

He'd been dismissed, Brent realized as he took a moment to check the shine on his high-laced shoes. Bending down to dust off the taut Congress gaiters, Brent conceded to the captain's opinion. "I'll get out of your way, then. Remember, though—at the first sign of trouble, too short and three long whistles. Right?"

"Right. Go on now and have a good time," Dazzle said, waving over his shoulder. "And don't forget to listen for the signal when we pass under the bridge."

Finally able to manage a smile, Brent pushed his way through the door, then descended the steep spiral staircase leading to the hurricane deck. There, instead of continuing on down through the boiler deck to the grand saloon where most of the passengers were celebrating in full force, he walked to the stern and leaned over the polished wood rail. The huge paddle wheel, painted bright red and highlighted with three white rings, churned the gray waters, kicking up a frothy wake.

Brent stared out toward the St. Louis skyline as the buildings grew smaller and wondered if he had finally found his niche, that special area in which he could excel and, in the bargain, make enough of a profit to restore the family plantation to its original grandeur. If he did succeed, then what? He would, he thought with a grimace, be subjected to a renewed effort by his family to seek a bride and begin a family of his own.

Brent thought of the women he'd known, of those still considered suitable by the Connors family, and slowly shook his head. Not likely he'd be settling down soon, given the prospects. Not likely at all. Instead of accepting a new way of life after the war between the states, instead of recognizing the changes that needed to be made, most of his neighbors' daughters seemed to want to go on living as if nothing had changed. They actually preferred living in the fantasy world of an antebellum society, apparently unconcerned that clinging to the past left them dangerously blind to the future.

"Southern women," he muttered into a fresh spray of water. He simply wasn't in tune with them, couldn't abide their silly games and fluttering eyelashes. The day Brent Connors decided to go after a gal with a lasso, she would have to be tough enough to jerk the rope out of his hands. Not likely to happen, he thought again, this time with a chuckle. Not in these parts anyway.

A sudden image of Jewel, the woman with many fathers, came to mind. Now there, he thought with a dash of admiration, was a tough little lady. The last time he saw her, she had cursed him like a deckhand as she stomped down the road to Topeka, leaving a trail of her own blood while Brent was hard-pressed to keep up with her. By the next morning she'd been gone, leaving her poor daddy behind—to work alone.

Tough, he thought again. Tough as old jerky. But she could also be cold, he remembered—colder than the Chicago wind in January. He thought back to the gunshot wound he'd inflicted. Her only reaction had been one of anger. Not once had he seen even the hint of a tear in her alluring green eyes. He'd expected a hysterical, wailing woman when he saw the blood on her sleeve, but she'd surprised him and lit into him instead.

She was tough all right. And cold. Brent suddenly wondered about the old coot pretending to be her father. Was he actually her husband? Her lover? Brent shook off an uncharacteristic stab of jealousy at the idea. It seemed unlikely that the balding gnome in Topeka was strong enough to tame the auburn-haired wildcat. Had anyone ever peeled away her tough hide and found a soft vulnerable woman beneath? Did such a woman even exist beneath that intriguing combination of wit and beauty?

Feeling a twinge of regret, wishing he'd had the chance to find out, Brent spun around and rested his back against the high rail. Suddenly eager to think of something besides the green-eyed temptress, he glanced up at the twin stacks. Also painted bright red, they loomed up nearly seventy feet into the sky, then gracefully bloomed, their chimneytops cut to resemble a crown of coiled plumes.

Black smoke spewed out of the stacks as the steamship neared the Eads Bridge, and Brent grinned in anticipation. The bridge, completed two years earlier, brought a steady influx of railway traffic from all directions. That traffic, ever growing, had cut into the already dwindling steamship business and threatened to bury it forever. But not if Sebastian Steamship lines could help it, he thought, knowing he'd gambled his entire savings on the public's love of luxury over convenience. A moment later, on cue as the twin stacks passed under the bridge, the fancy new five-toned whistle blew, announcing the ship's presence to any who cared to make note of her passing—and arrival.

Satisfied by the signal, Brent shook a triumphant fist into the air, then continued on his way to the grand saloon. When he stepped inside the magnificent cabin and his feet sank into the expensive Brussels carpet, he paused and hung his hat on a brass peg. "Luxury" and "opulence" were pale words to describe the scene, now that the ship was filled with glamorous guests. He'd divided the 300-foot cabin, designating the bow end for the entertainers and the stern half to games of chance, three championship billiard tables, and the bar. Tomorrow, after the celebrations had died down, he would separate the entertainment area from the gambling parlor with a large partition, but for now the room was open and enormous. Both halves were awash with light from twelve ornate oil-lamp chandeliers, and the saloon sparkled with a carousel of rich colors from stained-glass skylights. The cabin was the very height of elegance, an overt display of extravagance.

Brent took a deep breath, hardly able to believe it all belonged to him. The rich aroma of the fresh-sawn hardwood paneling and cherry ceiling drifted under his nose. Mingled with the scent, expensive perfumes and smoke from countless panatela cigars teased his senses, filling his chest with pride. He was home.

Ready now to blend in with the crowd, Brent stepped into the room and greeted the crowd in a seductively rich drawl. ''Ladies, it's a real pleasure to have you on board. Gentlemen,'' he added as he shook their hands, ''y'all be sure to take advantage of our fine new bar. We've stocked the finest cognacs and brandies available.''

Brent continued on his way, introducing himself to those he didn't know, and reacquainting himself with those he'd met before. He glanced over to the poker table and was relieved to see them crowded with card players. Then he looked up at the stage. A banjo player strummed along as a magician performed his sleight of hand for an enthusiastic audience. The backdrop for this and other acts was a huge ruby-red velvet curtain trimmed with gold cord. The heavy material swayed, gently following the rhythm of the river as the ship glided slowly atop the water.

Walking toward the polished mahogany bar in the stern for a visit with his saloon manager, Brent noted that several well-dressed gentlemen had already stepped up to the rail in search of a quiet midmorning nip.

All was as it should h   been. Laughter and gaiety surrounded him, putting life      his dream. Perhaps he'd worried needlessly about the we fare of the *Delta Dawn*, fretted in vain over the maiden voyage of the Sebastian Steamship Line's flagship—its only ship.

With renewed enthusiasm, Brent continued toward the bar. Then his eye caught something out of the ordinary, some little thing that hadn't been there before boarding began. What was it? he wondered, baffled. He slowly scanned the length of the saloon once again, and this time he spotted the disturbing object.

There, amidships, nestled between the round poker tables and theater chairs, stood a small square table that had apparently been taken from the dining saloon. It was covered with a gaudy green and gold drapery edged in black fringe. In the center of the table a crystal globe nestled like some giant egg in one of the *Dawn*'s engraved silver bowls.

Facing the bulkhead, an empty chair waited for its first customer. Opposite it, a high-back Windsor armchair sat unoccupied. Directly behind the table, tacked to the wall, was a sign: Madame Zaharra, the Gypsy Fortune-Teller. Fortunes Told with Dice, Dominoes, and Cards. Palm Readings and Much More. Two bits.

"What the . . . hell?" Brent's puzzled gaze returned to the bar, but Tex, his manager, was busy filling orders. He glanced back at the table just in time to catch sight of a head of unrestrained auburn curls bouncing along. When the owner of those flowing locks emerged from the crowd and revealed the rest of her enticing body, Brent felt his blood turn cold.

"No," he muttered as he studied her back. It couldn't be—could it? That hair, loose and flowing, was like hers, even with the little cap of black lace draped over the crown, but what about that garish outfit? Why would Jewel be dressed like a peasant?

Whoever she was, this was certainly no lady. She was costumed in a gauzy yellow drawstring blouse he could only guess was scooped in front to reveal the swells of her bosom. Long black lacy gloves met the sleeves of the blouse at mid-arm and matched the fabric tied around her waist in a wide sash. A diaphanous sequined scarf washed in hues of violet, rose, and soft canary yellow was draped across her shoulders, the tails flowing out behind her skirt like streamers. The hem of that wild paisley printed skirt was scandalously high. It fell to just above her shoes, exposing a tantalizing glimpse of her ankles as she worked her way to the table.

This was definitely no lady, he thought again. And even though she'd never pretended to be entirely proper, this couldn't be Jewel.

Brent continued to watch her as she slid into the Windsor chair and turned to face the passengers. Then his breath froze in his throat. When he finally managed to speak,

Brent's voice was ragged. "*No*. It can't be Jewel—not again!"

But it sure as hell was.

Uncertain exactly what propelled him—anger, shock, fascination, or a combination of all three—he caught his breath and pushed his way through the crowd.

Unaware that Brent Connors was bearing down on her, Jewel unwrapped the deck of cards she'd just gotten from Tex. After tossing the paper under the table, she split the deck and had begun to shuffle the cards when an indignant male voice startled her.

Cards shot up in the air. A few hearts and spades bounced off Brent's brocade vest as he said in a deceptively gentle voice, "What the hell do you think you're doing?"

Taken aback at first, Jewel stared up at him with huge round eyes, her mouth dropping open.

"Well, little lady? I know you can do better than that. Now, what the hell do you think you're doing, and how did you get aboard this ship?"

When she was able to react like a detective again, Jewel stood up and stepped out from behind the table. "Don't think you can push me around, mister. I have every right to be on this ship. What the hell are *you* doing here?" she demanded, jabbing her index finger into his shoulder. "Running into you once or twice may be a coincidence, but this is ridiculous. I'm beginning to think you're following me. What are you up to?"

"Me?" Brent circled her wrist with his hand and jerked her toward him. The sudden movement set the rows of cheap gold coins attached to her long necklace jingling. Through the clatter he warned, "You ought to be more careful who you mess with, little lady. I may be a southern gentleman, but if you think you can stand there poking me and get away with it, you got another think coming. I might just snap an irritating finger like that in half."

''Or blow it off, Mr. Sharpshooter?'' she blurted out recklessly.

Brent's honey-brown eyes narrowed and darkened like cold hard molasses. ''You've got one more chance to explain yourself before I pick you up and toss you overboard. I suggest you don't test my patience any further.''

Jewel's stubborn jaw tensed. Her expression slowly became thoughtful and calculating. She wrenched her hand free and began to wave it toward the bar, threatening Brent as she tried to get Tex's attention. ''This is one gamble you never should have taken. You've just bought yourself a passel of trouble. I wouldn't wager your entire stake on what's going to happen to you when the saloon manager gets over here and I tell him how badly you've been treating me.''

More amused than angry, he turned toward the bar and caught Tex's eye. With a short nod, he beckoned the man, then looked back at Jewel. His eyes soft and warm again, Brent spread his legs and drew a toothpick from his vest pocket. Using his tongue in a deliberately sensual fashion, he slowly moved the bit of wood from one corner of his mouth to the other.

''What's so damn funny?'' she demanded. ''You're the one who's about to get tossed off this boat, not me.''

Brent said nothing. Instead, he contented himself by watching her dig her own grave. His grin broad enough now to produce his dimples, he folded his arms across his chest.

Jewel glanced toward the bar and was relieved to see the manager approaching them. Looking back up at Brent, she mimicked his confident smile. ''There's a fellow about twice as big as you on his way over here now. He's going to wipe that grin off your face before you even know what hit you. What do you think of that, you shined-up dandy?''

Brent pulled the toothpick from his mouth, thinking she was in deep enough now to plant herself and a team of horses. His dimples split his cheeks, plunging to depths never before reached as he heard his manager shuffle up beside him.

"Yes, Mr. Connors?"

"Mr. Connors?" Jewel sputtered, cocking an eyebrow at Tex. "Where do you get off calling *him*—a man who is probably a stowaway—anything? I signaled you for a reason. I demand that you have this man removed from this boat. He's just a two-bit gambler, and I wouldn't be surprised to find he also cheats at cards." She sniffed and lifted her chin as she added, "He also insulted me. Please have him ejected."

Tex, a giant of a man who doubled as the bouncer, took off his visor and scratched his head. "Mr. Connors? What's going on? What do you want me to do?"

Brent held the toothpick in front of Jewel's face and snapped it in half. Then he turned to acknowledge Tex. "How did she get on board?"

"I hired her this morning, boss. I didn't think you'd mind, since you approved all the other acts I booked."

"I thought our entertainment budget was depleted."

Tex grinned, exposing a patchwork of neglected and missing teeth. "She signed on for room and board and whatever she can make from the passengers. Won't cost us anything but a few meals. I didn't think you'd mind."

Feeling left out, as if she'd never been a part of the discussion, Jewel elbowed her way back into the conversation. "Why do you care if he minds or not, and what's all this 'boss' talk? I thought *you* were the boss, Tex."

"I am in the saloon cabin, ma'am," he explained. "But Mr. Connors is the boss over all of us. He owns this steamship."

Her smile as counterfeit as the twenty dollar bills she'd tracked down in the past, Jewel kept her paralyzed gaze on Tex. "How very nice for him," she managed through a jaw so tight it would barely move. "How very, very lovely indeed. I—I guess I won't be needing you after all, Tex. I was just funning with Mr. Connors here. Thanks for taking part in my little joke."

Tex's eyebrow's drew together and he looked at Brent. "Mr. Connors?"

"Go on back to the bar, Tex. Thanks for coming over. I can handle this from here on out."

"Yes, sir." The puzzled giant began to move away slowly, then turned and hurried back to his post, shaking his head as he made his way across the long room.

Working to overcome her shock and wondering how, or if, she would keep her new job, Jewel reached over and lightly touched Brent's vest. "Nice fabric. Very expensive. It suits a big handsome man like you."

Again he circled her wrist with his fingers, but this time he held her arm up between them. "You have a decision to make and make now, little lady. You can come along to my cabin quietly and explain exactly who you are and why you are on this ship, or you can take a swim. Which will it be?"

"Why . . . stars and garters," she said in her best southern accent, "you don't leave a girl with much of a choice." Jewel stared up at him, pouting and fluttering her eyelashes. "I can't swim, you know, and going to your cabin is—how shall I say it?—not exactly the kind of thing a proper young lady—"

"Spare me the innocent act, all right? Are you coming with me or not?"

"Well, suh—"

"And get rid of the phony accent. If there's one thing I can't stand besides liars, it's southern belles. Now, what's it going to be?"

"I, ah . . . see." She shrugged. "In that case, I suppose a trip to your cabin is in order. I'm sure once I explain everything, you'll—"

"I'd just love to hear your story this time, but in private if you don't mind." Brent glanced around the saloon, noticing they'd already drawn more than a couple of curious stares. He began to walk away and was relieved when he heard her fall into step behind him.

Intent on dreaming up a story that would best serve her purpose, Jewel barely noticed the throngs of fancy ladies cautiously glancing her way as she wove her way through them. She kept her mind on business and her gaze on Brent's stiff shoulders—and caught glimpses of his taut behind when the tails of his coat split as he swaggered up the stairs. After they had passed through the texas deck where the passengers staterooms were found, then up to the hurricane deck, Jewel's attention was drawn to a part of the ship rarely seen by guests. Smaller than the other cabins, the area set aside for officers' quarters was every bit as opulent as the rest of the ship.

After glancing around the carpeted communal sitting room, Jewel watched as Brent unlocked a pair of polished rosewood doors. Above the porcelain knobs two oil paintings depicted the *Delta Dawn* and a view of the Mississippi at dusk. The river painting included huge cypress trees rising up out of the swamp, appearing ghostlike in the shrouded light. Jewel was engrossed in the Spanish moss hanging from the trees when the doors parted, depriving her of the view.

"Be my guest, little lady," Brent said with a smirk.

She took a breath and muttered, "Why, thank you, sir," then sashayed past him into the sumptuous stateroom.

He closed the double doors, then turned and issued an order. "Have a seat in front of my desk and we'll get down to business."

Regarding him over her shoulder, Jewel assessed the room before she took another step. The cabin reeked of money and elegance—everything she had supposed a man like Brent Connors was not. How could she have been so wrong about him? This was not the room, or the ship, of a two-bit gambler. She took slow steps toward a blue velvet armchair, making note of the filigree work on the ceilings, the gilt and ornate scrollwork above the doors and windows, and the heavy walnut furniture.

When she turned toward another set of double doors leading, she supposed, to the master bedroom, Jewel shook her head. She'd been so sure Brent was nothing more than a dandy, a lost southerner without a plantation to call home. As she continued toward the chair, she noticed an exceptionally well crafted billiard table clothed in blood-red felt. Again she wondered how she could have been so wrong.

"Sit," Brent said from across the desk.

"Huh?"

"I believe you heard me, Madame . . . Zigzag?"

"Zaharra," she corrected him as she slid onto the blue velvet chair.

"I'm a fairly patient man," Brent drawled as he glanced beyond her to the elaborate cuckoo clock attached to the wall. "I can spare five minutes for your little story. Let's hear it."

Thinking fast, she recalled the way he'd stared at her cleavage the first time they met. Jewel pushed her shoulders back and encouraged one sleeve of her low-necked blouse to slip down her arm. Then she leaned forward and began jerking on her chair in an effort to move it closer to the desk.

The act drew the expected response from Brent. His eyes lit up as her breasts jiggled and fought for a way out of the confines of the gauzy yellow material. This might be easier than she thought!

Brent cleared his throat of a sudden frog and looked into her calculating green eyes. The sight was no less disconcerting than the swell of her breasts, but when he thought of her numerous disguises and her obviously crooked reasons for using them, he managed a stern tone. "My patience is wearing thin. I said I would listen to your story, and I will, if you'll get on with it. Then I will have you removed from this ship—and perhaps arrested as well."

"B-but that won't be necessary," she sputtered, buying a little time in which to determine the best way around him.

"Then please tell me this: Why do I find a very proper Harvey Girl, the *daughter* of a kindly old gentleman, dressed up in this . . . this"—he waved a hand in her direction, unable to come up with a name for her Gypsy costume—"silly getup?"

"Oh, that." She laughed, still stalling for a little more time. "I can see how you'd misunderstand, after Topeka and all."

"By 'all,' may I assume you are referring to Chicago? You see, I haven't forgotten that little incident, either."

"Ah, well, yes, I suppose I am." Jewel's smile was strained as she realized what she was up against. Brent Connors wasn't going to be swayed by her feminine wiles as easily as she'd hoped. He wouldn't accept just any old thing she said as fact. Out of time and ideas, she laid her cards on the table.

"All right, Mr. Connors. I can see you're running a little short of tolerance, and I don't blame you one bit."

Brent kept his silence. Reaching into his vest, he withdrew a toothpick and popped it into his mouth. Fascinated, he gestured for her to continue digging her grave.

"I really haven't been quite the liar you think, sir," she began, her eyes wide and as innocent as she could make them appear. "Everything I told you about Chicago was true, and the same goes for Topeka." Deciding just a dash of helplessness would work in her favor, she tempered her earlier act. Her voice softer, lower, she absently rubbed at her injured arm as she told her tale. "After you shot me, I didn't have much choice but leave when my father ordered me to. I was no good to him, no good to . . . anybody." She slumped dramatically and raised a lace-gloved hand to her brow.

Brent stifled the urge to berate her and to demand that she drop the act. A spurt of residual guilt pushed a sigh from him instead. "Again I apologize for my poor aim. How is your arm? Healed by now, I hope."

"Nearly," she said, her voice even lower. "It was

broken, you know. I was forced to wear a cast for several weeks, but even without it, I'm afraid I simply do not have the strength I need to perform my usual chores.'' She raised her chin, issuing the barest of pouts and mournful glances. ''It is very difficult to serve meals and clean the homes of the rich with only one good arm. I—I took this job because it requires little physical strength. I don't plan to cheat anyone. I hope that's not what worries you.''

''Oh, good God,'' Brent groaned under his breath.

''Pardon me, Mr. Connors?''

''A crooked judge wouldn't pardon you if you offered him this ship *and* your considerable charms, little lady. You're just not to be believed.''

''But I'm telling the truth. I really do need this job—desperately! And I swear—get me a stack of Bibles—I swear that I will not cheat a soul on this ship. I'm just here to tell fortunes and watch all the rich folks have a good time. *I swear.*''

''I can certainly attest to that,'' he muttered through his thick mustache. ''The things I've heard come out of your mouth could make the captain of this ship blush.''

Jewel bit her lip and began to lecture herself in her mind—don't lose your temper, don't let him get the best of you, get even with him some other time—over and over until she was certain she could speak in a pleasant tone. Then she smiled sweetly and said, ''I do apologize for any vulgarisms I may have uttered in your presence. Life has been extremely trying for me lately.''

Brent stared at her for a long moment, a mixture of disbelief and admiration in his expression. Finally he shook his head, removed the toothpick from his mouth, and dropped it into the ashtray. Then leaned across his desk and said, ''You're either bolder than a June bug courting a bullfrog or so feebleminded you actually think I'm gullible enough to believe anything you've said.''

Suddenly wishing she could spill the entire story to him, Jewel felt the corners of her mouth waver as she tried to control the smug grin. "There's nothing else I can say," she admitted finally. "I wish you would believe me and let me keep the job. I promise you won't be sorry."

"I've been sorry since the first day I set eyes on you."

Her head flew up and her brows lifted.

"Fascinated, too," he added when he saw her injured expression.

Again fighting an irrational grin, Jewel began to push her chair away from the desk. "If that's all, then, I'd best be on my way to the—"

"We're far from done, sweetheart."

"But for heaven's sake! What else can I do or say?" she cried, frustration threatening to crack her calm. "I've bared my soul to you, been as honest as I can, and given my assurance you have nothing to worry about. Can't you just trust me a little?"

Brent's laughter was more of a chortle. "You surely don't expect that from me!"

"All right," she grumbled. "I'll confess that you have cause to doubt me, but if you really knew me, you'd realize that I can be trusted. I'm really an honorable person. It would mean a lot to me if just this one time you'd believe that."

More intrigued than ever, Brent cocked his head. "I wish I could. Talk. Maybe you can convince me if you tell me all about yourself. Start with your real name."

Caught off guard by the proposal and by the sincerity in his brown eyes, Jewel began to pick at a red and purple paisley pattern on her muslin skirt. If she'd been dealing with anyone else, some other man, her next move would have been routine. She would simply have beguiled him with her charms, hinted at her sensual nature and made promises she had no intention of keeping. Instinct told her that if she was foolish enough to make those promises to Brent Connors, he wouldn't rest until he'd collected.

The very thought of him sweeping her into his arms and demanding his due sent a surprising ache of desire throughout her. Jewel's shoulders slumped as she realized that she probably wouldn't put up much of a fight if she tried such a dangerous tack. Her plan to charm the handsome gambler could easily backfire. It would be an extremely foolish ploy. Why did the thought intrigue her so?

"Jewel Flannery," she finally said, deciding that honesty—as much as she could tender without revealing her occupation, anyway—was her best weapon with Mr. Brent Connors. "I was born in Chicago too many years ago to still be unmarried, but I am and I wouldn't have it any other way."

Startled by her candor, Brent felt his mouth open. Regaining his composure, he studied her, looking for signs of duplicity. She appeared to be remarkably in control and as fresh and guileless as a baby. Knowing she was anything *but*, he proceeded with caution. "May I ask why a lovely young woman, one who is usually dressed a little better than you are today, is so happy to be single at such an, ah . . . advanced age?"

Jewel bristled. "Are you suggesting I'm too long in the tooth to attract a husband, sir?"

"Oh, no, ma'am," he said, taking in her untamed appearance, the casual way her hair was arranged, the loose provocative clothing that no lady in her right mind would have considered donning. "You're quite attractive. I only meant to ask why you prefer life without a man to call your own."

"That,"—she spit the word out like a bad peanut—"is none of your business! But just for the record, please note that I've had plenty of men to call my own. I've just never seen any reason to marry one of you puffed-up jackasses."

"Puffed up? Are you including *me* in your highly inaccurate opinion of men?" he said, indignant.

"If the saddle fits . . ." She waved her gloved fingers at him and looked away.

Brent scowled, then caught sight of her upturned mouth and haughty demeanor. Unable to help himself, he laughed.

"All right," he said. "I guess I had that coming. Your personal life is none of my business, and that's really not the kind of honesty I was looking for." Or was it? he suddenly had to ask himself.

"Then if that's all," she said crisply, preparing to take her leave.

"I'm sorry, but it's not. You've lied about too many things." Giving himself a minute to prepare, Brent paused before he resumed his interrogation. "Flannery. That's not the name you gave me in Topeka. It's not the name of your elfin father, either. Would you mind clearing that little mystery up for me?"

Jewel let out her breath in a long slow sigh. What was it going to take to satisfy this man? Her entire life history, real or imagined? Choosing her words with care she grudgingly admitted, "Mac isn't my father."

"Now, there's a surprise."

Having expected that response, she went on. "Mac was only watching out for my welfare when he agreed to pose as my father. He's a good friend, that's all."

"A *very* good friend, I would think, since he was kind enough to share his suite with you," Brent blurted out, as unreasonable anger tore through him.

Her own temper flaring, she snapped back. "He's an excellent *friend*. Nothing more."

"Of course he is," Brent said sarcastically. "Why shouldn't I believe that when I stop to consider how easily you slip in and out of any man's room?"

Jewel pressed her lips together hard enough for the naturally rosy heart-shape to flatten and turn white. Done with the conversation and with him, she stood up. "I've been more honest than a pompous jackass like you could expect. I'd like to go back to work now."

"I'm not through with you yet."

"Oh? What else could you possibly want to know? My age when I received my first kiss? Or perhaps you'd like the name of the man who stole my virtue—along with all the juicy details!''

''That's enough!'' Brent pushed back from the desk and stood up so abruptly that the French carved chair toppled over with the force. He circled the glass-topped writing desk, intending to seize her wrist or an arm, but for some reason as he approached her, he impulsively clasped her into his arms instead.

''Enough lies,'' he demanded, wondering through a sudden fog what in hell he was doing. ''Why don't you just admit what you really are? Confess that you're a cheap little thief who uses any man who'll bed her to get what she wants!''

''Why, you''—Jewel struggled against his strength and worked to get her good arm free so she could drive her fist into his cocky mouth—''miserable son of a bitch! How dare you—''

''Tell me I'm wrong,'' he challenged, pinning her arms to her sides and pressing her body against the full length of his. ''I'll be happy to let you go if you'll give me give me one good reason why you broke into my room and spent half the night under my bed.''

Jewel went limp at the request she'd been dreading, the only one with which she was unprepared to comply. She worked to catch her breath now, struggling to ignore the steel hardness of his muscles pressing against her body through the thin cheap material of her blouse. Unable to think clearly, to formulate yet another story, she threw herself on his mercy. ''I—I wish I could tell you, but I can't and that's the God's honest truth.''

Inches from her sensuous mouth, freckle-kissed nose, and pleading eyes, Brent was a mass of contradicting responses. He could feel himself melting and hardening at the same time. His body urged his mind to believe her, but it also sent warnings. Signs flashed in his head: Danger—Bridge Out. She's a thief—take her to the nearest jail and forget her! his brain insisted. She's beautiful and voluptuous, and I want her more than I've ever wanted anyone, his body pressured. Take her, you fool!

"Please believe me," Jewel went on, suddenly desperate to make him trust her. "I meant you no harm." She hesitated, watching his eyes darken as he lowered his head. "I was . . . not in your r-room to rob you. . . . Please know that. I . . ." Her gaze suddenly shifted from his eyes to the thick sable wings of his mustache. He drew within an angel's kiss from her face. She looked into his eyes for only an instant before that mouth beckoned her gaze to return, begged her lips to meet his.

Then he plunged his fingers into her hair and began stroking the back of her head. "Oh . . . oh, Brent, I—I . . ." That was all she could manage before he captured her mouth.

She had one last rational thought as she met his heat, his passion: This is surely a match made in hell. Her response, devoid of her usual reliance on the dramatic, both frightened and thrilled her, intrigued and alarmed her. The flames of hell were flaring in her loins, heating her blood to temperatures she'd never even dreamed of. Brent Connors had to be the spawn of the devil to work this kind of magic on her. What else could it be? How else could she be feeling so much so fast? How else could she explain it? The man was only kissing her! Why was she coming apart so easily?

As she grew desperate to slow things down, Jewel sensed one last beam of logic striving to light up a glimmer of insight. She was very close to losing the one thing she'd always been able to count on—her own control. Against all that her body longed for, she tore herself out of Brent's arms.

"I—I have to go now," she gasped as she raised her gloved hand to her swollen lips, soothing them, convincing them this was for the best. Then, before he could reply or move, she jerked open his door and ran out of the room.

Choking for air, strangling on emotions too complicated to sort out, Jewel scrambled down the stairs to the texas deck, where she wheeled around the corner and ran head-long into a startled passenger.

"Oh, my dear—pardon me," Harry Benton said as he caught the distraught woman. "May I be of some assistance?" he suggested, noting the flushed cheeks and the frightened-rabbit glaze in her lovely green eyes.

Grateful for the support, Jewel nodded and allowed the stranger to steady her trembling body for a moment. Then, knowing she must look a sight, guessing her cheeks were on fire and her mouth was bruised and swollen, she pulled away without meeting the man's gaze. "Thank you, sir," she mumbled under her breath. "I must have taken a little seasick." Then she spun around and continued on down the hallway toward her stateroom.

Puzzled, Harry watched her retreating figure. "Excuse me, my dear!" he called after her. "Would you please tell me—am I missing out on some kind of costume party?"

# 7

Reba Thomas slid the glass of Chivas Regal across the bar top and waited for the nattily dressed customer to pay up. He dropped a single coin on the polished mahogany, then turned and walked away without so much as a thank-you.

"Enjoy the drink, Mr. Big Spender. I hope you choke on it," she muttered under her breath.

"Talking to yourself again, Reba?" Tex asked from behind her.

"Beats talking to the highfalutin passengers this voyage has managed to attract. I shoulda stayed on at the Gilded Bird in Natchez. I don't fit in with these folks."

"Ah, Reba, don't be so hard on yourself." Tex poured two frosty mugs of beer, then added as he passed behind her, "Give 'em a day or two to get used to the idea of a woman mixing their drinks. They'll come around."

"Humph. Like I'd care if they did." But she did care. At least she thought she did. Despite all she'd done during her forty-two years, respectability had never quite found its place on Reba's list of accomplishments. Why should it matter now? she wondered. Brent Connors, came the answer. He had given her a chance, perhaps her final chance, to rise up from the gutters of humanity. She'd taken him up on the offer, and now she felt she owed him something. But this wasn't working. Whatever had made her think she had what it took to be accepted by society's darlings?

"I ain't got the patience," she muttered to herself. "I've got no stomach for these high-society types who think I'm nothing but trash." She grabbed her bar towel and began to wipe down the storage wells, even though she'd done so only a few moments before. Then she caught sight of a new customer standing at the end of the bar.

Another high-society type, she decided as she tossed the rag into a bucket and started in his direction. Black silk top hat, tails, gray cravat, ruffled dress shirt, nose held at an upward angle, looking as if he'd sniffed a rotten egg. He was just another highfalutin, snob—too good to give her the time of day much less a tip. He would gct what he paid for, she decided, what they'd *all* paid for.

Harry Benton was too busy selecting the perfect bar stool to notice Reba's approach. He chose the wooden stool with padded black leather seat nearest the wall and slid onto it. From there he could study the crowd, his brain busy assessing and rating the financial status of the clientele, without worrying about other customers crowding in around him.

"What'll it be, mister?"

Amazed to hear a sultry feminine voice, Harry turned his head toward the sound. "My dear, what a pleasant surprise," he said, unable to keep his gaze from lingering on her marvelous, if slightly overblown, attributes.

"I split the duty with Tex," she explained brusquely. "So what'll it be?"

Harry spun around on the stool until he faced her. She was lovely in a timeless sort of way, even though the lines from her not altogether pleasant diary were deeply etched around her eyes and mouth. Her hair, bleached a pearly white, was piled high atop her head and fastened with a royal purple feather that matched her velvet gown. She was common, probably available to any man with the correct change, he thought absently—but somehow, Harry realized, surprising himself right down to his patent leather shoes, she was absolutely breathtaking.

Suddenly feeling frisky, he raised his stunted pinky and waved it, making sure she noticed the large diamond ring almost covering the pint-sized finger. "What would you suggest, my dear?"

Unimpressed, Reba began wiping a crystal glass with a fresh bar towel. "I'm not your dear, and I wouldn't have the slightest notion what you drink."

Nonplussed, Harry was momentarily at a loss for words. His impeccable manner of dress coupled with a faint accent that suggested all of Europe rather than a particular country, never failed to charm the ladies. Why did this one seem impervious to him? Even more curious, why would a woman of obviously common breeding attract him so?

Reba replaced the glass, waiting for her suddenly silent customer to order, and began to tap a polished fingernail against the bar. "Give me a holler when you've made up your mind," she muttered before twirling away.

"No—wait," Harry said, too fast, with far too little inflection in his voice. "I believe I'll have a cognac."

"Any particular brand?"

"Whatever you're having. I'd like to buy you a drink, my dear."

Cocking her hip, Reba raised one eyebrow over an ice blue eye.

"Forgive me," Harry said, instantly aware that he'd blundered. "Perhaps I can better refrain from offending you if we exchange introductions. My name is Harrison Poindexter, but you may call me Harry. And you are . . . ?"

Her eyebrow had dropped down to its original arch, but both blue eyes bored into him before she finally said, "Rebecca Thomas. My friends call me Reba. You may call me Miss Thomas. And by the way—thanks for the drink. Don't mind if I do." She stared at him for a long moment, her painted mouth lifted at the corners, then turned and slowly strolled down the plankway to where the bottles were propped up in bins.

*"Mon Dieu!"* Harry breathed to himself, appreciating the

seductive roll of her hips as she walked, even though he suspected the movement was deliberate. "What a woman!"

Content just to watch her, to be the prey rather than the predator for a change, Harry broke into a smile that brought his pencil-thin mustache absolutely level. When Reba returned carrying two glasses, he accepted his and raised it in a toast. "To your extraordinary beauty and what just may be a very memorable trip."

Her first impulse was to toss the drink down and walk away, but Reba hesitated, stopping for once to access the situation before reacting. Did he know her from somewhere? Did he think she could be purchased for ten minutes, or even for the entire night, as she once could have been? Or was he just being friendly?

Suspecting that the answer lay somewhere in between, Reba lifted her glass and touched it against Harry's. Then she winked and returned the toast. "Here's to customers who know how to tip well. Bottoms up." She raised the glass to her lips and downed the cognac in one gulp.

So completely captivated that his eyes were shining like those of a lad peeking through the keyhole at a whorehouse, Harry exclaimed, "Bottoms up indeed!" and tossed the drink down.

He closed his eyes as the cognac spread its heat, and when he opened them again, Reba's manner had completely changed. She'd gone from day to night, from storm clouds to sunshine. She smoothed the front of her white apron and produced a smile.

"Well, now, my dear," Harry murmured huskily, forgetting himself again. "To what do I owe this sudden—" He cut off his words when he realized he wasn't the cause of her new mood. She wasn't even listening to him. Following her gaze, he sagged as a younger man, his dark good looks marred by a frown, approached the bar.

"A whiskey, Reba. Make it a double," he said as he slid onto a stool next to Harry.

"Sure, Bre— Mr. Connors. Coming right up." She did a

half curtsy, grinning and fussing with her hair, then hurried over to the backbar.

In no mood to mingle with the customers, Brent ignored the man on his left and swiveled his head until he had a clear view of the Gypsy's gaudy little table. Still unoccupied. "Damn," he muttered, wondering why he hadn't just gone after Jewel and let things take their natural course.

"Tough day at the poker tables, son?" Harry inquired, eager to assess his competition.

Brent wheeled around, cognizant of his duty to his passengers, and offered his hand. "No, just looking for someone. "I'm Brent Connors, president of the Sebastian Steamship Line."

"Is that so? What an honor, sir. Harrison Poindexter at your service." Accepting the greeting, Harry made a fast study of the man. Thirtyish and apparently very rich, if he held such a prestigious position. Married? Harry glanced at the man's fingers and found them unadorned. Too bad, he thought. The challenge of stealing the wife of such a virile-looking chap was almost as interesting as the spoils he might have garnered.

Brent gave him a mock smile. "Very nice to meet you. I do hope you're enjoying your journey so far."

Reba returned with the whiskey at that moment, and as she handed it to Brent, Harry said, "I am having a wonderful time indeed, sir. In fact, everything has brightened considerably in just the last few minutes."

The innuendo was lost on Brent as he quaffed the whiskey. He wasn't interested in small talk or wealthy passengers. He was preoccupied by thoughts of a green-eyed vixen who'd set him on fire, then fled from the scene of the crime. A pyromaniac of the heart, he suspected. As a southern belle, a woman like Jewel Flannery could have destroyed the entire Confederacy without benefit of the Union army, he decided, his dark thoughts shadowing his eyes and twisting his features.

Weaving her fingers through the towel she used to wipe

the crystal, Reba ventured, "Everything okay, Mr. Connors? Can I get you something else?"

Brent glared into his glass, hesitated a moment, then shook his head. "Have you seen that little Gypsy fortune-teller in the last fifteen minutes or so?"

Reba checked up and down the length of the bar, rattling the platinum-blond ringlets spiraling off her crown in the process. With a shrug she looked back to Brent. "Didn't know we had one."

"Excuse me, sir," Harry interrupted, his eyes shining again. "Did I hear you mention a fortune-teller?"

Brent turned his head toward the stranger and nodded.

"Aboard this steamship?" Harry said, his excitement growing.

His interest in the man suddenly piqued, Brent turned all the way around and faced him. "Yes. Have you seen her?"

"No, I don't— Wait a minute. Maybe I have," he said thoughtfully. "Not twenty minutes ago I ran into a young lady on the cabin deck who may be the one you're looking for. I thought she'd been to a costume party, but perhaps—"

"Reddish brown hair, yellow blouse, black—"

"Black lace cap on her head? That description fits the poor young woman I collided with."

"The *poor* young woman?" Brent said with a grimace. "That's hardly the way I would describe her, but I think we're taking about the same one."

"When does she work?" Harry asked, feeling more vital than he had in months. "Where is she set up? It's been ages since I've had a decent palm reading, not to mention a comprehensive dream interpretation. Does she analyze tea leaves as well?"

His expression guarded, frozen, Brent exchanged puzzled glances with Reba, then gave her a barely noticeable shrug. Coughing to hide a sudden burst of laughter, Brent said, "You're asking the wrong person, friend. I wouldn't know tea leaves from chewing tobacco."

"That's all right," Harry said with a wave of his hand,

too alive with excitement to care about Brent's fit of whimsy over his beloved hobby. "Most people don't understand even the basic aspects of forecasting their own destiny through a simple cabalistic chart. I can hardly expect a layman such as you to appreciate the value of a truly expert palm reader."

"Hardly." Brent wondered what in the hell the man was talking about. "Reba?" He pointed to his glass and nodded emphatically.

"Now then," Harry went on. "Where can I find this gem of a woman?"

"If you'll recall, I mentioned that I was looking for this *jewel* of a woman myself."

"Yes, yes. Quite correct." Pressing his index finger to the shallow valley where the halves of his mustache almost met, Harry pondered his next move. "A schedule!" he blurted out. "You must have a schedule of her working hours. May I see it, please?"

"Ah, quite frankly," Brent said with a frown, "she was hired this morning by someone other than me. I'm not even certain I plan to offer the Gypsy's services."

"Oh, but you must!" Harry said, jumping off his bar stool. "You'll do your passengers a great injustice to have such a treat aboard ship and *not* let her ply her trade."

Brent frowned, then opted for something close to the truth. "The fact is, I'm not sure this girl's capable of telling your fortune. I have no way of guaranteeing her . . . authenticity."

Harry bowed slightly. "Allow me to perform that task, sir, if you please. I would be most honored to check the Gypsy's credentials. I'm certain I can tell if she's a fake. It would take a very smooth operator to put one over on me."

Then you've never met an operator like Jewel Flannery before, Brent thought as he mulled over the idea. Unable to find a reason not to accept the man's offer without having to explain the whole story, he let out a sigh. "As long as you're set on having the fortune-teller remain aboard, I suppose it would be best if you check her out. But let me give you a word of caution: Don't say I didn't warn you if she takes you for every penny you're worth.''

Harry's resounding laughter came from deep inside, hinting at his secret life without revealing it. He did his best to remove the smugness from his grin as he vowed, ''I believe I shall be able to parry any moves a little slip of a girl like that may try on me.''

''Uh-huh,'' Brent drawled, suddenly looking forward to the match. ''Better sharpen your sword, in any case.''

''Mr. Connors?'' Reba said as she refilled his glass. ''Is that the gal you're looking for?''

Following the direction of her gaze, both Brent and Harry spotted the mass of auburn curls moving past the shoulders of the taller passengers. Glancing at each other, the two men smiled, each entertaining his own thoughts, both filled with the same excitement.

''One more thing,'' Brent said, holding up a finger. ''I have a point or two to make with the little lady before she tells your fortune. You wait here. I'll give you a signal when she's ready to see you.''

''As you wish,'' Harry replied, his appreciative gaze again sweeping over the buxom bartender. ''I'm sure I can find a way to entertain myself while I wait.''

Brent slid off the stool, leaving Reba with an order as he made for the gaudy little table. ''Mr. Poindexter's drinks will be on the house today. See that he doesn't go away thirsty.''

Across the room, Jewel sat in the high-backed chair and watched as Brent chatted at the bar. Soon, she supposed, he would turn around and discover her. Then he would march up to the table, and . . . what? Toss her overboard in front of his distinguished passengers? Hardly. If she read him right, and she had to admit she'd been unable to figure him out as easily as she could most men, he would agree to some kind of compromise, something they could both live with. Hoping she was right, and that her body and mind could block out what had happened in his suite, Jewel took a deep breath as he crossed the room and approached her.

His usual grin in place, Brent reached for the spindle-backed chair across from her and bowed slightly. Then he spun the chair around, straddled the seat, and lowered himself onto it.

"Well, well, well," he drawled. "I see you didn't jump ship after all."

"Why would I do a thing like that?" she said, careful not to meet his gaze. "I've got a job to do. I was under the impression you were going to let me do it as long as I didn't annoy any of the passengers."

"As it turns out, you're right about that."

Trying not to look too surprised, she smiled and said, "Thank you. I promise, you won't be disappointed in me."

"I don't plan to be." When she didn't rise to the bait, he went on. "There is one little stipulation to your employment, however." Her attention and gaze finally drawn to him, Brent explained. "There's a gentleman on my staff"—he added the embellishment to make his proposal more authentic—"who just happens to be an expert on this fortune-telling business. If you can satisfy his requirements and prove that you're not here to reverse rather than predict my customers' fortunes, then I'll agree to keep you on."

Jewel gave him a short nod and began to shuffle her cards. If his employee wasn't *too* much of an expert, she thought with her usual confidence, her problems with the handsome gambler might just be over.

Glancing up at him, her green eyes sparkling, Jewel said, "I certainly can't object to that. What are you waiting for? Send him over."

"In a minute," Brent said, popping a toothpick in the corner of his mouth. "You and I have some unfinished business to take care of first."

Jewel drew her brows together. She banged the deck of cards against the table to stack them up as she said, "I don't understand. I thought we just settled—"

"I'm not talking about tea leaves, little lady. I'm referring to"—Brent hesitated, making a deliberate perusal of her mouth, then her bosom—"us. You and I, sweet lips." He moved the toothpick from one corner of his mouth to the other as he waited for her shocked reply.

"Oh," she said in a small voice as she carefully returned her attention to the cards, "that."

Jewel had expected this conversation. Her smile slightly crooked, she slowly raised her eyes and boldly caressed his features with her gaze. After lingering on his mustache, appreciating his full, slightly parted lips, her languid green eyes drifted down to his hands. She broke into a broad grin as she studied them one finger at a time. Exhaling an exaggerated sigh, she finally said, "I guess we do have a little unfinished business at that."

Stunned by her reaction, Brent let his mouth drop open, and the toothpick fell to the floor. Trying to cover his shock, he moistened his suddenly dry lips, then cleared his throat. "Wh-what do you think we ought to do about it?"

"Do we have to *do* anything?"

"Oh," he said, more in control, his confidence returning, "I definitely think we should. It'd be a real pity to let all this . . . this energy between us go to waste."

"Hmmm," she murmured, her voice soft and low. "I suppose you're right. How shall we handle it?"

Suddenly feeling like a schoolboy with a crush on his teacher, Brent curled his fist and coughed into it before he was able to say, "Why don't we just head up to my suite? We can finish our, ah, the conversation there."

"You really know how to turn a girl's head, don't you, Mr. Connors?" Jewel said as she resumed shuffling the cards. "How terribly original of you."

Again he coughed, but his mind was a sudden blank. "I . . . well, ah . . ."

"Why don't we both just think about this awhile?" she suggested, wondering how long she would be able to put him off, how long she would *want* to hold him at bay.

"Why don't we get this little test out of the way first? Then we can concentrate on other things."

Trying to ignore the heat building in his loins, Brent wiped his palms on his trousers and stood up. "Sounds fair to me. And just for the record," he said as he turned toward the bar and beckoned to Harrison Poindexter. "I'm beginning to hope you are on the up-and-up. Be a real shame to have to toss a lovely little lady like you overboard. A real shame indeed."

Caught by his words, the sudden change in his manner, Jewel began to wonder who had been teasing whom, but before she could come up with any answers, the employee was upon them.

"My dear, this is an honor," Harry said as he joined them and slid onto the chair. "Do you need to know my name, or is anonymity better in this case?"

Barely noticing his features, Jewel glanced up at him and shrugged. Then her gaze swept over to Brent, and she fell into her Gypsy accent. "Vell, Meester Connors? Zees ees your leetle test. How do you vish me to proceed?"

Brent rolled his eyes, but managed to reserve comment on her latest characterization. "Just, er, read Mr. Poindexter's cards or whatever it is you do with them."

She turned her attention to her customer. "Ees zees all right weeth you, sir?"

But instead of answering her, Harry pressed one index finger to his lips and narrowed his eyes. "My goodness . . . I believe we've met somewhere else, my dear. Have you done my chart before, perhaps?"

Finally looking directly at him, she stared into his smoky green eyes and caught her breath. There was something familiar about him, some little thing she couldn't quite identify. "I do not sink ve have met, sir."

"Oh, but, my dear, I'm quite sure that we have. I never forget a face—especially one as lovely as yours."

The stranger wrinkled his aristocratic nose, blending the light scattering of freckles into small islands. Why did he seem so familiar? she wondered again. She felt as if little kitten paws, their claws weak and pliable, had begun to hopscotch up her spine. Jewel shrugged them off, then smoothed her long black lace gloves.

"Shall ve proceed?" she said as she dealt the cards in threes using only her left hand in accordance with the Gypsy rules.

"Yes, I suppose we should," Harry agreed, still busy searching his memory.

Fifteen cards lay face down in a semicircle on the table. Jewel flipped over the king of clubs, the card she'd chosen to represent Mr. Poindexter, then turned up a group of three cards. "I see here zat you veel have a change of profession soon, but eet veel be a hard time."

"By golly, I have it!" Harry blurted out. "Philadelphia! Not two weeks past at the Fairmount Hotel."

Stunned, Jewel dropped the accent and stared across the table. "Wh-what are you talking about?"

"My dear, I never miss a good lover's brawl. You and your fellow were having a bit of a spat, and you had your arm in a cast. Did you ever let the rascal back in for the night?"

Full-grown cats seemed to dig their claws into the base of her spine, sending ominous impulses racing up to Jewel's scalp. She glanced at Brent's darkening features, then turned her attention to the customer. "I—I'm afraid you are mistaken."

Well versed in matters of the heart, Harry caught the exchange between the two, then laughed his suppositions off. "Of course I'm mistaken. Why, on closer examination, I see that you really don't look anything like her."

"Certainly, certainly," Harry said, anxious to right the wrong he'd done to the poor nervous girl. "Why don't we dispense with the cards? Anyone can interpret cards, but it takes a real expert to do an accurate palm reading. What do you say, my dear? How are you at palms?"

"Very good," she was able to say without reservation.

"Then I propose we make our decision based on her palm reading, Mr. Connors. It takes someone who knows what she's doing to give a correct reading, and I've had mine read by the best. If she's what she says she is, Madam Zaharra will concur with the others on my future."

"Fine," Brent bit off the word, anxious to have the charade over with. "Just get on with it, please."

Pricklings of foreboding loomed up inside her, making her uncomfortable and dry-mouthed. Unable to determine why she was having these feelings, again Jewel glanced up at Brent. His expression was rigid, unreadable. Somehow she managed a wan smile and held out her hand to receive her customer's palm.

Finally out of time, wondering why she was so reluctant to perform the fortune-telling feat with which she had the most experience, Jewel sighed and looked down at the man's palm. Then she brought her index finger to his life line and began her reading.

"Zees line ees sometimes called zee heart line, or cardiaca." She slowly drew her fingertip from the fleshy base of his thumb toward the outer edge of his hand, preparing her prophecies. Then she suddenly stopped, her finger frozen, her mind steeped in a horrifying discovery it couldn't accept.

"Madam Zaharra?" Harry inquired. "Have you detected some unfortunate message? I am prepared to accept any predictions you care to make. Please do not concern yourself with my fragile mental condition. I can take anything you may have to say."

The cat she'd imagined now grew to a mountain lion. It seemed to pounce on her shoulders, crushing the air from her lungs, then drag its claws through her awareness, tearing the logic from her mind.

"I say . . . Madam Zaharra?" When he got no answer, only the glassy-eyed stare of the young woman across from him, Harry glanced up at his host. "I—I don't know what to make of this."

Bending over, Brent peered into her eyes, noted the clouds muting their clear green color. Her cheeks were red, but her complexion was waxy and pasty. "Jewel? What is it?"

Suddenly aware, all *too* aware of the hand she held in her own, she dropped it as if his flesh had burned hers. *Harry Benton?* her brain screamed. Dear God, how could she have been so blind? *Harry Benton!* She glared at him, committing to memory the features that were so like hers, then returned her gaze to his stunted pinky.

Suddenly overcome, Jewel curled her hands into fists and stifled a sob. Unable to swallow the muffled cry that followed, she pushed out of her chair and ran from the room.

# 8

Sitting at the vanity in her cabin, Jewel stared at her reflection in the walnut-framed looking glass, then banged her fist against the matching dressing table. Something hot and acidlike stung her eyes. Leaning forward, she noticed a glassy sheen and blinked to clear her suddenly blurred vision. Again she banged her fist against the dresser.

"I will not cry—not for that bastard! I'll never cry over Harry Benton!" she vowed, swallowing a sob.

Tired of watching herself, of comparing the features she shared with the man who'd sired her, Jewel eased her head down on her folded arms and sighed as she plotted her next move. She'd quite literally had Benton in the palm of her hand, and what had she done? She'd turned and run away like a baby. *A baby!* Now what? Had she bungled the assignment? Had nearly ten years of planning and plotting her revenge just gone up in smoke?

"Oh, holy hell," she moaned, "what am I going to do now?" How could she ever convince Harry she was a professional fortune-teller after she'd behaved so stupidly? Then she thought of Brent, of her lack of credibility with him. How would he react? He would be furious with her at the least, she decided. He would probably— Jewel sat up straight, cutting off her self-recriminations.

Why the hell was Harry Benton working for Brent Connors? Were they running some giant scam aboard this ship? Gathering all of society's finest so they could fleece them all at once? Jewel's shoulders slumped. That didn't really seem likely. And yet, she had to remind herself, the first time she'd seen the handsome gambler, he'd been lurking in Scotty's room—a suite the dead crook had probably shared with Harry at some time during their visit to Chicago.

"Damn you, Brent Connors, just who the hell are you?" she muttered, as frustrated with him as she was with herself.

Then a new thought came to her, a way of vindicating herself. This was all Brent's fault. If he wasn't so damned attractive, so busy trying to get in her drawers, she wouldn't be in this mess. She would have noticed Harry the minute she stepped on board this ship, if not in Philadelphia. She was sure of that much. Almost.

Jewel stared back into the mirror. "Get hold of your-self," she mouthed. "Forget the shock of finding, of *touching,* Harry Benton, and work on a way to remain on board this ship." Now more than ever, continuing the voyage was imperative. What were her chances, she won-dered, of convincing Mr. B. S. Connors to keep her on? What part of her would she have to compromise this time in order to—

The door to her stateroom suddenly rattled as someone pounded on it, startling her out of her thoughts. "Yes?" she called out, cross and irritable. "Who is it?"

"You know damn good and well who it is!" Brent Connors shouted from the other side of the door. "But don't bother getting up. Just be sure your crooked hide is in my office in five minutes! You got that? Five minutes!"

"All right!" she shouted back.

"Fine!" came the retort, accompanied by yet another thump of his fist against the door. Then silence.

Again Jewel looked into the mirror, this time, amused. "Whatever shall I do with him?" she asked herself. "How can I get back into his good graces and ensure my position on this ship? How far am I willing to go to achieve my goals?"

She thought of Brent's weaknesses, of the things that seemed to attract him to her, and suddenly Jewel's eyes flashed with excitement. Grinning broadly, she stood up and removed the scarf, her lace gloves, and the cap. Reaching for the ivory-handled brush, she fluffed her hair and positioned a few curls across her shoulders. Then she loosened the drawstring around the neck of her blouse, revealing even more of her full bosom.

Stepping back a few feet, she twirled around before the looking glass, studying her appearance from every angle. With a satisfied smile, Jewel winked at her reflection and said, "You're a dead man, Brent Connors. By the time I'm done with you, I'll own you . . . and I might just own this ship as well."

When he heard a light tapping at his door, Brent rushed to it and nearly tore it off the hinges in his haste to be done with the auburn-haired trickster once and for all.

"Get in here," he ordered, deliberately ignoring the little pout she wore and the expanded cleavage. After she swept on by him, he slammed the door and turned on her. "I'm done with believing you and done letting you turn me and my passengers into fools. I'm putting you off at our first stop, Cape Girardeau."

"But Bre—"

"Don't bother. I'm not listening to any more of your lies. I brought you in here to make certain you know where I stand and to inform you that you will be under arrest until we dock."

"Arrest?" she gasped, clutching her bosom. "But what on earth for?"

"Fraud, for starters. I'm sure we can find other charges if necessary." In spite of his vows, his fickle gaze slid down to where her fingers were pressed between her breasts—and lingered there as she tried to plead her case.

"I really don't understand," she said, drawing in a huge lungful of air. "I have not committed fraud against anyone.

If you're referring to my sudden departure during the palm reading, I can easily explain that.''

''I'm sure you can, now that you've had time to think about it, but I guess you didn't hear me. I'm simply not interested in hearing the story.'' Too close to her for his own good, Brent wheeled around and stomped over to his desk. ''As soon as I can spare the personnel, I'll arrange for someone to guard you. In the meantime I'd appreciate it if you'd just have a seat and leave me the hell alone.'' He grabbed his logbook and made a great show of studying it.

Smiling to herself, Jewel strolled over to the billiard table, then slowly circled it, running her fingers along the soft felt railings as she walked. ''This is very unfair of you, Mr. Connors. I thought you were going to give me a chance to prove myself, but the second I took sick, you gave up on me. Not fair at all.''

Watching him out of the corner of her eye, Jewel saw him raise his eyebrows, but he continued to stare at his work, silent and brooding. ''I don't know what else I could have done, given the circumstances,'' she went on, her voice purposely weak and breathless. ''I suppose you would have preferred it if I had simply sat there and thrown up all over Mr. Poindexter and his diamonds. Would that have made you happy?''

''Please,'' he said heavily. ''I have requested that you spare me any more of your wild tales. I simply cannot abide hearing another of them.''

''But, Brent, this is not a lie. I haven't gotten used to the motion of this ship yet. I've been seasick since I got on board. Believe me, my hasty departure was only to save you and the gentleman from a perfectly horrible fate, not to mention a dreadful embarrassment to myself.''

Don't listen to her, his mind warned as he mulled over her words. She fooled you once, she'll fool you again! He returned to his work.

Swallowing a surge of anger, Jewel puckered up her mouth and tried another tack. She reached inside one of the table's leather pockets and drew out a colored ivory billiard ball. Tossing it in the air and catching it over and over, she sashayed toward Brent's desk. When she reached it, she caught the ball one last time, then slammed it down on the glass top.

"Hey!" he objected, leaping out of his chair. "What the hell do you—"

"I thought you were a gambling man," she challenged.

"I am," he answered automatically, checking his desk top for damage. "It's just that I've taken my last chance on you."

"But you haven't given me a real chance," she countered, hoping she'd assessed him correctly. "So I'm not asking for any more chances. Why don't we make a bet instead?"

"A bet?" he said quietly, more interested than he would admit—definitely more than he should have been. "What kind of bet do you have in mind?"

Jewel shrugged, although she knew exactly where she was going. "I only know what I want: I want you to trust me and let me go on with my fortune-telling for the rest of this trip. If I win the bet, you give me your trust and your assurance that you will not interfere in my business in any way."

"A damn tall order, little lady."

Again she shrugged, this time leaning forward slightly. "Not to me it isn't, because I know I can be trusted. It really isn't much of a wager if you know me."

Brent choked out a laugh, then circled the desk and propped his hips against the walnut edge. "And me?" he inquired, watching her from beneath drawn brows. "What do I get out of this bet when you lose?"

Drawing her lips into a coquettish pout, she said, "Whatever it is you want from me."

Brent slid his finger inside the collar of his shirt and loosened it. "Anything?" he managed through a suddenly tight throat.

"Anything," she said softly, her eyes wide and innocent.

Brent took a deep breath and furrowed his brow. "Ah, if we were to actually make this idiotic wager, what would we bet on? A game of showdown or something like that?"

"Ummm, I don't know," she said, piloting the conversation through imaginary snags. After taking a quick, unnecessary glance around the office, she reached across the desk and retrieved the shiny red ball. "I've got it—why don't we play a game of billiards?"

His mouth drier than an entire field of cotton, Brent glanced over at the table, then back at her. He was finally able to produce his voice, but it was high and incredulous as he said, "You play?"

Her eyes heavily lidded, her gaze fastened on his mouth, she said breathlessly, "Yes—a little. Do you?"

Brent's hands, the same ones that had deftly garnered him the Natchez billiards championship three years in a row, began to sweat. Trying to look sincere and unimpressed with his talents, he said, "A little. I enjoy a good game, but I'm pretty much an average player."

"Then you agree to the bet?"

"Sure," he said easily, knowing he was finally about to catch her in a trap of her own making.

"Great." Jewel stuck her hand out, setting the rules as she prepared to shake on them. "Straight eight, call your pockets?"

His confidence wavering slightly, Brent hesitated. "Ah, sure . . . but we have to set the wagers before we shake."

"That's an excellent idea. You first."

Brent cleared his throat—twice—then came right out with the demand he knew she'd never accept. "One night alone with you in my suite."

Jewel gasped. "All night long?"

Brent puffed out his chest, almost sorry the game was about to end, and stipulated, "From sundown to sunup."

Jewel stared into his honey-brown eyes as she considered his proposal and hoped that her trick-shooting talents were still as sharp as they'd once been. Then she tossed him a wicked smile and said, "All right."

His chest rapidly shrinking inside his shirt, Brent gulped. This was too easy, he thought, frantically trying to figure her game, equally eager to believe her. How could she possibly go through with this? What made her think she could get away with it? He glanced at her, gauging her manner, judging her sincerity. She was calm, still smiling at him in the way that turned his gut inside out.

Why did she seem so confident? he suddenly wondered. What would she do when it came time to pay up? Or worse, he thought, his mind filling with panic, what if she actually won the game? Was it possible that she was as good as or even better than he was at billiards? No—she couldn't be.

To make certain he understood her demands, he cocked his head and said, "And all you want—should you win, of course—is . . . ?"

"To continue on my way down to New Orleans with no further interference from you, period. Does that sound too difficult?"

Brent strangled on the air he breathed. Coughing into his fist, he collected his wits and decided to call her bluff. "Perhaps you didn't understand the terms of my wager. I'd hate to win the game and find that you and I weren't thinking exactly the same thing."

"I'm a big girl, Mr. Connors. I know what you expect— you want me to spend the night with you in your bed. To put it more bluntly," she added, trying to ignore a sudden case of internal gooseflesh, "you expect to make love to me all night long." She raised a skeptical eyebrow by way of punctuation, then looked away.

After clearing his throat yet again, Brent restated her wager. "And all you want is to continue your fortune-telling business? I find this extremely hard to believe."

"I want your assurance that I'll be left alone. And by the way, don't worry about me backing out on the deal if that's what's troubling you. I never renege on a bet, and I have no intention of doing so this time. It might even get a little interesting—should I lose, that is.''

His breathing suddenly became labored, and the air seemed too thick to find passage in his throat. Brent heard himself say, ''I always try to oblige a lady—you've got yourself a deal. When do you want to play?''

Jewel shrugged. ''Might as well get it over with. How about now?''

''Fine,'' he said, swallowing hard, trying to look as businesslike as she did. He stood up straight, surprised to find his legs wobbly. ''After you. Choose your weapons and we'll toss for the break.''

''No, no, Mr. Connors,'' she said, waving her finger in the air. ''Do you take me for a complete idiot? I'm not about to play this game in your cabin. I don't want any cheating or rigged balls on the table. We'll play downstairs in the saloon with a crowd watching so we both know it's all on the up-and-up.''

He shook his head, muttering, ''You realize, don't you, what a large and perhaps bawdy crowd we'll draw if you insist on playing downstairs? It isn't done, you know. Ladies simply don't play billiards in public.''

''Most ladies wouldn't wager their bodies for a boat ride either, but I have my reasons. Besides, I really don't give a damn what the other passengers think, do you?''

Unable to hide a grin of admiration, Brent shook his head and said, ''Not in the slightest.'' Then he wiped his damp palm on his trouser leg and stuck out his hand. ''So we have a deal?''

''A deal,'' she agreed, clasping his hand and shaking it slowly but firmly. Suddenly all too aware of his touch and of what would happen if she lost the bet, Jewel pulled her hand away and began to walk toward the door. When she realized he wasn't following, she stopped.

Not trusting herself enough to turn and look him in the eye, she said into the air, ''Well? What are you waiting for?''

"My, ah . . ." Brent groped around for an excuse, anything but the real cause—the fact his body was on fire for a woman who belonged in jail—and his obvious arousal at the thought of quenching those flames in her softness. Turning his back to her, Brent shoved his hands in his pockets and forced his clumsy legs to move him past the billiard table.

"I, ah," he continued, stammering, "ah, thought I'd bring my lucky cue downstairs."

Jewel whirled around at this. Brent was standing at the window, his back to her, staring out at the river. "Come on, now, Mr. Connors. I thought you said you'd be fair. You must realize I don't have my own stick with me. Shouldn't we both use the house equipment?"

Brent fought to keep from thinking of her, of the game, and mostly, of the prize. He thought instead of the battle the *Dawn* would have against the Mississippi. He imagined the snags, the dreaded sawyers rising up unexpectedly and gripping the hull of his new ship, tearing open her bowels, killing her. Brent shuddered, but it was finally with something other than desire.

"Forgive me," he said, facing her, then joining her at the door. "I wasn't thinking. Of course we should use the house equipment. I want this to be fair, just as you do." He turned the brass and porcelain knob, then pushed the door open. "Ma'am?" he said with a gallant sweep of his arm.

Holding her head high, but still avoiding his gaze, Jewel stepped across the threshold. You're in over your head, dummy, her inner voice warned as she made her way down the stairs, thinking of the long, muscular legs beneath Brent's tight pin-striped trousers. *Way over your head.* Her hands began to shake as she thought ahead to the game. What if he wouldn't let her break? What if he did, but she couldn't manage the trick she'd done so many times in the past? Doubts plagued her all the way down to the saloon. What if she *did* lose? She finally considered that a distinct possibility. What if he took her up to his suite and . . . ?

"Why don't you have a seat?"

Jewel jumped and gasped at the sound of Brent's voice.

"Sorry, I didn't mean to startle you. Have a seat here at the bar while Tex sets the table up." He turned as if to walk away, then hesitated and looked back at her. "How much money do you have on you?"

"Money?" Jewel wrinkled her nose.

"Look," he explained under his breath. "You may not care about your reputation, but I do—and I care about the reputation of this ship. If we don't make some kind of wager in front of these folks, they'll assume the worst—however true it may be."

"Oh," she said, not certain if she ought to be insulted or flattered. Jewel dug into the deep pockets of her skirt and pulled out the only coin she carried. A twenty dollar gold piece.

"That'll do," Brent said, eyeing the coin. "Hang on to it until it's time to decide on the break." Then he spun on his heel and disappeared.

Keeping a careful eye on Brent, Tex, and the tables, Jewel considered his words. He'd said he cared about preserving not only her honor but also the reputation of his ship. Those were not the words of a crook, she thought, not the declarations of man in partnership with Harry Benton, either. Her confusion about the handsome gambler was increasing. Who, she wondered again, was this Brent Connors? Out of the corner of her eye, Jewel noticed a round blond woman approaching.

Reba leaned an elbow on the bar and said, "Are you resting a spell or looking to wet your whistle?"

"Oh, I'm only—" Jewel interrupted her own sentence as she noticed her trembling fingers and felt butterflies unfolding their gossamer wings in her stomach. "Ah, how are you fixed for peach brandy?"

"Got some of the finest on board."

"Bring me a glass, please—and hurry."

"Right away," Reba said, rapping her knuckles on the

bar. When she returned a few moments later, the Gypsy was staring out at the crowd, looking as nervous as a blind man at a gunfight. "Here you go, honey. Got some troubles?"

"The likes of which you wouldn't believe," Jewel said before she took a long sip of the liqueur.

"Oh, honey, believe me, I've either heard or done it all. Nothing you could tell me would be a surprise."

"It's too bad I don't have time for a little side wager." Jewel laughed, relaxing at last. "I believe I've got a story to top them all." She reached into the folds of her skirt to collect some money for the bill, then remembered her bet. "Oh, dear! I'm afraid I don't have—"

"That's all right, honey," Reba assured her, feeling a kinship with the cheaply dressed woman. "This one's on the house. I don't think Mr. Connors will mind."

Jewel laughed. "I'm pretty sure he'd mind a great deal, but what Mr. Brent Connors doesn't know surely won't hurt him." Then she downed the rest of the brandy, nearly choking on the warm liquid as she suddenly heard his voice coming from behind her.

"I wouldn't be too sure of that, sugar pie," he whispered into her ear. Then he glanced up at the bartender. "Reba? Is there something I should know?"

"Oh, no, not really, Mr. Connors. The Gypsy, she didn't have any money on her, so I let her have one drink on the house. Didn't figure you'd mind."

Brent spun the barstool around and peered into Jewel's eyes. "Just one, you say?"

"One," Reba affirmed.

"Good," he said, his gaze locked on Jewel's. "I don't want you to default on me. You ready to play?"

"As ready as I'll ever be."

Brent grinned, his confidence on the rise, and wondered how or if she would try to back out. "Let's go, then," he said, more gruffly than he'd intended.

Jewel hopped off the stool and followed him over to the billiard area. As she walked, she took huge gulps of air, calming her nerves, steadying herself for the concentration she would need. When they reached the table, Brent stopped and turned to her.

In a loud crisp voice, he said, "Let's see your money, little lady."

Jewel reached into her pocket for the gold coin, then flipped it onto the rich green felt.

Brent produced a like amount, then said, "Do you want to flip for the break, or shall I?"

Using an innocent, almost childlike voice, Jewel said, "Oh, my. I thought, you know, as a gentleman, you'd just automatically give me the break." Then she inclined her head toward the gathering crowd and fluttered her eyelashes, making herself look as young as she sounded.

Rubbing his hand across his mustache, Brent regarded the men clustered around the table, gauged their expectations, and cursed under his breath. Damn her green eyes, anyway. Left with no choice, he began to back away from the table, but as he passed behind her, he whispered, "That's the last trick you'll pull on me, you hear?"

Jewel turned and smiled. "Why, thank you, Mr. Connors. Don't mind if I do break." Then she whirled around, her full Gypsy skirt billowing out behind her, and walked to the head of the table. "Would you mind explaining the rules concerning ship movements? What if the balls start rolling of their own accord?"

Brent pulled up a stool near the far end of the table and explained as he sat down. "We consider the rocking of this boat our third player. If the balls move, they stay where they land—except for the eight. If it drops into a pocket, it gets spotted. All right with you?"

"I guess so," she said gaily as she made her way to the rack on the wall behind her. There Jewel made a great show of choosing her stick, fussing over the pretty ones, complaining about the drab ones. The onlookers, their legions growing by the minute, began making side bets, laughing among themselves, wondering why a championship shooter like Brent Connors would be wasting his talents on a woman, for heaven's sake—a woman!

Finally settling on a medium-weight stick with a horse-hair wrap and mother-of-pearl inlays, Jewel snatched a cue ball off the rack and strolled over to the table.

"Well," she said lazily, waving to Brent from across the table, "are you ready?"

"Most definitely," he said, catching the gleam in her eye, the hint of her sensual nature in her upturned mouth.

Keeping that seductive smile in place, Jewel placed the white ball on the table and began to line it up with the cluster waiting a few feet away. She turned her head this way and that, her tongue peeking out the side of her mouth, then suddenly stood up straight and walked around the table.

Leaning over the triangle of balls, she frowned. "How's a girl supposed to make the eight ball on the break to win the game? That rack-job is way too sloppy."

Brent sighed heavily. "The odds of *me* making the eight on the break aren't very good, and for you, it's an even more unlikely event, but if you wish, I'll have Tex tighten it up a bit more."

"Please do," she said, facing him, her smile secretive, sanguine.

As Brent signaled Tex, his gaze met Jewel's. Trapped, unwilling to free himself, he looked into the emerald depths of her eyes and saw the jubilation lurking there. Oh, good God, he thought, stunned by the realization. She actually thinks she can do it. *She has done it before!*

Delighted by what she saw in Brent's expression, Jewel blew him a kiss, then returned to the head of the table. All business now, she waited until Tex finished his job and moved away from the table. Then she positioned the cue ball and drew a bead on the target. Mentally shutting out the noise, she studied all the angles and made her calculations, even though she realized this shot had more to do with luck than anything. When she was finally ready, Jewel drew back the stick and drove it into the cue ball.

The ivory sphere shot across the felt and exploded into the nest of balls, scattering them in all directions. Jewel held her breath as several of them, including the black eight, began to rattle against the leather pockets. A few balls, both striped and solid, dropped down into the pouches. The eight wobbled at the edge of the precipice, drawing a collective gasp from the crowd. Then it came to a sudden standstill, as if too frightened to follow the leader.

Jewel rushed to the site and stared down at the ball, willing it with her gaze to fall into the hole. It remained at the lip, its round white eye staring back at her, mocking her.

"Sorry, sugar pie. Nice try, though," Brent whispered into her ear as he walked by.

"No, wait!" she called to him. "We have to wait a few minutes—it could fall in, you know."

Brent leaned over the table and studied the angle. "I hate to tell you this, little lady, but since it hasn't fallen in yet, the only chance of that happening is with a little help from the waves. But of course, you know what we'll have to do then, don't you?"

"Spot it," she grumbled. Jewel glanced around at the crowd, at the expectant expressions, and heard the groans and laughter of the pitying men. Now she would have to play the game, test her rusty skills against those of a man who probably made his living at a billiard table. Her best—her only—chance lay in her ability to rattle him, but she would have to make damn sure she didn't allow him to do the same to her.

Taking several reviving breaths, Jewel calmly walked the circumference of the table. After choosing the balls sitting in the most strategic positions, she turned back to Brent.

"I'll take the stripes," she said with a confidence she didn't feel. Then she selected her best shot and drove the cue ball into a yellow and white stripe. The ball ricocheted off the corner pocket, then rolled impotently toward the center of the table. "Damn," she muttered to herself. Where was her usual panache, her normal coolness under fire?

"Tsk-tsk," Brent clucked as he held out his hands to his bouncer. He waited until Tex had sprinkled just the right amount of talcum powder into his palms, then finished the sentence as he rubbed his hands together. "Tough luck, little lady. I'll try to put you out of your misery as quickly as possible."

Carefully fitting a chalking cup to the tip of his cue stick, Brent slowly twisted it back and forth, caressing and stroking it as he grinned at her from across the table.

Jewel stepped back, alarmed by a sudden spurt of desire. Things were not going as planned, she fumed. Then she realized why. Brent Connors had planted that damn feather again, that mental tickle she'd had in her drawers almost since the first day they'd met. What in hell would it take to relieve it, she wondered recklessly—going to bed with him? Should she just forfeit the game, pay up, then get on with her life? She watched, absently running her tongue between her lips, as he expertly drilled the three ball into the side pocket. She flinched at the sound, at the masculine thrust behind his drive, and chanced a look in his eyes.

Brent returned her gaze, his brown eyes smoldering, guessing her thoughts, laughing. *Laughing?*

The feather reversed itself, moved up into her mind, and began jabbing her with its quill. Damn you, Brent Connors! she thought. I'll decide when, and if, you'll get a chance to relieve that tickle. For now she had to find a way—and no means were too devious—to beat him at his own game.

Smiling, Jewel began walking toward him as another of his solids dropped into a leather pocket. When she neared, he inclined his head and whispered, "Looks like you're in for a drubbing, little lady."

Jewel waited until he lined up his next shot before she answered, "That doesn't sound so bad. It's been a long time since I had a really *good* drubbing." Then she continued walking, smiling to herself when she heard his gasp and the squeak of a miscue.

She whirled around, her mouth a perfect O. "Oh, my! Did you miss?"

"Yes," he hissed from between his teeth. "And I'd appreciate it if, from now on, you'd refrain from talking while I'm shooting."

"Sorry." Jewel shrugged, then turned her attention to the table. His mistake had left her wide open, set her up for at least two or three shots—if she could keep control of herself. She wiped her palms on her skirt, then methodically began to remove the striped balls.

His confidence in his own abilities sinking, his hands shaking, and feeling uncharacteristically indecisive, Brent rested his elbows on the bar. Her luck would run out soon, he thought, loosening the collar of his shirt. It had to. Trying to gain the advantage, he waited until she circled in front of him for her third shot before he leaned over and whispered, "Enjoy yourself while you can—you're in for a *very* long night, little lady."

Jewel's knuckles blanched as she tightened her grip on the stick. Holding her breath and her words, she took aim and shot. The target ball careened off one of the solids, then spun dangerously close to the eight. She whirled around and glared at Brent.

He pushed away from the bar, lightly brushing against her as he whispered, "Strawberries and champagne all right with you for breakfast?" Then he waltzed down to the other end of the table, calling for talc, baiting her with his seductively expressive eyes.

Jewel gritted her teeth and waited for her next chance. It came when he was down to his last ball. Again waiting for the critical moment, she leaned in close and said in a breathless sigh, "Actually, I prefer *bathing* in champagne to drinking it. Don't you?"

Barely able to stop the shot before he miscued again, Brent turned to her and took a deep breath before he said, "Why don't you have a seat and let me finish this game?"

Even though he managed to appear calm, perspiration

had collected on his brow, giving him away. His hands, still trembling and unresponsive, felt as if he'd dipped them in ice water. Brent loosened his cravat and inhaled the stale air. "Tex?" he choked out. "More talc."

Jewel waited for him to dust himself with yet more powder, then closed in on him. "I'll be leaving now, but I want you to know something before I go sit down."

"Can't it wait?" he said warily.

"Nope." Then she pushed out her bottom lip and said, "I want you to know I'm pulling for you, Brent. I really do hope you win this game. In fact . . . I'm counting on it."

Then she slithered out of his range, but not out of his view.

Chewing on his lip, wondering how he could have soaked through a new dusting of powder already, Brent forced his attention back to the table. His final ball, the four, was sitting a mere two inches from the side pocket. It was a shot he could make in his sleep.

Grinning as he thought ahead to the spoils of his victory, Brent took aim through eyes fogged with desire, and drove the cue ball toward the four. The ivory globe remained in place, unscathed.

Groaning heavily, Brent slid his palms down over the expensive fabric of his trousers and left another trail of chalky white handprints. Shaking his head, he gestured for Jewel to resume shooting, then dragged himself over to the bar.

Their money in jeopardy, Brent's friends and customers gave him a wide berth and whispered among themselves as Jewel managed to sink her final two balls. A pregnant calm shrouded the group when she began to stalk the eight ball, examining the apparently simple shot from every angle.

Finally sure of the best strategy, Jewel searched the crowd for a pair of worried honey-brown eyes. She found them at the end of the bar. She smiled, then opened her mouth to announce the final resting spot for the black ball—for the death of his hopes for the night—but hesitated.

More than concern flickered in those expressive eyes. Jewel could see the expected frustration as well, but it was tempered with something else—regret? She glanced around the room at his incredulous friends. How would they react when she won? Would they ridicule him or commiserate with him? Laugh or buy him a drink and urge him to forget about it?

Suddenly angry—with herself for having these compassionate thoughts, with him for forcing her to put herself in this ridiculous situation in the first place—Jewel said, "Eight ball, side pocket." Then she took aim and fired.

The ball struck harder than she'd intended, but it was right on target. The cue ball lightly kissed the eight, nudging the black beauty into the correct pocket.

Jewel turned to face Brent and took a bow.

Behind her the crowd let out a collective gasp. Before she could spin back around, Jewel heard the clatter of ivory against ivory. Knowing what she would find, curiously resigned to the thought, she chanced a look back over her shoulder. The white ball was nowhere to be seen. She'd scratched on the eight.

"Congratulations, little lady," Brent said as he approached, his voice high pitched and odd, the sound loose and watery. "You lose."

Unable to meet his gaze, she gave him a tiny nod of acknowledgment. "What time?"

Brent glanced at the crowd of onlookers, grateful their attention was directed at Tex and the settling of their bets. Then he whispered, "Eight o'clock. That should be close enough to sundown to suit us both."

Again she nodded, but still refused to meet his gaze. "See you at eight," she said, preparing to take her leave.

Before she could move, Brent slid his index finger under her chin and forced her to look into his eyes. Badgering her, trying to get some kind of reaction, he said, "I'll have a light supper brought to my suite—something cold we can nibble on when we get time."

Jewel jerked her chin away and glared into his playful brown eyes. "Don't bother on my account. You know how easily I get seasick."

As she began to walk off, Brent caught her elbow and whispered one final order. "Be sure and wear something soft and slinky—something without buttons or hooks."

Then he released her and watched, laughing, as she hurried through the crowd muttering to herself.

Swept by laughter, relief, and a giddy sense of anticipation, Brent shook his head and studied her retreating figure. There goes one tough little lady, he thought with admiration. Tough as an old gator after a month-long sunbath, and twice as ornery.

Cold, too, he reminded himself.

Was this one of her many identities? Was it an act? Or was she as cold as she was tough?

Would she even show up at his suite tonight? Or would she instead find a way to jump ship, after taking Mr. Poindexter and others like him for all she could?

Brent drew a toothpick from his vest pocket and began to chew on it as he considered the only thing of any interest to him now. Tough or cold, real or fake? Suddenly he couldn't wait to solve those little mysteries for himself.

# 9

Jewel stood at the door to Brent's cabin, afraid to knock.

She'd had four hours.

Two hundred forty minutes in which to ponder the upcoming ten or twelve hours. To think about that segment of time in which she had promised to relinquish her body to Brent Connors.

Now she was out of hours. Out of minutes.

Out of time in which to think of Brent, to imagine his big hands caressing her, teasing her, to dream of sliding her mouth across his, to brush against his mustache. Jewel ran her tongue across her upper lip, shivering as desire blossomed, trembling as her muscles contracted and expanded. Her legs felt heavy, swollen. She moved her right foot, easing her legs apart, seeking relief from the congestion in her lower body. But it didn't help. If anything, she was more frustrated, more engorged.

Jewel raised her hand and brushed her fingertips across the painting of the *Delta Dawn*. Relief, if she was to find any this night, lay just beyond the door. Beyond the brass knocker with the angel Gabriel suspended in the center, beyond the metal tapper she'd thought of striking several times, but hadn't yet found the courage to do.

Why had she made that stupid bet in the first place? How could she—a professional woman, a *lady* for heaven's sake—have wagered her body, her intimate self, for a mere chance at trapping Harry Benton? *How could she have done such a thing?*

But she knew why, of course. She'd known from the moment she first stared into those honey-brown eyes: She wanted Brent Connors as much as he wanted her. Maybe more.

Jewel swallowed her apprehensions and allowed the barest hint of a smile to curve her lips as she acknowledged yet another ripple of desire. Then she raised her curled hand. Ignoring the brass knocker, she prepared to announce her arrival by pounding on the door.

Inside the suite, Brent stood at the window staring out at the dark, murky river. His thoughts, however fractured, were every bit as uncontrollable as the twisting, headstrong Mississippi. His breathing was rapid and shallow, as much from anticipation as from exertion. He'd been dashing from one corner of the room to the other, from the living room to the bedroom, darting like a firefly gone berserk.

Everything had to be perfect. Bedspread, smooth and inviting. Lamps and chandeliers, their flames low and provocative, barely flickering. Champagne, expensive, chilled, straining at the cork with abundant effervescence, as eager to explode as his own body. Brent drew in a ragged breath as another of those splintered thoughts shattered his concentration. What about the food?

He wheeled around, but at the last moment stopped himself from making another unnecessary trip to the Louis XV dining table. The bluepoint oysters were as fresh and icy as they had been three minutes ago; ditto the slabs of ham, sliced cucumbers, and boiled ox tongue. The rest—pecan pie, ladyfingers, and assorted fruits and nuts—would stay fresh until the wee hours.

Why am I doing this? he suddenly wondered. Why am I preparing for an event that will never take place? The last few hours had been a waste of time and energy. Jewel, if she even bothered to show up, would never taste the French mustard or sauce piquante, much less the entrées they would accompany. She wouldn't dream of raising her crystal wineglass to his in a toast. A toast to what? Insanity?

"Good God, Connors, what have you gotten yourself into?" he muttered into ribbons of foggy night air. How would he ever get *out* if Jewel happened to show up? If she did plan to go through with this—to pay up, as it were—he knew what he would have to do. Brent Connors was, if nothing else, a gentleman. He would have to assume the debt. Give her a way out. But could he actually turn down those alluring green eyes, that pouting mouth, the soft full body he sensed would be a perfect fit to his own? Brent gasped as another spurt of desire slammed into his loins. He took a deep breath and a few sluggish steps closer to the open window.

He tried to channel his thoughts, hoping to fill his mind with something other than the exquisite ache, that desperation he guessed he would continue to feel even if he bedded a thousand other women. Only one, he suspected, could relieve that. One bouncy, calculating, auburn-haired temptress who would most likely turn him inside out, then stomp him flat.

Brent shook his head, again trying to control his wandering mind. *If* she showed up, he mused, his only option as a gentleman, the only one he could live with, would be to release her from the debt. When that happened, he assumed she would flee from the scene of the crime, leaving him to pick up the ashes of what could have been. He sighed at the thought, and at that moment, the door on the gingerbread house of his Belgium clock banged open. A carved yellow and blue bird sprang from its bowels and began to announce the time.

"Cuckoo." Back inside the clock, then out again. "Cuckoo." Back inside the clock . . .

Brent watched, mesmerized, as he realized something was slightly out of tune, a thump that lagged behind the rhythm of the count. Although he was muddled enough almost to believe the bird had added a deft drummer to its merry little band, he finally understood the sound was coming not from the clock but from outside his suite. Someone was knocking on the door. *Jewel?*

Swallowing hard, Brent started across the thick carpet. When he passed the clock, the bird emerged for its eighth "cuckoo."

He reached for the doorknob, marveling at his growing nervousness. Brent Connors never had sweaty palms! At least not until he'd met that green-eyed vixen. Taking a deep, calming breath, he pulled the double doors open.

"Good evening," he said in a suddenly hoarse voice, carefully avoiding her gaze. "Please, come in."

Giving Brent a brief sideways glance, Jewel trudged into the suite on leaden legs and stood in the center of the room. Crossing her arms below her breasts as if caught by a sudden chill, she glanced around the suite. Her gaze was riveted on the marble-topped table laden with gourmet delicacies when Brent approached her from behind.

"Cold?" he asked, appraising the rigid downy hairs saluting him from her forearms. No longer in charge of his own mind, and although the evening was warm and sultry, he illogically suggested, "Perhaps you'd like a fire. I could stoke up the old—"

"No, please," she said, whirling around to face him. "I'm not the least bit cold. Just a little . . . surprised."

Taken back, again the schoolboy in love with his teacher, Brent became defensive. "Surprised? What did you expect—a mattress tossed on the floor and a quick 'Take off your clothes, ma'am, time's a wasting'?"

"Something like that," she said, her grin cooler than it felt.

Catching the humor in her eyes, the twitter of nerves in her voice, Brent relaxed a little. "Sorry about the outburst. I'm not real sure how to behave in a situation like this. It's rather new to me."

"Me too," she said, her eyes wide and guileless.

Brent released his breath, surprised to find he'd been

holding it, and took a long, objective look at her. She'd changed her clothes, as he'd suggested, but she'd switched from one Gypsy outfit to another. She still had the multi-colored scarf draped across her shoulders, its sequins sparkling—winking at him it seemed—and in place of the yellow blouse she wore a puff-sleeved white top with a much higher neckline. Her skirt, falling to just above her ankles, was bright red with clusters of tiny apricot-colored flowers planted in erratic patterns. Her hands were un-adorned. Her hair, loose and free, hung in cinnamon spirals across her shoulders and back.

She was dressed for business as Madam Zaharra, and yet she'd also managed to do as he'd asked. She *was* soft and slinky. In Brent's eyes, she was swaddled in puffy white clouds and sparkling stars, wrapped in the soft cocoon of his dreams, a place in which he imagined he could most happily die.

His breath clogged in his throat. Heat flared in his loins. Brent shoved his hands in his pockets and stared down at the expensive Wilton carpet. "Go on," he said with difficulty. "Get on out of here."

Jewel's arms dropped to her sides. "Wh-what?"

But still he kept his head bowed, his gaze fastened to the floor. "I said get out. You're free to go."

"Oh, now, just a minute here," she said, taking a step in his direction. "We had a deal, a bet. What's going on? What kind of game are you playing now?"

Testing himself, daring his very sanity, Brent raised his head and looked into her eyes. "All bets are off. You're free to go."

Jewel stood rooted to the spot, not sure she believed a word she'd heard. Was he making it easy for himself, trading her debt to him for her dismissal when they docked in the morning? She cocked one auburn eyebrow. "I have no intention of leaving this ship or this room. Now what's going on?"

Trying to ignore the way her full bottom lip trembled ever

so slightly, he shrugged and said, "I didn't think you'd show up. Now that you have, I realize we can't go through with this."

Suspicious and somehow disappointed, she demanded, "Why not?"

Brent took another long breath, knowing for sure that he, not some wooden bird, belonged in the little gingerbread house. No longer able to look in her eyes, he dropped his gaze back down to the gray and white carpet. "When I make love to a woman, it's because that's what we both want, not because of some bet made out of desperation."

"I've done nothing out of panic," she insisted, her precarious position as an employee and her recent discovery of Harry adding to the turmoil in her heated body. "A bet's a bet, and I'm here to pay up. I suggest we get on with it."

In spite of her boldness, the tightening of some of his muscles, and the hardening of others, Brent managed the lie. "Sorry, little lady. But I'm just not interested."

Jewel stamped her foot. This wasn't the way it was supposed to happen. She'd lost all control of the situation—of him—and had a very fragile grip on herself at best. What was he up to? He was lying—of that she had no doubt. She could almost *taste* his desire, feel the thundering of his pulse even though several feet separated them. She *knew* somehow that his need was as great as hers. Why the lie? Was he so intent on tossing her off the ship, ruining yet another of her assignments?

As determined to remain on board as she was needy, Jewel slid the scarf off her shoulders and tossed it aside. It fluttered to the floor, puddling on the thick carpet like shimmering lake. She moved toward Brent.

At that moment the *Dawn* chose to intervene, and made a few decisions of her own. She lurched, dipping her bow into a large swell, then abruptly righted herself.

Jewel staggered, off balance, and tumbled into Brent's arms. Instinct prompted him to draw her closer than necessary. Desire kept her locked in his arms long after the ship stopped its exaggerated pitching.

Jewel snuggled against his chest and slid her hands around his waist where her fingers clung to his linen dress shirt. Then she raised her head and looked into his eyes. "You want me. Admit it."

"Do not," he said hoarsely, avoiding her gaze, but recklessly staring at her mouth instead.

"I know you want me. Why are you pushing away what's yours for the taking?"

Why wasn't she taking the easy way out? he wondered briefly as he lied again, this time with a tongue that felt as if it were carved of Belgian walnut. "The only thing I want from you is your absence."

"Really?" Jewel's tongue peeked out the corner of her mouth as she tightened her grip on his shirt and molded her hips to his. "That's funny," she said in a breathless whisper. "I could have sworn you were unarmed when I walked into this room." With a half smile and a twinkle in her eyes, Jewel let her gaze slide to the his desk where his Colt .45 lay tucked in its belt and holster. When she looked back at him, her smile widened and became unmistakably carnal as she added, "Oh, my . . . I see that you . . . are."

The knot in Brent's throat grew huge and sprouted tentacles that coiled around his windpipe. Struggling for air, for a way to retain his sense of honor, he whispered, "You're . . . brazen. A brazen hussy."

Even though the heat in her own body was building to a fever pitch, so close to igniting them both she could barely keep her feet under her, she shrugged. "That may be, but at least I know when a man wants me. And you definitely want me."

"Do not," he insisted, knowing he was losing the battle, no longer sure whom he was fighting or why.

"Do," she whispered, sliding her fingers into his thick dark hair, lowering his mouth closer to hers.

"Do . . ." he choked out, "not."

"Don't," she said as her mouth brushed across his.

"Do," he groaned, defeated and relieved all at once.

Intent only on Jewel now, on tasting, touching, feeling her, Brent plunged his hands into her hair and wrapped the long tresses around his fingers. As he crushed his mouth to hers, as she matched his urgency, Brent inhaled and was suddenly filled with her essence. She smelled of violets—*fresh* violets, by God! Where had she found a field of flowers? Or was it all in his mind? Brent suddenly wondered if he even had a mind, and that not entirely lucid thought was his last as their passion ignited, consuming them both.

Entwined together, two candles twisting, melting in the heat of their own desire, they spiraled down to the thick carpet. Jewel knew she was out of control, out of her mind, but it didn't matter. She was frantic to have him inside her, to have him fill the source of her heat and extinguish the exquisite flames. Only then would she be able to think again, to become herself anew, and to return as the master of her own mind, ruler of her mutinous body.

Too eager, too much in a hurry for caution or regrets, she tore at Brent's cravat, ripped the buttons from his expensive shirt. Soothed for a moment, she let her fingers luxuriate in the thick mat of hair on his chest—but only for a moment. As Brent's kiss deepened, as their heated bodies rolled across the carpet, each one seeking dominance and the way to best find primal gratification, Jewel busied herself with his belt buckle and the buttons beneath it.

"Hold still," he said, the words thick and dark, as he poised just above her writhing body. "Let me touch you—I need to touch you."

Barely able to control her movements—to harness nature, as it were—Jewel spread herself beneath him and slid her hands around his neck. Intent on bringing his mouth back to hers, she pulled him toward her, but Brent only brushed her lips with his before continuing down her throat to the collar of her high-necked blouse. Caught up in her frenzy and his own foggy desire, he roughly tugged at the material until it separated, exposing her camisole and the taut nipples beneath. As impatient as she, he pulled the fabric aside and took her breasts in his hands. When his mouth followed, sliding across one full mound toward the crown, she cried out.

"No . . . forget that," she managed in a husky voice as she tugged at her skirts, pulling them up and out of the way. "Take me," she urged through a tortured gasp. "Take me *now*."

Barely hanging on to the last weak thread of his sanity, Brent was no longer interested in arguments. He tugged at her drawers, vaguely aware of the shrieks of ripping fabric, unable to distinguish whether the protest came from her underthings or his trousers. Or both.

Then at once they were free of clothing from waist to knee, as unfettered as they would take time to be. Brent lowered himself, hesitating only for a moment before he drove into her.

"Oh, God," she cried out, her voice weak, strangled. "Hurry Brent. Dear God, hurry . . . *hurry*!"

Every part of her body seemed to move of its own volition, but her hands, her needy fingers, seemed to be the most frantic. She dug into Brent's buttocks, her nails leaving moon-shaped welts, and urged him onward and faster, guided him closer, deeper. God, how she wanted this man, needed his touch. Had she ever needed anything or anyone like this before? She was swirling, lost, consumed by Brent, by his magnificent body, reduced to a quivering mass of nerve endings and demands. Jewel was beyond thought or questioning now, could only feel, wanted only to touch and be touched.

Without warning but with an intensity she'd never before known, the first wave of spasms struck, arching her back, forcing her nails deeper into his flesh. She tried to speak, to tell him, to thank him, to beg him to go on and on, but her mind was liquid, a gelatinous mass of pure pleasure as the spasms increased, moved on to higher and higher levels.

Brent loomed above her, watching her face, loving the joy radiating out from her features. He wanted to encourage her to go on, to lose herself with him, but his own voice, the rubble his mind had become, was lost in the chaos of his body. His pulse leapt and fluctuated wildly as she took what she wanted from him. Intense heat—hers, his, he couldn't be sure—sent the blood spurting through his veins at a reckless pace. Then it all came together in a series of white-hot jolts that shook him right down to his toes. Someone cried out in an anguished moan. Someone groaned in sweet agony.

And then silence. Damp, eerie silence punctuated only by the lapping of the water against the ship and their frantic gasps for air.

Jewel tried to think, to pull herself together, but all she could do was feel. A few lingering spasms pulsated quietly, fading along with the pounding of her heart. Brent's damp shoulder moved against her open mouth as he tried to control his breathing. Above them, a huge glass chandelier swayed gently—along with them or with the movements of the ship? she wondered through the mist of her mind. Then, too soon, as quickly as everything had happened, Brent pushed himself up on his elbows and looked down at her.

His eyes were swimming in a lazy haze. A lock of his sable hair, nearly black from his exertions, curled down over his forehead. He was in shock. A man emerging from solitary confinement into the bright sunlight. He blinked and rubbed at his eyes.

Jewel was still there, he realized. She was real, not imagined, and she was aglow with the rewards of their frantic lovemaking. Brent was touched, struck dumb, and slightly disgusted with himself all at once. ''I—'' He gave it up, knowing that even if he could find his voice, his brain would be unable to help him put a sentence together.

''I think I know,'' she whispered, sensing his confusion.

Suddenly feeling awkward and ashamed of his impulsive, dishonorable behavior, Brent rolled over and turned his back to her.

He began to pull on his trousers as he said, "Forgive me. I . . . that shouldn't have happened."

Jewel sat up and tucked her breasts back inside her chemise. Casting furtive glances his way as she worked at piecing her shredded blouse together, she said, "There's no need for you to apologize. After all, isn't that why . . ." She left the sentence unfinished, unable to say the words she knew were no longer true. This hadn't been the spoils of war, compensation for some foolish bet. She'd taken what she wanted. So had Brent. And while neither of them was likely to admit it, what had happened between them had absolutely nothing to do with a game of billiards.

"The reason doesn't matter," he said, angry with her for dismissing it all so casually, with himself for having lost control. "This simply should not have happened." His trousers finally on, held together at the waist by his white-knuckled fist, Brent climbed to his feet and examined the ruins of his shirt.

Over his shoulder he said, "I'll give you some privacy while I change my clothes. Do you need anything? A robe or . . ."

Jewel glanced down at her bosom, realizing she couldn't leave his room in such a state. "My blouse, what's left of it, is in tatters. I could use a drape of some kind if you can spare it. A shirt will do."

Appalled to think he was capable of such savagery, Brent forgot himself and wheeled around, catching her gaze, stopping his heart. Filled with remorse, he hunkered down beside her and glanced at her exposed breasts. She was flushed but, as far as he could tell, unmarked. "Good God, I can't believe I did that to you. If I've hurt you in any way . . . If you need—"

"Brent," she interrupted gently, "you didn't hurt me at

all. In fact, I don't believe I've ever felt quite so . . . so *healthy*.''

Brent swallowed hard, then lightly brushed her cheek with his fingertips. Speaking softly, his voice as rich and dark as molasses, he murmured, ''I sincerely hope you're telling the truth. I couldn't live with myself if I thought I'd hurt you.''

''P-please,'' she stammered, tongue-tied by a sudden case of nerves. ''Let's just forget about it.''

''Not likely, little lady. Not likely at all.'' He stared into her eyes, smiling, until crimson roses bloomed on her cheeks and she looked away. His dimples firmly in place, Brent stood up, forgetting about his damaged clothing.

''Oh!'' Jewel choked out through a burst of laughter as his trousers slid down over his hips. ''Sorry about that. Maybe I can mend them for—'' Unable to go on, thoughts of her previously inept attempts with a needle and thread making her laugh even harder, Jewel squeezed her eyes shut and wrapped her arms around her stomach.

Looking away from her, Brent pulled up his trousers and started for his room. ''Sorry about your blouse''—he waved his hand as he walked past her, irrationally unwilling to discuss something as intimate as her underwear—''and whatever else I may have damaged. I'll replace the items.''

''That won't be necessary,'' she said, laughter still sparkling the words. ''Why don't we just call it even?''

Trying to look as dignified as he could, he gave her a short nod before he said, ''As you wish, little lady.'' Then he stepped into his bedroom.

Watching his retreat until he disappeared behind the closed door of his bedroom, Jewel drew a long breath and shook her head. This night was to have been her way of bringing him to heel, of controlling him with that which he wanted so badly. It should have worked. She should have been able to escape, unscathed, unimpressed. Jewel remembered the words she'd mouthed into the looking glass—

"You're a dead man, Brent Connors."—and nearly laughed out loud.

She stumbled to her feet, still tingling from their love-making, and adjusted her clothing. There had been no corpses in this room tonight, she thought, amazed to realize the embers of passion were flaring in her again, only two very alive, extremely lusty, and voraciously greedy people. And there was no denying the result, of her plan either. She had set a trap for Mr. B. S. Connors, but she had fallen into it right along with him.

Now what? she suddenly wondered. How would those two lively people conduct themselves in the future? Could she ever look at him again without thinking of this night, of the incredible way he'd made her feel? And what about Brent? Would he still insist on dropping her off at Cape Girardeau? If he'd been as deeply affected by their love-making as she had how could he put her ashore?

The door to his bedroom opened, and Jewel turned away, her pink cheeks tattling on her again. As he approached, the sound of the boat's whistle joined his footfalls. Using only one of its five tones, the *Dawn* sent two short and three long notes into the sultry night air.

Brent froze in his tracks. "Good God! The *Dawn*'s in trouble!" Startled into action, he resumed his march across the room, tossing a shirt into Jewel's arms as he passed her. "Sorry, little lady, but I have to go to the boiler room."

"Why? What's wrong?" she said, alarmed by the concern in his expression.

"Probably nothing," he hedged as he reached the double doors and turned back to her. "Make yourself comfortable. Have some supper. Do whatever you like. I'll be back as soon as I can." Brent spun around, jerked open the doors, then looked back in the room one more time. "I know I've been saying this a lot tonight, but I really am sorry to have to leave you like this. I—It can't be helped." Then he blew her a kiss and closed the doors.

Mouth open, eyes unblinking, Jewel stared at the doors,

then glanced down at the garment in her hands. What in hell was going on around here? she wondered. Was the whistle a routine signal, or was the steamship in trouble? Should she stay—or go?

Jewel glanced at the profusion of edibles on the table, then remembered the terms of the bet: She was supposed to stay all night long. She shrugged. Whether Brent chose to return or not was inconsequential. She was obliged to keep her end of the bargain—wasn't she?

Ignoring her inner voices, Jewel stripped off the remains of her blouse and slipped into Brent's shirt. It hung down to her knees, but she gathered it up and tucked it inside her skirt. Determined to keep her feminine side hidden for the balance of the evening, Jewel strolled over to the marble table and examined the offerings.

She chose a plump oyster, plucked it from its shell, and downed it in one swallow.

"Ummm," she moaned, unaware until that moment how hungry she'd been.

After pulling up an armchair upholstered in burgundy velvet, she took a seat and filled her plate with ham, rolls, and relishes, leaving the boiled tongue for Brent. When her appetite was sated, Jewel wrapped a couple of ladyfingers in her napkin and pushed out of the chair. As she walked away from the table, the champagne bucket caught her eye. Hesitating for a moment, she stared at it, licking her lips, then shook her head and continued on her way to Brent's desk. She'd had enough excitement for one night.

She took a bite of the sweet cake, then cocked her head and slowly circled the glass-topped desk. Thoughtfully chewing, she glanced through his notes and calendar, hoping to learn more about the handsome gambler, but finding nothing. She finished the ladyfinger, then studied the napkin in her hand. A sketch of the *Delta Dawn* was embroidered in the center, along with "Sebastian Steamship Line, B. S. Connors." Brent Sebastian? Why had he named the company Sebastian instead of Connors? she wondered idly.

Jewel wadded up the napkin and glanced around the room. The door to Brent's bedroom beckoned. He'd told her to make herself comfortable and to do whatever she liked, hadn't he? Why not have a peek? She was, after all, expected to spend the night. Surely he didn't plan to keep her on the floor the entire time. Shaking off a sudden flutter in her lower body, trying to think of herself as a detective, not as a woman, Jewel dropped the napkin on the table and casually strolled over to the door. It wasn't quite closed.

Nudging the polished walnut door open with her toe, she gasped as she got the first glimpse of Brent's enormous bed. The custom-made, extra-long and double-wide mattress rested on an elaborate brass frame, but its cover was the thing that caught her eye. It was a patchwork of alternating squares of rich charcoal velvet and shiny silver satin. On either side of the bed, overlooking the river, floor-to-ceiling windows were draped with billowing charcoal velvet lined with smoky gray. The dressing table, freestanding looking glass, chiffonier, and upholstered rocking chair were all made of polished walnut and accented in brass.

"I'm impressed, Mr. Connors," she commented as she walked through the room running her fingers along the freshly oiled wood. "Very impressed."

Suddenly feeling coltish, deliciously feminine, and mischievous all at once, Jewel turned on her heel and rushed back to the dining table. With no further hesitation, she plucked the wine bottle from its icy nest and began to wrestle with the cork. By the time she'd loosened it enough for it to emerge under its own power, she'd shaken the bottle so much that the cork exploded from the glass sheath, spraying champagne everywhere, soaking Brent's shirt and most of her skirt.

Giggling to herself, undaunted by the unexpected shower, Jewel grabbed a crystal glass and a couple of clean napkins and hurried back into the sumptuous bedroom.

* * *

Several hours later Brent crept back through the double doors along the first hint of dawn. The lamps were still turned up, and some of the food had been eaten, but there was no sign of Jewel. Had she gotten tired of waiting for him and gone to her own stateroom? Or . . . ?

He glanced toward his bedroom. Not certain what he would do if she was in there or how he would feel if she wasn't, Brent quietly made his way to the door and pushed it open.

Jewel, dressed only in her camisole and torn drawers lay curled in the center of his bed on his pewter-colored silk sheets. He breathed a long sigh, acknowledging it was from relief, not exasperation, and wondered if he should announce his presence. As he silently made his way across the room, he noticed the bottle of champagne resting belly up on the night table and the rumpled napkins and crystal glass scattered across the carpeted floor.

Amused, touched, and more than a little eager to learn what she'd been up to all night, he slid the rocking chair over near the bed and eased down on it. Giving himself some time to collect his thoughts, he stared down at her. He could have returned to his cabin hours ago, he admitted with a twinge of regret, but staying away had seemed to be the proper thing to do at the time. Now he wasn't so sure. Had he been chivalrous—or a damn fool?

She looked impossibly tiny and defenseless lying alone in his big bed. Her hair, a deep rich sorrel, was spread around her, across his pillow, and down over her nearly nude shoulders. In slumber, her thick lashes brushing the rise of her freckled cheeks, she looked almost like a child, oddly vulnerable somehow. Was that a true side to her nature, one she'd been able, up to now, to hide from him? Did she conceal this gentle, susceptible side of herself from everyone or just from him? Finally accepting what he'd known since he first saw her on the ship, that he was trapped like a three-legged possum in a bog, he let his breath out in a sigh.

The sound reached Jewel's subconscious. She rolled over on her back and stretched her arms high above her head, where they stayed as she slipped back into the dark abyss of slumber, into an enticing wish-dream state where she could actually will her mind to produce the fantasy of her choice. Her choice that night, and probably for many to come, she acknowledged from the logic sector of her mind, was Brent Connors. Brent and his wonderfully exciting hands and mouth. Brent and the marvelous way he'd made her feel. Brent, with a feather for a whip. All he needed to do was wave that plume her way, and she would be his—anytime, any place.

Jewel lowered her arms, catching the pillow between them, and buried her nose in the flannel-covered down. She inhaled the hint of bayberry, the scent of the man himself, and issued a faint moan. Her smile serene, satisfied, she murmured through a sigh, "Brent."

Feeling guilty about watching her as she slept, Brent leaned forward, intending to announce his presence, but then she lowered her arms past her full, partially exposed breasts to her thighs, where her torn drawers afforded him just the tiniest peek of her auburn thatch and the satiny skin beneath. Once again she stretched, languidly, sensuously, twisting her hips from side to side as she slid her fingers along the length of her body on the return journey to the pillow.

Good God, he groaned inwardly, knowing he'd never get this sight out of his mind, her out of his heart. Thoughts of Jewel, of the way it felt to be inside her, of her fluid, natural movements as she responded to his touch, were destined to be a part of him for the rest of his life. Desire, intense and demanding, suddenly raged throughout him in a fire storm of passion. Brent leaned back in the rocker, struggling to get hold of himself, determined not to risk taking her like an animal again.

He looked around for a distraction, anything to keep him from staring at her beautiful face, from gawking at her luscious body. He found it on his pillow—on her hand. Not certain of what he saw, he leaned forward again and examined her little finger. It seemed to be exceptionally short, even for a pinky. He glanced at his own hand, at the graduating dimensions, then back to hers. It was definitely smaller than it ought to be—and just about the cutest thing he'd seen since his niece, using her voice as only a cocky two-year-old could, and begun calling him Unkee Bent. He was bent all right, he laughed to himself, twisted, to have thought he could waltz in here and watch Jewel without so much as—

Green eyes flew open, startling Brent, popping Jewel to an upright position like a catapult. "Holy hell!" she cried, snatching the sheet and covering herself. "What are you doing in my bedroom?"

"I—" Brent glanced at his surroundings, no longer sure he trusted his own mind, then said, "This is *my* bedroom. I belong in here."

Jewel's memory caught up with her at the same time her headache did. She managed a sheepish "Oh," just before a bolt of lightning split her forehead in half. With a heartfelt groan, she collapsed back on the pillow and held her forearm across her face.

Brent grabbed the empty bottle and waved it in the air. "Did you have a good time last night, little lady?"

"Shut up," she muttered. "Go away and leave me alone."

"This is my suite, remember? You go away."

One watery green eye peeked out from under his arm. "In a minute. Is the boat all right?" she asked, buying a little time for her pounding head.

"The boilers overheated, but we got them under control. Everything's new—the crew, the machinery. I think they just need a little time to get used to each other, but things should be all right from here on out.''

''Umm. That's wonderful. Absolutely wonderful.''

Brent stood up and banged the bottle down on the table. Laughing as she winced, he started toward the door. ''Why don't you get dressed? I'll have some breakfast brought in for us.''

Just the thought of food brought bile to her throat, but she held her tongue. As soon as Brent closed the door behind him, Jewel sat up and swung her legs over the edge of the mattress. What in God's name had possessed her to drink an entire bottle of champagne? her brain screamed. But she knew the answer. She'd tried to drown thoughts of Brent and their explosive passion, dilute them into pleasant memories she could deal with. It hadn't worked. Now she had to figure out a way to control herself for the rest of this trip, and she had to do it with the worst headache of her life. Her legs wobbly, her mouth tasting as if she'd mopped the floor of a saloon with her tongue, Jewel slowly dressed herself.

Then she trudged out of the bedroom and headed for the double doors, muttering as she passed Brent, ''If my time is up, I'd just like to go to my stateroom. I couldn't eat a bite, but thanks for the offer.''

''Wait a minute,'' he said, catching her as she reached for the doorknob. ''There's something I'd like to say, and we need to discuss a few things.''

''Can't this wait?'' she said wearily. ''I'm really in no condition for a debate.''

''Then just listen. That's all I really want from you right now, anyway.''

Jewel glanced up into his eyes, stunned by the sincerity, the sensitivity, she saw there. ''I'm listening,'' she said with a softness that surprised her.

''What happened last night . . . I just—''

''Can't we just forget about last night?'' she cut in,

alarmed at the direction the conversation was taking. "I think it would be better for us both if we did."

Brent raised one eyebrow, then slowly shook his head. "Maybe it would be better for you, little lady, but not for me. I don't know what goes on in your mind, but I do know my own. I can't just forget what happened here or how I feel about it today."

"Oh, Brent," she cried, not ready for this conversation, unwilling to search her own heart for her true feelings. "I don't want to know how you feel. Please don't tell me. Maybe you're making too much of this. It was just a silly bet, and even if the payment got a little out of hand, that's still the way we should look at it—as a payment, a way to settle the score."

*Cold.* The word leapt into his mind unbidden. Was this an act? Was she hiding something? Was there another man in her life? A husband, perhaps? Brent shook off the thought, but not his suspicion. This was not the same lady he'd seen asleep on his bed a few moments ago. Where was the sweet, guileless woman who'd turned his world upside down? How could he find the real woman, the truth? Too far from the answers he sought, Brent decided to let her think he was as unaffected as she—for now.

He popped a toothpick into his mouth and shrugged. "Most women—certainly most southern women—would demand much more than a short memory from me right now. They would expect me to restore their honor with a proposal of marriage."

*"Marriage?"* she nearly strangled on the word. "Please save yourself the trouble and embarrassment of showing me your misguided chivalry. My honor is just fine the way it is, thank you."

Again he shrugged. "Then we just forget about last night?"

"Absolutely. I've already forgotten it," she lied.

"Fine," he said. "Now that I think about it, I believe you could even say that last night meant nothing to me."

Jewel opened the door and stepped across the threshold, curiously piqued. She gritted her teeth and said, ''That's perfectly wonderful news, and rest assured, last night meant nothing to me either, do you hear me? Less than nothing!''

Then, forgetting about her dreadful headache, she slammed the door in his face.

# 10

"Zee seven of clubs on your queen of diamonds promises good fortune and happiness, but bids you bevare of zee opposite sex—hah! Truer vords vere never spoken!" Jewel added impulsively.

"I *beg* your pardon?"

Jewel looked up at the offended matron and rolled her eyes. "So sorry, Mrs. Astor. Sometimes zee cards take control." She looked back down at the table, hoping the explanation would satisfy the woman, and went on with her reading. "Now ve have zee ace of diamonds—humm. Zis means you veel soon receive a letter. Let us turn up zee neighboring cards to see from who and about vat."

She droned on with the reading, telling the woman what she thought she'd want to hear, automatically reciting the meaning of each card she turned up. But her mind was on Brent. Brent and the fact they'd studiously avoided each other for the past two days. When the *Delta Dawn* docked in Cape Girardeau the morning after the *incident*, as she now referred to that night, she had half expected him to demand she leave the ship. But it hadn't happened.

The best she'd gotten from Mr. Brent Connors over the last few days was an occasional perfunctory nod. A couple of times she'd actually caught him staring at her, but then he would just salute her as if she were some kind of regimental soldier and go on about his business. Had what passed between them really been so insignificant to him?

"Are you quite finished?"

The nasal voice startled her, and Jewel realized she'd been sitting there staring at the three of clubs as if she expected it to come alive.

"Pardon, madam, but zis is very interesting and I vant to be sure before I speak. Zee card says you veel be more zan once married."

Mrs. Astor choked, then began laughing into her diamond-laden fingers.

Working to keep her expression impassive, Jewel watched as the rotund matron cackled like an egg-bound hen, her bovine breasts jiggling beneath the bodice of her black silk dress. When the cackles became occasional clucks, Jewel pressed her lace-shrouded fingers into a tent, and raised one eyebrow. "Zee cards never lie."

"My, oh, my, Madam Zaharra," the society woman finally managed as she spoke through her perfumed hanky. "It's a good thing Mr. Astor didn't hear you say that."

Jewel shrugged. "Send him over to me. Perhaps vee can determine ven your next marriage will occur."

"Oh, my, my," the woman said through a chuckle, "you're quite impudent, aren't you?" Mrs. Astor dropped a couple of coins on the table, then labored at lifting her bulk from the chair. "Impudent," she went on, puffing for air, "but very entertaining as well. Thank you for the delightful card reading."

"You're velcome," Jewel replied, her smile strained. "And please be sure to geeve my regards to your husbands—all of zem."

The woman began cackling again, but once she was out of sight, Jewel collapsed against the back of her chair. She peeked around the end of the large partition Brent had installed to separate the men from the women, and glanced into the card room. The bar was crowded, but she saw no sign of Brent Connors or Harry Benton. She imagined that the shipowner would be up in the pilothouse, since the *Dawn* was due to dock at its next port in a matter of minutes, but where had Harry been hiding for the last two days? Although Jewel was an employee of the shipline and a confidante of the other workers, all she'd been able to learn was that he'd taken sick and was having his meals sent to his cabin. Was that true? she wondered, or was it part of another scam—a way for him to move about the ship in one of his famous disguises?

"Good morning, my dear."

Startled, Jewel lurched forward, nearly knocking the crystal ball out of the silver bowl. "Oh . . . hello."

"So sorry, my dear. I didn't mean to sneak up on you," Harry said as he deposited a teacup and saucer on the table and eased his wiry frame onto the chair. "And how are you this fine morning? Better than I've been these last few days, I hope."

"Oh?" she said, feigning surprise. "Have you been seek?"

Harry's fine black eyebrows drew together. "Something I ate, I suspect, but I'm fine now." Then he leaned closer, whispering conspiratorily, "And listen, dear, it's all right with me if you don't use the accent. I am one of the few people who understand that you don't actually have to be a Gypsy to be an excellent fortune-teller. Interpretation is really all that matters, wouldn't you say, my dear?"

"Ah . . . perhaps," she hedged, working to conceal her feelings, trying to forget he was her father. "Or perhaps you are still trying to prove to your boss that I don't belong on this ship. Is that it? Are you going to ask Mr. Connors to have me removed the minute we dock at New Madrid?"

"Oh, goodness no, my dear." Harry began to chuckle as he remembered their prior meeting. He looked down and smiled. "I am *not* an employee of this ship. I happen to have first-class accommodations. Mr. Connors merely borrowed me for the purpose of learning whether you were a fake or not after I informed him about my extensive knowledge of fortune-telling."

She wanted to believe him. She wanted to believe that

Brent was, if nothing else, an honest man who would never be in a partnership with such a vile excuse for humanity as Harry Benton. But she had to consider the possibility that these two men—both constantly on her mind—were cut from the same cloth. If she acknowledged the danger they represented to her, perhaps she could avoid becoming too comfortable around either of them.

"My dear?" Harry said, puzzled by her frown. "I hope that information doesn't offend you. Mr. Connors only wanted to be certain you were authentic. I told him you were, and he must have believed me—your business seems to be thriving," he said, pointing at her cash jar.

"What? Oh, yes, yes, it is."

Harry rumpled his brow. "Perhaps I should return at another time. You appear to be somewhat distracted today."

"No!" she said too fast, with too much emphasis. Recovering quickly, Jewel lowered her voice and adopted her best professional manner. "That is to say, I am truly interested in proceeding with your fortune. I think we might even make some very interesting discoveries." She held out her carefully gloved hand and smiled, determined to disregard the fact that this man had all but cut out her mother's heart. "Your palm, Mr. Poindexter?"

"Oh, no, my dear," Harry said. "I brought something much more interesting than my palm—I have my teacup from breakfast. The sign says you read leaves."

"Yes, of course," she said crisply, nearly thanking him for sparing her the chore of touching him. Jewel picked up the cup and peered at the contents, then shook it and made circles with it. When the particles were properly spread out for reading, she upended the cup on the saucer, allowed it to drain for a moment, then turned it over and set it on the table.

"There are a great many messages here," she began, hoping she could remember the different emblems represented by the leaves. "The ring here signifies marriage."

Harry laughed. "I think you will find that it says such a state will never be a part of my life."

Jewel slowly shook her head. "No, it says that you will be married. There's even an initial nearby, but I can't quite make it out—it's a little cloudy."

"Cloudy? That is not a good sign, is it?"

Jewel's expression was solemn and guarded. "It means you will most likely marry a very disagreeable woman."

"Oh, my. Then I shall have to avoid this marriage at all costs."

No longer able to look at him, resisting the urge to tell him he was probably safe from such a fate, that marrying *anyone* while behind bars was extremely improbable, Jewel peered down at the leaves. "Hmm," she muttered thoughtfully. "Here is an interesting grouping—a star surrounded by dots. This denotes—"

"Children." He laughed.

"Yes, and it means that *your* children may cause you grief and vexation."

"Impossible, my dear," he said, still laughing. "I have no children, nor do I intend to burden myself in the future with any of the little gargoyles."

Jewel narrowed her eyes, hardening her gaze until one green eye began to twitch. "Zee leaves," she said slipping into her Gypsy role, "say zat you have at least one child, sir."

"Zen zee leaves," he mimicked, "are quite full of shit, my dear."

Jewel gasped, and her mouth dropped open.

"Oh, goodness—pardon me, my dear. I never use such language, especially in front of a lady." Harry reached across the table and patted her hand. "Just the thought of having children is quite distressful for a man like me. I do hope you'll understand and forgive the slip of my loutish tongue."

She pressed her lips together and stared into Harry's smoky green eyes. You bastard, she said silently. You low-down rotten bastard. You can't even acknowledge me, can you? You won't admit, even to someone you suppose is a stranger, that you have a child—bastard that she may be. God, how I'd love to tell you that your daughter is sitting right across the table from you and that she'd like to stick her knife into your black heart!

Alarmed by what he saw in the young woman's expression, Harry pushed his chair away from the table. "Goodness gracious, I hardly think a harmless expletive, uncivilized as it may have been, is worth such a countenance of rage. Perhaps it would be best if I took my leave."

"Oh, no. Please excuse my manners," Jewel managed, barely able to resume her role and force herself to block out the past. Choosing to use the hurt and hatred to help her regain her advantage, she went on. "I'm afraid your words reminded me of a time best forgotten. They brought back some terrible memories of my childhood . . . things that cause me a great deal of pain."

"Oh, my dear, I'm so sorry."

"That's all right. How would you possibly know my own father thinks of me as an unwanted gargoyle."

Harry gasped. "Oh, my! He actually said that in your presence?"

Jewel folded her hands in her lap and gave Harry a cool stare. "He said it right to my face," *the dirty low-down, no-good bastard.*

"How terribly gauche of him." Harry slowly shook his head, then waved his hands in the air. "That's enough of that, then. You will kindly dispense with any further references to children, and I shan't mention my less than fatherly attitude toward them."

"Agreed." Jewel bit the word off sharply as she returned her gaze to the cup. "Now then, where were we? Have I mentioned the roads yet?"

"No. No, my dear I don't believe you—"

Harry's words and Jewel's reading were both rudely interrupted as the *Dawn* bumped against the dock at New

Madrid. Jewel looked into the cup, wondering if she could go on with her interpretations, but the movement had forced the leaves to coagulate. "I'm afraid it's too late for roads now, Mr. Poindexter," she exclaimed, tipping the china teacup toward him. "Would you like to try again with another—"

"Not now my dear," he said, waving her off as he pushed up from the chair. "I had no idea we were so close to New Madrid or I'd have waited until this evening." He reached into his pocket, but Jewel objected.

"You owe me nothing for this," she offered, knowing her best chance at trapping the man, of exacting her revenge, would come only if she presented herself as his friend. "Perhaps after the steamship leaves port this evening, we can try again."

"Thank you, my dear," Harry said with a short nod. "Until tonight, then. For now I believe a walk around town in the fresh air will be of immense benefit to my health. Good day."

"And good day to you, sir. Enjoy yourself." Jewel smiled up at him until he turned and made his jaunty way through the crowd. She impulsively made a face at his back before she returned her attention to the table and began to collect her cards and dice.

While she closed up her tiny shop for the afternoon, Jewel began working on a way to trap Harry. Now that he was well, back out in the open, surely he was in the process of choosing his latest target. A criminal like Harry Benton must be beside himself with delight, she thought as she watched the bejeweled passengers file off the *Dawn*—he sure as hell had no shortage of potential victims on this ship. Would following him into town provide her with any clues to his intentions? Or could she best learn of his latest scheme by breaking into his room and examining his personal effects?

While she was in the midst of indecision, Jewel's instincts unexpectedly jabbed at her subconscious. Brent was near; she could sense his presence without looking up. She knew his gaze was fastened on her even before she lifted her lashes and found his warm brown eyes. They were smiling, she noticed as he made his way toward her, friendly and inviting. What did he want from her today?

"How's business, little lady?" he said as he sauntered up to the table.

"I'm making a living," she said with a shrug.

"Got time for one more customer?" he asked, straddling the high-backed chair across from her.

"*You*?"

Brent popped a toothpick into the corner of his mouth and grinned. "I never did find out just how much you know about fortune-telling."

"Really?" she said, seizing the chance to learn more about his relationship with Harry. "I was under the impression your partner pronounced me authentic."

"My . . . partner?"

"Yes," she said, studying him for signs of duplicity, fighting the urge to reach across the table and touch him. "Mr. Poindexter, your expert fort—"

"Oh." Brent laughed, remembering. "He's not my partner. He's a passenger I borrowed after he offered to test your methods. The Sebastian Steamship Line is mine, and mine alone."

"If that's the case, then why Sebastian?" she asked. "I thought your last name was Connors."

"It is. Sebastian is my middle name and my mother's maiden name. I used it in honor of dear old granddad, who sired seven ravishing young ladies but not one son to carry on his illustrious name."

"How terribly . . . southern of you," she said through a quiet laugh.

"Yes, I suppose it is. What else do you know about southern men, little lady?" He took her hand in his. "Anything besides a few drawled expressions?"

In spite of her excellent instincts, forgetting all the vows she'd made to herself, Jewel finally dropped her guard and stared into his eyes, not as a detective but as a woman. A shiver darted up and down her spine, looking for an avenue of escape, as she pondered his words. All she knew of southern men, she'd learned from Brent Connors—and she knew far more about him than was prudent.

Sputtering, tongue-tied, as she always seemed to be around him, Jewel shrugged. "I guess I don't know much more about you southerners than how to say 'y'all' and 'much obliged, suh.'"

Brent laughed and pulled the toothpick from his mouth. "That's about all you need to know, little lady, at least as far as I'm concerned. Although I was born and raised in the decidedly southern state of Mississippi, I should inform you that I'm not exactly what most folks in these parts would call a *true* southern gentleman."

"That makes us about even, then." She chuckled. "I'm not exactly your average Gypsy, either."

As he joined in her laughter, Brent reached for her other hand and raised them both to his mouth. After kissing each finger through the black lace of her gloves, he murmured against the back of her hand, "God knows I've tried, little lady, but I can't seem to get what happened between us out of my mind. All I can think about is you and the way I feel when you're around. You been thinking of me, too?"

Jewel tugged at her fingers, trying to withdraw them and any little pieces of herself that she'd unintentionally given him, but Brent's grip remained firm. "Don't," she said weakly. "Please don't say things like that, and please let me go. I— Can't we just be friends?"

"We can be that," he said, looking up from her hands for a moment, "but we're also a whole lot more. I know it, and you know it, too."

"No," she protested, shaking her head in a lame effort to convince him. "We have to forget what happened in your room and make sure it never happens again."

Brent stopped kissing her hands and looked into her eyes.

"You don't mean that. I *know* you don't. Why can't you just admit it? You and I are made for each other—the perfect complement, a matched set."

Unable to speak through the shudder his words prompted, swallowing the knot of truth in them, again Jewel shook her head. Then she finally said, "We're a match made in hell. No good can ever come from us. Now please—let me go."

Dissatisfied, unconvinced by her answer, but too much the gentleman to ignore her request, Brent released her hands. "You're wrong, little lady. I intend to spend the rest of this voyage proving that to you."

"Don't waste your time," she replied in a strange and tiny voice. "This is as close as I intend to get to you from here on out."

His dimples firmly in place, Brent reached into his vest pocket and produced a coin. Flipping it onto the table, he said, "Wrong again, little lady. I'd like a palm reading. I believe that requires some physical contact, doesn't it?"

Smiling back in spite of herself, Jewel nodded, giving him a silent tribute, then reached for his hand. She slowly ran one finger from the base of his palm to the tip of his index finger, drawing an exquisite gasp from him. Then she said, "Zis is zee heart line or zee cardiaca. It says here zat you should run like hell from any woman whose hair glows with zee color of fire, zat zose flames—"

"Will incincerate me someday?" he interrupted, ready to meet the challenge. "Go ahead, little lady. It seems I've kindled at least a small blaze in you. I'm prepared to fight fire with fire. I dare you, sugar pie—strike your match."

Outside beyond the docks a hansom cab rounded the corner and pulled to a halt a few blocks away from where the *Delta Dawn* was tied. Allan Pinkerton climbed down from the plush carriage and paid the driver. Then he walked toward the "floating wedding cake," wondering anew how he would present himself, wishing he'd been able to think of a disguise clever enough to impress his best female operative.

As he stepped down off the boardwalk to cross the street, a scattering crowd caught his eye. Townsfolk and boat passengers spread out, revealing to Allan that they had been gathered around a wildly painted ox-drawn wagon. Bright red letters spelled out the words, Professor Harrington's Traveling Medicine Show. Laughing to himself, Allan resumed his progress, then stopped again.

Swivelling back toward the commotion, he observed as a tall silver-haired gentleman gathered his unsold merchandise and made his way to the rear of the wagon.

"Perfect!" Alan exclaimed as he started toward the man. "Absolutely perfect!"

His mind moving as rapidly as his feet, the detective devised his plans as he moved closer to the medicine show. When he finally reached the proprietor, the silver-haired gentleman had finished storing his wares and was engaged in conversation with the beautiful Oriental girl standing beside him.

"Excuse me, my good man," Allan apologized. "Might I have a word with you?"

Professor Harrington stepped away from Princess Ling Ling. "You may have just about anything you'd like, for a price. What can I do for you?"

"Just the words I wanted to hear." Allan laughed. "I am meeting a friend aboard one of the steamships dockside. I would like to buy or borrow your costume and perhaps a few bottles of tonic. Would that be possible?"

The professor flapped the sleeves of his colorful satin mandarin robe, then pulled a crimson silk scarf from inside the folds of the garment. "Not only possible, but done! Princess Ling Ling, four bottles of tonic, please—and grab my top hat while you're back there, too."

Then he draped the scarf around Allan's neck. "Do you intend to sell my product while in this costume, sir?"

"Well," Allan hedged, "I only wanted to play a little joke. I don't want to infringe on your—"

"Please, sir," the professor cut in. "I only ask so that you will be prepared with the proper speech. As it turns out, I'm in a bit of a hurry to leave New Madrid." He cast a nervous eye toward the center of town, where he knew the sheriff was in the process of locking up his partner, Chief Nogasackett. Then he swung the Chinese cape over his head and wrapped it around Allan's shoulders. His grin huge and completely genuine, the professor said, "You're welcome to my identity for the rest of the afternoon."

Princess Ling Ling returned with four bottles of medicine and the black silk hat. After handing them to Allan, she gave him a shy smile, then disappeared into the back of the wagon.

The professor adjusted the hat on Allan's head, instructing him as he arranged the bottles in the pockets of the detective's coat. "Be sure to refer to the tonic as 'the elixir of life.' Tell your customers that you have observed the authenticity of this product firsthand. You have also accompanied Chief Nogasackett on many an excursion as he picked just the right yarbs and roots, blended them with his own specially grown herbs, and added to them the mystical power contained in Princess Ling Ling's secret extract of poppy. And good luck to you, friend." Then he climbed onto the driver's seat of the wagon and extended his hand. "That'll be twenty dollars, sir."

"*Twenty?* No, I don't think so—not for a little joke." Allan made as if to remove the cape, but the professor spared him the trouble.

His worried gaze still darting toward the center of town, Harrington shrugged. "All right. Fifteen, then."

"Ten, or you get it all back."

The professor ground his teeth, then sighed. "Ten it is—but be quick about it. I really must be on my way."

Chuckling to himself, Allan paid the man and started down the street toward the *Delta Dawn*. As he walked, he read the label on a bottle of tonic: "Professor Harrington's Nature Cure and Worm Syrup: Guaranteed to heal liver ailments, eliminate all suffering from the pain of a toothache to the agony of childbirth, and restore health to those who endure any number of maladies."

Allan opened the bottle and sniffed. Grimacing, he replaced the cap and stuffed the bottle back inside his jacket pocket. "Ought to be outlawed," he grumbled to himself as he reached the ship. "Nothing but alcohol and codeine, mixed with God knows what all."

When he started up the gangplank, he explained to a deckhand as he passed by, "Just visiting a friend on board. No need to worry. I'll be off before she heads on down-river."

The deckhand shrugged and went back to his chore of taking on supplies.

Allan continued toward the saloon deck, where he supposed a fortune-teller might be working her trade. A quick glance into the huge room showed him Madam Zaharra and her colorful sign. She was sitting at her small table, staring down at a customer's hand as if deep in thought.

Slowly approaching her, Allan settled on the simplest way of announcing his presence, and at the same time he gave himself an identity Jewel wouldn't have to explain.

Proud of his creative disguise, he began to whistle as he drew nearer to his favorite employee.

The sound alerted Jewel. She looked up, stared at Allan for a moment, then gasped.

Prepared for her surprise, Allan threw his arms wide open and beamed. "My sweet little Zaharra! It's your wandering daddy come to see you! How's my little girl?"

# 11

Brent looked over his shoulder at what had to be some wild apparition, but the bizarre-looking man continued toward them, waving his arms as he approached.

"Now, is that any way to greet your dear daddy, girl?" Allan complained loudly. "Get up and give your old man a hug and a kiss."

"Oh, good God!" Brent rolled his eyes then scowled at Jewel. "Tell me he's kidding."

Jewel shrugged and tried to explain, but her tongue couldn't quite manage the assignment. "I—He . . . Well, you see, the thing is—"

Brent sighed as he stood up and shoved the chair close to the table. "Just one more question: Is this your *real* father?"

Jewel pushed away from the table and rose, her lips moving as her frantic mind searched for an acceptable reply. But no sound issued forth.

Allan circled around to where Jewel stood, his thick brows drawn together. "Have I upset you in some way, daughter?"

"I—ah . . . You—"

"Allow me to answer for her," Brent supplied, adding a caustic "daddy dear."

Allan looked down his nose at the handsome stranger and muttered indignantly, "And who might you be, sir?"

"I'm Jewel's long-lost twin brother. Sorry to spring such

a shocking surprise on you, Pop, but the midwife hid me under a cabbage leaf soon after I was born. I do hope you'll excuse my lack of manners and my irreverent attitude toward you, dear Father, but you have to remember that I was raised in a vegetable garden.'' Brent tipped an imaginary hat, then whirled on Jewel. ''When you're done visiting with Daddy here, stop by my office, sis. We have to discuss skeletons in our family closet.''

''If you'll just listen, please, I—'' Jewel began.

''Oh, I intend to. What's one more daddy story between us? I'll be in my office stoking up my *fire*. I'm not sure I've got enough fuel burning for this latest challenge. Five minutes, sis,'' he suggested, holding up his fingers for emphasis. ''That should give you and Pop plenty of time to come up with a good story.'' He spun on his heel and stomped off toward the bar.

Allan removed the stovepipe hat and scratched the top of his head. ''What was that all about?''

''Nothing,'' she sighed sinking onto the table top as she watched Brent disappear. ''Everything.''

''Jewel? What's going on here? Who was that?''

''Brent Connors.''

Allan whipped his head toward the bar and the nearby doorway, but the gambler was gone. Looking back at Jewel, he said, ''The man from Topeka? The fellow who—''

''Shot me,'' she said with a nod. ''The man who has now met at least *three* of my fathers.''

''Oh,'' Allan groaned, remembering all the details. ''I suppose this disguise isn't as clever as I thought, then, is it?''

''Not when you consider that Brent Connors owns this ship and I'm posing as one of his employees.''

''Oh, no! I'm sorry Jewel, but I had no idea. Do you think this will jeopardize your job?''

She only had to think a moment before she shook her head. ''Mr. Connors and I are a little . . . beyond such matters, but he's definitely going to want to know who you are and why you're calling yourself my father." Trying to hide the undeniable affection she felt for Brent from her employer, she looked down at the floor before she softly added, "I can't lie to him anymore, Allan."

The detective shook his head and offered his upturned palms. "I really thought I had the perfect excuse to visit you. I have an appointment in Memphis tomorrow and thought I'd stop by to check on you. I never dreamed—"

"Forget it. It's not important. This is—I have some information that may be of interest to you. Harry Benton is on board this steamship."

*"Benton?"* he said under his breath. "Are you absolutely certain?"

Again she nodded. "Without a doubt. If you'd shown up the minute the *Dawn* came into port, you'd have found me reading his tea leaves."

"That could have been disastrous. Harry would have recognized me in an instant." Allan glanced around the room. "Where is he? In this getup I'm bound to draw more than my share of attention."

"He's in town somewhere, but I don't know for how long. It might be best if you"—she gestured toward his robe— "get rid of this, this . . . Who are you supposed to be, anyway?"

"Professor Harrington, at your service." Allan clicked his heels together and handed her a bottle of worm syrup. "On the house, of course, but test it in the privacy of your stateroom. I believe you'll find it's quite intoxicating."

"Thanks," she said, taking the bottle from him. "Maybe I can use this to help soften Mr. Connors's opinion of me. I'm going to need all the help I can get."

Again he apologized. "Sorry, Jewel. What are you going to tell him?"

"Something I should have before now—the truth."

Allan winced. "Are you certain that's absolutely necessary?"

She thought for a moment, considered their newest

uneasy truce, then nodded. "Yes. I believe it is. What do you want me to tell him about you?"

Allan stroked his beard for a moment, then shrugged. "I think it'd be best if you leave my name out of it, but go ahead and tell him I'm one of your colleagues. You'll be telling the truth, if that's important to you."

Jewel didn't have to say a word. She looked into Allan's eyes and saw that he knew exactly how important it was to her. "Thanks," she said quietly.

His expression thoughtful, Allan asked, "Anything else I should know about before I leave?"

Jewel averted her gaze and shook her head. "I'll wire you from New Orleans, as we originally planned, and inform you of my progress—maybe before then, if Harry gives me a good reason to take him into custody."

"Is that a possibility? Maybe I should remain on board hidden away just to be on the safe side."

"No, Allan. Go on about your business. So far, Harry's been too sick to do much of anything. I doubt he's even had a chance to cheat at cards yet."

"You're sure you'll be all right?"

Jewel pushed away from the table and straightened her spine. Staring off to where she'd last seen Brent, she answered him in a preoccupied manner, with less confidence than usual. "I can take care of myself, Allan. You should know that by now."

Always the detective, Allan raised a skeptical eyebrow and warned her as he prepared to take his leave, "Be careful with this Connors fellow, Jewel. I don't want to lose one of my best operatives."

"Don't worry about me. I told you, Brent didn't mean to shoot me. He's just a rotten shot."

"I wasn't talking about the shooting, girl." Allan raised his bushy eyebrows and wagged his index finger. *"Be careful."*

Jewel caught his gaze just in time to see him wink. Then, with a great flourish, he turned, letting the cape billow out behind him and strode toward the doorway, his manner imperious. Laughing, Jewel waved good-bye, then made her way among the poker tables and started up the staircase leading to the officers' quarters.

Once she'd disappeared, Allan became more cautious, less flamboyant. It wouldn't do to collide with Harry in such an outrageous costume. As Allan looked around the ship, searching for a place to hide the cape and top hat, three men started up the gangplank toward him. His concentration centered on finding a handy hiding place, he casually stepped aside.

A hand shot across his body, grabbed his arm, and dragged him to the gangplank. "Not so fast, Professor Harrington."

Allan's chin jerked upward, and he squinted into the man's features. "Pardon me?"

"I can pardon you all the way to hell and back, but it ain't gonna do you one bit a good. You're under arrest, pardner."

"Now, just a moment," Allan objected, trying to wriggle out of the sheriff's grasp.

His captor's grip tightened. Before Allan could move, the sheriff wrenched his arm up behind his back and fastened his wrists together with manacles.

Satisfied his prisoner's hands were immobilized, the lawman said, "You'll get all the moments you need in my cozy little jail. Now get a move on."

"But I'm *not* Professor Harrington," Allan insisted. "I simply borrowed his clothing for the afternoon."

"Right." The sheriff reached inside the cape and pulled out a bottle of worm syrup. "This here bottle of cougar piss is just in case you take a little sick? Is that it?"

The detective stood his ground. "I can explain that. If you'll just look at my identification, I can prove beyond question that I am—"

The sheriff slammed his fist between Allan's shoulder blades, pushing him down the gangplank. "Tell it to Chief Knockaskucket, or whoever the hell he is, when you get to your cell. For the time being, just shut your goddamn mouth and *move*!''

Three decks up, unaware of her employer's plight, Jewel approached the shipowner's suite. This time she used the brass angel to announce her presence. When she heard Brent's muffled ''Come in,'' she turned the knob and stepped inside the room. He was bent over the billiard table, placing the final ball inside the wooden triangle.

''Just in case,'' he explained as he straightened up and met her halfway across the room. ''You never know when you and I might have to settle the score with a game of billiards.''

Her smile awkward, as shy as it was amused, Jewel said, ''I have a lot to explain, I know that. This time I promise to tell you to the truth.''

Brent stared into her eyes as he took her hand, searching for the real woman, seeking an expression of complete candor. But she was closed, guarded. With something less than enthusiasm, he pulled her over to his desk. ''Telling the truth should be a refreshing change of pace for you. Why don't you have a seat and give it a try?''

She pulled back. ''I don't want to sit down, I want to try to explain. I realize how difficult it must be for you to believe anything I have to say, and I don't blame you one bit. I'm asking you to please listen to me this one last time. I am prepared to tell the truth—all of it.''

Brent rested his hips on the edge of his desk and folded his arms across his chest. He reached into his shirt pocket for a toothpick, but shook his head and sighed instead. ''All right, little lady. I'll listen to your version of the truth—one last time.''

Jewel took a deep breath and began pacing in small circles. ''You've seen me in different costumes—the dance hall girl, the Harvey Girl, and now this. The outfits were disguises. Professional makeup.''

"*Professional*?" Brent jackknifed off the desk. "Just what kind of profession are you talking about?"

Jewel inclined her head and raised one offended brow. "What profession are you thinking of, Mr. Connors."

"Well, I don't know," he hedged, leaning back against the desk. "Just the word 'professional'—what do you mean?"

"I'm a detective," she said with a regal smile. "If you'll relax a minute, I'll show you my identification."

"A *detective*?" Brent lurched forward, stumbling as he got to his feet. "You mean you're the law?"

Jewel shrugged. "In a manner of speaking, I suppose I am. Quite often my work is government-related, but just as often I'm hired by a private party. I work for the Pinkerton Detective Agency based in Chicago, and I answer to Allan Pinkerton himself. Allow me to supply you with proof." She pulled a chair toward her and propped her left foot on it.

Rendered speechless, Brent stood open-mouthed and watched as she hiked her skirts to mid-calf and fumbled with the hem of her petticoat. Of all that he'd considered she might be, the word "detective" had never once crossed his mind. Was it really, *finally*, the truth? As she searched for her credentials, she exposed all of her slim ankle and a good portion of her shapely leg. Strapped to that beautiful leg, Brent noticed, was a stiletto—probably the same one she'd used on him. Startled as well as aroused by the sight, he cleared his throat and said, "The least you could do is have a little modesty and ask me to look away."

"Why should I bother?" she said, using the knife to slit open the hem of her petticoat. "You'd just peek anyway."

"Would not."

Jewel gave him a sideways grin, then pulled some documents from the secret pocket in her coarse muslin petticoat. "I hope you appreciate the trouble I'm going through for you. I abhor sewing, and now I'm going to have to stitch this hem together again." She lowered her foot to the floor and handed the documents to Brent. "Here, read these papers carefully. I believe you'll find everything in order."

But he didn't have to read a word to recognize the honesty in her voice, the naked truth in her eyes. He glanced at the papers, then dropped them on the corner of the desk. "Pinkerton, huh? I never would have expected you to be a secret government agent."

Unused to explaining her position to anyone but the crooks she apprehended, Jewel felt the color rising along the sides of her neck. "I've done a little secret government work, but my specialty is private cases—jobs like tracking down Jesse James. You do remember what happened to me on that job, don't you?"

"Oh!" Brent slapped his forehead and pushed away from the desk. "So that's how you knew who he was—and why you were so damn mad when I saved you."

"*Saved* me!" she echoed, rolling her eyes. "Too bad you couldn't have saved me from the wrath of Allan Pinkerton as well."

Brent closed the gap between them and slipped an arm across her shoulder. "I'm almost as sorry about that as I am about hurting you. I hope my assistance, however misguided and unnecessary, didn't put your job in jeopardy."

Intensely aware of his fingers as they massaged the back of her neck, she shrugged. "That's all right. Mr. Pinkerton is . . . Well, he treats me more like a daughter than an employee."

"Another of your many fathers?"

Jewel laughed, but it came out strangled. "Something like that. Mac in Topeka and the man you just met below—both are colleagues of mine. I was working with Mac, but the operative you just saw was a surprise to me. He had no idea you were aboard this ship or that you'd already met my 'father' a time or two."

Brent's fingers slid around to the side of her neck, pulling her closer. As he spoke, he began to stroke the length of her throat with his thumb. "I can't blame any man for wanting to watch over you, even if he has to dress up as your *mother* to do it. You're in a dangerous profession, Jewel, one I'm surprised your real father allows you to pursue."

As she listened, Jewel's fingers had instinctively trailed along his arm, stopping here and there to caress the man beneath the shirt. At his final words, she dug her nails into his forearm. "I do as I please, not as *anyone* allows."

Brent took one step back and furrowed his brow. "I was only asking about your real fath—"

"I don't have a father," she said, vowing to make that the final lie between them. "Please don't ask about him again."

Knowing only that he'd touched a very raw, very private spot, unable even to guess at the unhealed wounds accounting for the tender place, Brent moved forward again and pulled her into his arms. "Sorry, little lady. I don't mean to pry, only to understand. "

Too close to him, their bodies touching where his angles kissed her rounded curves, Jewel tried to push away.

"I said I'm sorry, and you know what else? I really do believe your story." He pulled her closer. "Why are you fighting me?"

Her brain heating along with her body, Jewel managed a feeble "I—I don't like the way you're watching me. Stop looking at me like that."

"Like what?"

"There—like that. Stop looking at my mouth as if you own it, as if you think there's some special bond between us."

Brent grinned. "Isn't there?"

"No. And there isn't going to be, so stop it right now."

"All right, I'll look elsewhere." Then slowly, with painstaking precision, he glanced up into her eyes, seducing her with his gaze, melting her resolve with his open hunger.

Jewel drew in a harsh breath. "Don't look at my eyes, either."

"Why not?"

"I— Because you're making me nervous."

"Oh?" His grin was crooked, sensual. "I don't think that is what's going on inside you at all. I think you want me."

"Th-that," she choked, her voice pubescent, "that's ridiculous."

"Is it?" he whispered, gently skimming her mouth with his. "I think not. You want me."

"Do not."

He laughed, reminded of another time, "Oh, yes, you do. You may think I'm the only one burdened by obvious displays of desire, little lady, but in many ways you're just as easy to read. I know how much you want me at this moment. You can't hide it any more than I can." He punctuated the sentence by pressing his hips against hers. At her gasp, he added, "You want me so badly right now, you can hardly stand the wait."

"Do not."

"Do." He grinned, his eyes warm, his expression open and inviting. "I can see it in your eyes, in your mouth. There," he whispered, rubbing a finger across her bottom lip. "See how you tremble with just the thought, how you shiver from my touch. You want me, Jewel. Admit it."

Not trusting herself to speak, she closed her eyes and bit her lip.

Still his rich melodic voice caressed her. "You want me so badly right now, your mouth is watering. Say it."

Jewel groaned and shook her head, but as her lips parted, she heard herself say, "Yes—yes, I do. I want you, Brent."

"Then you shall have me," he whispered just before he claimed her hungry mouth with his.

And then she was engulfed, by her own flames, by the heat of his touch. Her responses lightning quick, her patience nonexistent, Jewel reached for the collar of his shirt and began tearing at the buttons.

"No," he gasped, pulling away from her. "Not like that. Not this time."

"But, Brent," she said in a strangled cry, "I thought—"

"Put your arms around my neck," he demanded, seeking the impossible—complete control of himself. "I intend to make love to you, Jewel. I want to satisfy you as you've never been satisfied before."

Shuddering, her mind and body reeling with his words, she obeyed.

Brent scooped her into his arms and murmured endearments against her hair as he made his way toward the bedroom. When he reached the door, he nudged it open with the toe of his boot, then kicked it shut after he stepped inside.

He carried her to his immense bed, then hesitated before setting her on her feet. "This *is* what you want, isn't it? No games, no debts, no lies? Just you and I taking what we want from each other, giving all we can?"

Jewel drew in a ragged breath. "Yes. Oh, yes, Brent. Just you and I taking . . . giving . . . now, Brent. Now."

"We're going to take our time, little lady," he murmured as he loosened his grip just enough for her to slide down the length of his body. When her feet hit the carpet, she reached up to his shirt again, and this time Brent circled her wrists with his big hands. "Have a little patience, sweetheart. Let me get to know you Jewel, to learn everything I can about you."

"I think you already know me pretty well. I don't know what you're talking about."

"Then relax and let me show you." He lowered her arms to her sides and kissed her briefly, then began removing her clothing. "I want to know *you*, not Madam Zaharra or any of the other women you've pretended to be. I want *you*, and I don't intend to stop making love to you until I'm sure I've found you."

Jewel gasped, gulping in the air through an aching throat. No man had ever spoken to her like that, demanded so much of her—or offered so much of himself. *Run,* her mind shrieked. Run now while you still have some control. But her trembling legs stood their shaky ground. That was when

Jewel discovered that her mind controlled nothing but futile thoughts. Her body belonged to Brent and his sensitive hands, Brent and his thrilling mouth.

He quickly peeled off the layers of Gypsy clothing, then took his time with the laces on her camisole. When that was unfastened, he left it in place, forgoing the sight of her breasts for the time being. Instead, he slid his hands down over her spine and derriere and slowly sank to his knees.

Through a hoarse laugh he said, "I've always considered the treasure you women hide beneath your skirts to be a formidable weapon, but you do beat them all, little lady. You've got yourself a regular arsenal here."

Eager to get past the preliminaries, Jewel issued a nervous giggle as she started to remove her small pistol from the holster strapped to her thigh.

"No," Brent said softly. "Let me. Let me do it all, sweetheart—I especially want to remove this stiletto," he said tapping the leather sheath. "I want to know where this little beauty is at all times." He glanced up at her, narrowing one brown eye, then slowly removed her weapons. When he slid her cotton drawers from over her hips, Jewel's legs began to shake in earnest; when he brushed his mouth across her naval, her knees buckled and she lurched against his shoulders.

"B-brent," she managed through a tight throat.

"I know," he whispered, his own passion looming up inside him like a dark thick cloud. "I know."

"Then . . . *please*."

He'd wanted to make love to her slowly, construct an atmosphere of trust and caring before they became one, before they gave way to passion, but she wasn't having any of it. Brent got to his feet, still determined to build a stronger base for their lovemaking, stubborn in his need to know all there was to know of her. He would find the real Jewel Flannery or wear himself out trying. With a renewed sense of purpose, Brent removed her camisole, then slowly unfastened the pearl buttons on his own shirt.

Jewel stared at him, her green eyes dark with longing,

hazy with desire as he stripped off his clothing. When he finally stood naked before her, she drew in a shaky breath.

"Now, Brent? Now?" she whispered huskily.

"We're getting there, beautiful lady. You're looking a little wobbly. Perhaps you'd like to lie down?"

Sudden emotions, feelings she couldn't or wouldn't identify, joined in with the desire raging throughout her body, leaving her confused and incapable of speech. Jewel nodded violently and staggered toward the bed.

Brent caught her in his arms and deposited her in the center of the velvet and satin spread before he lay down beside her. "And you are beautiful, you know," he murmured, appreciating the dusky peaks of her full breasts just before he filled his palm with one of them. "Every little inch of you is beautiful, just made for kissing, for tasting," he continued, replacing his hand with his mouth.

Jewel cried out as his lips circled her nipple, then sucked in her breath as he continued his journey. "Brent . . . for God's sake."

"Slow down," he murmured against the hollow apex of her rib cage. "I only want to be sure you actually feel me touching you, that you know it *is* me. Is that asking too much?"

"No," she said plunging her fingers into his hair and forcing him to look into her eyes. "I'm really trying, but because I *do* feel you touching me, because I know without a doubt that it *is* you, I just can't wait any longer. Please—I wish you'd . . . you'd—"

"Really?" he said, glancing at her breasts, at the rigid sentries guarding the twin peaks. "But I was just getting to know your freckles, and this . . ." He ran a finger slowly, torturously down over her hip to the top of her thigh, "This cute little mole. I'm trying to think of a name for it." Recognizing that her groan was as much from frustration as from arousal, he continued making circles on her feverish flesh with his fingertips, sliding them along as if they were lazy ostrich plumes. "Which is the real you, Jewel? Are you just a mass of wanting now, or do you want *me*?"

"Y-you," she stammered through a tortured groan as Brent's hands and mouth worked their magic. "God, yes. I want you."

And although he knew she was ready for him, eager to have him become a part of her, Brent recklessly continued, piling her pleasure higher and higher until he was certain she'd reached new, glorious plateaus. Too late, he realized he'd pushed her too far. When he finally entered her, she was beyond control.

Brent rode with her, enduring her bucking and twisting with as much apathy as he could manage. When she finally calmed and her breathing became rapid but not labored, he pushed his own needs into the farthest corner of his mind and said, "Impatient little thing, aren't you?"

Jewel laughed, then choked out a reply as she tried to catch her breath. "I—I tried to slow down. Really I did."

"I guess you know what I'm going to have to do now," he warned against her flushed, damp skin.

"No," she breathed, liquid heat still throbbing in her veins.

"I'm going to have to start all over again."

And then he did just that.

Later—how much later, he couldn't determine—Brent jerked his head up off the pillow. He sorted through the ruins of his mind and pieced together his memories, trying to understand what had happened here. He glanced down at Jewel and found her skin damp and rosy, her eyes closed with a serenity of expression that touched him so deeply he had to look away.

He had taken her to places she'd never been before; that much he knew. He had also discovered mysteries in her body that even she was unaware of, and he'd definitely found the avenues that led her to the greatest pleasure. But had he actually reached the goal he sought? Had he touched

her heart? He didn't know, couldn't be sure. Somehow he'd
lost himself in the bargain.

"Jewel?" he whispered.

Her answer was a low, gratified moan.

Smiling down at her, sensing she was at some new level
of discovery within herself, he whispered, "Don't move.
Stay exactly the way you are. I'm getting out of bed, but I'll
be back in one minute."

Again she moaned, but her eyes remained closed, her
expression contented. Loving that look, sensing he was
closer to her now than anyone had been in a very long
time—maybe ever—he carefully eased himself out of bed
and padded over to his dresser.

Jewel heard Brent's words, felt him leave the bed, but she
couldn't speak, couldn't open her eyelids, which felt leaden.
She was lifted out of herself, floating above her own body
on a sensual cloud of the softest velvet. What had he done
to bring her to this state? Who had she become? No one had
ever given her so much and expected so little in return.
What *had* she given him? she suddenly wondered. More
than her body, came the answer. Some part of her she'd
never recognized, never allowed to surface before. What did
it mean?

In the midst of her thoughts, Jewel realized Brent had
returned to the bed. An instant later his gentle fingers began
to brush the errant hair from her brow. Her lids fluttering,
feeling drugged and unresponsive, Jewel tried to open her
eyes.

Brent kissed her cheeks and her damp eyelashes. "Stay
the way you are. Rest, think of us and how good we are
together. I'm going to cool your skin."

And then, before she could object—or thank him—Jewel
heard the trickle of water being poured into the washbasin
and felt the cool damp cloth as he drew it across her fevered
brow. Unfamiliar emotions swelled in her throat, threatening her air supply with their enormity. Why was he doing
this? she wondered as he methodically, lovingly, washed

her flushed body from head to toe. She felt stripped, symbolically cleansed right down to her soul, and deeply moved by an act that seemed somehow more intimate than their lovemaking. A new emotion—fear?—joined in with her already tangled feelings, pushing her to the edge of yet another unfamiliar response—Jewel Flannery was perilously close to tears. Choking back an enormous sob, she drew her knees up to her chest and rolled away from him.

"Oops," he said, unaware that she'd withdrawn her mind as well as her body. "Did I touch a ticklish spot?"

"Ah, no," she hedged, covering herself with the bedspread. "I was taking a chill."

"That's enough of this," he said, tossing the washcloth into the basin. Then he turned back to her and saw it. Her eyes were guarded, her expression wary. She looked like a frightened bird trapped by a wildcat.

"Oh, Jewel," he said with a sigh. "What is it? What happened to that beautiful, artless woman I just made love to?"

"Don't, please. I can't talk right now."

He stared at her for a long moment, then sighed. "If that's the way it has to be, all right." Moving to the edge of the bed, Brent retrieved his trousers and stepped into them, continuing as he tugged them up over his hips and buttoned them. "Every time I start to get close to you—begin to know you as a woman, not as some character you're portraying—you pull away from me and hide. Why can't you trust me?"

Jewel chewed on her bottom lip, seeking an answer for herself as well as for him. Her gaze followed Brent as he picked up his shirt and slipped it on, buttoning it as he circled the bed and crossed over to the side where she sat huddled against his pillows.

"Well?" he said again, easing down beside her. "Why can't I earn your trust?"

Although she knew the answer to that lay deep inside her, so deep that even she couldn't reach it, Jewel gave him the only reply she could. "Everything—not just our lovemaking—is happening too fast. Besides," she added, hoping it didn't sound too feeble, "I don't know enough about you to trust you. You have a little explaining to do yourself, you know."

Frowning, he said, "Like what?"

"Like the first time we met. I was on a special assignment. Why were *you* hiding in Scotty's room? I somehow doubt you had an invitation."

"That's a perfectly legitimate question," he said with a grin. "I broke in, too, but I had a very good reason to do so. Scotty had bragged to a couple of my friends that his newest partner was a high-class crook named Harry Benton."

*"Harry Benton?"* Jewel sat straight up, unconcerned about her nudity as the cover fell away from her body. "What kind of business did you have with him? How long have you known him?"

Alarmed by what he saw in her eyes, Brent held up his hands. "Hold on a minute. I didn't say I know Harry Benton. In fact, I've never met the man. He stole some things from my family—my mother's family jewels, to be precise."

*"He swindled your mother, too?"* she blurted out.

"Yeah," he said. "I guess you could say that. What do you mean by 'too'? Have you—"

Jewel cut him off. "Harry has a weakness for wealthy women and their jewelry. How long ago did he make off with your family ah . . . treasures?"

Brent shrugged, "A year or so ago."

"Umm, too bad," she said with a shake of her head. "He's probably unloaded them by now. I doubt you'll ever see them again. When I finally trap him, I'll keep a lookout for them if you like."

Brent's eyebrows slammed together. "When you trap him? Are you trying to track him down, too?"

Here was her opportunity to do something for Brent, to give instead of take. Sliding her hand across his, Jewel said,

"I've been trying to corner that man for years. He's the reason I had to get, and keep, this job. When I trip him up, I'll see that you get your pound of flesh."

Brent popped off the bed. "You mean to say he's on board this ship?"

Jewel raised a skeptical brow. "Are you trying to tell me you didn't know?"

"Hell, no, I didn't know! Where is he?" Brent demanded as he paced back and forth at the foot at the bed. "I'll have him tied him to the paddle wheel of his ship! He'll be separating the mud from the Mississippi until he tells me where those jewels are!"

"Before I can help you get your family possessions back, I have to catch Harry Benton at his own game."

"Then I intend to help." Brent stopped pacing and gripped the brass bed frame. "I know that passenger list upside down—Harry Benton is not on it. What name is he using?"

Jewel shook her head. "Sorry, but I can't tell you that."

Brent's features darkened. "I have a big stake in his capture. Surely you can trust me enough by now to give me that much information."

But Jewel was adamant. No one and nothing would come between her and Harry's darkest moment. Not even Brent Connors. "Stay out of it. You'll only jeopardize my chances of apprehending him."

"That's right," he snapped back, anger running his tongue. "I forgot—you're a professional. A coldhearted professional. And what am I? Answer me that, little lady. Just what part will I play in all this?"

"That's not fair!" she said, snatching the sheet off the bed and covering herself. "I've got a job to do. I'm just trying to do it to the best of my ability."

"Regardless of who you hurt in the process?"

Jewel glanced up at him, and her heart constricted. "I don't want to hurt you, Brent. I never asked you to care about me."

"No, you sure as hell didn't," he agreed, deep in thought. "But you have to admit you did lead me on a little. What about the pool game? Did you wager your body in the name of professionalism or—"

"I don't have to answer a question like that!"

"Then answer me this: Today, here in this bedroom—what did that have to do with your job?"

"Nothing, Brent!" Cornered, unable and unwilling to offer any more of herself, she blurted out, "I have . . . needs, like everyone else. Please don't think of what happened between us as anything more than that."

"Needs," he said softly, before raising his voice and shouting, *"Needs?* Is that what I am to you—just someone to see to your personal *needs?"*

"Stop it!" she shouted back, her hands cupping her ears. "You're not being fair. I refuse to discuss this any further until you calm down and think it through."

Brent was uncertain what controlled him now—anger, hurt, or hopelessness—as his rage reached a new plateau. He clenched his teeth and quietly said, "I have to agree with you. There is nothing to be gained by continuing this conversation. Will that be all, *little lady*? Is there anything else I can do for you? Any little need I can fulfill before I leave? A little room service, perhaps?"

Her breath was a painful ache in her throat as Jewel's fists curled around the sheet. "Yes, there is. If you care about me at all, lay off Harry Benton. He's mine."

Something in her tone—not the anger, but a desperation of some kind—gave him pause. In spite of it, Brent slowly shook his head. "Sorry, little lady. You're asking too much."

"Please," she begged, all anger gone from her tone. "I'm serious. Leave him to me."

Brent stood staring at her for a long moment, longing to go to her, to hold her in his arms, to feel her softness against his chest. She looked oddly vulnerable, so truthful and childlike. Then he reminded himself what a great actress she

was. Steeling his heart, he said, "Benton owes me and my
family. I can't let up on him until I get back what he stole
from us. If you won't tell me who he is, I'll just have to find
out for myself."

"Oh, please," she cried. "I promise I'll get your belongings back after I've dealt with him."

Brent cocked his head and took a toothpick from his
pocket. There was something more here than her job, some
sense of desperation he couldn't fathom. Jabbing the toothpick in the air he said, "Why is capturing Harry so damned
important to you? Has he got something on you?"

"Don't be absurd!" she snapped.

"Then stop being such a hypocrite! I thought you were
going to start being honest with me!"

"I am. I have been. I . . ." She stumbled around, trying
to find a way to remain truthful and keep her secret at the
same time.

"Or perhaps you are honest only when you choose to
be," he suggested as he broke the toothpick and tossed it on
the carpet. "Take your time getting dressed, little lady. I'll
give you some privacy now. Good day."

As he turned to leave, panic gripped her, and Jewel
blurted out the words she'd never breathed to another living
soul. "I have to get him myself because . . . because
Harry Benton is my . . . my father."

Brent had just plucked his hat off the dresser when the
final words reached his ears. He spun around, positioning
the derby on his head. "*What* did you say?"

Unable to repeat the loathsome words, horrified that
she'd said them at all, she lowered her gaze and hung her
head.

"I see," he grumbled. "So that's how it's going to be."
He turned, opened the door, then tossed over his shoulder,
"If that's how you want it, that's how you shall have it.
Maybe things between us are going a little too fast for me,
too." He crossed the threshold and slammed the bedroom
door behind him.

"But," she sputtered as she heard the doors to the suite open and close, "but Harry Benton really *is* my father."

This time the words were met with silence. Cold, hard silence. For the first time since she could remember, tears sprang into her eyes, then spilled down over her freckled cheeks. They rolled slowly at first, stinging her flesh like great drops of acid. Then they seemed to join forces, surprising her with the strength of their numbers, terrifying her with the depth of anguish behind them.

Tears she'd been saving for too many years to count raged out of her, soaking the muslin sheet, washing her body anew. Jewel Flannery Benton cried until she could cry no more.

# 12

Brent leaned over the ship's railing just outside the saloon deck and stared down at the Mississippi. Deep in thought, seeking a way to rid himself of this rage, he glared at the water, wishing it could dilute his anger.

He was still there thirty minutes later, still furious enough to turn the *Dawn*'s enormous paddle wheels by hand if he had to, but now he understood. Now he was able to direct his anger where it really belonged. At himself.

"Hell," he muttered under his breath. "I got exactly what I asked for." Here was a woman tough enough to jerk the lasso right out of his hands, Brent thought. Was it her fault if that strength also made it possible for her to turn the rope into a noose?

The river flowed on by, dispassionate and undaunted by his sudden fit of laughter as he realized he had indeed given her enough rope with which to hang him. Had he pushed her too far this time, injured her pride, and stepped on her professional toes? Gotten *too* personal? Tough as she was, Jewel Flannery was also a very frightened young woman. Skittish as a young colt caught in its first thunderstorm. What was she so afraid of? How would he ever earn the trust of the green-eyed hellcat who'd managed to steal his heart and bankrupt his mind? His blood still boiling, as much with thoughts of her as with the remnants of a quiet fury, Brent made his way to the bar and slid onto a stool.

"Can I get you something, Mr. Connors?" Reba asked as

she approached. Brent turned his melancholy gaze her way, and she gasped, stepping away from him. "Lord, Mr. Connors, are you all right? You got some problems with the *Dawn*?"

"No," he muttered. "Things are just fine. Business is good. So good, in fact, I feel like celebrating."

"Y-yes, sir. What can I get y'all? Some bourbon?"

"That'd be just fine. Bring the bottle."

"Yes, sir," she said, her worried glance flitting from here to there, landing on anything and everything but him. "Right away, sir."

"Thanks," he managed with half a smile before turning his attention to the gathering crowd. The *Dawn* was filling rapidly. Brent took his watch from the pocket of his vest and checked the time. The ship would shove off soon. The poker and billiard tables would be surrounded by moneyed guests, who would expect his presence and good-natured encouragement. He would have to stroll among the passengers, praising their wagers, laughing at their jokes, and generally pretending to have a good time. He would have to do this even though his thoughts would be with a woman named Jewel Flannery. Thoughts that were turning more serious— and permanent—every time he saw her.

"Here you go, sir," Reba said, cautiously sliding the bottle toward him. "Mind if I join you? Maybe a little company would put you in better spirits."

"Oh, I'm not really in bad spirits, just . . . a little pensive, I guess." Brent poured himself a glassful of bourbon and quickly downed it before he glanced at his concerned barmaid. Then inspiration lit his eyes. Reba was tough in her own way, not easily fooled or pushed around by anyone. In some ways she was a lot like Jewel. He leaned forward and said, "Mind if I ask you a question?"

"'Course not."

"If you were a single gal, and of course you are, what would you think my intentions were if I asked you to come on out and visit the family plantation when the *Dawn* pulls into port at Greenville?''

''You mean if you asked me to spend the night at Sumner Hall and meet your folks?''

''Yes, I guess that's what I mean.''

''Oh, Mr. Connors,'' Reba said with a definite twitter in her voice. ''Why, I'd think you were sweet on me, I suppose. I'd be real flattered.''

Brent stared down at the polished bar, then shrugged. ''But would you feel that I was pushing you? Would you feel cornered? Would you think I was trying to get some kind of obligation from you?''

''Well . . . I don't know.'' She poured herself a shot, then refilled Brent's glass. ''It's kinda hard to say when you're just speculating. Just what is it you're trying to do here, Brent? Ask me to your home or what?''

''Oh, good God, Reba, I didn't mean to confuse you. I— No. I was just wondering what you'd *think* about a man who'd do that. Forget I mentioned it.'' Eager to get past the suddenly awkward moment, he raised his glass and tapped the rim of hers before taking another pull on the numbing liquid.

Still confused, clinging to a ray of hope, Reba said, ''I want you to know that I'm here for you anytime you want. I'll always be here for you—just like you were there for me in Natchez.''

Brent looked up into her ice blue eyes. ''Thanks, but you don't owe me a thing. You'd have left the Palace on your own, even if I hadn't offered you a job. Enough talk about old times. How are people treating you aboard ship now that they're used to you?''

She raised her eyebrows, grateful for his understanding, and smiled. ''They're treating me pretty good—almost like I'm as human as they are. One in particular, Harrison Poindexter, is sniffing my trail like an old coon dog on his last hunt.''

"That a fact?" he asked, amused. "And just how fast are you running, sweetheart?"

Although she thought she'd lost the ability long ago, Reba blushed and looked away, shrugging, "I don't know—a little slower than I can, a little faster than I want to."

Brent took another swallow of liquid fire, then suggested, "Slow down, have yourself a good time. Hell, we don't get that many opportunities for happiness. Might as well take them when they're offered."

"Ah . . . maybe I will," she said, taking a sip of her own drink.

Cognizant of the suspicious gleam in Reba's eyes, Brent changed the subject. "What about the rest of the passengers? Are they still giving you trouble?"

"Nah, they're even starting to tip a little better. That might be 'cause I hold my hand out after I give em their drinks," she added with a chuckle.

His voice still a little stiff and unnatural, Brent laughed along with her before he said, "That may be the reason, but I think it's more likely that they just appreciate an honest woman. You're a rare breed, Reba. To you and all like you." He saluted her with the glass, then downed the remaining bourbon.

"So that's it," she said catching him off guard. "You were asking me how you ought to behave 'cause you're sweet on some woman, right?"

Brent shuddered as the alcohol raced throughout his system. Then he narrowed one eye at the bartender. "You are an astute judge of men, Reba dahlin', but I strongly suggest that you drop this line of questioning."

"Uh-huh," she murmured with a knowing nod. "It's not that little Gypsy, is it?"

"Our friendship will not guarantee your safety if you persist in pursuing this," he warned as he poured yet another glass of bourbon. "You'd best let it be."

"But, Mr. Connors," Reba persisted, "Why her? She's

nothing but trash—not even close to being good enough for a man like you."

Brent finished the drink and slammed his glass down on the counter. "I'm going to forget you said that, because I realize you don't know the woman, but that's all I want to hear from you, understand?"

Alarmed by the depth of his emotions, surprised at his apparent level of involvement with the fortune-teller, Reba took a backward step. "Lord, Mr. Connors, I didn't realize— I just thought you and she, you know, were just having a little fun and games! It never crossed—"

"Let it be," he insisted in a deceptively quiet tone as he reached for the bottle once again. "Not one more word about it." Brent poured another glass of bourbon, satisfied the conversation was at an end, but before he could bring it to his lips, a familiar voice called to him from behind.

"Mr. Connors? Oh, good, it is you," Harry Benton said as he rushed up to the bar. "I've been looking everywhere for you. I wanted to make sure I caught you before the *Dawn* left port."

Brent swiveled around on the stool. "I hope you haven't forgotten something ashore, Mr. Poindexter. We'll be leaving in a few moments."

"No, it's a little more serious than that." Harry looked past Brent's shoulders, trying to assure himself of their privacy. Reba read the message in his expression and moved on down the bar. "We've got a bit of a problem," he finally said, satisfied they would be unheard.

"We do?"

"Well, actually, *you* do. There's a thief aboard this ship. I assume you are the man to whom I should report any criminal activity."

*Harry Benton*, Brent thought, excited. Poindexter has stumbled over Harry Benton! "You most certainly have come to the right man. What's he done and where might I find him?"

"It's a *she*," he whispered, leaning in even closer. "I

caught her going through my things. I bound and gagged her so she wouldn't start screaming and disturb your other passengers. I left her tied to the bedpost in my room.''

"A woman?'' Brent said, strangling on the word, pretty sure he knew which woman Poindexter was talking about. "And you actually caught her in your cabin?''

"Incredible, isn't it? And, if you don't mind my adding, a little disgusting. However,'' Harry sniffed, "the deed has been done, and now I must ask you to dispose of her. It's that little fortune-teller. I should have known she wasn't quite right, but I did so want to believe in her.''

"So it is Jewel,'' Brent finally choked out, his thought processes slowed by the bourbon. "You've got Jewel tied up in your room?''

"I most certainly do. I caught her not ten minutes past.'' Harry squinted his eyes and studied Brent Connors, suddenly wondering if he shouldn't have meted out the girl's punishment himself. "I have noticed you've taken more than a passing interest in the Gypsy. Will you have a problem bringing her to task for her indiscretion?''

"No, of course not,'' Brent said absently as he hopped off the bar stool. "I'm just wondering why she'd go through your room. What on earth could she have been thinking of?''

"I believe she thought to rob me,'' Harry said impatiently. "Now will you see to her, or do I have to—''

"I'll take care of the matter immediately,'' Brent said, shaking his head to clear it. "May I have your key, please?''

Harry deposited the brass key in his host's hand. "It's the California Room. And I do expect you to return with a full report on this girl—what her punishment will be, where you intend to leave her, all of it.''

"Certainly, Mr. Poindexter,'' Brent said, suddenly wondering what the man's reaction would have been if he'd said "Mr. Benton.'' "You wait right here. This shouldn't take too long.'' Brent turned to leave, then called out to Reba. "Mr. Poindexter's drinks will be on the house today.''

"Why, thank you," Harry said, settling in at the bar. "I'll be right here, in that case."

"Good," Brent said, tipping his hat. "I want to know exactly where I can find you." Then he took off for the passenger deck.

There could be only one answer, Brent thought to himself as he hurried to the stateroom: Harrison Poindexter was, in fact, Harry Benton. Why else would Jewel have put herself in such a position? Why would she riffle through a passenger's belongings? What possible purpose other than the pursuit of Harry Benton?

Brent was still asking himself those questions as he unlocked and opened the door and stepped into the stateroom. But when he saw Jewel struggling against the silk ties that bound her to a solid walnut bedpost, the questions and their answers suddenly seemed insignificant.

"Good God Almighty," he said thickly.

She turned. Her eyes widened as he approached, but the cravat Harry had used as a gag kept her from saying anything but "Mumphhh. Greeaz?"

Brent reached for her, distress hoarsening his usually melodic voice. "What in hell were you thinking of? You could have gotten yourself killed!"

"Mufferenn—ake oaf!"

His features tense, concern carving deep grooves in his brow, Brent ignored the gag and slid his hands around behind her. After releasing the scarf from the bedpost, he reached down to untie her wrists. When she began to turn to accommodate him, Brent hesitated, then stopped her movement. "No. Wait a minute. We need to get a couple of things straight before I do something stupid like turn you loose."

"Gwat?" Jewel narrowed her eyes in warning. "Brmph."

"Sorry, little lady, but I've got some things to say, and I don't think you'll let me say them unless you remain my . . . captive audience."

Jewel rolled her eyes and groaned.

"I knew you'd agree with me," he said taking her into his arms. "I want you to know that I've finally realized how difficult I've made your life and, to some extent, your job."

Again she rolled her eyes, but this time she added a weary nod.

He grinned sheepishly. "I'll take that to mean you're usually a much better detective than you've been since you met me?"

Again a moan accompanied by vigorous nodding.

"Well, I'm here to tell you how really sorry I am and to inform you that things are going to change. I've decided that from now on—as long as you're on the Harry Benton case, anyway—I'm your partner. We'll work together toward the capture of Har—"

"Moffed *drmmfd*!" she said against the gag as she stomped his boot with the heel of her shoe. "Drwell?"

"Hey!" he complained, rubbing his injured foot against his pant leg. "Is that anyway to treat your new partner?"

"*Brmphhh*," she warned, one eye narrowed to a slit.

"Apology accepted, little lady. Now for the details of our new alliance. First I think we ought to set some rules. I could use your help with them. Can you keep a civil tongue if I remove the gag?"

Jewel nodded vigorously.

"Do you promise to listen to me? I can put the gag back on just as fast as I take it off, you know," he added, pointing to her bound wrists.

Once more she rolled her eyes and took a deep breath, but again she nodded.

"Very well." Brent pulled her close and reached around behind her head. As soon as he loosened the knot, she spit out the wad of silk and began to lick her dry lips.

Brent resumed his speech. "Now then, as I was saying, this partnership requires—"

"You're not a detective, and I'll decide when I need a partner!"

Slowly untying the cravat, Brent softly warned, "You're not listening."

She bit her lip, then said, "Go on, then. I said I'd listen, but I don't recall promising to agree with you."

"That's better." Draping the silk cravat across her shoulders, he pulled her close. "Now then, since we both know now that Poindexter is actually Harry Benton—"

Jewel gasped and raised her head. "Brent, you—"

"That's the first rule," he interrupted. "No more lies. I know he's Benton, and you know he's Benton."

Realizing there was no point in arguing with him, Jewel let out her breath in a low moan, then said, "Keep your voice down. We are in his room, you know."

"All right," he whispered, feeling decidedly clandestine. "As I was saying, since we both know who he is, why don't you just arrest him and get it over with?"

Jewel grimaced and leaned back. "You've been drinking."

"And you think Brent Connors has ruined you as a detective," he said with a crooked grin.

"He has!" she shot back. "This little incident alone could have cost me my job. I lay the blame for my lack of caution directly at your feet! Harry never would have caught me if I hadn't been in such a big hurry to trap him and get the hell off this ship."

"Ohhh," he groaned, his expression injured. "Now, you don't mean that. Say you don't mean that."

Jewel looked into his mischievous eyes, noting they were slightly out of focus, and had to bite her lip to keep from laughing. "No," she conceded in a gentle whisper, "I don't suppose I do, but you have had a dreadful effect on my concentration."

"So sorry to be such a distraction," he said with a lazy smile. "But since I am, and since you got caught, why don't you just arrest him?"

"I can't do that unless I actually catch him in the act of

swindling someone or find stolen goods in his possession.
As far as I can tell, this room is clean.''

"Then let's give him someone to cheat.''

"I'm going to do better than that, now that I have no
choice. I'm going to find a mark for him, and then I'm going
to help him pull the job.'' Loath to tell him exactly how she
intended to do that, Jewel tried one more time to persuade
him to back out. "Please promise me you'll stay out of it
and let me do my job this time?''

"No way, little lady. We're partners, remember?'' He
chuckled at her chagrin, then asked, "So how are we going
to pull this off? Do you have a plan, or should I think of
one?''

"I have a plan all right—one that does not include you.''

"Let's hear it. I'll decide if I think it will work or not.''

Jewel stamped her foot and said, her voice rising higher
than good sense dictated, "You can start by untying me!''

"If you don't agree to this partnership and keep me
informed of your progress with Harry,'' he parried, "I'll
march right downstairs and demand that he return my
mother's jewelry.''

"Oh, Brent, you wouldn't.''

"I don't want to. Do you have a better idea?''

She blew out a heavy sigh, then glanced up at him. "All
right. Partners. All the way.''

His dimples deepening, he grinned at her and said, "So?
What's the plan?''

"I'm going to talk him into teaching me his trade. Then
I'll convince him that he should make me his partner.''

He frowned, still trying to clear the cobwebs from his
brain. "Why would he do that? He's pretty successful on his
own, isn't he?''

"Yes, but I think he'll take me on.''

Brent shook his head. "It'll never work. He thinks you're
a two-bit thief and wants you removed from this ship. He'll
never take you on.''

"Yes, he will,'' she insisted, deciding to trust him with

the plan, if not the truth. "I intend to convince him that I'm his . . . his daughter."

"Oh, good God," he sighed, then drew in a huge breath.

"It will work. I know it will. I've got a stack of information that would reach my waist on that man. I know what I'm talking about, and I know it won't be any trouble for me to convince him that he's my father. You're simply going to have to trust me on some of this—all right?"

Again he drew in his breath, but this time Brent couldn't think of a single objection. "All right, then, but if it doesn't work—"

"If it doesn't work, I'll be more than happy to hear your ideas."

"It's a deal."

"Good. Will you untie me now so we can shake on it?"

Brent grinned down at her, his mouth crooked, his eyes playful. "In a minute. First we have a few more rules to discuss—personal rules."

"Why don't we discuss the rules later?"

"Nope, we're going to settle everything now."

"All right," she agreed, slumping her shoulders, steeling her heart.

"First," Brent began, "I think it's important that we keep our new partnership strictly on a business level. There'll be no more of that," he said wagging a finger in her face. "No more looking at my mouth as if you owned it, and no more staring into my eyes. You make me nervous when you do that."

Jewel recognized the effects of too much bourbon, saw the emotions he sought to hide through drollery. "Oh, Brent," she said with a soft sigh, "I'm so sorry about what happened in your room. If I could, I'd take back—"

"Shush," he said. "We'll just have to think of this as a silly day of . . . of *needs*. It never really happened. Didn't mean a thing."

"Brent—"

"There'll be no more interrupting, either. No more

looking at me, no more interrupting me"—he stared down at her mouth, caught the gentle concern in her eyes, and grew reckless—"and no more of this." He crushed his mouth to hers, desperate for a final taste of her, unable to stay away.

When some measure of reason returned, Brent released her and took a couple of steps back. "Definitely no more of that," he said thickly, his expression dazed.

"Brent," she said softly, more than ready to claim her share of the responsibility for his mood, "untie me now. Please—before Harry comes back and—"

"Right," he said. "We don't want to upset ole Harry now, do we?"

As he fumbled with the silk scarf binding her wrists, Jewel cautioned, "Try to use some other name when referring to Harry. You might slip up and call him by his real name otherwise. That would ruin everything."

"Yes, ma'am," he said, saluting her after he finished untying the knot.

When her hands were free, Jewel rubbed her wrists and glanced up at Brent. "About some of the things I said earlier. The—"

"Nope," he said holding his hand up. "No more of that nonsense, either." And then, because he couldn't stand her pity and couldn't trust himself to stay in the room with her any longer, he decided to let her think he was tipsier than he was. Brent staggered backwards, then said, "I believe I'd best get some air. Why don't you go on about your business with what's-his-name? I'll check in with you later and see how your daughter act went over. All right with you, sarge?"

"Are *you* all right?" she asked as she joined him at the door. "You're looking a little"—she grinned in spite of her promises—"wobbly."

Catching the innuendo, fighting the urge to take her in his arms, Brent led her outside the stateroom, then locked the door. "I'm just fine, little lady. Go on. Do your job, and for Christ's sake, see if you can't do it right this time."

"Thanks, partner. I'll give it my best." Then she turned and hurried on down to the saloon deck. Blocking all thoughts of Brent Connors from her mind, Jewel concentrated on gaining Harry's trust as she walked into the smoke-filled room.

Understanding that her newest plan was as dangerous as it was daring, Jewel took a deep breath and stepped up to the bar. "Mr. Poindexter, sir?" she said in a tiny voice from behind him.

Harry spun around, wide-eyed, then frowned. "You! Why are you running around free? Where is Mr. Connors?"

"He's still up above, sir. He said I could come down here and apologize."

"Apologize? My dear girl, that will hardly make restitution for your crimes. I thought I made that clear to Mr. Connors."

Jewel shrugged, blinking her eyes, feigning an innocent demeanor. "Yes, I know all that, but after I told him about . . . about myself, he thought it would be best for me to talk with you. Then if you still want to prosecute me, you'll be within your rights."

Harry sniffed and raised his chin. "I don't know what you could possibly tell me about yourself that I would find of any interest."

"I think there might be one little thing. Do you suppose we could step outside and talk privately?"

"Hah! Do you think can get me alone and try to rob me before you jump ship? Think again, you little scamp . . . but I do admire your audacity."

Jewel shrugged. "Then I guess we'll just have to discuss it here in front of the other passengers."

Growing impatient, Harry snapped, "If you really must speak to me, be my guest, but I can't imagine why you wish to waste my time."

Taking another long, deep breath, she began. "Do you

happen to remember a young woman you met around twenty-seven years ago by the name of Martha Flannery?''

Harry wrinkled his nose and brushed at her as if she were an annoying mosquito. ''That is a very long time ago, my dear, but in any case, the name does not sound familiar to me.''

Pushing her feelings and her outrage to a distant corner of her mind, Jewel hardened her heart and went for the kill. ''Perhaps the name of my grandfather's bank, the Chicago National, and that of the Lillie safe you robbed are a bit more familiar.''

His features alive with apprehension and alarm, he cocked one eyebrow and said, ''I am no longer amused by you or your impudence. I demand that you—''

''Forgive me for interrupting and for dredging up any, ah, memories that you prefer not to recall, but I'm trying to make a point here.''

''That being . . . ?'' he inquired breezily, his expression even haughtier and more aloof.

''Martha Flannery was my mother.''

Harry stared at her for a long moment, then said, ''How terribly unfortunate for her.''

Jewel gritted her teeth, but her eyes shone with triumph as she issued a hoarse laugh, then said, ''In many ways, I suppose having me was unfortunate for her—but I could turn out to be a real asset to you . . . Daddy.''

# 13

Harry grabbed his throat, choking on his breath, the drink, his heart. "Why, that's . . . that's *ludicrous*!"

Jewel shrugged calmly. Feeling in control, despite the fact that she was part of an actual performance of the drama she'd scripted so often in her imagination, she continued. "Knowing that you are my father has not been the highlight of my life, either, but it happens to be the truth."

Harry's mind instantly produced an image of his days—and nights—with Martha Flannery. Unable to hide a sudden rosy blush, he stole a sideways glance at the girl, then violently shook his head. "No! No, I tell you. I simply could not be— There must be some mistake." He raised his chin, but was unable to bring his nose to its usually lofty position.

Jewel leaned in close and said, "Like it or not, I am the product of a liaison between my mother and one Harry Benton. Either you will accept that fact or I shall hop up on this bar and see if anyone else does."

"No!" Harry cast an anxious glance around the room, then slid off the stool. "I don't know where you heard that name or why you've decided to attach it to me, but you are quite out of line. Perhaps this conversation would benefit from some fresh air after all. I suggest we reconvene at the railing. Shall we?"

Now it was Jewel's turn to balk. "I may not be much good at sneaking into rooms, but that doesn't make me stupid. If I go out to that railing now after all I've just told you, you'll try to throw me overboard.''

His gaze still bobbing from passenger to passenger, grateful to see none of those distinguished heads had been turned yet, Harry whispered, ''Give me a little credit, my dear. Do I look like the violent type? Does this body look capable of such a deed?''

''Looks can be deceiving, Father dear.''

Harry swallowed hard, studying her features as she spoke. He stared at the cool green of her eyes, the familiar freckled cheeks, the upturned nose, and gasped. ''I'd say that in your case, my dear, looks are very . . . revealing.''

Certain now that he was ninety percent convinced her claim was authentic, Jewel added the final validation. ''Excuse my poor grammar, sir, but you ain't seen nothin' yet.'' She tore off her lace gloves and tossed them on the bar.

''How many fingers can you count?'' she said in a little girl voice as she held her hands in front of his face.

''Yipes!'' Harry gasped as her stunted pinkies wriggled like two little grubworms. ''It's the Benton binkies!''

Jewel's hands fell to her sides, and her eyebrows shot up. ''The *what*? My, oh, my, did I have the right name for you after all, dear Father?''

But Harry was in shock, unable to say more at the moment. He stared down at her hands, his eyes glassy, and shook his head. ''Bloody hell!''

Now it was Jewel who glanced around the room, Jewel who noticed that others were beginning to take an interest in the little reunion. She slid one hand between Harry's ribs and elbow and steered him toward the doorway. ''I think now would be a good safe time to get some air. You're looking a little sickly.''

Dazed, Harry allowed her to lead him away, but before they could pass through the doorway, Reba intercepted them.

"Harry? Are you all right?" she asked, shooting suspicious glances Jewel's way.

"Oh, I, ah . . . just need some air," he managed.

Elbowing Jewel to one side, Reba glanced into Harry's glassy eyes and said, "The *Dawn*'s pulling away from the dock now, so I can't serve drinks for a few minutes. I wouldn't mind taking a little stroll around the promenade with you."

Himself again, or as close to himself as he would ever be in the future, Harry regained some control over his situation. Gently dislodging Reba's fingers, he said, "Thank you kindly for the offer, but I need a few moments of privacy with"—he glanced at Jewel, no longer certain how to refer to her, and finally shrugged—"this young lady. Do be a dear and understand. Perhaps we can take that stroll later?"

Jealousy flashed in Reba's eyes. She looked from Jewel to Harry, then jerked her chin up a notch. "Perhaps," she said brusquely. "And perhaps not." Then, her hips rolling like a maverick rum barrel amidships, she squared her shoulders and sashayed back toward the bar.

"Now, that's one hell of a woman," Harry commented, blissfully able to forget Jewel and the revelation she represented for a small moment.

Uninterested in his love life, in anything about him unless it had to do with his capture, Jewel snapped her fingers in front of his face. "Shall we?" she said, inclining her head toward the railing.

"Yes, yes, of course," he answered slowly, back to reality.

As they walked, the *Delta Dawn* began to pull away from the dock, lurching as she struggled sideways against the current. Her legs nearly swept from beneath her, Jewel stumbled and almost fell, but she rejected Harry's attempt to help her.

Once the pair made it to the railing, they clung to it and turned to face each other, measuring, studying, waiting to see who would be first to comment.

Unable to gaze into the girl's eyes any longer, Harry looked away and stared out at the churning waters. His voice heavy with resignation and tinged with guilt, he finally said, "The day you read my tea leaves . . . you were trying to tell me then, weren't you?"

"Yes," she said quietly, working to disregard her feelings about this moment, trying only to play a role.

"I must have sounded like a barbaric dolt to you. I was terribly cruel, and for that I apologize."

Jewel shrugged it—*him*—off. "You didn't know your daughter was sitting across from you then. I imagine I've grown some since you last thought about me."

"*Last* thought of you, my dear?" Harry said. "Today is the first I've ever heard of you, much less imagined that you might exist."

Trying to keep the cold hatred from her eyes, the curl off her upper lip, Jewel glanced across the water to the heavily wooded shore as the steamship made its way down the traffic lane toward Mississippi. How far would she have to go with this loving-daughter masquerade? she wondered, agitated. How much could she manage? Again struggling to keep her voice calm and nonjudgmental, she said, "I heard that you knew all about me, that you couldn't wait to get your hands on my grandfather's money and leave town the minute you found out I was on the way."

"Well, then, you heard wrong," Harry insisted. "I don't know what your mother told you, but until a few moments ago I was blissfully unaware that I was anyone's father. Sorry if that sounds callous to you, my dear, but it is the truth. I never wanted or intended to have children. I was always . . . careful, I thought, to preclude such a possibility."

"Oh, please," Jewel groaned. "Spare me the sordid details and the lies."

"Sorry, my dear, I don't mean to be indelicate, but I want you to understand that I never *meant* to leave your mother in such a . . . state."

"But the fact is that you did, and you left her to face the wrath and disillusionment of her very unforgiving father."

"Again, I must object. Martha never even hinted about her predicament to me. I can't imagine why she told you that she did."

Even though Jewel knew him to be a liar and a thief, something in Harry's eyes gave her pause and kept her next remarks on the tip of her tongue. Was it possible he hadn't known about her all these years? Was he now granting her the rare favor of telling her the truth? Jewel tried to think back, to recall a segment from the childhood she'd buried in the recesses of her mind, but the memory wouldn't come forward. Who had told her about Harry? Who had drawn him as a bastard—her mother or her grandfather? Or both?

"I—I can't remember exactly what mother said," Jewel finally stammered, her confidence shaken. "I just know that I am the bastard daughter of a bastard named Harry Benton, and I was treated as such."

"It might be best if you keep my real name to yourself for the time being, my dear," he suggested. Then, feeling a tenderness that surprised even him, he said softly, "As for your childhood, I do remember Lemuel Flannery quite well, and I am painfully aware of his capacity for cruelty. He was none too considerate of your poor mother even in the best of times. I can only imagine how beastly he must have been toward you."

Jewel's throat swelled painfully as acid tears formed behind her eyelids. Abruptly turning her head, she squeezed her eyes shut and swallowed hard. She had never dreamed that Harry might actually sympathize with her and understand what had driven her to this hatred and to her unrelenting need for revenge. Would he also guess her true purpose and ruin her plans before she could put them into action? She choked back a sudden sob, then stiffened as she felt his hand brush her shoulder.

"I wish I could find a way to wipe the indignities you

must have suffered during your childhood, my dear. I realize it's too little too late, but I wish I could do something.''

In spite of her struggles against them, the sobs increased and Jewel's shoulders began to tremble. Stop it, Jewel railed silently. Stop pretending that you care! I know you don't! You could never understand the torment of living with a grandfather who viewed you as vermin. You can't imagine begging for attention from an apathetic grandmother who didn't dare disagree with him, nor could you bear the pain of an adoring mother who could show her love for you only when no one else was around.

The girl's anguish, or whatever she was feeling, alarmed and touched Harry. For the first time in his life, he found himself unable to fathom a woman's mood. The only thing he knew for sure was that this woman, his daughter, was definitely in need of comfort. But how should he proceed? What could he do? What would a father do?

Feeling awkward and uncharacteristically humble, Harry reached for her. His hands hovered above her trembling shoulders for several indecisive moments before he finally gripped her and turned her around. Pulling her into his arms, he said soothingly, ''There, now, my dear. We shall get this straightened out. You will be all right, and I shall find a way to . . . to do right by you.''

Her eyes still squeezed shut, the lashes fringed with tears in spite of her efforts to control them, Jewel allowed him to hold her. It would be all right, she told herself. It might even serve her purposes by eliciting from him the sympathy and support she would need as she pursued her goals. All she needed to do, Jewel vowed as another sob nearly tore her throat apart, was find a way to ignore the surprising strength in his wiry arms, and disregard his clumsy attempts at comfort as his kind hands patted her back. Then Jewel gave up her struggles, convincing herself that this, too, would add to Harry's sense of obligation. She released the floodgates and permitted the entire reservoir of tears to drench Harry's cashmere dinner jacket.

Alarmed and increasingly disconcerted, Harry sputtered, "M-my dear, I—I told you I would do all that I can to make it up to you. Please see if you can't find a way to collect yourself. My dear little . . . ah, it's Jewel, isn't it?"

His final words gave her the courage she needed to swallow the last of her tears. Harry Benton, her long-lost father, wasn't even sure of her name. He didn't deserve the time of day from her, much less an honest tear. She drew in a painful breath and straightened her shoulders. Then, without requesting permission or glancing up at him, Jewel plucked the monogrammed hanky from his pocket and wiped her nose.

"Sorry," she said quietly as she stepped away from him. "I don't usually indulge in such displays."

"It's certainly understandable. After all, you have known about me much longer than I've known about you. I would assume this moment has been on your mind for some time."

Finally ready to look him in the eye, she gave him a cool stare. "Around twenty years."

"Yes, well, you certainly have the advantage on me," he muttered, still uncertain as to how he should proceed. "How is your dear mother? Well, I hope."

Her voice as flat and cold as a river stone, Jewel closed her heart and cut off her emotions before she could say, "She's dead."

"Oh?" Harry gasped. "I'm so sorry to hear that. I do hope she wasn't taken from you at too impressionable an age."

"I was away at Vassar when she died."

"College?" Harry said, his eyes bright with surprise. "You've had the benefit of a college education?"

Jewel balled the hanky into her fist and shrugged. "Grandfather Flannery was happy to pay for my education—anything to get me out of the house and out of his sight."

Again Harry reached for her, but she flinched and backed

away. Taking her cue, he lowered his arms and said, "I'm sorry for his lack of consideration, but he did give you an excellent opportunity, even if his reasons were suspect. Why didn't you take advantage of it?"

Too mired in her own pain and tangled thoughts to grasp his meaning, she stared at him quizzically. "What are you talking about?"

"Your education, my dear. You should have extracted as much as possible from it. Then you wouldn't have to pretend to be something you're not." He gestured toward her Gypsy costume.

"Oh, this costume? I only pretended to be a fortune-teller so I could catch up with you."

"Catch me? I'm afraid, my dear, that I—I don't quite understand."

Sensing his panic, she stepped forward and forced herself to pat his hand. "I've been looking for you for a long time, remember? When I heard you were back in the States, I decided to go where you might go and be what you might be looking for." Again she shrugged. "It worked."

His laugh nervous, his equilibrium still out of whack, Harry raised one thin black eyebrow. "And now that you've found me, just what do you expect from me, my dear?"

"That's easy." She led him into the center of her web. "I want you to supply the rest of my education."

"Money?" he sniffed. "You want me to pay you off, is that it?"

"No, Father dear," she said. "I simply want you to finish my training. I want to learn the family business."

Harry's thin brows formed a single narrow ebony line. "I don't know what you're talking about."

"Yes, you do," she said, glancing around to make certain they were still alone. "I studied dramatics in college and I am quite good at acting when the need arises. I've also inherited the Benton cunning. The only thing I need to carry on the family name in an admirable fashion is for you to teach me the nuances of the business. That is the only thing I want from you."

"You're out of line, young lady," Harry snapped, not willing to give up his secret life so easily. "It seems I have no choice but to admit my paternity—you have far too strong a case for me to do otherwise—but I will not stand here and listen to any more of this 'family business' nonsense."

Jewel made another quick survey of their surroundings. Then she moved in closer to Harry and whispered, "I know your business almost as well as you do. I have made it my life's work, to the extent that I have become friendly with several representatives of the law." She paused, giving him time to absorb that disturbing piece of news, then went on. "I have inside information about many of your jobs, from my grandfather's bank to some of your more recent conquests. One Countess DeMorney comes to mind, as does—"

Harry gasped, and his gaze darted from side to side. "Who told you about her?" he demanded.

"That really doesn't matter," Jewel said, knowing she'd finally gotten his attention. "What does matter is this—for every neglected highfalutin lady you strip of her jewels, there's at least one dear old man just waiting to lavish gifts on a sweet young thing like me. Think of it, Daddy! Imagine what a great team we could make!"

Harry stuck a finger between his Adam's apple and the starched collar of his shirt and loosened the material. "My dear, this is . . . Well, it's simply preposterous. I could no more teach you the business than I could fly. It simply isn't a viable idea. Please forget about it."

"Never," she said. "I intend to pattern my life after yours—with or without your help. I also intend to make sure the men I *borrow* from are aware they have been fleeced by the daughter of the famous Handsome Harry Benton. As I see it," she said, issuing her ultimatum, "there's only one question to be answered here. Doesn't it matter to you how well I carry on your name?"

Harry smoothed his mustache nervously as he stared at Jewel, measuring her, weighing his chances of calling her bluff. "May I have some time to think this over?" he said at last. "You have given me a lot to ponder."

"How long?" she said, a suspicious brow cocked.

"Just time enough for a brandy and some deep thought. One hour."

Her auburn brow still cocked, she said, "Long enough to jump ship, perhaps? If you do, I'll hunt you down like a dog. You know that I can and will do that, don't you?"

Harry sighed and lifted his chin. "If you've made such a thorough study of my activities, you must know that I would never jump ship."

"Hmmm, maybe not," she mused. "But as far as I know, today is the first time anyone claiming to be your child has come forward. No telling what you'll do in response to that."

"The idea of fatherhood was once repugnant to me, but now that is a fact, I do not intend to turn my back on you. Now, if you please, may I have some time to digest these rather startling revelations?"

Jewel hesitated for a long moment, staring into his smoky green eyes, then took a deep breath. "All right. I suppose I can grant you that much, but I warn you—"

"I know," he said with a chuckle, "you'll hunt me down like a dog."

"Like the shrewdest of bloodhounds," she agreed.

Bending slightly at the waist, Harry said, "In one hour, then. Where shall I find you?"

"I'll wait for you in my cabin. It's with the other employees' staterooms on the main deck. Don't look for any fancy oil paintings on the door. Mine is plain old room number three."

Harry nodded. "Till then."

"Till then," she echoed, watching as he spun on his heel and disappeared into the saloon. Once he was out of sight, Jewel made her way along the railing toward the stern.

There she stood watch over the giant paddle wheels, listening as the steady flap, flap, flap of the wooden slats pounded along with her heartbeat, flinching as the steam vents hissed like a giant dragon. Were they chastising her for treating her father less than honorably? Or were they cheering her victory over the master of deceit?

Brent suddenly loomed up from behind, ''Are congratulations in order? Do you have a new father yet?''

Jewel spun around, clutching her breast. ''Couldn't you have found a less startling way to announce yourself?''

''Sorry. How'd things go? Do you have a new father?''

''I do.''

''No kidding.'' Hugely impressed, Brent propped his elbow on the railing and smiled at her. ''So are you Jewel Poindexter now, or do you get a whole new name?''

''I really don't know. We haven't gotten that far. Harry's still trying to get over the fact that he has a daughter. He's going to think about that for a while, then come to my cabin and let me know if he'll teach me his trade.''

Brent raised a skeptical brow. ''Do you think he'll actually show up, or will he use the time to get away?''

''He'll show up.''

Brent laughed and pushed away from the railing. ''There really is honor among thieves, is that it?''

Jewel scowled as she marched past him. ''I'm going to wait in my cabin. I have better things to do than listen to your drunken rambling.''

Brent gripped her elbow. ''I'm not drunk and I'm not rambling. We're partners, remember? I was just inquiring about your progress. No need to get your back up.''

Jewel inhaled the sultry air and finally acknowledged her inner turmoil. The meeting with Harry had been no less startling and distressing for her than for him. She looked up at Brent and smiled. ''Sorry. I told you I'd keep you appraised of the situation, and I will. I guess I didn't realize how upset I would get. It isn't every day I announce to some poor fellow that he has a grown child who's come to haunt him.''

Seeing an opening in her armor, some glimpse of the sensitive woman beneath, Brent cupped her face in his hands. ''I saw you talking to him. I realize you're one hell of an actress, but it didn't look to me like you were having much fun playing the doting daughter role.''

Tears burned in her eyes, returning twice as potent as before. In danger of revealing too much about herself, Jewel nestled against his chest. ''Please don't say anything else,'' she implored him. ''Just hold me, Brent. Please hold me.''

''I'd be delighted to,'' he said softly. ''You know I always try to oblige a lady.''

Brent wrapped her in his strong arms, rocking her gently in rhythm with the *Dawn*'s rolling motion, humming no particular tune against her hair as he massaged her exposed shoulders. He wondered if this was the time to broach the subject of a visit to Sumner Hall. Would she be open to such an invitation or would she get defensive? He could feel her melting beneath his touch, the tense muscles in her shoulders softening as she relaxed. I could hold Jewel Flannery in my arms like this for the rest of my life, he suddenly realized. Was that why it was so important for him to take her on down home? If she agreed to visit Sumner Hall with him, what would her reaction be when she arrived? Would she finally understand how much he'd come to care for her—to love her?

Brent's mother would know the minute they stepped into the grand foyer. Miriam Connors would see the love in her son's eyes. She would spot the crackle of fire and the flashes of lightning between him and Jewel the second she observed them in the same room. Would she make some comment about their obvious fascination with each other and scare his green-eyed lady off before he got a chance to tell Jewel how he felt?

She pulled away from him then and looked up into his eyes. Her expression was grateful, almost loving. Brent knew then that he would have to take the chance. "Better now?"

She nodded, still too choked up to speak.

"Listen, little lady," he began, that awkward schoolboy tone creeping into his voice. "The *Dawn* pulls into her home port of Greenville, Mississippi, day after tomorrow. That's also my home port. I was wondering if you might like to ride out with me to my family plantation, Sumner Hall, and meet the rest of the Connors clan."

"Meet your . . . family?" Jewel blinked, struggling to organize her jumbled thoughts. "Well, I don't know," she hedged, trying to examine all the ramifications of such an invitation.

Hoping to coax her into accepting, he said, "I think you and my mother would really appreciate each other. She—"

"Of course!" Jewel cut in, slapping her own forehead. "I get it! Your mother—the heirlooms! We take Harry to your plantation and confront him there! Where did my brain go?"

"I'm sure I wouldn't know, little lady." Brent shrugged. Her acceptance and the reasons for it weren't exactly what he'd had in mind, but she *had* agreed to come home with him. "The *Dawn* will only be docked overnight, but that ought to give us plenty of time to trip old Harry and still enjoy a little rest among the giant oaks."

"Right," she concurred, but she really wasn't listening. Her mind was busy plotting new endings to her script and exploring new avenues in which to corner her quarry.

Brent tilted her chin, hoping to regain some small measure of her attention. "Did you bring any clothing besides these Gypsy costumes, or do we—"

"I have a traveling suit. That will have to do," she said briskly as she began to walk away. "Excuse me, but I have to get back to my cabin. Harry will be along soon, and I want to be ready for him."

Brent's excitement at the thought of seeing Jewel meandering among the wisteria and grandeur of his childhood home was rapidly diminishing. He puckered his mouth and offered some sarcastic advice. "Don't forget to invite your dear old dad to Sumner Hall, now—hear? Be a real shame to go all the way out there for nothing."

"Oh, don't worry," she called over her shoulder as she made her way along the deck. "You've actually come up with a pretty decent plan. I'll see to it that Harry accepts!"

Not long after Jewel returned to her cabin, she heard the expected tapping on her door. Daddy had arrived. Was she ready for him this time? Ready to change his mind if he'd decided not to take her under his wing?

And what if he'd fallen for the bait and come prepared to give her her first lesson? How would she act? What would she call him? Again, knuckles rapped against the door.

"Be right there!" she called out in as confident a voice as she could muster. Then she straightened her shoulders and marched across the tiny room.

"Do come in," she said as she opened the door and allowed her father into her private quarters.

"Thank you," he replied, tipping his hat as he crossed the threshold. After waiting until she'd closed the door behind him, Harry strolled into the center of her cramped cabin and slowly spun around.

Jewel raised her eyebrows. "Would you like to sit down?"

Harry furrowed his brow as he continued to peruse the room. Then he wrinkled his nose and said, "No, I don't think so. Why don't we get right down to business?"

"All right. What have you decided?"

Harry turned to her, squinting one eye as he studied her bawdy appearance. Then he cleared his throat and said, "The first thing we'll have to do, my dear partner, is get you a new wardrobe."

# 14

*Greenville, Mississippi*

Jewel stole surreptitious glances at her companions as the trio bounced along in the carriage. Harry was engaged in animated conversation with Brent, running on and on about his exploits across Europe, carefully leaving out, of course, his various occupations and disguises during his extensive travels. The two men had become immediate allies after she'd introduced Harrison Poindexter as her father, and Brent had fallen into his role as her enormously touched suitor with great aplomb. Now the pair, each playing the part that would most benefit two distinctly separate causes, were beginning to make her sick.

Harry, she noticed, was still droning on. Shamelessly dropping names like a whore soliciting customers, he told of kings and queens, barons and lords, positively raved about the enormous castles and secluded lakefront homes he'd been privileged to visit on the Continent. Brent seemed utterly fascinated and thoroughly impressed. Jewel was ready to scream.

How had she, the author of this scheme, become a mere observer as the drama unfolded? When had she lost control? She stared at Harry's graying temples and frowned. What was going on in his head? she wondered. What did he really and ultimately intend to do with her, this daughter he insisted he'd been blissfully unaware of? The man had positively dogged her heels since they'd formed their new alliance. Every time she turned around, there was Harry Benton, the contrite, ubiquitous father of her nightmares. Was it part of his act? Or did Harry Benton actually hope to step into her life and try to control it?

He was certainly trying to do so now. Even the simple little detail of deciding how she would address him had to be done his way and with panache. He insisted that she call him, Faathah, not Father. So European, he'd said, so very distinguished.

So asinine, she grumbled to herself.

When he wasn't correcting her diction, he was showing her how to become a proper lady—a *lady,* for Christ's sake, as if she didn't know the difference between a teaspoon and a soup spoon! When he finally decided her table manners would do, he began teaching her how to walk! Jewel Flannery, a woman capable of bringing the Royal Guard to its knees with one shake of her hips, had to be taught how to walk—by Harry Benton, of all people! If it hadn't been so laughable, she would have lost her mind over the last two days. Instead, it was beginning to look as if Brent had.

Where had he been during all Harry's careful tutoring? Hiding around corners, laughing when he got the chance, grinning when silence was the order of the day. Every time she tried to ambush him and work out a plan for actually pitting Brent's mother against Harry, he would change the subject or excuse himself and run off to the pilothouse. It was almost as if he had other reasons for bringing the ''Poindexters'' out to his family home—reasons she hadn't yet figured out.

Her frown deeper, more introspective, Jewel fanned her overheated skin and went back to work on her major objective: what to do when they arrived at Sumner Hall. Just let Mrs. Connors and her former lover bump into each other? Orchestrate an accident that would shake the truth from one of the most wanted criminals in America? Could the culmination of four years' work really be that easy? Not likely, she thought as the two men burst into another chorus of raucous laughter. Not likely at all.

Her discomfort increasing, Jewel smoothed the skirt of her gray serge traveling suit and wiped at her brow.

"Is the weather getting a bit too warm for you, ma'am?" Brent inquired, taking notice of her plight.

"It's more than warm, suh. It's hotter than hell."

Harry groaned, then scolded her. "Now, that's exactly what I was talking about just this morning, daughter. You'll never pass yourself off as a lady if you don't stop using vulgarisms."

"Pass herself off?" Brent inquired lightly, baiting him.

"Yes, sir," Harry said quickly, ever cool even near the hottest of fires. "Now that I have found this lovely lass, I intend to protect and harbor her until she meets a gentleman worthy of our family name."

After pausing as Brent choked on a sudden convulsive cough, Harry leaned across the carriage and took Jewel's free hand in his. "To that end, I have made it my responsibility to train this sweet young girl as my hostess until the happy event of matrimony descends upon her."

From behind Harry's top hat, Jewel watched as Brent rolled his eyes and mouthed the words, "Oh, good God!" Muffling a chuckle, she let out a long sigh and resumed fanning herself.

"So sorry for the vulgar outburst, Faathah dear, but I simply cannot abide this heat much longer."

"Yes, it is growing warm," Brent agreed, his southern accent increasing as the distance to his home decreased. "They say there's only one place more devastatin' to the body's cooling system than the lower M'sippi in July."

"And that would be . . . ?" she asked, playing into his hands.

"The lower M'sippi in August."

"Oh, ha-ha," she tossed off. "In that case, I'll just have to make damn—oh, pardon me, Faathah—I'll just have to make dang sure I'm back up north in civilization before August, then, won't I?''

''Tsk-tsk.'' Harry folded his arms across his chest and shook his head. Speaking to Brent, but staring across the carriage at Jewel, he said, ''You can see, Mr. Connors, that I have an awesome job ahead of me. My daughter is a bit flighty and quite headstrong, but I believe that, in time and with a considerable effort on my part, she'll be a woman even a grand duke would be proud to call his wife. Don't you agree?''

''My opinion is of no consequence,'' Brent answered, the words slow and deliberate. ''But yes, I believe any man would be proud to call Miss Poindexter his wife.'' He added softly, his gaze centered on Jewel's mouth, ''I know I most certainly would.''

Her eyes trapped by his, her mind vacillating between accepting his statement as truth and laughing it off as yet another shot in their verbal war, Jewel hesitated for a long moment. Then she opted for sanity and viewed them as banter. ''Before you seek any more of Mr. Connors's advice, Faathah, I feel you should know that his initials are B. S. I believe you'll find there's a very good reason for that.''

Harry leaned back against the leather cushion and turned to Brent. ''You see what I'm up against, my good man? The girl's mind is positively saturated with vulgarisms. I shall have my hands full wringing the filth out of her, yes, indeed, I shall. Perhaps a large bar of lye soap would help.''

''*Faathah dear*,'' Jewel warned, tired of his paternal gestures, whether genuine or theatrical. ''I agree with something Mr. Connors said earlier—what he thinks is of no consequence. Let us speak of other things.''

''Yes,'' Brent agreed as the carriage rounded the final bend in the road. ''We ought to speak of Sumner Hall. There she lies, dead ahead.''

Then father and daughter gasped in unison at their first glimpse of Brent's plantation home. The carriage, drawn by a matched pair of Palominos, rolled lazily along a lane framed by gnarled live oak trees that stretched for nearly a quarter of a mile up to the mansion. The trees arched inward as they rose, then bowed, scattering filigree patterns of sun and shadow across the cropped grass bordering the road. The scene was pastoral, cooling, and offered welcome relief from the broiling midday sun.

"Oh, Brent," Jewel said with awe as she caught a glimpse of the mansion's four soaring columns. Appearing to soar upward from the fertile alluvial soil, they rose like huge alabaster candlesticks and stood like sentries before the impressive terra-cotta brick building. "Your home is absolutely gorgeous!"

"Thank you," he said, pride coating the syllables. "It is impressive to a first-time visitor, I suppose, but nowhere near so grand as it was before the Yankees stormed it during the War between the States."

Jewel's eyes widened. "Battles were fought around here?"

"Not exactly. You might say the siege of Vicksburg spilled on up this way a bit. The Yankees burned Greenville to the ground, then destroyed as many homes and plantations as got in their way. Sumner Hall was badly damaged, but Dad managed to save it. We've spent the last ten years trying to put the place back together again, but we still have a ways to go."

"Goodness gracious," Harry breathed as the carriage rolled to a halt and he got a closer look at the Grecian-style home. "Goodness me."

The Bentons seemed to be totally involved in indulging their senses, so Brent gave them a few moments of silence as he helped Jewel down from the carriage and escorted her toward the fan-shaped front steps. Harry quickly joined them, but just before the trio reached the immense beveled glass and walnut door, he halted in mid-stride.

"Goodness," he repeated, fingering one of the giant

columns. "I haven't seen fluted columns the likes of these since my last visit to Greece!"

"You have a good eye," Brent said as he rang the bell. "They are Corinthian, and as authentic as the other embellishments you'll find in our home."

Harry turned back to the columns, but before he could comment further, the door opened and a large black man greeted them.

"Mr. Connors, so good to have you home again."

"Afternoon, Maxwell." Brent gestured for Jewel and Harry to precede him. "This is Miss Poindexter and her father. They'll be stayin' with us until the *Dawn* resumes her journey."

"Yes, sir." The butler nodded, then led the guests into the foyer. "I'll prepare their rooms. The gentleman should be most comfortable in the teak room, and the lady . . . ?"

Brent's gaze slid to Jewel as she glided across the black and white checkerboard pattern of the marble floor, and he grinned. "I think the lady will enjoy the magnolia room. It should be a nice change for her to inhale the scent of something other than violets."

Jewel tore her attention away from the impressive entryway long enough to make a face at Brent. Then she looked at the walls, trying to decide if the lush depictions of the Mississippi countryside were painted murals or wallpaper.

Maxwell clicked his heels together. "Will there be anything else, sir?"

"Where might I find the family?"

"The ladies are having their midday nap, and your father is resting on the veranda outside the library. I am not sure where your brother has run off to."

"Thanks. That will be all."

Maxwell nodded, then strode toward the seemingly endless curved stairway.

"Brent?" Jewel tugged at his sleeve, her eyes wide with alarm. "Did I hear right? Did that man say something about your *father*?"

"He most certainly did, little lady. Come on. I can't wait for you to meet him."

"But—but—" she sputtered as he led her toward a pair of burled walnut doors. "Your *father*?" she said again in a strangled whisper, aware that Harry was only a few feet behind them. "How could you have brought *him*?" she gave a slight jerk of her head, hoping he understood how appalled she was at the idea of his mother's two men meeting in such a manner.

Brent gave her a look that clearly informed her he thought she'd lost her mind, then pushed the twelve-foot-high doors open and showed her inside the library. "I thought bringing *him* here was the point," he said under his breath as Harry joined them. Brent glanced through the glass doors at the back of the library and saw his father. The elder Connors sat at the edge of the veranda staring out at the ruins of his acreage. Turning back to his guests, Brent said, "Dad has had a little trouble getting over his war injuries—mental as well as physical. I'll just go let him know he has company."

"Of course," Harry said before Jewel could open her mouth. "Take your time."

"I appreciate your understanding." Brent smiled at Harry, then chucked Jewel under the chin before he started for the glass doors.

When Brent was out of earshot, Harry turned to his daughter. "Look around you, my dear," he said in a barely audible but definitely unscrupulous tone. "Perhaps this would be a good place to start your lessons."

And finish yours? she thought, wondering if Harry realized he was a guest in the home of a previous victim. She looked around the library and slowly shook her head. "I don't think so, Faathah. I prefer to learn our business among complete strangers, if you don't mind."

"Humph. Then it's as I thought," Harry sniffed, raising his chin.

"What's as you thought?"

"This Connors fellow has been trifling with your affections. Just what has he promised you, and exactly what does he expect in return?''

Jewel's mouth dropped open and she turned on him, hands on her hips. "Now just a damn minute, Daddy! I've managed without you, without any facsimile of a father, for my entire life. I do not need your misguided opinions or rules on the care and feeding of men at this stage, nor—"

"Now see here, young lady. I realize that you did not have the benefit of a father's counsel during your formative years, but that was not by my fault.''

"Oh, *please,*" she said with a grimace. "Don't insult my intelligence by suggesting that you'd have come back to my mother and me if you'd known.''

"I have no way of knowing what I would have done back then," Harry admitted. "I intend to make up for those years, however, and I simply will not allow you to speak to me in such an insolent manner. Nor,'' he added, his tone more authoritative, "will I allow you to be taken advantage of by some riverboat gambler with things other than your respectability on his mind. I hope I've made myself clear.''

"I can't *believe* this!" she sputtered. "I'm twenty-five years old, for God's sake! What makes you think you can waltz into my life and tell me what to do and whom to see?''

"I'm warning you, young lady! Age has nothing to do with the way you're behaving. It's all too apparent that your mother spoiled you into thinking you could always have your own way. Too bad she didn't give your backside a good thrashing more often. If you were a bit younger, I'd spank you myself!''

Jewel's mouth dropped open again, and she gasped. "How . . . dare you talk to me like that!''

Harry met her green-eyed gaze with one of his own. "You of all people should know better than to issue a challenge to a Benton. Until I'm able to discern an alternative method for bringing an adult child to heel, I'd appreciate it if you would find a way—''

"Excuse me," Brent cut in as he strolled back into the

library. "I hate to interrupt this touching exchange between you two, but my father is feeling a little weak this afternoon. I would so like for you both to meet him before he retires. Can I trust you together in the same room?"

Jewel's eyelashes fluttered of their own volition as she turned her back on Harry and faced Brent. "Please forgive Faathah's poor manners. He and I are . . . new at this father-daughter business. I suppose these little squabbles are bound to occur now and then."

"I'd be beholden to you both," Brent said with a curt nod in Harry's direction, "if you would please find a way to keep them for the future. Perhaps when we return to the ship you can resume your . . . discussion."

Chagrined, Harry nodded. "Of course, Mr. Connors, and I am indeed sorry if we have caused you any—"

"No apology is necessary. Shall we?" He made a sweeping gesture with his arm, then bent his elbow and offered it to Jewel.

Stifling the urge to stick out her tongue at the man she now called Faathah, Jewel consoled herself with a withering sideways glance, then slid her hand into the crook of Brent's arm. "I'd be charmed, sir."

As they made their way across the room, Harry lagged behind, blocking thoughts of his daughter and their lost years from his mind as he kept a lookout for the subtle and not so subtle indications of wealth, along with any obvious signs of spurious attempts to merely indicate great wealth. The floor-to-ceiling shelves were filled with beautifully bound books. The furnishings—desk, chairs, sofas, and occasional tables—were all from Louis XV, carved from walnut, and ornamented with gilded bronze. Authentic, Harry observed, or the best damned imitations he'd ever seen. But just as he was about to decree the Connors family as truly wealthy, he noticed the tattered and stained rug covering most of the hardwood floor. Glancing up as he passed through the doors leading to the veranda, he also realized that sheer beige curtains hung in stark simplicity where heavy draperies should have billowed.

Suddenly unsure about the wealth of Sumner Hall and its inhabitants, Harry circled around behind the chair Brent directed him to and awaited his introduction.

"Dad," Brent said to the wizened man in the cane wheelchair, "this is Jewel Poindexter and her father, Harrison. My father, Raiford Connors."

"A pleasure to meet you, sir," Jewel said as she extended her gloved hand.

Raiford squinted up at her as he raised her hand toward his mouth and thin gray beard. "Y'all ain't from 'round these parts," he commented in a breathless drawl before kissing the back of her hand.

"Ah, no, sir," Jewel said, unable to keep from staring at the outline of his withered, useless limbs beneath the thin blanket draped across his lap. "My father and I are from Chicago."

Taking her cue, Harry extended his hand. "Harrison 'Harry' Poindexter, sir. An honor to meet you."

Again squinting a chocolate brown eye as he studied the unfamiliar face, Raiford said, "Likewise, I'm sure. Y'all kin to the Tennessee Poindexters?"

"Ah, no, sir, I'm afraid not."

"Shame. Real shame," he muttered, shaking his head. "The Tennessee Poindexters are right good folks. Right good. Now, why don't y'all sit a spell? I'm bound to get a powerful crick in my neck if I have to keep staring up at y'all much longer."

Jewel and Harry obediently slid into high-backed wicker chairs, and Brent sat next to his father.

Just then a young girl appeared in the doorway. "Afternoon, Mr. Connors. Kin I get y'all somethin' to eat or drink?"

"Thanks, Loanne," Brent said, looking to his guests. "Why don't you bring us some mint juleps and a few snacks?"

"Right away, sir." The girl made a little curtsy, then disappeared into the house.

As if he'd forgotten about his company, Raiford tugged at the huge wheels on his chair and propelled himself over to the railing. Looking out at his beloved plantation, he said absently. "How's the shipping business coming along, boy?"

Brent shot an apologetic glance toward his guests, then said, "As I was telling you before, fair to middling, sir."

"We gonna meet the tax bill on time this year?"

Again Brent looked at Jewel and Harry, then turned his palms up and shrugged. "That and at least enough extra to restore Mama's rose gardens."

Raiford whipped his head around. "That right, boy? Y'all hear that?" he shouted as he looked back out at the farm. Slapping his atrophied thighs with glee, he laughed and hollered at imaginary soldiers. "By God, you hear that, you bastids? By dern, you Yankee boys thought you could wipe us off'n the map, but I guess y'all got another think coming! By God, ya dirty bastids do!"

"Take it easy, Dad," Brent said softly, with no hint of condemnation in his voice. "Maybe you forgot—we have a lady visitin' us. Won't do for you to go on like that."

Quickly looking over his shoulder, Raiford blanched, then turned his gaze back to the fields. "Pardon my dreadful manners, little gal. I swear, sometimes I think those damn Yankees blowed away my ability to think as well as walk. I do hope y'all can find it in your heart to forgive me."

"Don't worry your head about it, Mr. Connors. I think—"

But Jewel's thoughts were put on hold as a boisterous male voice shattered the gentle conversation.

"Brent! You ole coon dog! How'd I miss you in town?"

"Good God, Beau! See if you can't get a grip on yourself. We got company."

The younger, more gregarious version of Brent, froze in mid-stride, then surveyed the occupants of the wicker chairs. After setting a tray of drinks and snacks on a table, he bowed at the waist. "Glory be, if we don't," he said, his voice lush and rich with southern masculine pride. "Glory be if we don't got us some right pretty company at that."

Barely acknowledging Harry as Brent introduced the two men, Beau lingered over Jewel, keeping her hand sandwiched between both of his as he heard his own name repeated, ". . . my brother, Beauregard Sumner Connors."

"Meetin' you is a pleasure, ma'am. A real *pleasure*," he repeated, openly admiring her from head to toe.

Jewel cocked one eyebrow as the younger Connors leaned closer to her. His eyes, nearly the same honey brown as Brent's, lacked the depth, the sensitivity, but seemed filled to overflowing with gaiety and frivolity. His face—round, smooth, and free of whiskers—was boyish and hopelessly adorable. Beauregard Connors was a cuddly bear of a man, Jewel decided, but probably infinitely more dangerous to the ladies of Washington County than the real item.

"Excuse me, Beauregard," she said with a saucy lilt, "but are you feeling all right?"

Beau raised his brow and said, "Pardon me, ma'am?"

"I was wondering if you'd taken ill, sir. Your tongue seems to be lolling out the corner of your mouth."

Just as her little comeuppance began to sink in, a big hand crushed down on the nape of Beau's neck. Then Brent's voice, low and dangerously polite, raised the hair on his spine.

"Perhaps I can interpret for the little lady, brother. I believe she's concerned y'all might drool all over her nice dress. Y'all wouldn't want to do a disgustin' thing like that, now, would you?"

"Uh," Beau stammered with a nervous chuckle as he straightened his spine. "No, 'course not." He turned, his eyes bright and innocent. "Just tryin' to be polite, Brent. You know me, 'bout as polite as a fella kin get."

"Yes, li'l brother, I *do* know you, and you're damn lucky that I do." Then, his grin broad, Brent pulled the younger man into his arms for a brief hug. When he released him, he reached for the tray and offered refreshments to his guests, inquiring as Jewel helped herself to a mint julep, "Why didn't y'all meet us at the *Dawn,* Beau? I was hoping you'd stay on board while I visited the folks."

Beau grabbed a chair and pulled it up beside Harry as he answered. "I rode on up to the levee, but I got sidetracked some. Stopped off to the McAlexander place for a spell, and I guess the time got away from me."

Brent cocked an inquisitive eyebrow as he sat down next to his father. "That little McAlexander gal still single?"

"Yep." Beau laughed. His dimples were arresting but not as deep or carved in appearance as Brent's. "She's still lots a things, and lots of fun and—"

"Do mind your manners, Beau."

"Oh, yeah," he said through a muffled chuckle as he finally dared another glance at Jewel. "Sorry, ma'am. Anyways," he went on, speaking as if he'd never been interrupted, "time I got to the ship, y'all had gone, so I come on home."

"No harm done." Brent shrugged. "Tex and Reba assured me they could take on supplies and passengers."

Beau's boyish grin was still in place, but his obvious boredom with the business side of the conversation shone in his impish honey-brown eyes as he turned to Harry. "You a passenger on my brother's steamship, Mr. Harrison?"

Harry cleared his throat and took a sip of his julep before he said, "Poindexter. My name is Harrison Poindexter"—he looked down his nose at the young man—"but you may call me Harry."

"Harry? That's a good easy name. That real, Harry?" Beau said, pointing to the three-carat diamond adorning his gold stickpin.

"Good God, Beau," Brent groaned. "Do button your lip and save us from any more of your observations."

"That's all right." Harry laughed, genuinely amused by the childish curiosity that seemed so much a part of the younger Connors's personality. "Many people wonder the same thing."

"That may be, sir," Brent said, decidedly unamused, "but how many of them are idiotic enough to ask you about it?"

Again Harry laughed. "Please do not concern yourself about Beau's curiosity. I find it refreshing." He turned to the younger brother. "Yes, son, it is quite real. In fact, this particular diamond was a gift to me from the Prince of Wales."

"Whales?" Beauregard began to laugh. "Where in tarnation is that?"

"Not *whales,* son, *Wales.* Let me explain . . ."

As Harry spoke to Beau, Brent observed the pair, concentrating on his brother's reactions to their 'esteemed' guest. Then he realized Jewel was speaking to him.

"I'm sorry, little lady. Did you say something?"

"Yes," she said, ignoring the lively discussion between Beau and Harry. "I think your father has fallen asleep."

Brent glanced to his right, then looked back to Jewel. "Happens often. Perhaps I ought to take you two to your rooms now and let you freshen up. The womenfolk should be coming downstairs before too long. You might want to take a short nap yourself before you meet the rest of my . . . little family," he added with a wink.

"They can't be as . . . well, as—" For lack of respectful word, she glanced at Beau and raised her eyebrows.

"Worse," Brent said through a chuckle.

"Then perhaps I'd best retire for a short while." She laughed along with him as she rose from the chair. Her amusement soon died as she took another look at Raiford Connors. In sleep he appeared even more fragile, and so close to the end of his life that she wondered how his sons could bear to look at him. Again she fretted—how could Brent possibly subject his father to the scene between Harry and his mother? How could he allow the poor man to discover that he was a cockold?

Abruptly turning away from Brent, she snapped at Harry. "Let's go to our rooms, Faathah. I suddenly have a headache."

"Probably the mint julep, my dear," Harry said, oblivious of her sudden anger. "Is it possible you did not realize you swallowed a dash of Kentucky whiskey in that very refreshing drink? Perhaps it didn't agree with you."

"Perhaps," she agreed, tired of the charade, dreading the inevitable confrontations to come. "In any event, I'd like to rest now."

"Of course." Harry finished his drink, then joined her and Brent.

As the group started on through the library, Brent issued an order to Beau. "Go on ahead and round up Maxwell. Have him take Dad to bed. He'll need plenty of rest if he's going to join his company at the supper table tonight."

After waiting until his brother was out of earshot, Brent explained to the Poindexters as they made their way to the stairway, "You'll have to forgive Beauregard's lack of common sense. He means well, but at twenty-four years of age, I'm afraid he's still got a heap of growing to do."

"Oh, I think he's delightful," Harry said with a laugh. "You don't often find an innocent sort like him."

"No," Brent said, barely able to hold back a knowing sneer, "I don't suppose you do." He had turned to Jewel and was about to show her the way up the winding stairway when a feminine voice called to him from above.

Like the whistle on the *Delta Dawn,* she spoke in a rare combination of five tones. Sweet, soft, and lilting, Miriam Sebastian Connors's voice could also carry an underlying strength and the distinct crack of a cat-o'-nine-tails.

"Why, it is you, Brent," she said, using only the first three tones. As she made her way down the steps, her soft gray eyes widened and she gasped, "And I see you've brought some friends home with you."

# 15

Three pairs of eyes glanced up to the top landing where the sound of gently rustling crinolines heralded the descent of an ethereal figure. The flounced hem of Miriam's white muslin wrapper swished back and forth, lightly dusting the hardwood steps as she made her way toward the trio, her ghostlike appearance becoming more dense with each step she took.

"Sorry if we disturbed you, Mama," Brent said, climbing several steps to greet her midway. "I brought some folks home with me. I do hope you don't mind the surprise."

"Not at all, son," Miriam said as she kissed his cheek and allowed him to escort her down to the foyer.

Jewel's gaze flitted from Harry to the woman, and back to Harry as she looked for some sign of shock, recognition, fear, or a combination of all three. She saw Miriam's cool, clear appraisal of her, but no acknowledgment of the man standing beside her. By the time the Connors's were within a few feet of the Bentons, Jewel's heart was thundering in her ears, and her mouth was dry with anticipation.

Brent, amazingly calm and collected, smiled at her and said, "I'd like to present my mother, Miriam Sebastian Connors. Mama—Jewel Poindexter and her father, Harrison."

"A pleasure to meet you, dear," Miriam purred, lightly touching Jewel's hand before she finally looked at Harry and extended her greeting. "Sir, welcome to our home. I do hope you both understand and forgive the state of disrepair. These have been trying times."

"The honor is mine, madam," Harry responded as he lightly kissed the back of her hand. "And never apologize for a stately mansion like Sumner Hall, Mrs. Connors. It is truly one of the finest showplaces I've ever had the pleasure of visiting."

Jewel's gaze, piercing and perceptive, remained riveted on the pair as they exchanged pleasantries. She studied the handsome woman, looking for some glimmer of surprise, but her countenance was serene and contained no more than a casual interest in her guests. Miriam's features, alive with animation, were, Jewel decided, nearly a mirror image of her older son, right down to the dimples. But there the resemblance ended. Where Brent's hair was dark, as his father's had once been, Miriam's curly locks were faded blond, almost washed out in appearance. Her pale gray eyes were almond shaped and thoughtful, whereas her son's, honey brown in color, were round and playful.

Jewel stared into those silver eyes, forcing herself to forget the son and search instead for signs of familiarity with Harry. But the woman remained warm, polite and not much interested in the dashing stranger. Had Harry been so well disguised during his assignation with her that he was now unrecognizable? If so, what about Harry himself? Where was the shock of discovering he was in the home of a former paramour?

Miriam abruptly turned her pale eyes back to Jewel, lighting the first sparks in their depths since she'd reached the landing. Again touching her hand, she said, "You'll be staying to supper, I hope?"

Brent drew up close to Jewel as he addressed his mother. "I have extended our hospitality through the entire night, Mama. I do hope that won't inconvenience you."

"Oh?" Miriam glanced at her son, a smile tugging at the corners of her mouth, then looked back at Jewel. "No trouble at all. It's been too long since we had guests at Sumner Hall.'' Focusing her attention on her auburn-haired guest, she offered a deep-dimpled smile. ''I expect you'll want to go to your room right away to freshen up and change into something a little cooler.''

Jewel waved her off as she said, ''Oh, thank you, Mrs. Connors, but I'm afraid I've brought nothing to change into. My, ah, luggage and other clothing . . . I, ah—''

''It's a very long story, Mama,'' Brent cut in, saving Jewel the trouble of making up yet another story.

''Well, then,'' Miriam said, her amused gaze swinging between her son and Jewel, ''perhaps we'd better save it for later. I think Mary Mildred will be able to find something suitable for your guest to wear.''

''Oh, but I couldn't,'' Jewel objected.

''Nonsense,'' Miriam insisted. ''The girls have an abundance of frocks. Now, if you'll excuse me, I have to run into the kitchen and see about supper. Brent? Would you mind showing the Poindexters to— Oh, by the way,'' she said, interrupting herself as she turned back to Harry, ''you wouldn't be related to the Tennessee Poindexters by any chance, would you?''

''No, madam, but I understand they are a lovely family.''

''Yes, they are lovely indeed,'' she agreed, before resuming her conversation with Brent. ''Son, would you mind seeing your guests to their rooms now? And do stop by Mary Mildred's room and see about a dress for your . . . friend.''

Brent frowned, then narrowed one eye in warning as he assured his mother, ''We were just heading upstairs. I'll join you downstairs in a few minutes.''

''Good. I need to go over . . . the books with you. See you all later, then,'' she said, patting Brent's arm as she nodded to her guests and glided down toward the hallway.

''Lovely woman,'' Harry commented as he started up the long staircase. ''You have a lovely family, Brent, and an extraordinary home. You must be very proud of them.''

"I am, sir, and I thank you for your opinion of them," he answered, guiding Jewel toward the top landing. At the apex, the hallway branched off to both sides, leaving a short walk straight ahead to the gilded double doors leading to the master bedroom suite. Brent led Harry and Jewel to the right down the carpeted path to the guest rooms, where he opened the first in a series of elaborate hand-carved doors.

"I think you'll be comfortable in here, Harry."

"Yes, yes, quite, I should think," Benton concurred as he stepped across the threshold and took in the small but well-appointed room.

"If you should require any assistance," Brent offered, "simply pull the cord just outside your door. Maxwell will see to your needs as soon as he can. We are a bit shorthanded, so don't be surprised it it takes him a while to arrive."

"Don't give it another thought," Harry said, waving him off as he resumed his financial appraisal of the Connors family.

"If you come downstairs in about an hour," Brent said, "you and I can have a bourbon before supper. Turn left at the foot of the steps and you'll run into the study."

"I'd be delighted. I'll see you in one hour."

With a nod, Brent closed the door, then grabbed Jewel's hand. "Come on," he said under his breath as he pulled her down the hallway, "you and I have a couple of things to straighten out before the girls wake up."

When he reached a door with a large white magnolia painted in the center, he pushed it open and dragged her inside the room. After checking up and down the hallway to make certain it was still deserted, Brent closed the door and gestured for her to follow him to the window.

Whispering conspiratorially, he said, "It looks like old Harry is a lot more cunning than I first thought. He didn't even blink when I introduced him! Shouldn't we have gotten more fireworks than that?"

"Well . . ." she hesitated, still appalled by the whole

plan and Brent's apparent lack of compassion where his father was concerned. "Yes, I suppose I expected them to be startled at the very least."

"Then how come Harry wasn't recognized? Could he have worn some kind of disguise when he lifted the jewels?"

Jewel shrugged. "He's been described in so many ways that it's difficult to get a clear picture of him from his victims. Even so, Brent"—she took time to examine her choice of words—"don't you think your mother, or any other woman he'd been with, would have shown at least *some* sign of recognition?"

"My mother? What do you mean by 'been with,' and why in hell would she recognize Harry?"

Jewel heaved a frustrated sigh as again she looked for the correct words. "Something should have clued her. His voice, something in his eyes, the way he kissed her hand. A woman doesn't forget subtle little things like that once she's been a man's lover."

*"What?"*

"Shush!" She glanced around as if she expected the door to bang open. "I thought you wanted to keep this little meeting secret."

"I do, but talk sense, little lady! What's all this about lovers and mothers?"

Jewel furrowed her brow and took a backward step. "Why, your mother and her little fling with Harry, what else?"

Brent's eyes widened and bulged. "Have you gone completely mad, woman? How can you even *think* such a thing?"

Taking a couple more backward steps, she stammered, "B-but I thought that's what this was all about. I thought Harry stole your mother's jewelry and that we were—"

"He did steal her emeralds, lady detective, but he stole them from Beau, not from my mother." Brent cocked his head, and leveled a finger at her. "What in God's name made you think it could be otherwise?"

Retreating in earnest now, Jewel circled the canopied bed and ran her nervous fingers across the embroidered white coverlet. "It was an understandable error," she muttered, trying to reconstruct the crime in her mind. "Relieving wealthy women of their jewelry *is* Harry's specialty, you know. What else was I to think?"

"Maybe a little more of me," Brent grumbled, facing her from across the bed. "I find it insulting both to my mother and to me that you could actually believe I'd bring Harry into my home under those circumstances."

"It did seem a little . . . callous on your part, but I still don't know what else I could have thought. The very idea of Beau losing the jewelry to Harry is so ridiculous, I can't even entertain the notion."

Still frowning, his feelings injured, Brent shoved his hands in his pockets and walked back to the window. Staring out at the cedar trees lining the pathway to the barns, he said, "The war shattered this family's spirit for a while, but it did not rob us of our honor. My mother is a true wife to my father and an extremely noble woman. Perhaps I need to question Beau a little further, but if he says Harry stole the jewels, then Harry stole the jewels. Understand?"

"Not really, Brent," she said softly as she approached him from behind. "Why don't you tell me exactly what happened to Beau? Maybe then we can get this all straightened out."

"There's not much to tell," he said, still staring out the window. "Beau went on down to New Orleans about a year and a half ago to make a loan so he could pay the taxes on Sumner Hall. He was going to use the emeralds as collateral."

Jewel waited a long moment, then prompted, "And?"

"And nothing." He shrugged. "He said Harry stole them out of his hotel room before he had a chance to find a lender."

"And you're absolutely certain he said the man's name was Harry Benton?"

Brent recalled the night his brother, wild-eyed and trembling, related the story of the theft. "Yes, I'm positive the name was Harry Benton."

"But that's absolutely ludicrous," she said, more baffled than ever.

Spinning to face her, Brent gripped her shoulders. "Why do you keep saying that? What's so ridiculous about a crook like Harry Benton stealing a diamond and emerald necklace of considerable value?"

As Jewel stared up into his sensitive brown eyes, it became increasingly difficult for her to make the objective observations of a detective. Fighting the sympathetic woman inside, she tried to explain. "Please try to look at it from my side, Brent. I've made a thorough study of Harry Benton, and while he may be a lot of things, most of them unsavory, he is definitely not a thief."

"Excuse me, little lady?" Brent said, his brow high and incredulous.

"All right, that was a bad choice of words." She laughed. "But if you put him in the picture you're trying to paint, he simply isn't a thief of that sort. Harry has had a long and checkered career, to be sure, but he *always* takes his payments from ladies. That's one reason he's been so difficult to catch. Most of his victims do not want him prosecuted for one reason or another."

"Those reasons being . . . ?"

"Their husbands or fathers, for one. All of his victims were attached to very successful men." No longer able to look into his honey-brown eyes, Jewel blushed and glanced out the window.

"What's the other reason?"

"He, ah . . ." She sputtered around, her usually glib tongue unable to speak of Harry in such terms. "He apparently leaves most of them happy. They, ah . . . The women generally decide that he's entitled to whatever he helps himself to."

In spite of his earlier dark thoughts, Brent burst out in laughter. "That definitely does not match Beau's story."

"No, it most certainly doesn't." Turning back to him, she pleaded, "Why don't you have a long talk with your brother and see if hasn't confused Harry with someone else?"

"Doesn't sound as if I have much choice," he said, sliding his hands off her shoulders and down her back to her waist. "What do we do if he has made a mistake, partner?"

"Why don't we worry about that later? For now, I'm just glad to hear he wasn't involved with your mother. I really couldn't understand how you could be so nice to him all the way out here. You can happily drop that little act now. It was beginning to get on my nerves anyway."

"It wasn't that much of an act, little lady. In spite of the fact that I still believe he stole my family heirlooms, I think Harry's a pretty likable fellow."

"Just don't become too enamored of him," she grumbled, disturbed by the idea of Brent and her newfound father becoming friends. "One way or another I intend to put that man behind bars for the rest of his life."

"Do you also intend to masquerade as his daughter right down to the end?"

"Yes, and don't you dare even hint that I'm only pretending to be the heir to his throne!"

"Some throne," he laughed, pulling her close. "More of a gallows, if you ask me."

"Well, I didn't. You just go on downstairs and talk to your brother; then let me know what you find out. Can you manage that, *partner*?"

"I believe so." Brent linked his fingers, tightening his grip around her waist as she tried to back away. "Don't run off yet. What do you think of my family so far?"

Vaguely uncomfortable with the new direction the conversation was taking, and with the fact that she was so close to him, Jewel pressed her palms against his chest. "I think they wouldn't approve of you being alone with me in my room.''

''And here I thought you didn't understand southerners.'' He leaned forward and kissed the tip of her nose before indulging himself with a quick taste of her mouth. ''I've missed holding you, Jewel, missed touching your skin and kissing your lips—I've missed all of you. Perhaps I was a bit hasty in setting the guidelines for our partnership. Maybe this would be a good time to remove one of the more stupid rules,'' he murmured softly, hovering above her parted, trembling lips. ''There's no reason I can think of that we shouldn't do this. No reason at all.'' And before she could agree or object, he covered her mouth again, this time in a deeply satisfying kiss.

The door opened at the same instant a young woman's voice called out, ''Brent? Is that you?''

He released Jewel and quickly stepped back from her, but not fast enough to escape the inquisitive cinnamon eyes of his youngest sister. He turned, speaking in a hoarse voice, and scolded, ''Good God, Brandee Leigh, you should know better than to walk into a room without knocking.''

She giggled into her hand. ''I'm sorry. I didn't know you had company in here. I thought I heard your voice, so I've been running up and down the hall looking for you.'' Standing on tiptoe, she craned her neck and peeked behind her brother's shoulders, then acknowledged Jewel's presence with a little curtsy. ''Excuse me, ma'am.''

Her cheeks in full bloom, Jewel managed a quiet ''That's all right.''

Brent beckoned his sister to cross the room as he said, ''Jewel, this is my nosy sister, Brandee Leigh.'' Addressing the young woman as she approached, he explained, ''Miss Poindexter and her father are our guests for the night. See if you can't mind your manners and stay away from their bedrooms until after they leave tomorrow. Mr. Poindexter is in the teak room. I'm sure he wouldn't want you barging in on him the way you just burst in on us.''

She giggled again. "He didn't mind too much."

"Pardon *me*?"

"It wasn't my fault," Brandee said, lowering her gaze. "I told him I was looking for you. How could I have known there was a strange man in the house?"

"Oh, good God," Brent complained again, this time under his breath.

"Don't worry about it," Jewel said. "I'm sure my dear faathah has been through much worse."

Brandee's cinnamon eyes lit up and she blurted out, "Did you hear that, Brent? She said 'faathah.' How exciting these two are! When I looked in the teak room, the man said, 'Goodness, my dear,' or something like that. Oh, golly, you both sound so deliciously *foreign*. Where are y'all from?"

Her mouth curved up at one corner, Jewel glanced at Brent, then addressed the girl. "Chicago."

"*Chicago?*" she echoed in a sigh. Clearly disappointed, Brandee pulled one of her caramel-colored curls across her shoulder and began to twirl it. "But your daddy sounded so—"

"Foreign. I know. But that's understandable," Jewel explained. "Faathah has traveled extensively in Europe. I suppose some of the accents he's been exposed to have just naturally become a part of his speech."

"Doesn't matter whether Harry's got an accent or not," Brent grumbled as he bore down on his sister. "To Brandee Leigh, anyone who comes from east of Kentucky is a foreigner. And for a young girl of fifteen—"

"Sixteen," Brandee interrupted with a pout.

Brent raised his brows. "Since when?"

Brandee's gaze drifted around the room as she gave him a tiny shrug. "Next month."

"As I was saying," Brent continued, taking Brandee by the arm. "For a girl of fifteen, this one spends entirely too much time thinking about foreigners and about men in general." As he started toward the door with his sister in tow, he whispered a warning into her ear. "I don't want to see you making a fool out of yourself in front of Miss Poindexter's daddy. Behave yourself, you hear?''

Brandee turned mournful eyes on him and slowly nodded.

''Good.'' Brent glanced across the top of her head to the window where Jewel stood grinning. Keeping his gaze locked on her laughing green eyes, he said to Brandee, ''I'm afraid we left our luggage on the *Delta Dawn*. Go get Mary Mildred. Mama says you gals can find an extra dress for Jewel to wear to supper.''

''Oh, sure!'' she said with high-pitched exuberance, forgetting her reprimand, looking ahead to the events of the evening instead. ''I won't be but a minute, Miss Jewel! We have a pile of gowns you can choose from.''

Brent waited for her to brush past him and scurry on down the hallway before he bowed slightly at the waist and said, ''Welcome to Sumner Hall, Miss Flannery—there's two more like her on the way in here as we speak. Think you can manage them?''

Through her laughter, Jewel said, ''I think Brandee and Beau are delightful. I'm sure I'll enjoy the rest of your family as much.''

''Mary Mildred and Trilonnie Georgette are older and more formidable than Brandee Leigh,'' he warned. ''I suppose you ought to count yourself lucky that my married sister, Mildred Mary, who lives in Vicksburg will not be joining us this evening.''

Still laughing, she said, ''Mary Mildred *and* Mildred Mary?''

''Oh, yes, ma'am. We southerners do like to keep our names going 'round and 'round.''

Jewel's chuckles eased, then increased just as suddenly when she recalled her earlier meeting with Brent's brother. ''I guess,'' she gasped, ''that holds true for you boys, too, then. I noticed you both have the same initials—B.S.''

Through his laughter he said, ''So the detective in you has not been completely disarmed by my charms. Yes, there are two B. S. Connorses. Until the Yankees robbed him of his pride and his mobility,'' Brent explained as he stepped out into the hall, ''my father was not without a sense of humor. See you at supper, little lady. And good luck with the Connors gals. You'll be needin' all you can get.''

He pulled the door shut on her laughter and carried the sound with him as he negotiated the hallway and staircase and headed for the study. Finding the double doors open, he stepped inside, then closed them behind him when he spotted his brother working at the rolltop desk in the far corner.

''Got a minute, Beau?'' he said as he strolled over to the side table set up as a bar.

''Huh?'' Beau looked up from the column of figures and grinned as he saw his brother take two glasses from the shelf. Pushing away from the desk, he sauntered across the room. ''I've always got time for a snort with you.''

Brent chose a bottle of Kentucky bourbon from the row of decanters, then poured two fingers neat into each glass. After handing one drink to his brother, he raised the other and said, ''To the brothers Connors—and to truth.'' He fixed Beau with a narrow gaze as he tapped the rims in a quick salute.

''Truth?'' Beau said before taking a long pull on his drink.

''Yes, brother, the absolute truth.'' Brent sipped the bourbon, testing the flavor, then downed it. After a long sigh, he explained. ''I have been chasing up and down the Mississippi looking for this Harry Benton fellow you told me about. It has come to my attention during my travels that the thief in question could not possibly have stolen our mother's jewels from you in New Orleans, or anywhere else for that matter. One of us is mistaken about the name of the man who robbed you. Now which is it—you or me?''

''Gee, Brent. I don't know. I'll have to think on that some.''

''You have five minutes,'' he said, refilling both glasses.

"I'm always happy to give anybody five minutes to come up with a story. Just make sure the one you come up with this time is the God's honest truth—you hear?"

Keeping his head down, Beau glanced up at his brother, then nodded before he slowly turned around and walked over to the fireplace. Resting his elbow on the lace runner that covered the oak mantel, he closed his eyes and raked his fingers through his hair.

Keeping his word, Brent waited in silence for several long minutes. Then he joined Beau at the fireplace. "Well?" he quietly said. "Surely your memory's had a chance to return by now. Just exactly what did happen to Mama's emeralds, Beauregard?"

After finishing the last of his drink, Beau lowered his head and muttered, "They were stolen, just as I said, but maybe I got the name wrong. Now that I think about it, I guess it wasn't Harry Benton after all."

Brent clenched his teeth, waiting until he could speak in a calm rational vice. "Why did you give me Benton's name if he wasn't the thief, Beauregard?"

The younger Connors shrugged and picked at a loose strand of thread hanging at the edge of the runner. "I read about him in one of those mystery books. It said he liked jewels and fancy ladies and made his living off'n them."

Knowing any display of anger would spook his overly sensitive brother, Brent swallowed his rage and went on. "Why? Why did you give me a name in the first place? Why in the name of all that's holy did you have me peeking into hotel rooms and places I had no right to be, searching for a man who never did our family wrong? Answer me *that,* Beau!"

"I—I can't! I don't know!"

Forcing a coolness he didn't feel, Brent took a deep breath and placed a gentle hand on Beau's shoulder. "Take it easy, now. Don't get yourself all in a stew. Just tell me the truth so I'll know what to do next."

The younger Connors glanced up at his brother's expression, then furrowed his brow. He began tracing the brick patterns along the low hearth with the toe of his boot as he tried once again to explain. "I didn't think you'd really go after Benton. And I never believed you'd actually find him." Beau's next thoughts lifted his chin and popped his eyes open. "*Did* you find him? Oh, glory be, is that it? What happened?"

"That's what I've been asking you, little brother. I'm still waiting for an answer."

"Oh, glory be, glory be," Beau muttered as he began wringing his hands. "I went on down to New Orleans. I was gonna—"

"I know all that. What happened to Mama's jewel's?"

"She— I— Well . . . damn it all, Brent." Beau stepped away from the fireplace, away from his brother, and circled around behind his mother's gold velvet settee. "I only wanted to show Mama I was as good as you. I wanted to help in a big flashy way, like you done when you won the *Delta Dawn*. I never thought . . ." His words trailed off as he tried to find a way to explain his incredible stupidity.

Brent slowly made his way to the couch and stood facing Beau. Keeping his tone low and nonjudgmental, he said again, "What did you do with the jewels?"

Beau lowered his head and voice before he was able to admit the truth. "I lost them."

"Lost them? How did you do that? Did you put them somewhere, then forget where? Did you take them to—"

"I used them to cover the biggest pot I've ever seen—ten *thousand* dollars."

"You *wagered* Mama's emeralds on a game of chance?" Brent's color rose, and his mustache began to twitch. "What in God's name were you using for a brain, if you don't mind my asking?"

"Glory be," Beau cried, once again wringing his hands. "If you'd been there, you'da done the same, I swear! I had it won. I knew I did, Brent! God Almighty, wouldn't you bet the farm on a full house, queens over nines? Wouldn't you?"

"Depends, little brother," Brent answered, his nostrils flaring. "Where did you find this little game and who were the other players?"

"I told you—down to New Orleans. I was at a place called the Purple Turtle."

"Oh, good God," Brent said with a heavy sigh of resignation. "Who—and believe me, I'm almost afraid to ask—was running this game?"

Beau looked up at his brother, then averted his gaze and said in a very quiet voice, "Skinner. That was his whole name. Just Skinner."

"Jesus, Beau!" Brent shouted, his vow to remain cool dissolved in a flash of white-hot anger. "He's the biggest crook this side of the Mississippi! What in God's name could you have been thinking?"

"I told you!" Beau shouted back, his voice high, wavering. "I just wanted to win big, like you!"

Brent held up his hands, acknowledging that his anger wasn't really directed at his brother. He lowered his voice to just above a whisper and said, "I know you did, Beau, but couldn't you have thought about the difference between us? I was the manager of the Gilded Bird when I won that ship. I knew the players, and I ran the game myself. I knew it was an honest poker game, because I was in charge. Understand, Beau?"

He nodded slowly. "You were Skinner."

Brent winced, then shrugged. "In a manner of speaking, yes, but never mention my name in the same breath with his again, brother—you got that?" At Beau's miserable nod, Brent sighed and circled around behind the settee. "I know you only wanted to do something big to help the family, and I do appreciate that fact. Next time, however, make sure it's something you're an expert at. Understand what I'm saying?"

Again Beau nodded. Then he glanced up at his taller

brother. "I think I understood right after it happened, but it was too late." His honey-brown eyes pleading, he faced Brent. "You aren't going to tell Mama, are you? Please don't—"

"'Course not. I'll make some inquiries about the necklace when the *Dawn* pulls into New Orleans. Maybe we'll get the emeralds back yet."

Beau's eyes lit up. "I know what Skinner did with 'em! Let me help you get 'em back!"

His mustache twitching again, Brent paused and sighed. "I'll have to think on that awhile. What did Skinner do with the jewels?"

"He gave 'em to that Cajun gal who runs the . . . upstairs trade at the Purple Turtle. She's right fond of me! Maybe I could—"

A light tapping at the door cut off his words. Then Miriam stepped into the room. "Did I hear my boys scrapping in here?"

"No, Mama." Brent assured her as he squeezed his brother's arm. "Beau and I were just having a little fun."

"That's some powerful noisy fun you were having—I could hear your voices all the way down to the kitchen." Miriam shot her older boy a perceptive look, then addressed her younger son. "Beau, darlin', do me a favor and run out back to the garden. Loanne is picking some vegetables and gathering fresh eggs. I think she could use your help. After that, you go on up and dress for supper. It's getting late."

"Yes, ma'am." Beau's eyes sparkled, and his expression reflected open admiration as he took a moment to smile up at his brother. Then he practically skipped out of the study and down the hallway to the kitchen.

After he was gone, Miriam closed the doors and approached her firstborn. "Everything all right 'tween you and your brother?"

"Things are just fine, ma'am. Nothing for you to worry your head about."

Lifting the flounced hem of her wrapper, Miriam settled

down on the couch and regarded her son. "I have a few minutes to spare before I have to dress for supper. Isn't there something you want to tell me?"

Staring into his mother's intuitive gray eyes, he wondered how long she had been outside the door to the study. Had she heard the conversation about her grandmother's emeralds? His voice uncharacteristically hesitant, Brent shrugged and said, "I don't think so."

"Come now, Brent, you don't expect me to believe you brought that girl and her father out here just to pass the time of day. Don't you think it's time we had a little talk?"

Brent eyed his empty bourbon glass and wondered if another drink would make it any easier to have this conversation with his mother. How could he find a way to explain the ill-conceived poker game and still keep his promise to Beau? Could he explain it without hurting her or his brother? Again he glanced at his glass.

Miriam spared him the decision. "Aren't you suddenly the shy one." She laughed, teasing him. "Why, if I didn't know better, I'd think I was talking to Beauregard."

Brent cocked his head and raised an eyebrow. "Ma'am?"

"Don't go thinking you can pull one over on me," she went on, a knowing gleam in her eye. "When were you planning to let us all in on the surprise? Tonight at supper?"

"Surprise?" Brent scratched his head. "Mama, I'm sorry, but I guess I just have too much on my mind right now to make sense of your conversation. What in tarnation are you talking about?"

"Why, Jewel of course." Miriam shook a finger at him. "Brandee Leigh told me what she saw in the magnolia room. I realize you weren't expecting her to pop in on you, but I do think I taught you better manners than you exhibited, you rascal."

"Oh, that," he muttered quietly, not sure if he was relieved or distressed at the unexpected choice of topics. "I beg your pardon. It won't happen again."

"Oh?" Miriam said, one eyebrow raised high. "I expect

it will. Don't think I didn't notice the sparks between you two when I first met her and don't think I didn't notice she's not one of our own kind, either. Are you sure you know what you're doing, son? Have you thought this over carefully?''

Brent cleared his throat and acknowledged his mother's assumptions with the barest of nods. ''Jewel does mean an awful lot to me. I'd appreciate it if you would treat her like one of our own, without referring to our relationship in any way. She is a very special and intelligent woman, but skittish as all get-out. Jewel won't cotton to any of us suggesting I brought her out here for reasons other than business.''

''Business?'' Miriam wrinkled her nose. ''What kind of business could you possibly have with her?''

''Ah, not with Jewel. With her father. They are both passengers on the *Dawn*, and he expressed an interest in Sumner Hall. I thought it prudent to indulge his curiosity.''

''Oh, is that all?'' Miriam sighed, then slowly shook her head. ''And here I thought you were finally ready to settle down. I suppose this means you aren't planning to announce your engagement at the supper table, then.''

''*What?* Good God, no! If you even suggest that, Jewel will head on out of here like a pack of coon dogs is at her heels.''

''Oh, dear me,'' Miriam said as she lifted herself off the couch. ''I'd best go have another talk with your daddy, in that case. You know how he can be.''

Brent groaned under his breath. ''You've gone and mentioned this to Dad?''

Thinking ahead to supper, and to Raiford's penchant for blurting out the most embarrassing statements at the most inopportune moments, he groaned again, then sighed, ''Good God all Friday.''

# 16

Ten months younger than Brent, Mary Mildred was the Connors child most affected by the War between the States. A bride at eighteen, a scant year later she had lost her young husband and a good part of her sanity at the siege of Vicksburg. Now thirty, Mary had settled into a kind of permanent truce with herself and her circumstances.

Draped in a bouffant gown of deep indigo, she stood on the marble floor of the foyer, one hand caressing the newel post at the bottom of the curved staircase, and told Brent about her afternoon with Jewel. Mary's periwinkle-blue eyes sparkled with open adoration as she spoke to her favorite sibling. She turned her head, displaying her new hairstyle, and pointed to the rows of blond spirals. "Look back here at the crown," she said enthusiastically. "Jewel says this is the latest style from New York. Do you like it?"

"You look downright stunning, li'l sis. A blinding vision of beauty."

"Oh, you flatterer," she drawled in a voice so soft, so faint, it was barely more than the kiss a butterfly. "But really, don't you think Jewel did a lovely job? I know it's the latest fashion, too, because I saw a recent issue of the *Harper's Bazar* over to Noland's Dry Goods Store. Every last one of the models wore her hair like this."

Indulging her, acknowledging the special corner of his heart he kept just for his oldest sister, Brent lightly pinched her cheek. "I told you I thought you looked absolutely beautiful. What can I possibly add to that without puffing your head up like a big old gourd?''

''Oh, Brent,'' she said, giggling and glancing at the top of the stairs.

Catching the expectant look in her eyes and recognizing the conspiratorial gleam, he followed her gaze, then furrowed her brow. ''All right, li'l sis, what's going on, and where is Jewel? Everyone seems to be downstairs but her. What have y'all gone and done with her?''

''She's on her way,'' Mary said with a coy smile. ''Ought to be at the top of the stairs any minute now.''

''Is that why I'm standing here like a doorman? I'm waiting for Jewel's grand entrance, is that it?''

Mary's quiet laughter sprinkled the air before she said, ''I guess you might say that.''

''Then I guess you might also say that I'm leaving.'' He gave her a dramatic bow as he turned and started for the study.

''No, Brent! Please wait up.''

In spite of his better judgment, he halted his progress. ''Look,'' he said heavily. ''I've been through all this Jewel business with Mama. Why can't y'all get it in your heads that I just brought the Poindexters to Sumner Hall as our guests? Why do you insist on making so much of it?''

''But Brent,'' she said in a soft cry, puffing out her bottom lip. ''I thought she was right special to you. I only—''

''Oh, now, don't go getting all upset.'' He walked back to her and put his arm around her shoulder. ''What Jewel is, or isn't, to me at this point is still a private matter. You'll be the first to know when it isn't. Does that make you feel any better?''

''Some,'' she answered with a sniff of her nose.

Footfalls from above caught Brent's attention. Raising an eyebrow, he whispered sternly to Mary, ''I believe Jewel is coming down to supper now. Only one of us is going to be standing here waiting for her entrance. Will that be you . . . or me?''

''Oh, but . . . Oh, Brent you are such an old pooh,'' she complained with a stamp of her foot. ''You, I guess.''

He grinned and tugged one of her curls. ''Then skedaddle on out of here.''

Mary Mildred lifted her chin and the hem of her skirts, then flounced on down the hallway at the same moment Jewel appeared at the top of the stairway.

After making sure Brent was alone, she cleared her throat to catch his attention, then quickly turned her profile to him. Dressed in a billowing rose-petal ball gown of delicate pink taffeta, Jewel posed theatrically on the top step and fluttered a matching pink hanky trimmed in white satin.

''I do declare, Mr. Connors,'' she breathed in an exaggerated drawl. ''I just feel so completely *suhthen*, I have the insane urge to rush out to the fields and pick some cotton. Y'all *do* raise cotton, don't you?''

''Oh, good God in heaven,'' he said with a laugh that was more of a groan. ''What have my sisters gone and done to you?''

''I declare,'' she repeated as she slowly began her descent. ''I don't know that y'all could be talkin' about. I'm the same innocent li'l old thang I've always been.''

Laughing, content just to watch her—to love her, he acknowledged from deep inside—Brent said nothing, but his dimples were bottomless pits as she gracefully made her way down the stairs. The old-fashioned gown, cut in a deep V at the bodice, afforded him a tantalizing glimpse of Jewel's ample bosom, yet somehow made her look pristine at the same time. Her hair was arranged like Mary's, with careful tubes at the crown and one long auburn spiral that grew from the center petals, then coiled down over her shoulder. That curl bounced, skimming along the soft rise of her breasts, as she came within four steps of Brent. Then, without warning, Jewel lurched to one side and dropped into a heap of petticoats and skirts on the third step.

"Oweeee," she cried as she thudded down on the hardwood. Moaning softly, she complained, "I guess I'm just too damn awkward to be dressing up like a fancy southern lady."

Brent vaulted up the stairs and hunkered down beside the mountains of fabric. "You all right, little lady?" he asked, lifting her chin. "What happened, sweetheart?"

"I turned my ankle," she groaned, rubbing her hand up and down her leg. "And it's all because of these—" She glanced around the foyer and down the hallway, making sure they could not be overheard, then lowered her voice in a bare whisper. "It's because of these damnable slippers Trilonnie insisted I wear. They match this dress, but they're too tight in some places and too big in others. I'll be lucky if I don't break my neck before the night's over."

"Then take the damn things off! We can't have you falling all over the house." His expression solemn with concern, Brent tried to brush her skirts aside and wade through the yards of material to remove the offensive shoes.

Jewel slapped at him, still grumbling. "I can't go around barefoot, you idiot. What would your family think?"

"Since when do you care what anyone thinks?" he said with more directness than he'd intended.

Taken aback, her injury forgotten, Jewel rested one hand on his forearm. "Oh, but I do care, Brent. Your sisters have been absolutely wonderful to me. They've treated me almost like one of them."

Touched by her words, by what he saw in her eyes, Brent took her hand from his arm and raised it to his mouth. Against her palm he said, "I know you care, sweetheart. I wasn't trying to imply that you don't." He gently nipped the fleshy part of her thumb with his teeth, then released it and stared into her eyes. His voice breaking, he said, "Go ahead upstairs and put on your own shoes. No one will notice the difference."

Jewel slowly shook her head as she turned away. Reaching for the banister, she pulled herself to her feet and insisted, "If Trilonnie can wear these damn things, so can I." Then she cautiously resumed her descent.

Brent shrugged as he got to his feet and joined her at the foot of the stairs. He slid his hand around her waist to the small of her back, warning. "Don't blame me if you're crippled for life. Are you ready to make your grand entrance?"

Jewel glanced down the deserted hallway and listened to the sounds of muffled conversation. Lowering her voice again, she said, "Just give me one more minute. I have to know what happened with your brother. What did he say when you asked him about Harry?"

Brent frowned and took a quick look toward the study. "This is not the time or the place to discuss that, but I will tell you this much—Beauregard made a little mistake. Harry Benton was not the swindler who stole our mother's emeralds."

"I knew it!"

"Hush!" he cautioned, again looking down the hallway. "We'll have to talk about this later, but for now here's a word of warning: From here on out, as far as I'm concerned, Harry is an honored guest in my home. *All* of us, including you, will treat him as such—you hear?"

"But he's still—"

"Later," he said, firmly pressing his palm against the hollow in her spine and pushing her forward. "If we don't make our entrance now, the tongues will start wagging all over again. Let us resume our earlier conversation. I believe you were discussin' an unholy urge to do in our cotton crop."

Jewel gasped and her mouth dropped open, but before she had a chance to scold him, Brent gave her backside a nudge and propelled her into the crowded study.

Thirty minutes later the entire family and their guests were gathered around the enormous dining table. Seated majestically in his wheelchair at the head of the table,

Raiford Connors droned on, leading the group in a halting, befuddled prayer. Jewel sat at his right, her thoughts as distracted as his sermon. Unable to keep from gawking around the cavernous dining room, she peeked up through her lashes. The room was rich in embellishments from the cherrywood paneling and the Italian marble fireplace to the rich solid walnut Louis XV dining table and chairs. But something was inconsistent here. Some little thing nagged at her, insisting that things weren't quite as they seemed.

Jewel ran her hands along the satiny emerald brocade covering the arms of her chair, wondering why the furniture seemed so familiar. Then the cause of her sense of discord suddenly struck a clear note. The dining room chairs, as well as other pieces throughout the immense home, were mates to those she'd seen on the *Delta Dawn*. Many similar pieces were displayed in the offices and quarters of the ship's handsome owner. Faint color variations on the mansion's walls added credence to her theory. Ghostly outlines testified that numerous paintings had been removed and were now hanging elsewhere—presumably on the cabin doors of the *Dawn*. Why had Brent stripped his family home of its priceless antiques?

Raiford suddenly increased the volume and pitch of his voice, signaling the climactic end to his incoherent speech. Her attention now drawn to him, Jewel studied him through her eyelashes. The nap had left the senior Connors keen-eyed and bright, allowing Jewel to glimpse the rakish gentleman he must have been some twenty or thirty years ago. His features, sharper and more angular than those of his sons, were proud and strong, a fine chiseled base for the full silver beard he kept trimmed and carefully groomed.

His dark chocolate eyes flashed in Jewel's direction just as his deep gravelly voice ended the prayer with a booming "A-*men*, y'all! Pass the eats."

Jewel stifled her laughter and glanced across the table through the brightly burning candelabra, to where Brent sat sandwiched between Trilonnie Georgette and Brandee

Leigh. He was listening to his young niece as she tried to make her thoughts known through a two-year-old's limited vocabulary, leaving Jewel to watch him, unobserved.

"My present, Unkee Bent," Melissa Mary pouted, extending a chubby hand as far across her plate as it would reach. "I want my present!"

"So that's it," he said, winking at the child's mother, Mary Mildred. "I brought you a present all right, Missy darlin', but I'm not giving it to you till after supper. First you've got to sit up like a good girl and eat your gumbo."

"Unkeeee Bent," she cried, the pout in full bloom, her big blue eyes round and pleading, "*peeze*?"

"You must listen to Brent, Melissa Mary," Miriam instructed from the end of the table. "It's not polite to ask for gifts. They must be offered."

Beaten, as he always was by the beguiling toddler, Brent dug into his coat pocket and produced a coin depicting a likeness of the Eads Bridge in St. Louis. "It's all right, Mama," he said, reaching across the table. "Here you go, Missy girl, but you got to promise to eat all your supper now, you hear?"

Melissa squealed, nodding vigorously as she snatched the coin from his hand.

Miriam slowly shook her head. "You spoil that child something awful, son."

"Begging your pardon, ma'am," he answered back. "But while I may spoil the girl a little, you flat out indulge her."

Her grin smug, her gray eyes flashing triumphantly, Miriam glanced at Brent and said, "I am Missy's grandmother. It's my *job* to spoil her." She lifted a steaming platter, then turned to her right and offered it to Harry Benton. "Have some spoon bread, Mr. Poindexter?"

Completely fascinated by Brent's mother, Jewel studied the older woman as Miriam passed the serving dishes around the large table. Dressed in a plain but elegant black silk gown, she looked every bit the matriarch, and com-

pletely at ease. Then Jewel looked into her tired gray eyes,
noticed the strands of silver in her faded yellow hair, and
saw that her proud carriage and composed expression
couldn't quite hide the frailty of a woman burdened by
troubles for too long.

"It's right good, you know," came the deep male voice
on Jewel's right.

"What?" she said, turning to Beau.

"The spoon bread. Have some. Loanne makes the best in
the county."

"Oh, why, thank you." Jewel spooned a portion of soft,
hot corn bread from the dish, then passed it on to Raiford.
As she accepted the platter of ham that followed, she
noticed the one remaining oil painting centered between the
six enormous arched windows that constituted the north
wall. The portrait was of a young woman with haunting dark
eyes and flowing black hair. While her features were unlike
Brent's, they seemed familiar somehow. Jewel cocked her
head, studying the woman from every angle as she tried to
identify her.

Noticing her guest's curiosity, Miriam supplied the answer. "The painting is of Raiford's mother, Mildred Mae
Sumner. Her daddy built this plantation over one hundred
years ago."

"Oh?" Jewel said. Looking back at the portrait, then at
Raiford, she said, "I thought the young woman looked
familiar, but I couldn't decide where I'd seen her before.
Now there's no question in my mind as to which side of the
family she's from."

"It's interesting you should say that," Miriam commented as she passed a bowl of black-eyed peas. "It purely
amazes me how often the resemblance between father and
son will be noticed and remarked on immediately, but for
some reason, the reverse is true of father and daughter. How
often are you told that you favor your daddy?"

"Oh, I—" Jewel blanched and looked down at her plate.
"Not often," she finally said, keeping her features hidden.

Still busy serving supper, Miriam didn't notice Jewel's sudden distress. "Exactly my point," she went on. "Why, save for the fire in your hair, you and your daddy could be cut from the same bolt of cloth. Was your mama a redhead, honey?"

Her gaze still fixed on her plate and the slab of ham swimming in maple syrup, Jewel could only shake her head.

Harry elaborated. "Jewel's mother had lovely dark blond hair like Trilonnie," he said, acknowledging the girl directly across from him. "My daughter inherited her auburn locks from my own mother, who got her flaming red hair from her Scottish forebearers, the Mulls."

Jewel drew in a sudden painful breath at the reference to the ancestors she'd never known, the nameless relatives she'd ceased to speculate about sometime during her childhood. Surprising herself, she blurted out, "I'm Scottish?"

Harry leaned across his plate and craned his neck in her direction. "Part of you, Jewel dear. We're English on my father's side, but your grandmother was Maureen Mull from Scotland." Straightening his spine, he regarded his hostess. "I hope you'll forgive this lapse in our manners, Mrs. Connors, but my daughter and I have only just recently discovered each other. Due to circumstances beyond our control, we were separated when Jewel was quite young."

"Oh, I'm so sorry to hear that."

"Thank you, but your sympathy is truly unnecessary. Jewel and I are grateful to have this second chance. We're having fun getting to know each other." Again he looked down the table at Jewel. "Isn't that right, dear?"

Jewel took another breath, uncomfortable with the personal conversation, then chanced a quick look in Brent's direction. His arms were folded across his chest, his expression a combination of disbelief and amazement. Quickly averting her gaze, she nodded toward Harry and Miriam and gave them a tiny smile before she cut into the ham slice on her plate.

"This is so special," Miriam said, turning to Harry with

a sunny smile. "I think it's wonderful you two have found each other after so long. Were you married to Jewel's mother for long?"

"Ah . . . married?" Harry said, his cunning mind working on a suitable answer to Miriam's inquiry.

From the head of the table, Raiford, a forgotton presence, boomed out, "Married? Did someone say married?"

Raising her voice a notch, Miriam said, "It's nothing to worry about, Raif. We're talking about Jewel's—"

"Jewel? By God, that's right—I almost forget about her!" Raiford cut off his wife's explanation as he turned to the guest on his right. "So what's this all about, gal? Brent's mama tells me you got your cap set for our older boy. You got it in your head to marry up with him?"

Jewel choked on the piece of ham she was chewing, and coughed.

Miriam, her voice cracking like a cat-o'-nine-tails, gasped, *"Raiford!"*

After a long, exaggerated groan, Brent collapsed against the back of his chair and muttered under his breath, "Good God all Friday."

The Connors girls, not entirely surprised, glanced around the table, their eyes wide with excitement, their mouths open.

Only Beau seemed to be unaffected. "Mama?" he asked quietly. "Would you mind sending the spoon bread back over this way?"

Harry sat as if frozen in time, then suddenly came to life. He slammed his hand, palm down, on the tablecloth and demanded, "Now, see here! Why wasn't I consulted about this, young man?"

"Sir, I, ah—"

Not waiting for Brent's explanation, Harry leaned across the table and caught his daughter's gaze. "Jewel? Shouldn't you have sought your father's counsel? At the very least, shouldn't I have been informed before such an announcement was made?"

Jewel threw her hands up in the air and rolled her eyes before pinning Brent with a heated gaze. "I wouldn't know the correct etiquette regarding you, Faathah, but I do think it's generally advisable for a beau to give the young lady in question some warning! Wouldn't you think so, Mr. Connors?"

"I have to apologize for my family," Brent said, having considerable difficulty finding his voice. "They have overstepped their bounds, but please rest assured that this is all a big misunderstanding." Facing Harry, he continued his explanation. "Dad sometimes has a little trouble with reality. I'm sure he didn't mean—"

"Don't speak for me, boy!" Raiford shouted, his color rising. "Your mama said something about this gal and you getting married." He paused a minute, scratching his head, then looked down the long table at his wife. "You did, didn't you, Miriam?" he asked, his voice quieter, less certain.

"Ah, yes, Raif, we did talk about Brent and Jewel some, but I think you have have, ah . . . misunderstood. I don't recall mentioning the word 'marriage.' Ahhhh, why don't we just forget all this and drink a nice welcome toast to our guests?"

"A toast?" Raiford's eyes lit up. "Yes, by God. Let's have a toast." He reached for his wineglass and raised it high. "Welcome to Sumner Hall."

"An excellent toast, darling," she answered back, relief clearly showing in her eyes.

As glasses clinked against each other, creating a staccato ditty in crystal, Brent offered his own silent toast across the table to Harry. Smiling broadly, hoping to reassure and pacify the man, Brent bowed his head. Much to his relief, Harry responded in kind, and tapped the rim of his glass. Then Brent's spine stiffened as his gaze fell upon the large diamond glittering on Harry's pinky. Stunted, minuscule by anyone's standards, the finger was a duplicate of the dainty feminine version he'd so recently adored as it lay on his pillow.

Brent gulped, stunned by the realization, staggered by the display of absolute proof. Harry Benton really was Jewel's father, he realized with alarm. Confused and troubled, he swallowed his wine, then took a deep breath and stared across the table, his gaze flickering between Jewel and Harry.

As Jewel ate, she could feel Brent's eyes on her, and she knew his thoughts were dark and intense. Guessing at the cause, unwilling to deal with either Brent or Harry just yet, she chose to ignore them both and finished eating in silence.

When supper was over, Miriam rose and addressed her guest. "Why don't you join the girls and me in the drawing room now, Jewel? We generally do a little needlepoint before retiring for the evening and leave the men to enjoy their cigars and brandy in the study."

"Thank you, Mrs. Connors. I'd be delighted." Jewel dabbed at her mouth with a napkin, more to hide the grimace as she contemplated her lack of sewing skills than to clean her face, then rose and followed the women out of the dining room. As they started down the hallway, Brent caught up with her from behind and pulled her aside.

"Hold up there, little lady," he whispered.

"Brent!" she muttered under her breath. "Your mother is waiting for me. Let me go."

"In a minute." Tucking her into a hallway alcove, he slid his hands up along her arms and gripped her shoulders. "Do you remember where the library is?"

Her eyebrows drew together as she said, "Yes. Why?"

"As soon as you gals finishing talking, or whatever it is you do in the drawing room, and y'all start heading upstairs, I want you to stay behind. Tell them your legs are stiff or something and you need to take a walk. Tell them anything you want—you're good at making up stories."

Jewel pressed her lips together in a smirk and cocked her head. "You're not so bad at spinning tall tales yourself."

"After they go up to their rooms," he continued, talking as if she'd never interrupted him, "you duck into the library. I'll meet you there as soon as I can. Be there."

She lifted her chin defiantly. "What for? Don't you think we've both had enough trouble for one night?"

Brent released her and stepped back. "You be there, little lady. We have a few things to discuss." He added as he stepped away, "If nothing else, we ought to discuss our upcoming wedding, wouldn't you say so, my darling Miss *Benton*?"

# 17

After only ten minutes, Jewel grew bored waiting in the library, with its collection of first editions. Drawn by the thought of the cooler night air and the steady drone of the crickets' song, she strolled over to where the beige sheers were drawn together for the night. She pulled the curtains aside, then opened the door and stepped out onto the veranda.

Cognizant of the balcony directly above her, she stayed back from the railing and leaned over the low side wall instead. There she drew a huge lungful of jasmine-spiced air and tried to collect her thoughts.

Tonight those thoughts were not of Brent but of Harry and a faceless red-haired woman named Maureen Mull. "Grandma," she murmured as a huge fist squeezed its icy fingers around her already aching heart. Why tonight? she wondered. Why, when she was so close to bringing Harry to justice, did he have to become so . . . so mortal? Why did she have to learn of the family she'd long ago ceased to think of? Why had he given a name to the man and woman whose union had made her existence possible? Why *now* at this critical period of her life?

But she knew, of course. All of this had been a possibility since the day she'd settled on using the fact she was Harry's daughter as a snare to trap him. In the beginning she'd been sure she could handle anything he might toss her way. Then he'd managed to call her bluff not five minutes after he accepted her as his own. He'd made her cry—inadvertently, to be sure, but cry she did. He'd prompted a show of weakness no one had been able to accomplish in all her twenty-five years. What would happen to her now that he was revealing bits of information from her past and tying her to the history of the Benton family? Would she survive? Could she steel her mind and her heart against any further information he might disgorge about this lost family of hers? Jewel found herself trying to imagine Maureen and Grandfather Benton cavorting in the fog-shrouded Scottish Highlands. Then she bit her lip in frustration and lowered her head with a heavy sigh.

From the other side of the curtain, Brent stepped into the library and quickly closed the door behind him. He glanced around the room, frowning, and whispered under his breath. "Jewel?"

But no answer was forthcoming. Then he noticed the slight movement of the sheer drapes. The door leading to the veranda was ajar. Thinking she might have stepped outside for a breath of air, he silently crossed the room and peeked outside. Jewel stood with her back to him, her posture suggesting she was deep in thought. Brent studied her for a long moment, wondering how best to approach her, how to broach the subject of Harry without raising her ire. Then he suddenly broke into a broad grin. Squaring his shoulders, he quietly stole through the doors and crept up behind her.

Keeping his rich melodic voice low and menacing, he crooned, "Don't scream."

Jewel gasped, then relaxed as she felt Brent's gentle fingers slide up behind her ear.

"Now turn around," he ordered, clicking his tongue to mimic the sound of a gun's hammer. "Nice and easy—no sudden movements." As she turned, he ran one fingertip along her jawline, caressing her, until it finally rested under the tip of her chin. Sliding his thumb up and down her throat, the movement deliberate and sensual, he whispered,

"Talk, little lady. Tell me what I want to hear. Tell me how much you want me, how much you . . . love me."

Unwilling to deal with Brent and his words of love on this night of painful revelations, she kept her manner cool and and impassive. Batting her eyelashes playfully she went limp against his chest and softly drawled, "Oh, suh! Puhleese, suh, don't shoot li'l ole me! Don't hurt me with your great big ole . . . gun." As she spoke, she maneuvered her own finger into the V of his crotch. Then she gave him a little poke.

Brent hopped, taking an impulsive backward step, before he warned, "That'd better be your *finger*, little lady."

"And that'd better *not* be your gun, suh."

"You really are brazen," he said, sliding his hand around to the back of her neck, "a brazen hussy who deserves everything she gets."

And then he gave her what she'd asked for. Covering her mouth with his, he buried himself in her softness, wanting nothing more than to be lost in her eager embrace for the rest of his life. Would it ever be possible? he wondered. Could there ever be an honest, loving relationship of any duration between them? Reminded of his purpose, of his reason for meeting her, Brent reluctantly pulled his lips away and stared down at her.

In the moonlight her hair had taken on a coppery sheen, creating a ring of fire around her head, an unholy halo of sorts. Half angel, half devil, he thought to himself, the ideal combination in a lover, but an impossibly difficult woman to corral as his own.

Tempted by the tantalizing she-devil, hopelessly in love with the angel, Brent took her back into his arms. He kissed the corners of her mouth, the sweet inviting center, and then returned to the upturned corners once again before he was finally able to let her go.

Shoving his hands in his pockets, he moved farther down the railing and faced the darkened fields. Drawing in a breath of air, sweet with the scent of honeysuckle and jasmine and heavy with evening moisture, he said, "A lot happened at the supper table tonight. A lot you and I weren't expecting. Are you willing to tell me the whole truth about yourself—about anything?"

Glancing at the balcony above them, she approached him, whispering, "Let's go inside. I don't want any of this to be overheard."

Still staring out to the fields, he shrugged. "It's not necessary. No one can hear us out here. The room above us is mine, and the windows of the other bedrooms are down at the corner of the building."

Her sense of privacy satisfied, she pressed against his ribs and looped her arm through his. "What do you want to know?" she said quietly, without cunning or forethought.

Inclining his head, Brent kissed the top of her hair and sighed. "I think you have some idea what concerns me. Why didn't you tell me Harry really was your father?"

Giving him a tiny smile, she shrugged. "I did . . . once."

Brent furrowed his brow, trying to remember.

"In your room," she reminded him as wings of a shyness that was not part of her personality fluttered in her breast. "You know, after we . . ."

"Oh," he said with a short laugh. "Yes, of course—a day I shall never forget." Sliding his arm around her waist, he squeezed, loving the feel of her against him. "Now that I think about it, I do recall you telling me to lay off Harry because he was your daddy, but did you really expect me to believe it then? Hell, little lady, you get a new father as often as a southern belle recovers her virtue. How was I to know you'd finally told the truth?"

Jewel cocked her head, toying with him. "Are you so certain I'm telling the truth now? What makes you think Harry really is my true and natural father? Surely not because we both have a few silly freckles."

Brent spun around and faced her. "The freckles helped," he said, grinning as his gaze followed a trail of them across the bridge of her nose, "but you've got a lot more than that in common with old Harry. Hell, I don't know why I didn't see it sooner." He reached up and stroked her cheek as he studied her features. "Those beautiful eyes are a dead giveaway—not the exact shade so much as the look— there's something cool and crafty in those Benton eyes."

Lowering his fingers, Brent's voice followed suit as he murmured, "There's also the shape of your jawline and chin—it's stubborn and ornery, a match to that of one of the country's more accomplished jewel thieves. Speaking of which"—he cut himself off with a chuckle—"I wonder if Harry's put that together yet."

Before he could expound on that thought, Jewel finished it for him. "I don't know if *he* has, but I certainly haven't missed the irony in a jewel thief siring a daughter named Jewel." Then, and not for the first time, she had to pause and wonder if perhaps her mother hadn't concealed a healthy sense of humor beneath that stern and very proper exterior. Had she actually named her daughter Jewel to spite crusty old Lemuel Flannery?

With a short laugh, Jewel snapped out of her musings and blinked up at Brent. "Your observations about my parentage are merely interesting at best. I don't see how you've discovered conclusive proof that Harry and I are related in any way."

"I wasn't quite finished with my appraisal." He let his hands slide down her neck, following the contours of her shoulders before they came to rest at her elbows. "The most incriminating—please forgive the use of such a descriptive word—link you have with old Harry," he said, pausing dramatically as he reached for her hands and held them up between them, "is the fact that you both have these odd, but completely adorable, half-grown pinky fingers."

"Damn." She pulled her hands from his and lowered them to her sides. "Betrayed by the Benton binkies."

"The what?"

"Binkies," she said, frowning as her good humor sank

into the dark sea of her troubled thoughts and injured feelings. "It's what Harry called them the day I stuck my hands in his face and informed him that I was his daughter."

Hearing the change in her voice, the brittle edge to her tone, Brent slid his index finger back under her chin and forced her to look up at him. "I saw you that day, you know. I watched as you went into what I thought was just another role. At the time I thought you were the best actress I'd ever seen." He paused, observing her expression, noting the pain in her eyes. "None of it was an act, was it, little lady? It hurt. It still does."

Jewel twisted her head away from him and raised her fists to his chest. "I don't want to talk about this. Not now. Not ever. Let me go, Brent. I—I'm getting cold. I want to go to my room now."

Understanding that his next words would either pound some sense into her or drive her away, Brent hesitated only a moment before he took the chance and said, "If you've taken a chill, little lady, it's not coming from this warm night air. It's coming from here." He pressed his palm against the exposed part of her breast. "Sometimes you can be very cold inside, Jewel. That's a mighty difficult kind of chill to ward off."

Her back went rigid as his words, far too close to the truth for her to acknowledge, scalded her ears. Jewel's eyes blazed as she snapped, "I'm not cold inside! I don't know how you can say such a thing. You always seem to be well heated in my presence!"

"That's not what I meant and you know it." He couldn't ignore the sudden anger her denial sparked in him. After taking a deep breath, he softened his tone and tried once again to explain. "I only want you to take a look at your feelings, Jewel, your heart. Hell, every time I think I'm on solid ground with you, something happens. Whenever I begin to get close, you freeze up and I seem to fall through the ice."

She opened her mouth to object, but closed it when she

saw his pain and the sincerity in his eyes. She swallowed the sudden ache in her throat instead, then uncurled her fists. Lowering her head to the comfort of his broad chest, she murmured against his cotton shirt. "I don't mean to do that to you, Brent, really I don't. It's just that now is such a . . . difficult time for me. I really can't deal with you and Harry, too. If you'll just not push me till after I settle the score with him, maybe things between us can be a little different."

"What do you mean by 'settle the score'? Help me to understand, sweetheart," he whispered against her hair. "Now that we know my family was not victimized by him, I can't see anything but a happy future for us all. What's left for you and Harry but to get to know each other a little better?"

She raised her head and leaned back. "Have you forgotten who I am, Brent—what I am? Harry Benton is a thief, remember? My job is to find evidence of his crimes, then bring him in. I can't let this go until I've done just that."

Brent released her and moved far enough away to get a clear view of her expression. His voice incredulous, he said, "You can't possibly expect me to believe the Pinkerton Agency requires its operatives to arrest members of their own families."

"Please," she whispered, scanning the veranda and its surroundings. "I know you said we couldn't be heard here, but I'd appreciate it if you'd keep your voice down and not mention the name of my employer again."

"All right," he agreed softly, glancing around for a more private spot. "Why don't we take a stroll down the path to the oak grove. There's a nice little summerhouse right smack in the middle of the trees."

Jewel glanced up at the windows and looked for telltale shadows, but the curtains were all drawn. Assured their walk would be unobserved, she agreed. "I think that would be wiser than standing out here waiting to be discovered."

"Come on, then."

Reaching for her hand, Brent gave it a little squeeze before he guided her down the few short steps leading to the brick pathway. As they passed through the ruins of Miriam's rose garden, the scent of jasmine and honeysuckle grew stronger, beckoning to Jewel through the gnarled branches of purple-shadowed live oaks. A chorus of bullfrogs joined in with the crickets, and suddenly the peaceful countryside didn't seem so quiet anymore. Just as they reached the wooden steps leading to a small circular gazebo, a sparkling shower flashed before Jewel's eyes, startling her, then just as quickly darted out of her vision.

"Brent?" she said, searching the semidarkness for the images, doubting her usually excellent eyesight. "I thought I saw some tiny lights or something."

"Lightning bugs," he said as he guided her up the steps and onto the wooden platform. "Can't usually see them in the moonlight."

"Fireflies?"

"Yes, little lady. Fireflies looking for the perfect mate." Pausing, he made sure he had her full attention before he finished with "They're not so very unlike people."

At his final words, the heavy innuendo behind them, Jewel pulled her hand away and began to walk around the circumference of the summerhouse. She casually studied the lattice roofing and its covering of heavy vines, noting the small white blossoms and the heavy scent of honeysuckle. Taking a few more steps, she reached a small table with several cast-iron chairs ringing it. Jewel slowly ran her fingers over the scrollwork, then continued her silent, distracted inspection.

Growing impatient, assuming her careful perusal of the gazebo was only a way of avoiding his attempts at a personal conversation, he reverted to the previous discussion. "Why don't you have a seat and explain this nonsense about trapping your own father?"

Stopping at one of the chairs, she looped her fingers around the back and gripped the iron as she stared across the table at him. "It isn't nonsense, Brent. I intend to bring Harry in if I have to follow him for the rest of my life."

His extravagant eyebrows drew together in disgust. Leaning over the table's glass top, he asked, "How can you even *think* of doing such a thing?"

Jewel set her jaw and leveled a defiant gaze at him. "I won't have any problem at all. It should be as easy as it was for him to abandon me twenty-six years ago."

"You mean he left when you were just a baby?"

Her fingers tightened around the scrollwork as she explained, "He left before I was born. He says he didn't know about me, that meeting me on the *Dawn* was the first he knew he even had a child. Hah," she added with a bitter laugh.

"It might be true, you know," Brent offered hopefully.

Jewel shrugged. "It doesn't matter one way or another to me. Let's just drop the subject. All right?"

Brent circled the table and reached out for her, but she eluded him and backed away. Holding his hands up, as much to ward off the sudden chill in her demeanor as to keep her standing before him, he said, "Take it easy. I'm just trying to understand—remember? I can't fathom your anger. What Harry did or didn't do in the past shouldn't matter too much now. He seems to enjoy being around you. I think he really likes being your father. Why not give him a chance?"

Turning her back on Brent, Jewel marched over to the waist-high wall and drew in a long breath before she answered him over her shoulder. "I appreciate what you're trying to do, but it's impossible for you to understand how I feel about Harry or what I have to do now." Her voice taut with the strain of holding her emotions in check, she spun around and said caustically, "You'll never understand because you can't know what it's like for a girl to be raised without a father."

"I can't?" he said, cocking his brow. "What about my niece, Missy? She doesn't have a father, but I believe she'll grow up to be a happy, well-adjusted young woman in spite of it.''

''That's different,'' she grumbled. ''Her mother was widowed, not deserted. I'm talking about growing up a bastard.''

''I can't say I'm any too fond of your choice of words, but so far I don't see the difference between you and Melissa.''

Jewel narrowed her eyes, waiting for him to laugh and tell her it was all a joke, but his expression remained dead serious. ''Do you know what you just said?'' she breathed.

Brent leaned back against the railing and thoughtfully popped a toothpick into the corner of his mouth. Looking across the distance between them, he said, ''I most certainly do, little lady. Mary Mildred was widowed, all right, but her husband was killed some twelve years ago during the War between the States.''

Unable to comprehend the circumstances of the child's birth, Jewel sputtered, ''But she said . . . I mean, Mary led me to believe that her husband was the girl's father and that she'd been married only the one time. I—I don't understand.''

''Regular miracle, isn't it?'' He grinned at the family's private word for Melissa's conception, then explained. ''After Mildred wed and moved to Vicksburg, Mary took to visiting her every six months or so. She come home from one of those trips in a family way. First thing she did was sit me and Beau down to explain that she wouldn't be marrying the baby's father and that there was no point in trying to find him or in doing something stupid like demanding a chance to defend her honor.''

''You mean *she* refused to marry *him*?''

Brent shrugged. ''We don't know if he ever even knew about Missy. From that day on, Mary insisted we never mention it again.''

Her balance suddenly shaky, feeling as if she were negotiating the promenade deck of the *Dawn*, Jewel made her way to back to the table and steadied herself against a chair. ''But your family is so . . . affectionate toward Missy. They treat her like . . . like—''

''One of their own?'' he supplied. '''Course they do— she is, you know. We all love her very deeply. Why would we feel otherwise? Missy never did anything wrong. For that matter, I'm not sure you could say that Mary did, either. Having that child has been a blessing for my sister. Missy has brought joy and laughter back to a woman who lost her spirit when her husband died.''

Unable to fathom the kind of love a family could possess to be so completely accepting of a child born out of wedlock, Jewel turned her head and squeezed back a sudden rush of tears.

''Jewel darling?'' Brent whispered softly as he closed the gap between them. ''What is it, sweetheart? Please talk to me. Don't run away from me this time.''

But her tears were gathering momentum. Afraid of making a fool of herself, she said, ''I—I can't talk about this.''

''But of course you can,'' he gently persisted as he took her shoulders in his hands and pulled her away from the chair. At that moment the moonlight caught the sparkle of dew on her cheeks, illuminated the trembling lips and eyes that sought to hide this sudden vulnerability from his gaze. ''It's all right, little lady,'' he whispered. ''Go ahead. Maybe crying will do you some good.''

Jewel's eyes flashed opened, spilling their contents in a sudden rush as she insisted, ''I—I don't cry. I *never* c-cry!''

One corner of Brent's mouth curled up in a warm grin as he removed the toothpick and tossed it over the railing. ''Come here, Jewel,'' he said tenderly, the words thick and dark. ''Let me hold you while you don't cry.''

And because she needed *something* from him at that moment, because her mind was too far in the past for rational thought in the present, she threw herself into his arms and allowed the tempest to run its course. After several minutes of tortured sobs and occasional whimpers, Jewel's humiliation and anger at this, her second bout of foolish weeping in less than a week, slowly evaporated along with her teardrops. Gathering herself, she drew comfort from Brent's strength and the depth of his compassion.

When she felt able to speak in complete sentences again, Jewel lifted her face off his damp shirt and sniffed. "I swear I'm really not one of those weepy females. I'm sorry if I—"

"Don't you dare apologize for having some honest emotions, little lady," he interrupted as he pulled a hand-kerchief from his back pocket and gave it to her. After waiting until she finished dabbing at her eyes and nose, he went on, choosing his words carefully, speaking in a voice that was almost a caress. "Please don't feel that I'm pushing you into a corner, but it would mean an awful lot to me if you'd tell me what that was all about."

Stifling a hiccup as she considered his request, she drew in a calming breath and offered something close to the truth. "You wouldn't understand, Brent, not coming from a . . ." She hesitated as another, deeper sob erupted, then finally stammered, "N-not coming from a f-family like yours. You couldn't possibly imagine what it was like being raised in a home where you were thought of as something less than human."

Jewel dried yet another trickle of tears before she finished what she had to say. "I—I was treated like a repulsive aberration, bound to that . . . that"—she swallowed hard, nearly unable to speak the word as she thought of the Flannerys—"*family* only by the accident of my birth. I'm surprised they didn't drop me on a stranger's doorstep. At times, I wish they had."

Brent felt as if his gut had collided with the hub of the ship's wheel. His breath came in a short gasp as he whispered, "Good God, little lady. I had no idea."

"You still don't," she said, curiously willing to share some of her past with him. Her strength renewed, Jewel stepped away from him and resumed her trek around the summerhouse. "How do you think I learned to play billiards?" she went on, her fists clenched. "It sure as hell wasn't because someone took the time to teach me!"

Resisting the urge to follow her, to take her back into his arms and comfort and soothe her, he kept his silence, hoping she would feel secure enough about him to reveal more of herself.

She did. "I taught myself, that's how!" she replied, answering her own question with more pride than hurt in her voice. "Whenever Grandfather Flannery had guests, whether they were business associates or members of my own family, I was hidden away in the bowels of his mansion. More often than not, I chose to disappear in the billiard room."

Unable to follow her logic, he asked, "Why did you hide if it upset you to do so?"

"I guess I didn't make myself clear," she said, kicking at a wooden post as she passed by. "I wasn't given a choice, Brent. I was *ordered* to vanish."

At his expression of disbelief, she balled her fists and closed her eyes. Memories of long ago came flooding back, images of Lemuel and his spiteful eyes, Lemuel and the judgmental tone in his voice whenever he spoke to her. The man was fuelled by hatred. He thrived on watching her cringe whenever he rapped his cane against the countertop. "You're long overdue for a good cuffing, you misbegotten daughter of Satan! I'll show you what happens if you behave improperly around me, I will!" he would say, rationalizing yet another unjustified beating.

Lemuel's image was suddenly so clear that she could almost feel the ivory cane biting into her tender flesh, so vivid she could smell the sour venom of his breath mingled with the scent of freshly minted money. Jewel gasped, and her eyes flew open. After taking in her surroundings, assuring herself that she was not in the Flannery mansion, she straightened her spine and began pacing again.

Through a jaw so tight and aching she could barely form

the words, Jewel forced a nonchalant tone and finished her explanation. "You see, Brent, the way Grandfather figured it, if his rich clients didn't know about me, he wouldn't have the chore of explaining my presence." She stopped pacing and turned, looking Brent square in the eye. "How does the very snobbish president of a bank explain that he harbors a bastard in his otherwise proper home?"

"Jesus Christ," he growled, the acerbic taste of anger and disgust filling his mouth, turning his stomach. "Did he behave that way toward other members of your family, too?"

Looking away, she said slowly, painfully, "I wouldn't know my own cousins if I fell over them."

"And your grandmother?" he asked, his anger growing, "Hell, your *mother*? She let him get away with that kind of cruelty?"

Jewel shrugged, surprised she was able to relate the story. "I wouldn't know what to say about Grandmama. I usually have pretty good instincts about people, but that woman was the most closed-up, untouchable person I ever met. I don't know what she thought about me, my mother, or even Grandfather, except that she was afraid of him—we all were."

His heart going out to her, still he fought the urge to touch her, to break the spell. His tone carrying his feelings across the distance, expressing the depth of his emotions, Brent asked, "Didn't you have anyone, sweetheart? No one to turn to—to love you?"

Feeling strangely impassive about such a personal question, Jewel glanced across the table, seeking his gaze. When it connected with hers, she felt the breath whoosh out of her, and her heart seemed to skip in her breast. Her mouth trembling, her mind racing, she said, "I—I don't think I really know what love is, Brent. My mother cared about me. I do know that much. When Grandfather wasn't around, she always made a great fuss over me and tried to make up for his cruelty. We had some good times together."

"When Grandfather wasn't around," he qualified.

Embarrassed, as much for her mother as for herself, she

slowly nodded and lowered her eyes. "Yes," she said, her voice so faint it was nearly carried away on the sultry evening breeze. "Mother had no trouble loving me when we were alone, but I could always count on her to betray me the minute Grandfather walked through the front door."

No longer able to stay away from her, his need to comfort her desperate somehow, Brent edged closer and tentatively took her hands. "I wish I had the power to let you relive your childhood in a home filled with love. Maybe if you let me try, I can help wipe those terrible memories from your mind."

Suddenly feeling stripped, as if her mind were a bashful nude exposed for all the world to see, she stammered, "Th-they don't usually bother me so much. I figure if you just refuse to think about a thing, it can't hurt you."

Brent recognized her discomfort, assumed this was the first time she'd ever discussed the indignities of her childhood at such length, and decided a change of subject was in order. "You remind me of the Mississippi, little lady," he said, his grin back in place.

"Oh?" she said through a nervous laugh, relieved he was no longer interested in dwelling on her tormented childhood. "Why? Do I have mud on my face?"

Chuckling along with her, he squeezed her hands, then explained. "You and the river have the same characteristics. You're both wild and untamed, and you both do whatever you damn well please, no matter how hard people try to change your direction. Like the river," he said, "you're unpredictable, exciting . . . deceptive. And like the Mississippi, little lady, it seems that whenever I relax and think I've got you tamed—when I drop my guard, so to speak—you rise up and overwhelm me, sinking me."

Jewel shivered at the thought. She glanced out of the summerhouse, smiling as she spotted the distant courtship of a few fireflies, and forced a tiny chuckle. "If the Mississippi was that bent on sinking me, Mr. Steamboat

Owner, I think I'd make it my business to stay the hell away from it.''

But he wasn't letting her off so easy. Not this night. He grinned back and quietly said, ''She draws me to her, little lady. I can no more stay away from the Mississippi than I can stay away from you.'' Brent released her hands and cupped her face. His voice a lover's caress, his eyes dark with something more than passion, he pulled her mouth within inches of his own and murmured, ''I happen to love that river, Jewel . . . and I love you.''

Her heart began to race, and her mind suddenly exploded with a thousand fragmented thoughts. Jewel tried to pull out of Brent's embrace, but his grip was as determined as the man. In desperation she said, ''Please, don't—don't say things like that. I'm not ready to have anybody love me, especially not you. I—I don't know how to handle it or what to do.''

''Then you need a teacher.'' He was ready for her arguments this time. ''I have enough love for both of us until you've learned your lessons. Have you ever been in love before, Jewel? Ever done some poor young man the honor of lending him your heart?''

She strained against him, pleading, ''Don't do this, Brent. You don't know what you're asking of me.''

But he held fast, sure of his course. ''Then I invite you to tell me.''

Jewel gave up the fight then and allowed him to tilt her head back until their eyes met again. No longer as firm in her convictions, she said, ''I've never loved anyone before, and I don't want to be in love with you, Brent. It's that simple. Love is for the feebleminded, those who are unwilling or unable to rely on themselves.''

Remembering the supper conversation, the musings of Raiford concerning her intentions toward Brent, she added, ''After listening to the comments of your family, I have to assume you plan to marry sometime in the future. I care enough about you to make sure you understand that I can never be that woman.''

His heartbeat suddenly irregular, vibrating with foreboding, he recklessly said, ''How can you be so sure of that?''

''I don't ever intend to get married—to anyone. I will never be caged by any man again, not like I was in Grandfather's house, and not by the law and some silly wedding ring.''

''But, Jewel,'' he protested, unaware he was practically asking for her hand, ''marriage doesn't have to be like that. You simply haven't had the chance to see that for yourself. Our life together would be one hell of a lot better than anything you've described here tonight.''

That hand squeezed her heart again, constricting the vessels, inflaming her chest. She raised her fingertips to his mustache and began stroking the silken hairs. ''I'm sorry, Brent, but my answer is no. My freedom is all I can depend on. It's my very sanity. I'll never give it up.''

Brent's thick eyebrows inched toward each other as he considered her words, the one in particular—*no*. Had he asked Jewel to marry him? he wondered, alarmed. When? Had he spent thirty-one years dodging the question only to ask it by accident, with only a foggy notion of what he'd said? His expression flickering between disbelief and speculation, he began to wonder—had he proposed automatically because Jewel really was the one, the only woman for him?

She was watching him, her new best friend, guilt coaxing a tear from the corner of her eye. Unable to bear the sight of his torment any longer, she said, ''I'm sorry, Brent. The last thing I want to do is hurt you. It might be easier if you consider how much worse it could have been if I'd let you go on thinking we might have some kind of future together.''

Her words brought him back to earth. ''That's all right,

little lady,'' he said, backing away from her. Feeling a curious blend of relief and disappointment, he laughed it all off. ''I never seriously planned to marry, anyway. I've always been the independent sort myself. We're probably both better off on our own.''

Unconvinced of his sincerity, feeling lower than the river in October, Jewel followed him to the railing. Reaching for his shoulders, she began to massage them through his shirt, kneading the hard ridge of muscle all the way to the back of his neck. ''Brent,'' she murmured, ''I wish I could show you how much I *do* care.''

Spinning on his heel, he faced her and took her in his arms. ''Maybe you can, little lady.'' He glanced beyond her to the house. Only one light flickered in the distance, the soft glow of the lamp in the library. Looking back down at her, seeing the warmth in her usually cool green eyes, he grinned. ''If I just had a blanket with me, I'd make you finish paying off your debt from the billiard game. If you remember, we were rudely interrupted.''

''Oh, I remember,'' she said, her expression wicked. ''And if you're thinking you need that blanket for this wooden floor, you might be interested to know your sisters have piled enough petticoats around me to carpet the saloon deck of the *Dawn*. I'd be most agreeable to losing a few of them.''

''Is that a fact?'' Brent said, his voice deep and throaty as he began to unbutton her dress, stroking her satiny skin as his gentle fingers worked their way down her back.

Jewel gasped at the depth of emotions his touch elicited from her. Brent's caresses were as soothing as they were exciting. They comforted the injured child in her even as they heated the needy woman. Moaning with pleasure, her voice catching with expectation, she murmured, ''Here's another fact, Mr. Connors, one I hope you haven't forgotten: I always pay off my bets.''

''Oh, I remember,'' he breathed as he slid the pink dress

down over her shoulders. "I just hope you remember that our bet was for all night long."

Through a husky laugh, she whispered, "Remembered and doubted—this is one bluff I can't wait to call."

# 18

The following morning as the Connors family carriage bounced past the heavily vined woods on the outskirts of Greenville, Jewel fought to suppress yet another unladylike yawn. She turned her head away from Brent and Harry, who were seated across from her, and rubbed at her eyes. Her usually supple eyelids felt heavy and scratchy, as if they were lined with wool and burdened by curtain weights. Then she yawned again.

Harry, alert and ever the astute watcher of people, regarded his daughter. She looked drawn and worn, yet curiously flushed and girlish. Beside him, Brent drew in a ragged breath, then lapsed into a kind of exhausted stupor. No one spoke.

His suspicions growing along with his irritation, Harry thought back to Martha Flannery, to the kind of mother she might have been. Mousy and plain, quiet and shy, the woman had probably been too timid to instruct her child on the ways of men and life. Obviously, he thought to himself, she had never even taken the time to sit Jewel down and teach her how a fine lady should conduct herself.

Again he glanced at his weary daughter. Then Harry shook his head. This wouldn't do at all. Not for one more day. Jewel was a woman in possession of far too much intelligence and style to be wasted in such a manner. Taking another quick look at his traveling companions, Harry noticed a brief exchange of glances between the two, caught the hint of a blush on her cheeks, the contented grin of his host, and decided it was time—way *past* time—for him to have a little talk with his daughter.

His mouth set, his mustache puckered with disapproval, he abruptly slapped his hand against Brent's shoulder and said, "A perfectly lovely morning, wouldn't you say, old chap?"

Startled but too groggy to react, Brent lurched forward and nearly fell into Jewel's lap. He saved himself by grabbing her knees through the fabric of her traveling suit and pushing himself back into the carriage seat.

With a lethargic groan, Jewel smoothed her skirts and opened one eye to its fullest. Training her bleary gaze on Harry, she said, "Why are you so full of vinegar today?"

"Why shouldn't I be?" he countered, drawing in a lungful of fresh morning air. "Look around you, dear girl. Look at the marvelous lush countryside and the quaint albeit somewhat war-torn city ahead."

Propping her chin up with one hand, she cast an indifferent glance toward the rows of buildings as they passed by them, then shrugged. "Adorable little town. A bit rough around the edges, but simply adorable."

"Quite so."

Suddenly alert, Brent recognized the knowing timbre in Harry's voice, could actually feel the disapproval of a man bent on protecting his precious daughter. Forcing a light tone, he explained the city's disheveled state. "Greenville was leveled during the war, but it was rebuilt and enlarged not four years later. The ruins and reconstruction you're looking at now are the result of a couple of bad fires, one in 1874 and another just last year."

"How terribly unfortunate," Harry commented, although he couldn't have cared less. "And you've lived in this quaint little village all your life?"

Brent nodded, sighing as he began to relax again.

But Harry was leading him down a carefully constructed path. He went on, speaking casually, his query deadly serious. "Then I must assume you've had quite a string of young ladies following along after you. How is it one of them hasn't drawn you into her web—or is there someone you haven't mentioned?"

Jewel's heavy eyelids were suddenly feather-light. She straightened her spine and cocked her head so she wouldn't miss one word of Brent's reply.

Fully awake now, he was staring at Harry, his brow wrinkled, his expression curious and slightly piqued. Through another sigh, he said, "I suppose I've had my share of interested ladies, but I have never considered forming a lasting attachment."

Until I met your beguiling daughter, that is, he added to himself.

Before Jewel, Brent recollected, he'd had his share of close calls and had somehow managed to dodge the matrimonial bullet. A careful study of women and their tricks had served him well, taught him how to spot a woman who was more interested in the respectable state of marriage than she was in him. Who'd have guessed that Brent Connors would be felled by one so completely forthright? Forthright, stubborn, and . . . still a little too cold, he thought as his loving gaze drifted over her features.

Jewel was staring out toward the woods, her spring green eyes dreamy and languid, her full lips parted, still swollen and bruised from their incredible night of lovemaking. There had been no chill in her during their long night and early morning together. He'd found and ignited every source of heat in her luscious body, as she had done for him. Would the love he felt for her be enough to thaw the barriers to her heart as well? Did he have the means, the insight, to do whatever was necessary to make her truly his? Or would it be impossible for her to break from the past and build a future with him? Again Brent thought back to the day he'd asked for a tough woman. Once more he understood that he'd gotten more than he bargained for. Laughing to himself, he wondered if it was too late to temper that order just a bit.

Harry's irritation grew as he saw the private amusement in his seatmate's expression. He pressed forward, still seeking answers. "Am I to assume, Mr. Connors, that you have designs on my daughter?"

"Ah . . . sir?" Brent choked.

"Harry, for heaven's sake!" Jewel blurted out.

Raising his chin defensively, Harry said, "I don't see the harm in such a question. It is a father's right to have some idea what a man's intentions are toward his daughter. Surely you concur with that, Mr. Connors."

"I'm afraid we'll have to discuss this later," Brent said, grateful to have a reason to cut him off. "We're nearly at dockside, and I have many chores to see to."

"Oh, of course," Harry agreed as the carriage lurched up the final incline to the levee. "Perhaps over a brandy at the bar this evening."

"Ah . . . perhaps," Brent agreed as the carriage rolled to a stop and he climbed out. Reaching up, he slid his hands along Jewel's ribs and helped her out of the rig. Then, keeping one eye on Harry as he disembarked from the other side, Brent leaned over and kissed her soundly.

When Harry rounded the carriage and approached the pair, Jewel was giggling and Brent's silly grin was back in place. Loudly clearing his throat, Harry said, "Jewel dear, I need to have a word with you in private. Please join me in my suite."

"In a moment, Faathah," she said, reluctantly tearing her gaze from Brent. "Mr. Connors has a very interesting problem that you and I might be able to help him solve. I have a few more questions to ask him, but I'll join you before too long."

Grumbling to himself, Harry said, "Very well, dear, but do hurry along. My suite is—"

"I know which room is yours, remember?" she said.

Harry pressed his fingertips to his mouth for a moment,

then gasped as he recalled tying her to his bedpost. "Oh, my—but of course you do. My dear girl, I am so sorry. Had I but realized you were—"

"Of course you would have." She laughed, dismissing him. "I'll see you in a few minutes."

"Quite so," he said, starting up the gangplank. "But please don't dawdle."

Waiting until Harry was out of earshot, Brent raised a worried eyebrow. "You may be in for some trouble, little lady. I don't believe your father is near as fond of me as he once was."

Jewel watched as Harry disappeared, then shrugged. "I can handle him. As for the sudden loss of affection," she added coyly, "I suppose I'll just have to be fond enough of you for the both of us."

"Is that a fact, ma'am?" he said, enormously pleased. "And just how fond might that be, now that we're standing in the glare of morning light—if you don't mind my asking, that is?"

Jewel frowned. "I do mind your asking, but if you must know, just plain fond is all you're going to get out of me."

Even though she'd said it half in jest, experience told Brent she was ready to erect her icy shield. Soon she would close herself off from his love. Sighing, he took her hand and began walking toward the ship. "Come on, little lady. It won't do to keep your daddy waiting."

As they neared the gangplank, his gaze shifted between the two most beautiful things he'd ever seen—the *Dawn* and Jewel. The steamship glistened in the morning sun, owning up to a magnificence she'd never known in her previous life as a troop transport ship. Still amazed by the fact the *Dawn* belonged to him, he turned, intending to inform Jewel of his awe. She, too, was staring up at the steamboat, her eyes wide with wonder, and at that moment, Brent was suddenly struck by an unwavering certainty: Without hesitation, he would gladly trade the ownership of the one for the love of the other.

Aware of Brent's intense gaze, Jewel glanced over at him. What she saw in his eyes frightened and thrilled her, caused her heart to lurch forward even as she took a backward step. She brought her nervous gaze back to the *Delta Dawn* and made a great show of studying the gleaming decks, noting the white gingerbread woodwork and following the skyward path of majestic twin stacks and the endless circles of the red and white paddle wheel.

And still she felt his eyes on her, more intense and heated than ever. Refusing to acknowledge him, to hear the words that would accompany such a look, she casually said, "You must be very proud to own such a magnificent boat, Brent. I don't think I've ever seen a more splendid display of craftsmanship."

The frost warnings were in effect. Bowing to them, he expelled a heavy sigh and returned his gaze to the ship. "I thank you for your observations—but to fully appreciate her grandeur, you should have seen her the day I won her."

"Won?" she said, wrinkling her nose.

"In a poker game about four years ago," he supplied. "She was the *Delta Star* then and a bigger mess than you can imagine. The Confederates commissioned her for their use during the war until she ran aground. That's where she stayed until I won her. I spent all my time and every bit of my money restoring her."

Astounded, she looked back at the *Dawn* and let out a long, low whistle. "I thought . . . I just assumed your family was quite wealthy." Again she whistled, adding, "This is all very impressive, Mr. Connors. Almost as impressive as your stamina."

Jewel clapped her hand across her mouth, then blushed, instantly regretting the impulsive reference to their very long and satisfying night together. She looked away from him and stared across the river, her eyelashes fluttering furiously of their own volition, her throat dry and growing tighter by the second.

Equally ruffled, more by the surprising honesty of her

observation than by the words themselves, Brent gave her a
practiced shrug as he tugged at the collar on his shirt. His
dimples small caves, he was finally able to say, "Again I
thank you, but I believe that must have something to do with
the company I keep."

"Perhaps," she mumbled under her breath. Still unable
to look at him or to believe this new shy person was actually
a part of her personality, she abruptly changed the subject.
Glancing across the river, noticing the tiers of lush cottonwood and willow trees spilling down the bank to the
waterline, she asked, "What's over there? Louisiana?"

"Not quite," he answered, as relieved as she at the new
topic. "It's Arkansas."

Clumsy at small talk, she spoke in a higher pitch than
normal, her enunciation stiff and boardlike. "I've never
been to Arkansas—or to Louisiana, for that matter."

Brent's reply, only slightly less formal than hers, was
accompanied by a much needed breath of fresh air. "You're
in for a real treat when we dock day after tomorrow. New
Orleans is a very exciting and lively town."

At the mention of the city, Jewel felt her usual calm
return. Once again the detective in lady's clothing, she
turned and faced him. Reasonably certain she could conduct
a conversation without another thought about their passion-
ate evening, she lifted her chin and said, "I really should be
going now. Is there anything else you can tell me about this
Skinner fellow or the Cajun girl? Are you sure Harry will
recognize her without you or Beau to point her out?"

Frowning, vexed somehow by her ability to repress her
emotions, he grumbled, "Are you still set on going through
with this?"

"You know I am. I thought we got our plan all worked
out early this morning."

Still frowning, he nodded. "Yeah, I guess we did at
that." No longer capable of being angry at her now that he
understood her better, Brent considered the good that might
come from her plans. At best, the Benton team would steal

back his mother's emeralds, and in the process, Jewel might come to realize how much she needed and cared for her father. Miriam would have her heirlooms, and Jewel would finally have a part of the loving family she'd never known.

At worst, he had to acknowledge, they could all be caught in their own trap, tried and found guilty by a jury of their peers, then tossed in jail for the rest of their natural lives. Were a few precious stones and a young woman's quest for revenge worth the risk?

"Hello?" Jewel called to him, waving her hand in front of his face. "You're not listening to me. Brent? What's the Cajun girl's name again?"

No match for the determination he saw in her eyes, Brent gave in and said, "Monique. That and Skinner are the only two names you need to know."

"Right," she agreed, turning back toward the gangplank. "Now all I have to do is give this information to Harry. I'll bet it won't take him any longer than *that*," she said, snapping her fingers as she started up the footbridge, "to come up with a plan."

"And not much longer than *that*," he muttered back, snapping his fingers at her retreating figure, "for you to break the man's heart into a thousand pieces."

Jewel stopped and looked over her shoulder. Cupping her hand over her ear, she called down to him, "What did you say?"

Brent waved her off. "I've got a thousand things to do. Take a nap when you're through talking with Harry. I'll see you at supper."

Back in his stateroom, Harry circled around the settee where Jewel sat waiting for his reaction. "And that's all there is to it?" he remarked, pleased by the simplicity of their first job together. "This Monique works at the saloon, and she always wears the Sebastian emeralds?"

Jewel shrugged. "That's what Beau told his brother."

"Hmm," Harry murmured as he resumed his pacing.

"Well, if you're determined to go through with this, I suppose they're as safe as any pigeons we could find on our own."

"Oh, I'm determined, Harry. Don't ever question my determination or my willingness to do what is expected of me."

Harry stopped in mid-stride and faced her. His expression wounded, he said, "I realize our relationship is as new to you as it is to me, Jewel dear, but do you think you could refrain from calling me Harry? It seems disrespectful."

Trying to smile, even though her mouth felt pinched and tense, she gave him a slight nod. "Of course, Faathah dear. I'll try not to forget myself in the future."

Harry's expression remained hurt, even after she made her promise. Keeping his tone light, he suggested, "Perhaps you'd be more comfortable calling me something other than Faathah. The way you say it, the word sounds almost vulgar."

"Sorry, Faathah," she said, forcing a soft easy lilt to her voice. "I'll do better from now on. I'm just a little overtired today."

"Hmm," he murmured again, regarding her for a long moment before he resumed pacing. "I wish to speak to you about something else before we go on with our plans."

"What?"

Coming to a halt in front of her, Harry stared down into her eyes. "This Connors fellow and you—just how involved are you two?"

"Just a minute!" she blurted out, struggling to get to her feet.

Nonplussed, Harry took both of her shoulders in his hands and pushed her back against the blue velvet cushions, reassuring her as he insisted, "Try to remain calm and keep a respectful tongue in your mouth, young lady. I'm only interested in what's best for you."

"But you couldn't possibly know what's best for me, and I resent the fact that—"

"Jewel, please," he interrupted, his voice calm but uncompromising. "I cannot think about bringing you into this business until we come to some sort of understanding. Either you will behave as a daughter should and acquiesce to your father's reasonable demands, or I shall have to forget the whole thing."

"But—" This time, Jewel cut herself off. She looked into his eyes, found the stubborn verdant depths so like her own, and knew she and Harry had reached an impasse that only she could bridge. Unwilling to jeopardize her plans at this stage, she took a deep breath and quietly said, "What do you want to know?"

"Nothing terribly personal or improper, if that's what distresses you," he said, his smile more appreciative than triumphant. "First I have to know this: Do you love him, daughter?"

Jewel snapped her head up, and her mouth dropped open. "I—I . . . no," she finally said, surprised at her own hesitation and at the difficulty she had vocalizing the denial.

"Good, then. Love can be a most annoying obstacle to overcome." His relief visible, Harry explained his objections. "I took the liberty of examining the Connors family at length during our visit at their plantation, and I discovered they are not nearly as well off as they might appear."

"If that's what this is all about, don't bother with the rest. I know Brent won the *Delta Dawn* and that his family is practically penniless. So what?" she said, amused.

"So plenty, dear girl." Harry pulled up a three-legged footstool and straddled it. "I've been doing a lot of thinking about you and your future, and I have a lot of exciting plans for us after we finish this necklace business in New Orleans. How would you like to tour Europe with your father?"

Jewel gasped, and her hand fluttered to her throat. "Oh, I don't know what to say. I appreciate your including me in your vacation plans, but—"

"Not a vacation, Jewel. A tour." He patted her knee, then explained further, "I can introduce you to some of the most

powerful and influential men in the world: barons, earls—
*kings*, even!''

''But, I don't care about such things, Har—Faathah. My
head isn't turned by—''

''Listen to me, girl,'' Harry cut in. ''Believe me, it's best
if your head isn't turned by titles, but think of the possibil-
ities for your future! Why, with your looks and my
experience, we'll take Europe by storm!''

Disturbed by his apparent interest in her life, no longer
sure how she felt about it, she asked, ''Are you saying you
expect me to rob someone like the king of England? Are
you running a little low on funds or what? I don't understand.''

''Goodness, no, my darling girl,'' Harry said through a
rare burst of laughter. ''I have enough capital for us to live
on comfortably for the rest of our lives. It just seems to
me that you might as well fall in love with a member of the
nobility. I thought you might even be pleased with the
idea.''

Unable to look at him any longer, to see the childlike
enthusiasm with which he discussed her future, Jewel stared
down into her lap and began to pick at the satin braid on her
jacket. ''Thanks, but I really can't agree to such a plan. Not
now.''

''That's quite all right, and understandable, too. I simply
want you to think about it for a while. In the meantime, I
believe you'll be better off if you follow a few simple
rules.''

Jewel glanced up at him and raised her eyebrows.

Harry explained his stipulations. ''I must ask that you go
out of your way to avoid Brent Connors. He is obviously
smitten with you, but I don't believe he pays you the proper
respect.''

Jewel's shoulders slumped, and she spoke in a voice that
was very nearly a whine as she complained, ''But, Faathah,
he's harmless enough, and I *do* like him a lot. Why can't I
keep seeing him until this trip is over?''

"Because, daughter dear, even though you say you don't love him, I recognize a few not so subtle signs in you suggesting otherwise."

Jewel's pout was genuine as she tried to think of a way to convince him that she could ward off this evil thing called love. But she was out of arguments, beyond examining her feelings, or unable to predict where those nebulous emotions might lead her. With a resigned sigh she said, "If that's the way it has to be, then, all right. But I really don't see how we can pull off this job in New Orleans if I'm not allowed to see him."

"Well, of course you must see him and even talk to him, but never allow Mr. Connors to get you alone. Is that understood?"

Hoping to end the discussion, Jewel gave him a short nod.

"Good. I think you'll be much happier this way." Harry stood up and resumed pacing as he continued planning the assignment. "Now then, back to business. Since the *Dawn* will stop in New Orleans for only one night, we won't have much time to put our plans into action." He rubbed his index finger across his chin as he studied her appearance. "Is this truly your only decent dress?"

"I'm afraid so."

"No problem," he said, resuming his thoughtful march in front of the settee. "We dock in Natchez for a few hours tomorrow. That would be an excellent place to get you a few outfits and perhaps even the costume I'll need to gain this Cajun woman's trust."

"Costumes?" she said, bright-eyed again. "You're going to be in costume?"

"Oh, my yes, Jewel dear." He spread his arms dramatically. "Your father is known as a consummate master of disguise."

Jewel chuckled to herself as she recalled the varying descriptions splitting the seams of the Pinkerton files on one Harry Benton. Grinning, she said, "I think I remember hearing *something* about your penchant for masquerade."

"Believe it, dear girl," he said with a sly chuckle. "Believe that, and the fact that after the Bentons have made an appearance in the Crescent City, it will never be the same again."

# 19

*New Orleans, Louisiana*
*Two days later*

"I don't like it," Brent grumbled. "There isn't one damn thing I like about this idiotic plan."

"The only thing wrong with this plan," Jewel snapped back as they started across the massive width of Canal Street, "is the fact that you decided to show up and ruin it!"

Forced to rely on his longer stride to keep up with her, Brent waved a hand as he continued his objections. "Is that the thanks I get for coming along to ensure your safety? Do you honestly think you should berate a poor fellow who's only trying to protect you from harm?"

Waiting until they reached the corner to comment, Jewel turned on him, unmindful of the other pedestrians. "I never asked you to come along as my bodyguard, you know! I can take care of myself, Brent. How many times do I have to tell you that?"

He sputtered for a minute, then pointed to her costume. "That may be true in Chicago, but you're in New Orleans now. Do you have any idea what might happen to you if you parade around this town alone dressed like *that*?"

She glanced down at the outfit she and Harry agreed would be most likely to catch Skinner's attention. The skirt was a plain brown sheath with a stylish, if undersized, bustle, but the black silk jacket was not so simple. Though

286

high in the back, the entire front of the bodice was cut away in the shape of a large heart, exposing more of Jewel's breasts than would have been considered decent in any town. Her hair, pulled back at the sides and fastened at the crown with a saucy little hat, hung in loose coils and swung free across her back and shoulders.

She was, they had decided, half whore and half lady, wholly capable of bringing Skinner to his knees with the shrug of one soft white shoulder. She and Harry apparently had figured on everything but Brent's objections to their methods. Now here he was, threatening to throw away what might be their only chance of recovering his family's jewels over a little display of flesh.

Touched by his concern, yet equally worried about his determination, Jewel lowered her voice and tried to assure him. "I'll be all right—really I will. You must turn back. You know we can't let Skinner see you with me. That would ruin everything." She gently laid her hand on his forearm and implored, "Please, Brent, go back to the dock and wait for Harry and me on the *Dawn*. This shouldn't take too long."

This time he listened and carefully thought over her suggestions. But in spite of his good intentions, Brent was unable to see anything but the woman he loved bared for all the world to see. He narrowed his thoughts to the overt exhibit of her generous breasts, the picture of availability she presented, and finally to the reactions of every man who happened to pass close enough for a view of her charms.

His determination renewed, Brent issued an ultimatum. "I will not leave you alone. I'll stay out of Skinner's sight, but I am going to follow you to the Purple Turtle, and I will continue to follow you after you get him to agree to help you. You hear?"

Jewel rolled her eyes, sighing when she realized arguing any further would be pointless. Shaking her head, she said. "I hear you, Mr. Connors. If you insist on jeopardizing this job, please be sure you stay out of sight. Understand?"

"Understood," he agreed, enormously relieved.

"Fine, then. I'm going now. I don't want to see you or hear from you until we're back on the ship." She began walking away, waiting for his reply, but there was none, Jewel turned back. "Brent?" she said, too late to notice he was nowhere in sight.

Smiling to herself, feeling more cherished than smothered, Jewel wheeled around and continued on her way to the Vieux Carré. Although she fought to keep her attention on the part she was about to play and not on the charming houses along her path, again and again she found herself admiring them. Each home, no matter the size, seemed to have a little inner court alive with the vivid hues of abundant shrubs and flowers. Rows of balconies beckoned to her with the heavy scent of the numerous varieties of flora peeking through the intricate iron lace railings. Almost too soon, she arrived at Bourbon Street. Now only a block from her destination, she forced her attention to the gathering throngs.

The sounds of music and gaiety filled her ears as Jewel made her way past the shops and stores that seemed crammed on top of one another. She began to encounter men who had never heard the word "gentleman," much less expected it to be applied to them. Ready for them, she was able to ignore the expected whistles and grunts of those few, and most of the pedestrians were late afternoon shoppers who were either uninterested in or unimpressed by her charms. Several feet ahead she spotted a large turtle fashioned from cast iron and painted a bright, garish purple. Squaring her shoulders, Jewel picked her way through the sparse crowd and peeked through the swinging doors of the saloon.

A large upright piano graced the wall to her right, its bench unoccupied. The center of the room was filled with card tables and games of chance, but only a handful of men lounged there. On the back wall, the expected portrait of a nude woman spanned several feet of decaying plaster.

Beneath it, its counter top scarred and pitted by discarded cigarettes and careless knives, the bar stretched the entire length of the wall.

Sitting on one of the dozen or so stools facing the nude was Harry. Beside him a woman with hair the color of an overripe orange stood with her back to the bar, her elbows draped on the counter.

Taking care to avoid any eye contact with the woman, Jewel shifted her gaze and settled on the man who best fit the description Brent had given her of Skinner. After drawing a deep breath, as much to save her lungs from the clouds of acrid smoke hanging in the stale saloon air as to expand her bosom, she pushed her way through the doors and stepped inside the darkened room.

Slowly making her way to the table nestled in the farthest corner, she caught the attention of a man with slicked-back hair and reptilian eyes. "Mr. Skinner? Is there a Mr. Skinner in this bar?" she called out, innocently glancing around the room.

"Over here," he rasped, his ruined voice bubbling over in his throat like cheap champagne. "Who wants him?"

Jewel turned toward the sound, aware that Harry's eyes were on her, and gave the stranger a coquettish pout. "Are you Mr. Skinner?"

"Maybe. What's it to you?"

As she approached him, a booming voice from behind her said, "If he ain't the fella you're looking for, honey lips, I am!"

Never breaking stride, Jewel shut her ears and mind to the chorus of guffaws and ribald laughter that followed and pulled up just short of the gambler's chair.

Speaking softly, with just the hint of a giggle in her voice, Jewel leaned forward slightly and said, "Oh, I do hope you are Mr. Skinner. I'm desperate for your help, and I'd be ever so grateful if you could spare me a few minutes."

The reptilian eyes shone with the barest suggestion they might be human as he gestured her toward a chair. "Sit a spell, woman. What kind a trouble you in, and who sent you here?''

Shuddering at the thought of even touching a piece of furniture in the establishment, Jewel demurred. ''I would so like to join you, but I don't have time. You see,'' she said, fluttering her eyelashes, ''it's my sister, Mr. Skinner. She said you might remember her and . . . help her out.''

''Your sister, you say?''

Jewel nodded. ''Lillibeth Benton—remember? I'm her sister, Marabelle.''

Skinner lowered his pockmarked face as he rolled, then lit, his twenty-fifth cigarette of the day. He finally shook his head and stared up at her, his eyes flat and cold again. ''Sorry, gal. Name don't mean a thing to me.''

''Oh,'' she said, giggling, ''you've just got to remember Lillibeth! 'Course, she was just a baby a couple years back and has filled out some since then. She told me she spent some real special time with you. You must remember her. She's lots prettier than me with that gorgeous silky yellow hair of hers just a-streaming down her back. Oh''—she gasped dramatically—''and surely you remember her big blue eyes and soft round . . . Well, you know what I mean. Lillibeth is heaps prettier than me.''

''That right?'' The legs of Skinner's chair groaned as he scraped them backwards across the wooden floor. He pushed himself upright, then drove his index finger into his left nostril. Regarding Jewel as he probed for the source of his irritation, he finally withdrew his finger and wiped it on his grease-stained trousers before he said, ''I still can't say I remember this Lillibeth gal, but if she insists she knows me, maybe I'd best look her up. You say she's in trouble?''

''Just a little.'' Jewel shrugged, impulsively backing away.

''What'd she do?'' he rasped, his smile showing as much snarl as grin.

Still backing away, she said, ''Not much. It's like this, you see. She, ah . . . just wanted to show this fella over on

Canal Street a little fun . . . you know. It's getting real hard for a gal to make a living these days.''

Those eyes showing more radiance than they appeared to be capable of, he advanced on her. "What'd she go and do—rob him while he had his pants down?''

"Well, ah, Mr. Skinner, like I said''—she giggled nervously—"it's getting real hard to earn a living in these parts, and Lillibeth and I are just a couple of—''

"Don't get all in a twitter,'' he cut in as he took a long drag of his cigarette, then crushed it out beneath his bootheel. "Sounds real interesting,'' he rasped through a sudden fit of coughing. "Real interesting, indeed. Where is she?''

Backing away in earnest now, certain that at any moment he would touch her, Jewel gestured for him to follow. "Lillibeth's over on Canal Street, like I said, but if this fella has his way, he's gonna drag her off to the sheriff, so we don't have much time. Come on.''

"I'm a coming, gal. Just make no mistake about what I expect in return.'' Skinner caught up to Jewel and gripped her arm. Jerking her toward the doors, he stated his terms. "Once I persuade this poor fella to let her go, I expect you gals to come down here to the Purple Turtle and work for me a spell. Month or so ought to do it.''

"A month?'' she gasped.

Skinner stopped just short of pushing his way through the doors. "If that don't suit you, then *you* go convince the poor fool that you and your sister are pearly white and pure as fresh-picked cotton.''

"A month will be fine,'' she agreed. Resisting the urge to grin or to peek back inside and see how Harry was doing with the Cajun woman, she followed Skinner through the doors and out into the late afternoon sunlight.

Inside the bar, Harry's gaze flickered over the top of Monique's head to the swinging barroom doors. Jewel and the vile gambler were out of sight. Confident his eloquence had kept the redhead too attentive to realize that her boss had left the bar in the company of another woman, Harry smiled.

"And you know what else, my dear?" he said, baiting the trap. "If you'll let me paint a small sample portrait of you right now, I shall make a gift of it, free of charge."

"Yeah?" She giggled, completely captivated by the dashing stranger. "But won't I have to strip down to my gooseflesh to do that?"

Harry laughed, adjusting the large plum-colored beret he'd donned for the assignment. "Please rest assured, my dear, that you will be painted in the most modest of costumes. I have several drapes suitable for a portrait such as this." He gestured to the nude above the bar and went on. "I also have a completely private dressing room, which will guarantee your privacy."

"Umm, I don't know," Monique said, hesitating. "I'd sure like to have my picture hanging up there instead of that homely no-name we got there now, but I don't know if my man will agree to it." As if to answer the question herself, she glanced around the room. "Maybe if I ask him . . . Oh, looks like he's gone."

"Too bad," Harry said, feigning disappointment. Then he lit up with excitement. "Or perhaps it's not so bad. Maybe we can incorporate an element of surprise."

Monique squinted up at him, crinkling the corners of her eyes as if she'd suddenly been struck blind. "Huh?"

His expression one of patience, Harry cleared his throat and said, "Mademoiselle, I suggest that we paint you as a gift to your beau—a surprise of sorts. How could he then resist engaging me to enlarge such a portrait to replace this"—Harry flipped a disdainful wrist in the direction of the amateurish nude—"this rubbish?"

Monique's dusty blue eyes rivaled the sparkle from her emerald and diamond necklace as she stared up at the portrait and imagined herself gracing the place of honor. Pressing her fingertips against her painted mouth, she giggled, "How long would it take?"

"If we hurry and catch the last of the sunlight, no more than two hours."

Her giggles increased, and she squeezed her shoulders up with delight. "Sounds swell, but I got a little problem with doing it, Mr. LeBonde. Skinner always tells me to keep away from Jackson Square and you types—says your kind can't be trusted and that you artist folk carry every manner of disease."

Harry raised an indignant chin, but didn't dare take even one extra breath of the stale tobacco-laden air. "My dear, apparently you haven't been paying attention to me. Jackson Square is a lovely place in which to paint a landscape, I suppose, but I am Paris-trained and a consummate artist. I have taken a suite at the St. Louis Hotel. It is there in my room that I have created my studio. I believe you will find my credentials impeccable."

Her features crumpled once again with confusion, Monique focused on the one name she did understand—the St. Louis Hotel. "You really got a suite at the St. Louis?"

"Most assuredly," he said, sliding down off the stool with unerring confidence.

Grinning broadly, Monique turned back to the bar. "Hank? Be a pal. I'm working on a right fancy surprise for Skinner. When he comes back, tell him I had some errands to run and that I'll be gone for a couple of hours."

"Sure thing, Monique," the bartender answered, barely acknowledging her, not even glancing in Harry's direction.

Pleased the assignment was working so smoothly, Harry flared his painter's smock out behind him as if it were a satin evening cape, then turned and escorted Monique out of the dingy bar.

In the opposite direction and several blocks to the west, Jewel and Skinner approached the foot of Canal Street. Comfortable in her presence now and confident of his plans for the evening, he linked his arm around her waist as if she were his best girl. When he came to a stop just before the intersection, he pulled Jewel up tight against his body and made a more careful study of her.

"You sure that li'l sis of yours is prettier than you, Marabelle?"

"Heaps." She choked the word out, gagging on the breath of a man whose teeth had gone to decay.

"Once we round that corner, no telling what kinda trouble we'll run up against," Skinner went on, fondling a lock of her hair. "You and me could have us a real good time right now and let your sister find her own way outta her troubles. Yes sir, we could do just that." He leered as he lowered his head and began to nuzzle the lobe of her ear.

From behind them, Brent loomed up out of nowhere and increased his stride to a near gallop as he growled, "That's *it*!"

By the time Skinner and Jewel heard the remark, Brent had already torn the gray striped cravat from around his own neck and looped it over Skinner's head.

Nearly garroted, the vile gambler clawed at his throat, desperately trying to loosen the silk noose, but the pressure increased as his assailant dragged him off the street and into a deserted alley. Once in the shadows, the garrote loosened for just a second before something cold, hard, and metallic crashed against the side of his head. Then there was only icy darkness.

"Holy hell, Brent! Have you gone completely *mad*?" Jewel cried out as she dropped to her knees at Skinner's side and pressed her fingers to the hollow of his throat. "What if you killed him?"

"I hope I did," Brent said, kicking the man squarely in the shin with the toe of his boot. "That son of a bitch doesn't deserve to live after putting his greasy hands and mouth on you. Why I ought to—"

"Hush!" she insisted, still searching for the man's pulse. When the faint but steady signs of life bumped against her fingertips, she sat back on her heels and sighed. "He's not dead."

"Well, I can sure as hell take care of that!" Brent threatened, waving the gun he'd just bashed against Skinner's head.

Jewel climbed to her feet and ran her fingers along Brent's arm until she reached the hand holding the pistol. "Darling," she said in a reassuring whisper, "put the gun away. I'm all right, and Skinner's out cold. Nothing's really ruined here. I was just supposed to keep him busy long enough for Harry to get Monique out of the saloon, anyway." She glanced down at the unconscious man. "I'd say we've managed to do that."

Recognizing the signs of insanity in his behavior, Brent took a long calming breath. Then he holstered his gun and pulled Jewel into his arms. "He *touched* you."

"He kissed me Brent, but he didn't hurt me. If I promise to boil every spot he touched for ten minutes before I go to bed tonight, would it make you feel better?"

Brent grumbled to himself, then stomped over and kicked Skinner in the ribs. At the corresponding rush of air and strangled groan, he said, "Now I do."

"Then come on," she said, shaking her head. "Let's get out of here before someone comes along."

But Brent held back. "I may have gone too far. I don't think we should leave him here wondering why he was dragged across town or thinking about who may have set him up." Then he snapped his fingers and hunkered down beside his old enemy. After gingerly opening the man's stained vest, he reached inside the pocket and pulled out several gold coins. Then he dropped them into his own pocket, and tied Skinner's hands behind his back with the cravat he'd donated to the cause.

"Brent!" Jewel said through a strangled whisper. "You can't do this! I can't be involved in an *actual* robbery! Do you realize what you're doing?"

"I think I do," he whispered back, joining her and

glancing around the corner. "We'd better go now before he wakes up."

"In a minute," she said, turning her back on him and lifting her skirt. Jewel removed the large orange and brown checkered shawl she'd tied around her waist like a petticoat. She wrapped the shawl around her shoulders like a fichu, adjusted it over her low neckline, and stepped back out onto the boardwalk.

Plaiting her loose hair into a long braid as they walked back toward Jackson Square, she continued voicing her displeasure. "Do you have any idea of the spot you've put me in? I'm a Pinkerton agent! I can't go around robbing people just to make things look better!"

"You didn't rob him. I did," he said, proud of his logic.

"That's just wonderful," she muttered. "And what am I supposed to do? Turn my head as if nothing happened? Act on the side of the law when it suits me?"

Brent glanced over at her and frowned, no longer convinced he'd come up with such a great plan. Then the impressive triple steeples of the St. Louis Cathedral caught his gaze from across the street. His honey-brown eyes twinkling as he revised his earlier strategy, he excused himself. "You wait right here, little lady. I believe our good friend, Skinner, is about to make a healthy little donation to the neighborhood church."

Without waiting for her reply, he dashed off, navigated the circular park directly in front of the immense structure, then bounded up the steps leading to the high-arched doors.

When Brent returned a few minutes later, he pulled his empty pockets inside out and gave her a dimpled grin. "Happy?"

"Almost," she said with a grudging smile. "Go back to the ship and I'll be ecstatic."

"No. Not for all the sugarcane in Louisiana. You need me around, whether you want to admit it or not. Where do we go next?"

Jewel spun on her heel and began walking back toward

Bourbon Street. "I'm going to the hotel, Mr. Connors," she said over her shoulder. "You are not."

"We'll just see about that," he promised as he popped a toothpick into the corner of his mouth.

But Jewel ignored him and increased her stride. Digging into her reticule for the spectacles and the hairpins she'd purchased earlier, she kept up her hurried pace until she flounced into the lobby of the magnificent St. Louis Hotel. Wandering over to the center courtyard, she ducked under one of the moss-draped trees in the lush gardens and donned the glasses. Then she wound her braid into a coil at the nape of her neck and fastened it with a handful of hairpins. Satisfied that these important changes transformed her into a woman who bore little, if any, resemblance to Marabelle, Jewel stepped back out into the lobby.

She spotted Brent lounging on a settee. Most of his features were buried in the pages of the newspaper, but as she neared him, she felt his watchful gaze from over the top edge. Muttering to herself, she climbed three flights of steps and finally arrived at the door to Harry's suite.

After knocking as she turned the doorknob, she poked her head inside the room and announced her arrival. "Excuse me, Faathah?"

Harry wheeled away from the brocaded chaise longue and waved his sable paintbrush in the air, "Yes, daughter? Do come in."

"So sorry to disturb you," she said softly, the picture of a reticent young woman who knew her place. "The manager has requested your presence in the lobby, sir. Something to do with my plea for a more private room."

"Is that a fact!" Harry boomed, playing the artistic temperament to the fullest. "Who do they think they are dealing with? Did you tell them; you are the daughter of *the* LeBonde?"

"Yes, sir, I did, but still he insisted that you come to him and make the arrangements yourself."

Dramatically slamming his paintbrush onto his palette, Harry ignored the few splatters of yellow raining down on his shoes and the thick white carpet. He turned back to Monique, his arms spread wide. "You see the indignities a great artist must endure, my dear? Please forgive me, but my daughter's privacy is of the utmost importance to me. I shall return shortly."

Monique shrugged and pulled the strategically draped length of crimson organdy up across her shoulders. "I guess it'll be all right, but I got to get back to the Purple Turtle 'fore too long, you know."

"No! No, my dear girl! Do not move!" Harry brought his hands up and rushed to the long couch. "Relax if you must while I'm gone, but please do not change your pose. It will take us all that much longer to reposition you when I return."

"Oh, sorry, Mr. LeBonde," Monique said, nervously glancing around as she tried to remember exactly how she'd been fashioned across the hard little couch.

"I shan't be long—I promise," Harry said, spinning toward the door. As he neared Jewel, he winked and said, "Be a dear, daughter, and keep Miss Monique company while I'm gone. And make sure she doesn't move a muscle."

"Yes, Faathah, I shall." Jewel casually walked over toward the canvas Harry had propped against the easel in the center of the suite. Glancing at the door connecting the extra bedroom to the living room, she checked to see that it was tightly closed, then smiled at the girl before turning her gaze to the painting.

What she saw forced her to rely on her dramatic talent. The only sketching Harry had done, except for a few lopsided clouds and an off-center globe representing the sun, was the outline of an oval face. The crude features of this rudimentary portrait comprised a single hair growing out of the top of the head and a pair of unmatched eyes. The pupils—two dots staring in at each other—completed Harry's portrait of a cross-eyed moron.

Pressing her quivering lips together, Jewel forced her gaze away from the cartoon and drew a huge lungful of air before she trusted herself to address the woman on the chaise longue. "Is this painting for someone special, or are you one of Faathah's models?" she asked as casually as she could.

Monique giggled, trying to conceal her nudity from the obviously pristine young woman. "Shucks, I don't think I could ever be anyone's model. I'm having this done for my . . . beau."

"How nice," Jewel softly breathed as her gaze flickered between Monique and the drawing. How could this woman, *any* woman, allow a man like Skinner to become so important in her life, much less *touch* her? she wondered. What good could her future possibly contain?

Feeling sorry for Monique and knowing such emotions could only jeopardize her assignment, Jewel made a great show of studying the painting and observed, "I'll just bet your beau is the kind of man who can really appreciate Faathah's work."

Monique shrugged. "Sure. Rudyard Skinner knows just about everything about anything."

"Rudyard?"

Monique giggled and slapped her hand across her mouth. "Don't know if you'll ever meet up with him, but if you do, don't say that name and don't tell him I told you. I'm not even s'posed to know it."

Jewel fought the urge to roll her eyes and began to fidget instead. Just how long did it take a man of Harry's talent to creep into the adjoining room, remove the necklace and the garments they would use to alter their appearance, and then return to the studio and save her from this inane conversation?

Harry burst into the room then, answering her questions and relieving her of her burden all at once.

"This is the most ill conceived and poorly staffed hotel I've ever had the misfortune of visiting," he complained, striding forcefully into the room. "But I believe you will find your newest accommodations more to your liking, daughter."

Harry turned his attention to the chaise longue, apologizing profusely, "If you'll have the grace to excuse me once again, Miss Monique, I shall show my daughter to her quarters and make certain she is safely ensconced in her room before I resume work on your portrait."

"Well . . ." She hesitated, glancing out the window at the setting sun.

"I shan't be more than five minutes, my dear. If I am, I invite you to return to your fine establishment of employment."

Monique shrugged, and a wan smile lifted her worn features. "All right. I guess I can wait around a little longer."

"This masterpiece," he said, pointing at the canvas, "will most assuredly be worth the wait, wouldn't you say daughter?"

In complete control of herself, Jewel gazed at the cartoon as she cocked her head this way and that. Then she finally said, "I can honestly say that I've never seen anything quite like it, Faathah."

"There, now—you see?" he said, addressing Monique. "You have nothing to worry about."

And with that he took Jewel by the arm and led her out of the suite, carefully closing the door behind them. Once they were a few feet down the hallway, he began speaking rapidly and barely above a whisper. "On the couch ahead— your bonnet and my top hat. Get them while I dispose of my beret and smock."

Working quickly, Jewel and Harry performed the simple chores, then met again at the top of the stairs. While he positioned his top hat, she tied the long ribbons of her plain brown bonnet beneath her chin and made certain her shawl covered every inch of her bodice.

Offering his arm, Harry turned to his daughter and said, "Come with me, my darling. We have a steamship to catch."

# 20

Back aboard the *Delta Dawn*, Jewel and her father sat in Brent's office and watched as he locked his mother's heirloom necklace in the wall safe. With a sigh of relief, he replaced the oil painting he used to hide the vault, then turned toward to his accomplices.

Thinking back to the caper, Jewel burst out laughing. "And there's something else," she managed to say through her chuckles. "You should have seen the sketch Harr—Faathah made of Skinner's girlfriend!"

"I said I could pull this job off," Harry said, sniffing and raising his chin in mock indignation, "but I do not recall laying claim to any artistic talent. How do you think dear Monique liked my portrait of her?"

At the reference to the saloon girl, Jewel's laughter faded in her throat. "Oh, I don't know. . . . I feel sorry for her. I really can't say I enjoyed duping her so much as I did her miserable excuse for a boyfriend."

Harry reached across the table and patted her hand. "While your compassion is commendable, Jewel dear, you would do well to remember one unerring truth: No two people will be equally happy with the same comforts or with the identical station in life. She's probably as well off in her circumstance as she'd be anywhere else. As the French would say, *c'est la vie.*"

Jewel wrinkled her nose. "Still, just the thought of her

calling a loathsome creature like Skinner her beau turns my stomach."

"Again, my darling, I must remind you that even a three-toed horned toad is considered beautiful by someone—even if that someone is another three-toed horned toad." Pausing while she laughed, he added, "If you think Skinner is disgusting, just try to imagine the pair of misanthropes who begot him!"

Laughing along with them, Brent addressed Harry. "I can't think of a better name for old Skinner than three-toed horned toad."

"I can!" Jewel gave it to another burst of laughter. "Try Rudyard."

"Rudyard? Skinner's given name is Rudyard?" At her nod, Brent shook his head and laughed along with her. "Silly as it is, it almost sounds too human for him," he commented, his attention back on Harry. "I want to thank you for getting my mother's emeralds back. I can never repay you, but if there's anything I can do—"

"It was my pleasure," Harry cut in, accepting Brent's outstretched hand. Dismissing the caper, he went on, "Just the fact that a woman as lovely as your mother is once again in possession of what was rightfully hers is thanks enough for me." He rose then, gesturing to Jewel to follow suit. "Now if you'll excuse us, my daughter and I have some traveling plans to discuss. Perhaps we'll see you in the dining hall at supper tonight."

Brent's suspicious gaze shot to Jewel, but she deftly avoided acknowledging him. "Traveling plans, little lady?" he said to her back as she joined Harry over near the door.

"Yes, old chap," Harry answered, eager to protect his daughter's heart. "Jewel has decided to accompany me on a tour of Europe. We shall be going abroad as soon as we can make all the arrangements."

"Jewel?" Brent persisted, trailing after them. "What's he talking about?"

Unable to avoid him any longer, she turned back and

managed a halfhearted smile. "It's something Father and I discussed on the way back to the steamship, Brent. I'll let you know all about it after we've gone over the details."

"Good day, Brent," Harry said, tipping his hat. Then he ushered Jewel out through the door before the handsome gambler had a chance to digest her explanation.

Slowing making his way to the side bar, Brent drew a toothpick from his pocket and stuck it in his mouth. Jewel had to have some kind of ulterior motive for allowing Harry to think she'd join him on a European tour, he decided, some new little twist in the Harry Benton saga he hadn't figured out yet. She would return, he reassured himself as he poured a shot of bourbon. Soon she would come back to his office and explain this newest puzzle in the life of Jewel Flannery Benton. Lifting his glass high, he addressed it before he downed the liquor. "She'll come running back to explain before we move two feet from the dock. I can bet the *Dawn* on it."

It was a good thing Brent was no longer a betting man. He sat in his office poring over the ship's operating expenses, wondering why Jewel had been so difficult to corner over the last two days. She was all he could think about—all he seemed to be able to acknowledge. He stared at the rows of numbers, but saw her stunning green eyes. He rubbed his palms against the coarse fabric of his trouser legs, but felt instead the soft satin of her skin and the silky texture of her hair. Guessing her scent would fill his senses, he didn't take a breath of air.

Why was she doing this to him? he wondered for the thousandth time. They'd met for dinner the last two evenings and even managed to have a few strained conversations, but Harry was always lurking nearby, cutting in or actually dragging Jewel away to her next lesson in etiquette.

And Jewel was allowing it. She was acting as if she and Brent were casual acquaintances, as if nothing had passed between them save a brief handshake or two. Was she really so involved with learning how to be a daughter that she had no time for him? Or was it something else? Had he made some thoughtless remark or gesture or inadvertently offended her?

A light tapping at the door interrupted his thoughts. In no mood to be disturbed by yet another deckhand, Brent barked a quick "Come on in—it's open," then rubbed his eyes and forehead in a feeble attempt to clear his head.

The door opened and closed. Then he heard the faint rustle of silk. Before he could open his eyes to identify his female visitor, the barest hint of fresh violets drifted under his nose. *Jewel.*

Brent jerked his hands away from his face and pushed out of his chair. "Good God, little lady, it's about time," he complained, but the relief in his voice belied the anger it contained. Sighing heavily as he rounded his desk and started toward the center of the room, he added, "I was just about to fashion a lasso from one of the drape pulls and go round you up myself."

"I'm sorry," she said with more nonchalance than she felt. "I was just trying to make things as easy as I could for all of us."

But Brent was filling his senses, not his logic, as he took a good look at her. She wore a dress of lilac and white candy-stripe silk that fit her like a wet camisole from the lace ruffle at the throat to the curve of her hips. Then the overskirt and bustles flared out, tumbling down past her heels into a fashionably long train. Never before had he been privileged to view her dressed like a woman of high breeding.

"Good God, little lady," he repeated, his breath catching in his throat. "If you aren't a sight."

Jewel raised one eyebrow and advanced a few more steps. "Am I to assume, then, that you like my new dress?"

"It's—you're absolutely stunning—if you don't mind my saying so, that is," he added, finally regaining his usual balance.

"Thank you. I'm sure Harry thanks you, too, since he bought it for me back in Natchez. It's a Charles Frederick Worth, you know."

"No, I didn't know, and," he added raising one corner of his lip. "I wouldn't, since I've never heard of the fellow."

"He's a Parisian designer who's all the rage in New York. Father says he's—"

"I don't care who he is," Brent cut in as he gently pulled her into his arms. "I just care about you, little lady. Now, why are you so dressed up, and why in hell have you been avoiding me the last couple of days?"

Jewel looked up into his warm brown eyes, then quickly turned away as she thought of what she had to do next. Bracing herself against his broad chest with both gloved hands, she whispered, "Fath—Harry told me to stay away from you."

"*What*? After all we've been through together—and I'm talking about the three of us—what possible purpose would that serve? What have I done wrong?"

"Brent, please—let me go. I can't think when you hold me like this."

But he was a starving man, hungry for the sight of her, craving a taste of her sweet lips. Brent stubbornly fit her against his body and said, "No, dammit. I want to know what's going on, and I want to know now." He took her chin between his thumb and forefinger and forced her to look into his eyes. His gaze intense, demanding, he said, "What's happened to you?"

Jewel steeled herself, expecting the inquiries, and quietly answered, "When the *Dawn* arrives in Memphis—and I'm told we'll be docking shortly—"

"Within the hour," he interrupted, impatient, uneasy. "Go on."

"When we get to Memphis, Harry and I will be leaving the ship." Her eyes grew cold as she prepared for his next remarks. "We're going on to Chicago by train."

Brent stared at her, the blood frozen in his veins, the air

trapped in his lungs. Finally his system sprang to life, and he whispered harshly, "*Chicago*? You can't still be planning to turn Harry in, can you?"

Even though she'd been expecting the words, Jewel's defenses were stifled, trapped as much as she was by his grip. Using surprise as her only leverage, she tore out of his arms and spun away from him, nearly tripping on the fine ecru lace edging the silk hem of her train.

Brent watched incredulously as she stumbled over to the billiard table. Then he raised his voice a notch and repeated, "Is that what this is all about? You still have it in your mind to put your own father away?" When she didn't answer right away, he persisted, "And he's *agreed*? He's just going to let you haul him off to Chicago and put him behind bars?"

Hanging her head, she quietly said, "He thinks we're just stopping off there to collect my things."

"Oh, great plan, lady detective. You should be real proud of yourself."

Facing him again, Jewel gripped the felt railing of the table and raised her chin defiantly. "I don't see why you're so interested! Your precious family and its heirlooms are all safe, sound, and secure. What I'm compelled to do with my own family shouldn't be of any concern to you."

"Aw, Jewel," he said, his voice softer, lower. "I know you don't believe this. You think a little more of our relationship than that, and," he added, crossing over to the billiard table, "I also happen to believe you care more about Harry than you're letting on."

Circling the table, keeping just out of his reach, Jewel grabbed a billiard ball and tossed it down the eight-foot span of felt. The ivory sphere ricocheted hard off the opposite rail, then began its return journey toward her open palm as she tried once again to inform him of her plans

"I didn't come here to argue with you about Harry, Brent. I just wanted you to know we were leaving the ship.

It doesn't mean that you and I can't see each other again. Maybe when the *Dawn* returns to—''

"Stop it," he snapped. "There's a lot more at stake here than when and where we meet again."

"I don't see why!" she bit off, again thrusting the eight ball down the burgundy felt. "I've spent my entire life just waiting and planning for the day I could bring Harry to justice. My job as a Pinkerton operative *demands* that I bring him in now. I fail to see what either of those things has to do with you and me."

This time Brent caught the ball before it could start the return trip. Holding it up, he squeezed it until his knuckles turned white. Then said the things he knew he would regret, the thing he *had* to say in spite of those regrets. "Oh, I believe your plans and your sense of justice have everything to do with you and me, little lady. At least as far as I'm concerned they do." Brent positioned the cue ball on the table, then gave it a vicious twist that sent it spiraling off the corners of the railing before it finally came to rest in front of Jewel.

Eyeing the ball, then looking up at Brent, she said, "Then you and I have come to a major difference of opinion."

He regarded her from across the table for a long moment as he searched for a way to reach her heart. Raising his eyebrows, he finally said, "Maybe we do have slightly different views on a few things, but I don't see any obstacles we can't overcome if we're honest with each other."

"I've been honest with you," she insisted, plucking the slick ebony ball off the felt and passing it from one hand to another.

Brent shrugged. "Maybe, but I have to wonder how honest you've been with yourself. Do you really know yourself, sweetheart?"

Jewel smashed the ball down on the table. "Look, I'm simply not interested in having my brain picked right now. I only stopped by to let you know—"

"Hear me out," he demanded. "I think you owe me that

much.'' Taking her silence as acquiesence, he went on. ''I happen to know how I feel about everything, little lady, especially when you're talking about my family. They are everything I value in my life, except for you.''

''I realize that,'' she said, her tone softer. ''You're not telling me anything I don't already know.''

''Maybe—maybe not.'' He leaned down and gripped the railing, spearing her with a pointed gaze. ''Do you know that the Connors family—all of us—survived the war only because we knew we had one another? Can you understand what I'm saying about us? We could have lost everything— hell, we damn near did—and it wouldn't have really mattered because we still had one another. That's the kind of honesty I'm talking about, little lady.''

Suddenly nervous, her breast fluttering with sensations she couldn't identify, Jewel took the ball in her hand again, this time content to hold it and stroke the smooth surface. ''I know your family is wonderful and that it means a lot to you, but I still don't see why you expect me to relate to it. Have you forgotten the kind of home I was raised in, the people I have to call family?''

''Not at all, little lady. Perhaps you don't understand what I'm trying—''

''I understand perfectly! You're trying to fit me into a place I don't belong. Don't you see that?'' she cried, suddenly desperate for his compassion. ''Try to imagine how living in that home has made me feel in here,'' she said, striking her bosom, ''how awful I feel inside when I think of those few people I have to call . . . *family*.''

Brent closed his eyes and shook his head. Still seeking the right words, he glanced back up at her and gently whispered, ''I can't know your pain, Jewel, but I do recognize the good fortune in that fact. That's my point—you don't know how *good* it feels in here,'' he said, placing his palm on his heart, ''when I think of the word 'family.' I had hoped to share some of those feelings with you. If you thaw out a bit and allow me to try, it might even dissolve most of the hurt.''

Jewel stared at him a long moment, trapped by his intense gaze, locked in place by her own erratic heartbeat. Tears, more alkaline than acid, formed against the back of her eyes, and threatened to expose a part of herself she'd never before seen. Unprepared for what she might find, Jewel blinked back those tears and thrust the billiard ball toward the rail where Brent's fingers were draped. Then, her usually glib tongue unable to form the words ''good-bye,'' she spun on her heel and stomped toward the door. When her hand touched the knob, Brent's voice reached her from across the room.

''Before you open that door,'' he cautioned, his voice heavy and grave. ''I want you to understand one thing. I happen to love the woman you are. I love her very much. But know that if you walk out of this office now and proceed with your plans to destroy your father, a man I have embraced as family''—Brent hesitated a moment, making himself aware of the challenge in his next words—''if you can do that, don't bother to come back through that door.''

Anger and fear collided, forming a huge knot in Jewel's throat at his final words. Not daring to face him, she let her hand remain poised above the doorknob as she asked in a strangled whisper, ''You say you love me in one breath, then tell me not to return in the next. May I ask why not?''

''You may,'' he answered softly. ''I love you, who you are today, Jewel. But I repeat: Family means everything to me. I could never love the woman you'll become if you find yourself capable of ruining Harry.''

Those new, softer tears pressed forward, broke through the dam of her eyelids, and joined forces with the knot in her throat. In a blind rush, Jewel tore open the door and slammed out of the room—out of Brent's life.

Brent stared down at the eight ball in his hand, and snarled at the cruel white eye as he imagined it laughing up at him. Then he heaved the globe through his office window, splintering the glass in a parody of his own shattered heart.

The following day as the northbound train rattled its way through Mount Vernon, Illinois, Harry returned to the small compartment he shared with Jewel. He found her moping as she had been since they boarded the train in Memphis. She was staring out the window, looking at the landscape, but seeing nothing.

In an effort to boost her spirits, Harry plopped down on the plush hinged seat across from her and said, "I realize these accommodations are far from perfect, my darling, but tomorrow evening when we leave Chicago, I shall see to it that you travel in style. Princess? Did you hear me?"

At the mention of his newest pet name for her, Jewel looked away from the window and managed a wan smile. "I'm comfortable enough. You don't have to spend extra money for first-class accommodations on my account."

"Don't be silly, dear. Where do you think we'll find all the lords and kings you'll bewitch with your great wit and beauty—in steerage?"

Jewel chuckled, brightening in spite of her dark mood.

"That's better," Harry said, surprising even himself with the depth of emotion behind the words. "You're so very beautiful when you smile. I wish I'd had the chance to watch you grow. Were you a simply adorable little girl?"

Again in spite of herself, she laughed. "Are you kidding? With these freckles and this hair, which I should tell you was the color of a rusty mop bucket until I turned thirteen."

Enjoying another rare burst of laughter, Harry sighed, blissfully, eager for more information on the daughter he was proud to call his own. "Tell me some more about yourself, dear. We've hardly had a chance to become acquainted. Given these cramped quarters, I'd say you've got my undivided attention for the next twenty-four hours."

"Oh, ah, I—I'd rather not talk about my past, if you don't mind."

Harry leaned forward and took her hands in his. "Oh, but I do mind, Jewel darling. I've grown quite fond of you since learning your true identity, and I cannot seem to get enough information about your childhood. I've missed so much of your life." He released her hands and sat back, angry as he thought of all he'd been deprived of. "I still cannot believe your mother was selfish enough to keep this from me!"

Finally able to believe that he was telling the truth, to accept that he'd had no knowledge of her birth, Jewel bit her lip and stared out at the rolling hills as the train chugged on by them.

Harry sat forward abruptly. "Goodness me! Jewel darling, perhaps Martha wasn't aware of you herself the last time we met! Isn't it just possible she couldn't tell me what she didn't yet know."

The idea had occurred to Jewel more than once. She merely shrugged.

"When were you born, darling?" he asked, his eyes shining with excitement.

"On October 22, 1850. I'll be twenty-six this year."

Harry rolled his eyes toward the ceiling as he made his mental calculations. "Assuming you were not premature, that means you were . . ." He stopped just short of overstepping the bounds of good taste, and continued his addition in silence. Jewel had to have been conceived in late January or early February, he determined. But what had he been doing in the year 1850? Then it came to him.

"My goodness," he said, his eyes glazing with memories of another time, another life. "I think the odds are your mother had nothing to say to me but good-bye the last time we met. That was most definitely on Valentine's Day. She made some small heart-shaped cakes for us to share and then . . ." Harry snapped back to the present and straightened his shoulders. "I know that's the correct date because I brought her a dozen red roses that night. I wanted to leave her with something special. Little did I know," he added, "that it would be you."

Jewel blushed and stared down at the white satin ruching on her skirt panel.

"Please don't be offended, princess," Harry apologized, again reaching for her hands. "I don't mean to be indelicate, but I had to make sure of the dates. I know the last time I saw Martha was on Valentine's Day because the following morning I cleaned out old Lemuel's safe and took off for New York."

This pulled a chuckle from Jewel. Returning her gaze to his again, she smiled and said, "I have to tell you, that hurt Grandfather more than anything you did to my mother. I think you could have bedded the entire household, Grandmama included, and he'd have forgiven you, but once you stole his precious money—"

"I know," Harry said, holding up one hand in submission. "I remember him quite well. Why do you think I never tried to see your mother again?"

"Because your job was done?" she ventured with a knowing grin.

Harry shrugged. "All right, you have me there, but perhaps you don't have a very clear picture of your mother. Even if she had known about you before I left, I doubt anything would have come from it. Had I proposed marriage—"

Jewel's sudden burst of laughter cut him off.

"All right," Harry grumbled, grinning at her insight. "On the *off* chance that I might have proposed, I do not believe she would have have married me—at least not if I insisted she move out of Lemuel's home and start a life away from him."

As she thought back to her days with her mother and remembered the blind devotion her mother had for Grandfather Flannery, Jewel recognized that there was probably a lot of truth in Harry's words. Suddenly uncomfortable with the conversation, with the thoughts it seduced from her mind, she shrugged it all off.

"There's really no point in all this conjecture. What's

past is past, and no amount of scrutiny will change any of it.''

"I'm aware of that, Jewel darling. I'm only trying to find out more about you, to become a significant part of your life, I suppose." Humbling himself, Harry did something he would never have done before he discovered this lovely link to his immortality. He begged. "Please, princess, I beseech you. I'll be happy for the rest of my life if you'll allow me into your life and give me a chance to become the kind of father you deserve."

Her throat swelled, and again Jewel had to look away. Why was he doing this? she wondered. What did he have to gain now? A daughter? Could she really have become that important to him in so short a period? Knowing she couldn't afford to think such thoughts, mentally or professionally, Jewel tried to raise the protective shield. Oddly enough, she remained vulnerable.

Interrupting her moment of silent introspection, Harry ventured forth, "Princess? If you doubt my sincerity, I want you to realize just how determined I am to become a man you'll be proud to call your father. As of this moment Handsome Harry Benton is officially retired."

Jewel snapped her around at this. "*Retired*? B-but—"

"I know," he interrupted, grinning. "I promised to teach you the business, but I'm afraid I must decline."

Jewel leaned forward in her seat. "But I don't understand. Why would you?"

"Please, darling. Try to look at it from my standpoint. I'm getting on in years, although I'm still as spry as a man half my age," he qualified, raising his chin a notch. "And frankly, in my profession, one never knows when one might be—how shall I say it?—incarcerated."

"Oh, holy hell!" Jewel groaned as she collapsed against the back of her seat.

"You may be disappointed in my decision now," Harry went on, assuming he'd ruined her plans for fleecing all of Europe, "but one day you'll thank me. I couldn't bear the idea of you practicing such a dangerous profession, anyway. We'll both be much happier this way, and as I've said before, I have plenty of money to sustain us until you land some wealthy baron.''

Jewel slowly shook her head and stared down at her fingernails. Why was all this happening to her? Why now? The next thing she knew, Harry would be telling her how much he loved her—*loved* her, for Christ's sake! All her life she'd looked for some kind of affection, for some sign of love from the few men in her life. The best she'd ever received was strained tolerance. Now she had Brent professing his love, however many qualifications he put on it. To top that off, she had Harry sitting across from her, the word "love" forming on his lips even as she stared at him. Why was she working so hard to push them both away? she suddenly wondered, struck by a bolt of insight. Why wouldn't she just—

Jewel's thoughts were abruptly interrupted as the train's wheels screamed an agonizing protest against the steel rails. Groaning, objecting mightily, the locomotive puffed and screeched to a sudden stop. The force crushed Jewel's shoulders and head back against the wall. Harry, off balance and caught by surprise, was catapulted across the small compartment and smashed against the opposite wall.

Stunned, the breath knocked out of her, Jewel remained pressed against the wall for a long moment before she was able to lean forward and try to make sense of it all. She glanced at Harry and gasped. He was sprawled half on her seat and half off, his headed wedged against the corner farthest from her. A crimson puddle was beginning to form just above his right ear.

Movement caught her eye, and Jewel swiveled back toward the window. Three horsemen galloped on by, a fourth following along behind. As the last rider neared, Jewel could make out the sinister features of Jesse James. When he rode past her window, he seemed to grin at her. Then he moved beyond her field of vision.

Shocked into action, Jewel hiked up her skirts and reached for the pistol she kept strapped to her leg. Then she jumped to her feet, intending to race through the train to the baggage compartment. But her eye caught Harry's form as she was about to step over his legs.

Jewel gasped in horror, as she reached for the door handle. The puddle had grown to a small scarlet lake.

# 21

"Oh, my God!" Jewel cried. "Dad?"

But Harry didn't answer or move a muscle. With only a halfhearted glance toward the compartment door, Jewel tossed the pistol on the seat and dropped to her knees.

"Dad," she whispered, her voice taut. "Can you hear me? Wake up!"

She stroked the top of his head with one hand and pressed the other to the hollow of his throat. Chewing on her bottom lip, Jewel sought the vibrations of life, but her panic urged her fingers upward before she was able to find even an irregular heartbeat. She raised his eyelid, then recoiled at his blank stare.

"Oh, Dad!" she cried. "Please don't die! You *can't* die now—not *now*!"

Jewel searched her normally sharp brain for a lucid thought, for a way to help him, but for some reason, her mind was as blank as Harry's gaze. She continued stroking his hair, allowing her fingers to drift down to the side of his head. Suddenly she connected with something warm and sticky. She snatched her hand away and stared for a long moment at the trail of ruby-red blood rolling down her fingers.

Then Jewel Flannery Benton, who had always been indifferent to the sight of blood, did something she'd never done even in the most terrifying of situations as a Pinkerton agent. She screamed.

Pushing away from Harry, she jackknifed to her feet and tore open the compartment door. Still screaming, she stumbled into the hallway. Unmindful of her bloody fingers smearing the fine silk of her dress, she hiked up the hem of her skirt and ran headlong toward the other passengers.

"Help!" she cried, making her way down the aisle between the seats. "Help me—*please*! My father's been hurt. I think he's dying! Someone help me, please!"

But no one seemed to care. Mothers were too busy calming the pitiful cries of their small children who'd been dashed against the seats in front of them. Adults, caught off guard by the sudden stop, moaned and groaned as they searched their own bodies for injuries. Those who'd remained unscathed were swept up in the general confusion and bewildered muttering of the other passengers.

Jewel frantically searched the crowd for a calming influence, for the features of someone, *anyone*, who appeared to be unruffled by the surprise attack on the train. As she scanned the faces, she continued to cry out, "Is there a doctor on board? Isn't there someone here who can help my father?"

Then her gaze connected with a pair of indifferent eyes. Rushing toward the stranger, she called out, "What about you? Can you help? Do you know anything about head injuries? My father's bleeding profusely!"

The man glanced up at her and removed his broad-brimmed hat, revealing a head of thinning chalk-white hair. "Maybe—but I ain't no doc."

Jewel hesitated for a moment as she stared into his close-set piggish eyes. They were the palest blue, rimmed with watery pink rings. He blinked those ghostly eyes rapidly as he looked up at her, and Jewel had to glance away from them. His skin, she noticed, although nearly translucent, was mottled with dried reddish patches, monuments to its many defeats by the unforgiving sun.

"Want me to take a look at him?" the man said, as

apathetic about her perusal of his unusual features as he was to the confusion around him.

Jewel made another quick scan of the crowd, then turned back to the albino. "All right, but let's hurry! He's bleeding badly!"

She took off down the hallway, glancing behind her to make sure the man was following, and finally arrived back at the compartment she shared with Harry. He was sitting in the middle of the floor, holding his head with both hands.

"Dad!" she cried, squeezing onto the seat beside him. "Are you all right?"

"I don't think so, princess," Harry groaned.

The albino hunkered down in front of Harry and said, "Howdy. Name's Phineas Moseley. I come to have a look at your head."

Without waiting for an invitation to do so, the man bracketed Harry's head between his meaty hands and twisted the side with the damp, matted hair toward the sunlight filtering in through the window. The albino parted the viscous shafts of hair and began picking at Harry's skull, apparently oblivious to his patient's moans of pain. Then he finally stopped probing.

Glancing up at Jewel, the man said, "give me a length of your petticoat."

Obeying instantly, she raised her skirt and began tearing at the cotton fabric, asking as she removed the bottom ruffle, "Is he going to be all right? How bad is it?"

The albino shrugged. "Don't look too bad. Head wounds bleed a lot—usually look much worse than they are. Got an ache in the old noggin, fella?"

"Abominably so," Harry moaned, wincing as his pulse thundered in his temple.

"We'll get the bleeding stopped in a minute. Ought to be fine in a few days, even if you are concussed." Those eerie blue eyes looked back at Jewel. "Got that petticoat torn up yet, ma'am?"

"Just about," she said, straining as she ripped the last bit of stitching from the hem. When the ruffle fell free, Jewel lifted it and began to bunch it up in her hand. Then her Pinkerton documents dropped into her lap. Quickly burying them in the folds of her satin ruching, she tossed the length of cotton to the albino.

Unaware or unmindful that anything was out of order, Phineas tore the cloth in half and folded one part into a neat square pad. After pressing it against Harry's wound, he began wrapping the remaining cloth around his head and tucked the tail into the edging at the top. "There ya go," he said, dusting his palms. "Ought to be just fine." The albino got to his feet then and slid his hands under Harry's arms. After lifting him as if he were a child, Phineas gently deposited him on the seat across from Jewel.

When the man turned to leave, Harry called out to him, "Thank you kindly, sir, or should I say 'Doctor'?"

" 'Sir' will do," Phineas said as he stepped out of the compartment.

"You're not a member of the medical profession?" Harry asked.

The albino shook his snow white head. "I run a slaughterhouse up to Mattoon."

Harry groaned and rested his head against the wall.

Jewel quickly said, "Thank you very much, sir," then turned her attention back to her father as Phineas bowed his head and disappeared down the hallway. "How do you really feel, Dad?"

"Terrible," Harry groaned, "but the man is correct—I shall be all right. What happened?"

"It was a train robbery," she answered nonchalantly. "Jesse James and his gang are back in business again, and they don't seem to be wasting any time."

"The James gang?" Harry raised his head. "How can you be so sure it's them?"

"They rode past the window." Jewel regarded her father, knowing if she said much more, the words might raise questions as to her true profession. Suddenly it didn't matter anymore. She smiled and said, "I recognized Jesse."

But Harry's attention was not on her implied familiarity with one of the West's most lawless men. His gaze was riveted on the gun lying on the seat beside him. "Goodness," he muttered, reaching for the weapon. "That nice man left his pistol behind. Perhaps you ought—"

"It's mine," she cut in, reaching out for the weapon.

"Yours, princess?" In spite of the dull ache pounding in his head, Harry's eyes and mind sharpened. "Goodness me, dear, whatever do you need with such a weapon?"

The time for lying was past, she knew. Jewel pushed back against the brocaded cushion and turned her head toward the window. She resumed chewing her lower lip as she pondered her next move and tried to visualize the rest of her life. Had all the years of seeking revenge, of plotting Harry's ruination, really come to this? A sob loomed up in her throat, but this time no amount of swallowing would lessen the pain. Tears, soft and dewy as those of a newborn baby, formed on her eyelashes. She drew in a ragged breath, but still she couldn't speak.

"Jewel dear?" Harry whispered across the short distance. "What is it, princess? What troubles you so about this gun? Have you . . . Goodness me, have you *killed* someone with it?"

Harry's words brought the necessary relief. Jewel laughed, the sound strangled with emotion, then looked back at him and said, "I've used this gun to frighten a few men and to bring several more to justice."

Harry brows rose high over his slightly unfocused eyes.

Jewel explained. "I wear it strapped to my leg. I carry a stiletto on the other. It's useful as a lock picker more than anything, but it comes in handy as a weapon as well."

"Jewel dear?" Harry said, concern raising the pitch of his voice. "Just what kind of activities have you indulged in during your past? I believe I have a right to know—especially if you're wanted by the law."

Again she laughed. This time the sound was slightly giddy. "Quite the opposite, Dad."

"I—" Harry interrupted himself, wondering if perhaps his wound had rendered him incapable of rational thought. Then he shrugged and went on, "I simply don't understand. My head must have suffered more damage than I realized."

"I think your head is all right," Jewel said. "If either of us has an addled brain right now, I'm afraid it's me. Here," she said with a rashness that surprised her, "these are mine, too." Casually, as if they were nothing more than the morning newspapers, she tossed her identification records onto the seat beside her father. Harry reached for the items, then flinched as if they had suddenly become a nest of hissing rattlesnakes.

"Good Lord!" he gasped, recoiling as he read the letters, P-i-n-k-e-r-t-o-n. Harry shot an incredulous glance at Jewel, then reached for the papers. After quickly reading them, he allowed the documents to fall from his hand, then slowly raised his anguished gaze to his daughter.

"Am I to assume, then," he said, his voice a painful whisper, "that your interest in me over the past few years has not been entirely . . . personal?"

Suddenly ashamed of herself, Jewel began to pick at a loose strand of lilac silk hanging from the sleeve of her dress. "I would say," she began slowly, "that assumption is correct."

Unable to meet his gaze as she heard Harry's tortured groan, she tried to explain. "I thought capturing you would free me from the past somehow, that I might cut out all the pain and indignities of my childhood if I brought you in. In all that time I never once thought of you as a person, as . . . my father."

"And now?" Harry said softly.

Jewel swallowed hard, and again, she had to look away. "Now I just don't know what to think or do—about anything."

"I see," Harry muttered under his breath, although he

wasn't quite sure that he did. "Then may I also assume that you have no intention of taking me to your home when we arrive in Chicago?"

The train lurched to life again, jolting them, and Jewel had to wait a moment until she found the nerve to say, "Correct again, I'm afraid. I planned to march you right to the home of Allan Pinkerton instead. I figured we'd arrive just about tea time, and then he could arrest you."

"Goodness me," Harry murmured, at a loss for his usual river of words.

Jewel sighed. "I can't do it, Dad. I can't take you in, and I can't be a detective anymore. I've made a dreadful mess of everything."

His normal insight and intuitive nature again intact, Harry leaned forward in spite of the increased pressure at his temples. "Jewel darling, I have to assume you mean that you cannot turn me in. May I also assume the reason for that is because now that you've discovered *who* your father is, you rather enjoy being with him?"

Keeping her head down, she slowly nodded. "As usual, all of your assumptions are correct."

"Jewel," he whispered, his voice low and clogged with emotion. When she didn't respond, Harry stood up and swiveled around. Then, even though space was tight, he managed to squeeze in beside her and drape his arm across her shoulders. "Do you have any idea what it means to me to know that you return my love?"

*Love*? Who said anything about love? she thought for a brief moment. Jewel raised her head then and forced herself to look at her father. It was as if she were seeing him for the first time, as if they'd both been reborn. Had her father chosen the correct name for these feelings after all? Was love responsible for this fierce protective person inside her that seemed to loom up from nowhere and prevent her from turning him in? And what about his injury, the blood? What about the panic, the terror and fear, all the things she'd never truly experienced before? Were those things also a part of this emotion called love?

A single tear rolled down Jewel's cheek, but her eyes were shining with something other than pain as she said, "Yes, Dad. I think that may be it. I—I do . . . love you. All I want now is for you forgive me and be proud of me."

"That I am, princess," Harry said, his voice deep and unsteady. "That I am. I'm also particularly fond of your new name for me—Dad. It sounds so . . . real." Then he hugged her shoulders and lightly kissed her forehead.

"It *feels* real . . . Dad."

Those deep, wonderfully disturbing emotions, as new to him as they were to Jewel, left Harry off-balance. He cleared his throat and straightened his spine, then tried to speak with his usual composure. "Tell me," he said, hoping to relieve the ache in his throat. "What's all this nonsense about you ruining everything? If anything, I believe you've managed to patch together the broken pieces of our lives and fill in the empty spaces."

Jewel sighed. "Maybe I've mended a few fences with you, but I'm afraid I've ruined every chance I ever had with Brent."

Harry took his arm from her shoulder and stood up. Waiting until an attack of vertigo passed, he returned to his seat and stared across at his forlorn daughter. "So I was right all along," he said.

Jewel regarded him through her eyelashes, then pouted. "I don't know what you mean."

"You *are* in love with this Connors fellow."

Jewel's gaze drifted around the small compartment, landing on the iron scrollwork decorating the wooden doors, admiring the tufted velvet of the seat back, scanning the window, and basically settling on anything but Harry before she finally shrugged and said, "I don't know."

"Humph. I'm quite sure you do know, princess, but we'll discuss that later. Has the scoundrel told you that he loves you?"

Not quite meeting his gaze, she nodded.

"Perhaps you shouldn't be too flattered by that," Harry said with a lilt in his voice. "Many a young man will say those words in the heat of the moment, or even just hoping to *get* to the heat of the moment, but rarely do they mean them. To say 'I love you' is just another way—"

"Brent meant it, Dad," she cut in, defensive and distraught all at once. "I've had my share of beaux, and I've heard enough declarations of love to know the truth from a lie. Brent loves me"—she raised her chin and looked into her father's eyes—"and I love him."

"Ah, quite so," Harry murmured, not in the least surprised.

"Quite so," Jewel echoed, curiously relieved.

Smiling across the short distance, again Harry leaned forward, this time taking her hands in his. "So what is your problem, dear? Go to him and tell him of your love—but be sure to explain also that you're probably giving up a title and more money than a gambler such as he will ever see in his lifetime."

In spite of her fears, Jewel laughed, "Thanks for the advice, Dad, but you don't understand. I said and did some dreadful things the last day on board the *Dawn*. I threw Brent's love back in his face and slammed the door to any future we might have had. I'm sure he doesn't ever want to see me again."

"Balderdash!" Harry said. "If your heart is set on this young fellow, and I suspect that it is, nothing will stop you from getting him. You are, remember, a Benton. And I intend to see to it that my little girl gets everything she wants."

Harry straightened his jacket sleeve and looked down his nose at the smears of blood staining the fabric. Grimacing, he turned from the sight and went on. "Mr. Connors hasn't got a prayer against two Bentons. Surely by the time we return to the steamship, we'll have thought of a way to get back in his good graces. Now then, is there anything else troubling you?''

Grinning as she listened to him, warming at his unwavering optimism, Jewel tried to think of a gentle way to remind him of her professional obligations. Taking a deep breath, she said, ''There's just one more thing—Allan Pinkerton and my responsibilities to him and to the agency. I still have a lot of explaining to do. He trusted me to do my job. I even wired him from New Orleans and told him I would bring you in within the week.''

''Oh, goodness me,'' Harry muttered as he pressed his fingertips against his mustache. ''I take it working for Mr. Pinkerton has been more than a simple job to you.''

Much more,'' she softly replied. ''Although I didn't realize it, I know now that I have allowed Allan to act as a sort of father to me. I can't disappoint him like this without some kind of explanation.''

''I see,'' Harry said, working to ignore a tiny stab of jealousy at the thought of another man guiding his daughter's career, her life's decisions. ''But I have run out of ideas, princess. I haven't a clue as to how you might assuage the man's ire if you don't bring me in—and you no longer plan to do so. Correct?''

''Correct.'' She laughed as the image of Harry, his hands over his head, marching up the brick pathway to Allan's home, suddenly took form in her mind. Sobering again, she slowly shook her head and sighed. ''I do have to report to him though. I do have to tell him at least a part of what's happened between you and me. After that''—she shrugged, unable to draw on her experiences as Madame Zaharra and read the future—''I don't know what he'll do. He may even bring charges against me.''

''Utterly ridiculous!'' Harry snapped. ''I simply won't have it. Why, from the little I do know about you, I'm quite certain you must be a valued employee of the . . .'' Harry scowled, then lowered his voice as he said, ''The Pinkerton Agency.''

Chuckling again, Jewel gave him a short nod and a gratified smile. "Allan says I am one of his best operatives, male or female. One of my famous captures was that of Cole Jennings. I brought him in single-handed."

Harry whistled at the mention of one of his more accomplished peers. "Very impressive, princess. Jennings, while not endowed with my considerable talent, was truly a plum in your basket. That alone should be enough to inspire your employer to overlook this one little misstep."

"I don't think so, Dad. There's also the matter of the stolen necklace. I *was* an accomplice in that caper. If I don't turn you in, how can I justify my participation in the robbery?"

"Robbery?" Harry sniffed. "If it was that, it was a robbery worthy of Robin Hood himself. I can't believe Mr. Pinkerton is as shortsighted as all that."

"I really don't know what he'll do or how he'll feel," Jewel said, wringing her hands. "How am I going to explain all this to him?"

The following afternoon Jewel stood staring out the window of the dusty Chicago streets below.

Deep in thought, Allan Pinkerton slowly circled his desk, his normally pleasant features drawn and morose. After several long minutes he propped his hip against his desk and cleared his throat. "These are serious charges you've brought against yourself, Jewel. I'm not sure how I should go about investigating them. I'm not even sure an investigation is warranted."

Jewel whirled around, the tight skirt of her day dress twisting around her knees. After adjusting the material, she marched over to Allan. "Not warranted? I just walked in here and told you that I had Harry Benton in my hands and I turned him loose. If that's not enough, I also opted to stay with Harry while Jesse James robbed the train. I didn't make any attempt to stop or apprehend the James gang, and Harry is busy plotting his escape to Europe. Just what evidence do you need to call an investigation, Allan—a photograph of the outlaws laughing at us?''

"Now, Jewel," Allan said, "I hardly think you're relating the story exactly as it happened, but no, I do not see a need for an investigation. For one thing, I have always been aware of your attachment to Harry.''

Jewel gasped and pressed her fingertips to her mouth.

"Why are you so surprised? I am a master detective, after all.''

"B-but if you thought Harry might mean something to me, why did you let me follow up on his leads?''

"Would you have given up the search if I forbade it?''

Jewel shook her head and averted her gaze. "I'm sorry, but with all due respect to you and the agency, I have to say no.''

Allan turned his palms up and grinned. "I rest my case.''

Giving in to his attempts at dollery despite her feelings of guilt, Jewel smiled back at him. "How long have you known Harry was my father?''

"I never knew for sure. I went as far as looking up a copy of your birth certificate, but—''

"I know. Grandfather Flannery hated Harry Benton so much that he let me live my life as 'Jewel Flannery, Father Unknown,' rather than have the man's name on a legal document tying him to our very proper family.''

Allan raised one bushy eyebrow, then shook his head in disbelief. "Your Grandfather must have been a real prince.''

"No more talk about Lemuel Flannery. I've heard his name often enough over the last few weeks to last me a lifetime.'' She took a few more steps toward Allan, then perched on the edge of the chair directly in front of him. "Even if you understand why I was so obsessed with Harry, how can you ever forgive me for turning him loose? For tending his wounds when I should have been confronting the James gang?''

"First of all, Jewel," Allan said, his voice authoritative

and stern, "I did not expect you to confront the entire James gang while they cleaned out the baggage compartment! You should know better than that."

Jewel inched back in the chair until her spine touched the padded cushion. "Of course, sir, I do understand procedure. What I mean to say is that, at the very least, I should have gone back there to see if there was any way I could thwart or—"

"Please," he interrupted, "spare me a reading of the manual on such occurrences. The only thing you may have to answer for is your deliberate release of Handsome Harry Benton, a man who has been skirting the fine edge of the law for years. That is a more serious offense and one you and I shall have to find a way to deal with."

"Yes, sir, I know that. That is why I'm here. Unless you intend to fire me, I want you to know that as of this morning, my resignation is official."

"Over my dead body!" Allan pushed himself off the edge of the desk and shook a finger at her. "I remind you that I am in charge here. I have chosen to disregard any neglect of your duty that may have occurred where the James gang is concerned, but I will not accept your resignation over this Harry Benton thing. The Pinkerton Agency is not without a heart, you know."

"But, Allan, I only meant—"

"Please let me finish. The way I see it, you really had no choice. I was foolish to think you would handle your job and confront Harry at the same time. We're both at fault here, so I suggest that instead of resigning, you accept a temporary leave of absence."

"A leave to— B-but I don't understand," she sputtered.

Allan's smile was warm and fatherly as he gazed down at her. "You need some time off, Jewel. As you know, we really have only one woman who may come forward as a witness against Harry—and she's doubtful. Perhaps if your father made some kind of restitution along with a promise—"

"He's retired!" she cut in. "I mean, if he really was responsible for any of these robberies, he wouldn't—"

"I'm sure he wouldn't," Allan said with a smirk. "Whatever he does or doesn't do is going to be your problem over the next few weeks. I also heard a few things in your explanation you probably didn't expect me to catch. Maybe you'd also like to use some of your free time to go back downriver and clear up the troubles you seem to have had with your young man."

Jewel blushed and looked away. With a tiny shrug, she said, "It's true I could use a few extra days to try to explain a couple of things to Mr. Connors. He deserves much more than the lies I threw at him the last time we met."

"I'm sure Mr. Connors deserves at least that much, Jewel. All I know is that it's time you allowed yourself some happiness. Take several weeks, or a couple of months if necessary, but I would like to see you back in here on the job someday soon. You're still the best damn female operative I've got. I'll miss you."

Perilously close to those newfound tears, Jewel blinked them back and took several deep breaths before she could say "Thank you, Allan. From the bottom of my heart, thank you."

"You can thank me," he said, reaching for her hand to pull her to her feet, "by finding a way to smooth things out between yourself and Brent Connors. Don't think I didn't notice the spark between you two. A match like that is too rare to ignore."

"Even if it's made in hell?" She laughed.

"*Especially* if it's made in hell," he countered. "All the better to keep you two warm at night."

Smiling broadly as she walked to the door, Jewel linked her hand through Allan's arm and said, "Dad and I worked on my getting back into Brent's good graces during the train ride to Chicago. He came up with some pretty wild ideas and one absolutely insane suggestion that might even work."

"Listen to him," Allan suggested with a knowing grin. "Harry's about the best in the business when it comes to matters of the heart."

Chuckling to herself as she thought of her father's remarkable prowess with women, she turned to Allan and gripped his hand. "I'll do that. I'm sure whatever Harry decides will be the best course of action."

Allan raised an eyebrow. "Whatever he *says*, Jewel? I thought he was on his way back to Europe."

She shrugged. "Well, that's about right, Allan. The last time I saw him, I'm quite sure he was pointed in the direction of England or France."

Allan nodded. "One other thing, Jewel. While I don't expect you to bring your own father to justice, I cannot condone his . . . methods of operation. Should I find he's back in business, I will instruct my operatives to hunt him down. For Harry's safety and your new sense of family, I hope that he *has* packed off for parts unknown."

Jewel smiled at her employer, then impulsively threw her arms around his neck and gave him a heartfelt hug. When she released him, she stepped back, murmuring, "Thank you again, Allan. Thank you for everything. I'll let you know when I plan to return."

"See that you do," he said, waving as she walked through the door to the outer office. Misty-eyed, thinking himself too old for such nonsense, he prepared to return to his desk when he suddenly stopped and called to her just before she passed through the outer door. "Jewel? Speaking of your beau and his steamboat on the Mississippi . . . did I tell you that I was arrested as I was leaving the *Delta Dawn* in New Madrid?"

She whirled around, her eyes wide. "*Arrested*? What on earth for?"

"I . . . Oh, never mind. It's a long story. I'll tell you some other time," he chuckled. "Just remember the moral of that story: Think twice before you borrow the costume of a stranger. I wasn't in jail for long, but frankly, now that I think about it, it was a rather interesting experience.''

Waving good-bye, he gave her a final order. ''Go on, now. Find your young man and be happy. And be sure,'' he added with a wink, ''to say hello to your father for me.''

# 22

Brent stared out the window of the *Dawn*'s pilothouse and thought the city of St. Louis had never looked so bleak. He began counting the other steamboats tied up at the levee, but stopped after he'd tallied only twelve. Nothing was going to divert his troubled mind, he knew, certainly nothing as tangible as his competition's growing numbers.

His mood as dark as the circles beneath his lusterless eyes, he straightened his charcoal waistcoat. As he adjusted his new gray and white striped cravat, he watched the first of the *Dawn*'s passengers start up the gangplank.

He ought to have been overflowing with enthusiasm. The ship's maiden voyage had more than fulfilled his expectations financially, and now she was booked to near capacity for her second trip down the Mississippi. He should have been delirious with joy, filled with optimism for the future. Happy, at the very least.

Instead, Brent Sebastian Connors felt depleted of energy. Thoroughly drained, as if some vicious claw had torn the cork stopper from his aorta.

"Mr. Connors?"

Brent turned his head toward the voice and struggled to focus his weary eyes on Captain Randazzo. Sighing wearily, he muttered, "Did you say something, Dazzle?"

The captain shook his bushy head and pointed out to the landing. "Don't you think it's about time you went down to greet the newest load of cattle?"

"Passengers," Brent corrected, "clientele, even, but not cattle, Dazzle. You talk like that in front of me, you're bound to slip up in front of the customers. Won't do. Simply won't do at all."

"Do as well as the hound dog face you been wearing for the last week," Dazzle grumbled. "You look like someone poked you in the eye with a sharp stick."

Brent uttered a short chuckle and wondered where he might find a bandage large enough to cover the wounds inflicted by one bouncy green-eyed heartbreaker called Jewel Flannery. Shaking off the thoughts, he forced a grin as counterfeit as the captain's hat he sometimes wore, and said. "Is this better, friend?"

Distracted, Captain Randazzo kept his gaze on the docks below and suggested, "Might have to pump yourself up a little more than that. Looks like we got royalty coming on board."

Brent moved back to the window and looked down at the commotion. An elaborate carriage drawn by four white horses had just arrived, and already a crowd was beginning to form. The liveryman opened the door, and a portly old gentleman climbed out of the covered rig. He extended his hand to receive the elbow of a heavily veiled woman, then carefully helped her from the fancy carriage.

"What the hell?" Brent said, guessing the white satin gown and billowing veils were her wedding costume. "Give me a copy of the passenger list, Dazzle," he said, watching as the couple made their way up the gangplank.

When the captain handed him the long sheet of paper, Brent tore his gaze from the odd couple and ran his finger down the list. Nowhere could he find any mention of a wedding to be performed aboard the *Dawn*, or any names that even suggested royalty. After rereading the document, he glanced back out at the dock, but the man and woman were gone.

Determined to find and question the mysterious pair,

Brent started toward the doorway, then nearly collided with a young deckhand as he rounded the corner.

"Sorry, Mr. Connors," the lad gasped, out of breath. "But there's a king or somethin' wantin' to talk to ya. Johnny Roy is takin' em to the sittin' room outside your office."

"Thanks, Billy," Brent muttered. "I'm on my way."

One deck below, Jewel settled onto the couch next to Harry. "This is insane," she whispered under her breath. "It's never going to work. We'll be lucky if the only thing Brent does is toss us overboard."

"Relax, princess, and please do us both the favor of keeping your very lovely mouth shut until you hear your cue. I know what I'm doing." Harry tugged at the ties securing the bustle he wore as padding for his trim middle. "Trust me, dear," he added.

"But—" Harry's elbow nudged her ribs, but the act was unnecessary. The sight of Brent, *her* Brent, as he strode into the sitting room, was enough to take the words, and her breath, away. Jewel watched him through the heavy veils, wishing she could tear the yards of lace from her face and gaze into his dreamy brown eyes. Instead, she slumped her shoulders and lowered her head.

Harry slowly rose from the couch. "Mr. Connors, I presume," he said, rolling the *r* in a thick Spanish accent. Extending his hand, he introduced himself before Brent had a chance to respond in kind. "I, sir, am Duke Alfonso, directly descended from Queen Isabella the Second. My daughter, the duchess, and I would like a word with you in private."

Openly staring at the pompous man, Brent returned the brief handshake, and wondered if he could be for real. The duke wore a tall stovepipe hat that covered most of his head but allowed a crop of coarse white hair to hang down from the brim to the top of his jacket collar. His thick mustache and full beard, the same bluish white as his hair, covered the lower half of his face. One of the duke's eyes was covered with a chic black leather patch, but the other bloomed larger than life, appearing grossly distorted as it peered through a silver-framed monacle.

Brent took a backward step as he stared at the large, unsightly mole blocking the man's left nostril, then turned and opened the door to his office. "Please, do come in, ah . . . sir."

Harry reached for Jewel's hand and pulled her to her feet. "Please call me Duke Alfonso," he said, his nose cocked at a lofty angle as he escorted Jewel through the doorway and into the room.

When the regal pair swept by him, Brent's sensitive nose caught the scent of violets. His heart constricted, and he had to bite his lip to keep from calling Jewel's name. The woman, her head bowed in submission, glided over to the farthest chair and eased down onto the cushion. *God help me,* Brent's heart cried out. Would he ever be able to bear the scent of violets without thinking of Jewel, without wanting her?

"Sir!" Harry rapped the long black umbrella he carried against the glass-topped desk. "We come on a mission of the utmost importance. Our meeting must be concluded before this ship leaves the dock. Please join us."

Brent shook his head in a vain effort to rid his mind of Jewel, then walked over to his desk. His dislike of the grandiloquent man growing, he said, "This ship and her passengers are my most immediate concerns, sir. I have already checked, and your name is not on our passenger list. Please state your business—the *Delta Dawn* will be heading down river soon, whether your mission is concluded or not."

"That, *sir*, remains to be seen."

Brent inflated his chest and stiffened his spine, stretching to his full six feet two inches. "Just what is it you want . . . Duke?"

"That's Duke Alfonso, to you," Harry said, sniffing the air with disdain. "And what I want is justice!"

Again he rapped the cane against the desk, and when he stared up at Brent, the distorted eye appeared to be wobbling in its socket.

Trying not to stare at the stranger's bizarre features, Brent warned, "I'll give you exactly five minutes to explain yourself."

Harry grinned. "I'll give you two minutes to do the same!"

Some of the air seeped out of Brent's lungs as he tried to make sense of the strange conversation. "You'll have to make your business clearer than that. I have no idea what you're talking about."

"I'm talking about honor, sir! You southern gentlemen are supposed to know all about that. I've come to avenge my daughter's honor, to extract my pound of flesh from your silver-tongued hide!"

Brent leaned forward and gripped the edge of his desk. "*Excuse me*?"

"I doubt that I shall ever be able to do that, but I'm willing to try if you'll accept your responsibility and restore my daughter's good name."

"Your daughter?"

"Yes," Harry hissed. "You have stripped her of her good name and compromised her exemplary reputation. For that, sir, you shall pay one way or another."

"But—"

"To that end," Harry went on, stepping on Brent's words, "I've taken the liberty of procuring the services of a preacher and the sheriff. Both are waiting in the carriage below. At my signal, one of them will board this ship and perform his duty. Which gentleman shall I summon, sir?"

Again Brent's mouth dropped open. Then all he could manage to say was "What the hell is going on here? I've never even *seen* your daughter, much less compromised her."

Barely able to hide his delight, Harry turned to Jewel.

"Daughter? Is this or is this not the man who used you in such a vile manner?"

Slowly, dramatically, Jewel rose from the chair. She took dainty, halting steps over to where her father stood, then straightened her shoulders and looked across the desk at the man she loved. Unable to contain her grin or the pulse that seemed to be leaping from her throat, she tore off her headpiece and the mounds of veil connected to it.

"That's him, Daddy!" she cried, pointing to Brent's chest. "I swear on my word as a fine young lady, that's the man who robbed me of my . . . honor."

"*Jewel*?" Brent choked out as his throat, his entire system, seemed to shut down.

"Did you say 'Jewel'?" Harry chuckled, dropping the Spanish accent. "Are you prepared to admit that you are acquainted with my daughter and, therefore, guilty?"

Before Brent could compose himself enough to answer, Jewel repeated her claim. "Don't listen to his lies, Daddy. That's him all right. In fact, right here in this office—"

"*Jewel*!" Brent cut in, finding his tongue. "Good God!"

She shrugged and turned to Harry. "Would it be indelicate of me to mention that right here in this office is where Mr. Connors gave me my first kiss?"

"Quite." Keeping his tiring eye trained on Brent, Harry issued his ultimatum. "Well? Which is it—do you wish to speak to the sheriff, or would you prefer to restore my daughter's good name?"

His initial shock wearing off, Brent stared through the monocle at the smoky green eye and said, "*Harry*? Is that you under all that hair?"

Harry flipped the patch up to his forehead, then popped the monocle out of his eye socket. "I believe," he said, tipping his hat and the gobs of silver hair attached to the inside band, "you'll find me inside of here somewhere."

Steadying himself, Brent straightened his spine and hooked his fingers through the spindles of his chair back. Slowly shaking his head, he choked out, "I—I just don't

know what to say, or— This is the last thing I expected.''
He glanced from Harry to Jewel, lingering there as he saw
the contentment, the happiness, shining in her eyes. Then he
looked back to Harry and adjusted his vest. ''Yes, I do know
what to say. You can rest assured that I will do the right
thing by your daughter—whatever that may be.''

Harry nodded, then turned to Jewel. ''I don't believe we
can ask more from the man at this juncture. I think it would
be in your best interests if I wcre to allow you to spend a
few minutes alone with Mr. Connors so you can explain the
type of commitment we expect from him. I shall be
downstairs visiting a special lady at the bar if you need my
further assistance.''

Harry leaned over and kissed her cheek. Then he tipped
his hat and his hair, spun on his polished bootheel, and
strode over to the door. Just before he crossed the threshold,
he turned back, a thoughtful finger pressed into his cheek.
''One more thing, old chap—you wouldn't happen to know
how Reba feels about poetry, do you? To be more precise,
rhyme?''

Utterly confused, Brent could only shrug and turn his
palms upward.

''That's all right. I suppose it is something one should
find out for oneself. Let's see,'' Harry muttered as he
resumed his retreat. ''I wonder how she'd respond to
'Hickory dickory dock, the mouse ran up the . . .'''

The door closed behind him, muting his voice, leaving
Jewel to face Brent alone. He stood there slowly shaking his
head, muttering, ''What the *hell* is going on around here?''

Jewel shrugged. ''I'm afraid I can't explain Harry's
sudden interest in poetry. He recently suffered a severe blow
to the head. Maybe—''

''That's not what I'm talking about,'' Brent said, finding
his voice, finally understanding that the woman standing
before him was no mirage. He circled the desk and drew her
into his hungry arms. ''You,'' he growled, unable to find his

normal timbre, "Harry. Me. Tell me what's happening here. Can all this be true?"

Jewel grinned up at him and slid her arms across his shoulders. Indulging herself, she wound the dark curls at the back of his neck around her fingers as she said, "I guess you might say I finally had a spring thaw." She withdrew one hand and placed it on her breast. "In here, Brent."

He found he couldn't speak. He closed his eyes, drew in a huge breath, and hoped he understood what she was trying to say.

Jewel sensed his apprehension. She brought her hand back to his neck, then plunged it into the thick waves of sable hair just behind his ear as she explained. "I find I'm suddenly full to overflowing with love for both you and my dad. I've found enough runoff in me to keep the Mississippi high for the next twenty years. Please tell me," she whispered, the words low and dark, "that I'm not too late."

"Oh, my Jewel," he breathed, his own heart full to the point of bursting. "My beautiful gypsy Jewel. You could never be too late to become part of my life."

Her grin huge, wicked, she asked, "So what are we going to do about it?"

Brent shrugged, then slid his fingers up to where she'd pinned her hair into a knot at the top of her head. Slowly removing the hairpins, he suggested, "How about a game of billiards?"

Jewel's eyes brightened as her hair fell in waves across her shoulder. "Straight eight, call your pockets?"

"If I win," he whispered, lowering his mouth to hers, "we get married. Sumner Hall, bridesmaids stretching the length of the oak grove, and everyone we know witnessing the event."

Jewel gave him a crooked grin and warned, "My daddy isn't the kind of man to make idle threats. That carriage outside isn't empty."

Brent's eyebrows drew together. "You mean there really is a sheriff gunning for me?"

Jewel waited a long moment before she let him off the hook, and said, "No, but we did bring a preacher along—just in case. If I win, I say we bring him in now. Otherwise, Mr. Connors, it's going to be a very long time before we can start our honeymoon."

She saw the unspoken questions in his eyes. "Having a dad, a real dad to call my own, has rewards I never dreamed of," she explained, "but it also presents a few problems. I'm afraid Harry isn't going to let me out of his sight again until I'm properly wed."

Brent thought about that for only a second before he whispered against her lips, "In that case, little lady, I do."

421

717